The Lost Princes: Darius, Cassius & Monte

RAYE MORGAN

Published in Great Britain 2014
by Mills & Boon, an imprint of Harlequin (UK) Limited,
Eton House, 18-24 Paradise Road, Richmond, Surrey, TW9 1SR

THE LOST PRINCES: DARIUS, CASSIUS & MONTE
© 2014 Harlequin Books S.A.

Secret Prince, Instant Daddy!, Single Father, Surprise Prince! and *Crown Prince, Pregnant Bride!* were first published in Great Britain by Harlequin (UK) Limited.

Secret Prince, Instant Daddy! © 2010 Helen Conrad
Single Father, Surprise Prince! © 2010 Helen Conrad
Crown Prince, Pregnant Bride! © 2011 Helen Conrad

ISBN: 978 0 263 91184 8
eBook ISBN: 978 1 472 04479 2

05-0514

Harlequin (UK) Limited's policy is to use papers that are natural, renewable and recyclable products and made from wood grown in sustainable forests. The logging and manufacturing processes conform to the legal environmental regulations of the country of origin.

Printed and bound in Spain
by Blackprint CPI, Barcelona

Raye Morgan has been a nursery school teacher, a travel agent, a clerk and a business editor, but her best job ever has been writing romances—and fostering romance in her own family at the same time. Current score: two boys married, two more to go. Raye has published over seventy romances, and claims to have many more waiting in the wings. She lives in Southern California, with her husband and whichever son happens to be staying at home at that moment.

SECRET PRINCE, INSTANT DADDY!

BY
RAYE MORGAN

This book is dedicated to Ineke
and all my Dutch cousins

CHAPTER ONE

PRINCE DARIUS MARTEN CONSTANTIJN of the Royal
House of Ambria, presently deposed and clandestinely
living under the name of David Dykstra, was not a heavy
sleeper. Ordinarily the slightest unusual sound would
have sent him slipping silently through his luxury pent-
house apartment with a lethal weapon in hand, ready to
defend his privacy—and his life.

The sense that his life might be under threat was not
outrageous. Since he was a member of an overthrown
monarchy, his very existence was a constant challenge
to the thuglike regime that now controlled his country.
And as such, he had to consider himself in constant
jeopardy.

But tonight the instinct to defend his territory had
been muted a bit. He'd hosted a cocktail party for fifteen
rowdy London socialites and they'd all stayed much too
long. That had a consequence he didn't suffer from often
anymore, but its effects were not unfamiliar to him. He'd
had too much to drink.

So when he heard the baby cry, he thought at first
that he must be hallucinating.

"Babies," he muttered to himself, waiting to make
sure the room had stopped spinning before he risked

opening his eyes. "Why can't they keep their problems to themselves?"

The crying stopped abruptly, but by now he was fully awake. He listened, hard. It had to have been be a dream. There was no baby here. There couldn't be. This was an adult building. He was sure of it.

"No babies allowed," he murmured, closing his eyes and starting to drift back to sleep. *"Verboten."*

But his eyes shot open as he heard the little rule breaker again. This time it was just a whimper, but it was for real. No dream.

Still, in his groggy state, it took time to put all the pieces of this mystery together. And it still didn't make sense. There was no way a baby could be in his apartment. If one of his evening guests had brought one along, surely he would have noticed. And if this same ill-mannered person had left that baby behind in the coat room, wouldn't they have come back for it by now?

He tried to shrug the whole thing off and return to peaceful slumber, but by now, that was impossible. His mind was just awake enough to go into worry mode. He'd never go back to sleep until he was sure he was in a baby-free abode.

He groaned, then rolled out of bed, pulled on a pair of jeans he found in a pile on his chair and began to stalk quietly through his set of rooms, checking one after another and wondering grumpily why he'd leased a place with so many rooms, anyway. The living room was littered with cocktail napkins and empty crystal wine goblets. He'd sent the catering crew home at midnight—a mistake, he now realized. But who knew his party guests would stay until almost 3:00 a.m? Never mind, the cleaning lady would arrive in just a few hours and make everything clean and sparkling again.

"No more parties," he promised himself as he turned back to his search, kicking a long feather boa someone had left behind out of the way. "I'll just go to shindigs at other people's homes. I can still maintain my information sources and let others deal with the hassle."

But for now he had an apartment to search before he could get back to bed. He trudged on.

And then he found the baby.

It was asleep when he first saw it. He opened the door to his seldom-used media room and there it was, tucked into a drawer that was serving as a makeshift crib. The little mouth was open, the little round cheeks puffing a bit with each breath. It looked like a cute kid, but he'd never seen it before in his life.

As he watched, it gave an involuntary jump, its chubby little arms lurching upward, then falling slowly back again. But it didn't wake. Dressed in a pink stretch jumper that looked a little rumpled and a lot spit up on, the child seemed comfortable enough for now. Sleeping babies weren't so bad. But he knew very well what happened when they woke up and he shuddered to think of it.

It was pretty annoying, finding an uninvited baby in your home and it was pretty obvious who was to blame—the long, leggy blonde draped rather gracelessly across his cantilevered couch. He'd never seen *her* before, either.

"What in blazes is going on here?" he said softly.

Neither of them stirred, but he hadn't meant to wake them yet. He needed another moment or two to take in this situation, analyze it and make some clear-headed decisions. All his instincts for survival were coming alert. He was fairly certain that this was no ordinary sleepover he'd been saddled with. This must have something to do with his royal past with its messy rebellion history and his precariously uncertain future.

Worse, he had a pretty strong feeling it was going to turn out to be a threat—maybe even the threat he'd been expecting for most of his life.

He was fully awake now. He had to think fast and make sound judgments. His gaze slid over the blonde, and despite his suspicions about her, his immediate reaction was a light frisson of attraction. Though her legs were sprawled awkwardly, reminding him of a young colt who hadn't got its bearings right just yet, they were shapely legs, and her short skirt had hitched up enticingly as she slept, showing the aforementioned legs off in a very charming way. Despite everything, he approved.

Most of her face was hidden by a mass of wiry curls, though one tiny, shell-like ear peeked through, and she'd wrapped her torso up tightly in a thick brown sweater. She wasn't really all that young, but her casual pose made her seem that way and something about her was endearing at first glance. There was an appeal to the woman that might have made him smile under other circumstances.

But he frowned instead and his gaze snapped back to stare at that gorgeous little ear. It was decorated with a penny-sized earring that seemed familiar. As he looked more closely, he could see it was molded in the form of the old Ambrian coat of arms—the coat of arms of the deposed royal family he belonged to.

As adrenaline shot through his system, his heart began to thump in his chest and he wished he'd picked up the weapon he usually carried at night. Only a very select set of people in the world knew about his connection to Ambria, and his life depended on it being kept a secret.

Who the hell was this?

He was pretty sure he was about to find out.

"Hey. Wake up."

Ayme Negri Sommers snuggled down deeper into her place on the couch and tried to ignore the hand shaking her shoulder. Every molecule of her body was resisting the wake-up call. After the last two days she'd had, sleep was the only thing that would save her.

"Come on," the shaker said gruffly. "I've got some questions that need some answers."

"Later," she muttered, hoping he'd go away. "Please, later."

"Now." He shook her shoulder again. "Are you listening to me?"

Ayme heard him just fine, but her eyes wouldn't open. Scrunching up her face, she groaned. "Is it morning yet?" she asked plaintively.

"Who are you?" the man demanded, ignoring her question. "What are you doing here?"

He wasn't going away. She would have to talk to him and she dreaded it. Her eyelids felt like sandpaper and she wasn't even sure they would open when she asked them to. But somehow she managed. Wincing at the light shafting in through the open door, she peered up through her wild hair at the angry-looking man standing over her.

"If you could give me just one more hour of sleep, we might be able to discuss this in a rational manner," she proposed hopefully, her speech slightly slurred. "I'm so tired, I'm hardly human at the moment."

Of course, that was a lie. She was human alright, and despite how rotten she felt, she was having a reaction to this man that was not only typically human, it was also definitely feminine. Bottom line, she was responding to the fact that he was ridiculously attractive. She took in the dark, silky hair that fell in an engaging screen over his forehead, the piercing blue eyes, the wide shoulders and the bare chest with its chiseled muscles, and she pulled in a quick little gasp of a breath.

Wow.

She'd seen him earlier, but from a distance and more fully clothed. Up close and half-naked was better. She recommended it, and under other circumstances she would have been smiling by now.

But this wasn't a smiling situation. She was going to have to explain to him what she was doing here and that wasn't going to be easy. She did try to sit up and made an unconvincing attempt at controlling her unruly hair with both hands. And all the while she was trying to think of a good way to broach the subject that she'd come for. She had a feeling it wouldn't be a popular topic. She would have to introduce it just right and hope for the best.

"You can do all the sleeping you want once we get you to wherever it is that you belong," he was saying icily. "And that sure as hell isn't here."

"That's where you're wrong," she said sadly. "I'm here for a reason. Unfortunately."

Little baby Cici murmured in her sleep and they both froze, staring at her for a moment, full of dread. But she sank back into deep slumber and Ayme sighed with relief.

"If you wake the baby up, you're going to have to take care of her," she warned him in a hushed voice. "I'm in a zombie trance."

He was sputtering. At least that was what it sounded like to her, but she wasn't in good judging form at the moment. He could have been swearing under his breath. Yes, that was probably it. At any rate, he wasn't pleased.

She sighed, shoulders sagging. "Look, I know you're not in the best shape yourself. I saw you when we first got here. You had obviously been enjoying your party a little too much. That's why I didn't bother to try to talk to you at the time. You know very well that you could use more sleep as much as I could." She scrunched up her nose and looked at him hopefully. "Let's call a truce for now and…"

"No."

She sighed, letting her head fall back. "No?"

"No."

She made a face. "Oh, all right. If you insist. But I warn you, I can barely put a sentence together. I'm incoherent. I haven't had any real sleep for days."

He was unrelenting, standing over her with strong hands set on his very tight and slender hips. The worn jeans rode low on them, exposing a flat, muscular stomach and the sexiest belly button she'd ever seen. She stared at it, hoping to deflect his impatience.

It didn't work.

"Your sleep habits are none of my concern," he said coldly. "I'm not interested. I just want you out of here and on your way back to wherever you came from."

"Sorry." She shook her head, still groggy. "That's

impossible. The flight we came on left for Zurich ages ago." She glanced at the baby, sleeping peacefully in the drawer. "She cried almost the whole trip. All the way from Texas." She looked up at him, expecting sympathy but not finding much. She made a face and searched his eyes, hoping for a little compassion at the very least. "Do you understand what that means?"

He was frowning like someone trying to figure all this out. "You flew here straight from Texas?"

"Well, not exactly. We did change planes in New York."

"Texas?" he repeated softly, as though he couldn't quite believe it.

"Texas," she repeated slowly, in case he was having trouble with the word itself. "You know, the Lone Star state. The big one, down by Mexico."

"I know where Texas is," he said impatiently.

"Good. We're a little touchy about that down home."

He shook his head, still puzzling over her. "You sound very much like an American," he said.

She shrugged and looked up with a genuine innocence. "Sure. What else would I be?"

He was staring at her earrings. She reached up and touched one of them, not sure what his interest was. They were all she had left from her birth mother and she wore them all the time. She knew her original parents had come from the tiny island country of Ambria. So had her adoptive family, but that was years ago and far away. Ambria and its problems had only been minimally relevant to her life as yet.

But then, she was forgetting that the Ambrian connection was the reason she was here. So naturally he would notice. Still, something about the intensity of his interest made her uncomfortable. It was probably safer to go back to talking about Cici.

"But as I was saying, she wasn't happy about traveling, and she let everyone know it, all across the Atlantic." She groaned, remembering. "Everyone on that plane hated me. It was hell on earth. Why do people have babies, anyway?"

His eyes widened and one eyebrow rose dramatically. "I don't know. You tell me."

"Oh."

She gulped. That was a mistake. She groaned internally. She really couldn't afford to goof up like that. He'd assumed Cici was her baby, which was exactly what she wanted him to think, at least for now. She had to be more careful.

She wished she were a better actor, but even a professional performer might have trouble with this gig. After all she'd been through over the past week, she really ought to be in a straightjacket by now. Or at least a warm bath.

Just days before, she'd been a normal young first-year lawyer, working for a small law firm that specialized in immigration law. And then, suddenly, the world had all caved in on her. Things had happened, things she didn't dare think about if she was to keep her wits about her. Things she would have to deal with eventually, but not yet…not now.

Still, she was afraid that nothing would ever be sane again. She'd turned around and found herself in the middle of a nightmare, and suddenly she'd had very limited choice. She could give up and go to bed and pull the covers over her head for the duration—or she could try to take care of what was left of her family and get baby Cici to where she belonged.

The question was moot, of course. She was used to doing what was expected of her, doing the responsible thing. She'd quickly decided on the latter course and now here she was, single-mindedly following the path she'd set for herself.

Once her mission was accomplished she would breathe a sigh of relief, go back to Texas and try to pick up the pieces of her life. That would be the time for facing what had happened and deciding how in the world she was going to go on now that everything was gone. But until then, for the sake of this tiny life she was protecting, she had to maintain her strength and determination no matter how hard it got.

In the meantime, she knew she had to lie. It went against her nature. She was usually the type who was ready to give her life story to anyone with a friendly face. But she had to squelch that impulse, hold back her natural inclinations and lie.

It wasn't easy. It was a painful lie. She had to make the world around her believe that Cici was her baby. She hadn't been a lawyer for long, but she knew a thing or two and one of them was that she would put this whole plan in jeopardy if people knew Cici wasn't hers, and that she had no right to be dragging her around the world like this. Social workers would be called in. Bureaucrats would get involved. Cici would be taken away from her and who knew what awful things might happen then.

Despite everything, she already loved that little child. And even if she didn't she would have done just about anything for Samantha's baby.

"Well, you know what I mean," she amended a bit lamely.

"I don't really care what you mean," he said impatiently. "I want to know how you got in here. I want to know what you think you're doing here." His blue eyes darkened. "And most of all, I want you to go somewhere else."

She winced. She could hardly blame him. "Okay," she said, pulling herself up taller in the seat. "Let me try to explain."

Was that a sneer on his handsome face?

"I'm all ears."

She knew very well he was being sarcastic. He didn't seem to like her very much. That was too bad. Most people liked her on sight. She wasn't used to this sort of hostility. She sighed, too sleepy to do anything about it, and went back to contemplating his ears.

They were very nice and tight to the sides of his head. She admired them for a moment. Everything about this man was pretty fine, she had to admit. Too bad she always felt like a gangly, awkward teenager around men like this. She was tall; almost six feet, and she'd been that tall since puberty. Her high school years had been uncomfortable. She'd been taller than all the boys until her senior year. People told her she was willowy and beautiful now, but she still felt like that clumsy kid who towered over everyone.

"Okay."

She rose and began to pace restlessly. Where to begin? She'd thought this visit was going to be pretty straightforward, but now that she was here, it seemed much more complicated. The trouble was, she didn't know all the sorts of facts a man like this was going to want to know. She'd acted purely on instinct, grabbing Cici and heading for London on barely a moment's notice. Panic, she supposed. But under the circumstances, she had to think it was understandable. She'd done the only thing she could think of. And now here she was.

She closed her eyes and drew in a deep, shaky breath. She'd come to this man's apartment for a reason. What was it again? Oh, yes. Someone had told her he could help her find little Cici's father.

"Do you remember meeting a girl named Samantha?" she asked, her voice cracking a bit on the name. Now it was going to be a chore just to keep from crying. "Small, blonde, pretty face, wore a lot of jangly bracelets?"

He swayed just a little and looked to be about at the end of his tether. She noticed, with a bit of a start, that his hands were balled into tight fists at his side. Another moment or two and he was going to be tearing his hair out in frustration. Either that or giving her shoulders a firm shake. She took a step backward, just in case.

"No," he said, his voice low and just this side of angry. "Never heard of her." His brilliant blue eyes were glaring at her. "And never heard of you, either. Though you haven't provided your own name yet, so I really can't say that, can I?"

"Oh." She gave a start and presented herself before him again, chagrined that she'd been so remiss.

"Of course. I'm sorry." She stuck out her hand. "My name is Ayme Sommers. From Dallas, as if you couldn't tell."

He let her stand there with her hand out for a beat too long, still looking as though he couldn't believe this was happening. For a moment, she thought he was going to refuse to respond and the question of what she was going to do next flitted into her head. But she didn't have to come up with a good comeback, after all. He finally relented and slid his hand over hers, then held on to it, not letting her go.

"Interesting name," he said dryly, staring hard into her dark eyes. "Now tell me the rest."

She blinked at him, trying to pull her hand back and not getting much cooperation. She was suddenly aware of his warm skin and hard muscles in a way that stopped the breath in her throat. She tried not to look down at his chest. It took all her strength.

"What do you mean?" she said, her voice squeaking. "What 'rest'?"

He pulled her closer and she gaped at him, not sure why he was playing this game of intimidation.

"What is your tie to Ambria?" he asked, his voice low and intense.

She gasped, her eyes wide, and gazed at him in wonder. "How did you know?"

He inclined his head in her direction. "The Ambrian shield on your earrings pretty much gives it away."

"Oh." She'd forgotten. Her mind was full of cotton right now. It was amazing that she even remembered who she was. She touched one ear with her free hand. "Of course. Most people don't know what it is."

His eyes narrowed. "But you do."

"Oh, yes."

She smiled at him and he winced, and almost took a step backward himself. Her smile seemed to light up the room. It was too early for that—and inappropriate considering the circumstances. He had to look away, but he didn't let go of her hand.

"My parents were from Ambria. I was actually born there. My birth name is Ayme Negri."

That sounded like a typically Ambrian name, as far as he knew. But he didn't really know as much as he should. This girl with the shields decorating her ears might very well know a lot more than he did about his own country.

He stared at her, realizing with a stunned, sick feeling that his true knowledge of the land his family had ruled for a thousand years was woefully inadequate. He didn't know what to ask her. He didn't know enough to even conjure up a quick quiz to test her truthfulness. All these years he'd had to hide his identity, and in the process he hadn't really learned enough. He'd read books. He'd talked to people. He'd remembered things from his early childhood. And he'd had one very effective mentor. But it wasn't enough. He didn't know who he was at his very core, nor did he know much about the people he came from.

And now she'd arrived, a virtual pop quiz. And he hadn't studied.

Her hand in his felt warm. He searched her face. Her eyes were bright and questioning, her lips slightly parted as though waiting for what was going to happen next and slightly excited by it. She looked like a teenage girl waiting for her first kiss. He was beginning to think that the alarm, which had gone off like a whistle in his brain, was a false one.

But who was she really and why was she here? She seemed so open, so free. He couldn't detect a hint of guile in her. No assassin could have been this calm and innocent-looking.

It was pretty hard to believe that she could have been sent here to kill him.

CHAPTER TWO

"AYME NEGRI," he repeated softly. "I'm David Dykstra."

He watched her eyes as he said the name. Was there a slight blink? Did she know it was an alias?

No, there was nothing there. No hint of special knowledge. No clues at all. And it only made sense. If she'd wanted to finish him off, she'd had her chance while he was sleeping.

Still, he couldn't let his guard down. He'd been waiting for someone to arrive with murder on his mind since that dark, stormy night when he was six years old and he'd been spirited away from the rebellion in Ambria and across the countryside in search of a safe haven.

The palace had been burned and his parents killed. And most likely some of his siblings had died as well—though he didn't know for sure. But he'd been rescued and hidden with a family in the Netherlands, the Dykstras. He'd been spared.

All that had happened twenty-five years ago, and no one had ever come to find him, neither friend nor foe. Someday he knew he would have to face his destiny. But maybe not today.

"Ayme Negri," he said again, mulling over the name.

He was still holding her hand, almost as though he was hoping to gain some comprehension of her motives just by sense of touch.

An Ambrian woman, raised in Texas. That was a new one to him.

"Say something in Ambrian," he challenged quickly. At least he had a chance of understanding a little of the language if she didn't get too complicated. He hadn't spoken it since he was a child, but he still dreamed in his native tongue sometimes.

But it didn't seem she would be willing to go along with that little test. Her eyes widened and a hint of quick anger flashed across her face.

"No," she said firmly, her lovely chin rising. "I don't have to prove anything to you."

His head reared back. "Are you serious? You break into my apartment and now you're going to take on airs?"

"I didn't break in," she said indignantly. "I walked in, just like everybody else you had here to your party. I...I sort of melted into a group that was arriving and no one seemed to think twice."

She shrugged, remembering how she'd slipped into the elevator with a bunch of boisterous young city sophisticates. They seemed to accept her right to come in with them without a second thought. She'd smiled at a pretty young woman in a feathered boa and the woman had laughed.

"Look, she's brought a baby," she said to her escort, a handsome young man who had already had much too much to drink. "I wish I had a baby." She turned and pouted. "Jeremy, why won't you let me have a baby?"

"What the hell, babies for everyone," he'd called out

as the elevator doors opened, and he'd almost fallen over with the effort. "Come on. If we're going to be handing out babies, I'm going to need another drink."

Laughing, the group had swelled in through the door to this apartment and left her standing in the entryway. No one else had noticed her. She'd seen the host in the main room, dancing with a beautiful raven-haired woman and swaying like a man who'd either fallen in love or had too many rum drinks. She'd sighed and decided the better part of valor was to beat a hasty retreat. And that was when she'd slipped into the media room and found a drawer she could use as a bassinet for Cici.

"I don't remember inviting you," he noted dryly.

"I invited myself." Her chin lifted even higher. "Just because you didn't notice me at the time doesn't make me a criminal."

He was ready with a sharp retort, but he bit his tongue. This was getting him nowhere. He had to back off and start over again. If he was going to find out what was really going on, he needed to gain her trust. Making her defensive was counterproductive at best.

And he did want to know, not only because he was plain curious, but because of the Ambrian connection. There had to be a reason for it. Young Ambrian women weren't likely to just appear on his doorstep out of the blue. In fact, it had never happened before.

"Sorry," he said gruffly, turning away. Taking a deep breath and calming himself, he looked back and his gaze fell on the little child. There had been a period, while living in his huge adoptive family, when he'd spent a lot of time with babies. They didn't scare him.

Still, he could take or leave them. They were often just too much work.

But he knew very well what happened when one of this age was woken from a sound sleep, and the results were never very pretty.

"Listen, let's go to the kitchen and get a cup of coffee. Then we can talk without waking up your baby."

"Okay." She stopped, looking back. "Shall I just leave her here?" she asked doubtfully.

Cici had been practically glued to her body ever since Sam had left her behind that rainy Texas day that seemed so long ago now. And yet it hadn't even been a week yet. She smiled, suddenly enchanted with the way the child looked in the drawer.

"Look at the little angel. She's sleeping like a lamb now."

He frowned. "How old is that baby?" he asked suspiciously.

That was another question she wasn't confident enough to answer. Sam hadn't left behind any paperwork, not even a birth certificate.

"Her name's Cici," she said, stalling for time.

His glare wasn't friendly. "Nice name. Now, how old is she?"

"About six weeks," she said, trying to sound sure of herself and pretty much failing at it. "Maybe two months."

He stared at her. Skepticism was too mild a term for what his gaze was revealing about his thoughts on her answer.

She smiled brightly. "Hard to remember. Time flies."

"Right."

She followed him out into the living room. He snagged a shirt from the hall closet as they passed it, shrugged into it but left it open. She made an abrupt turn so he wouldn't find her staring at him, and as she did so, she caught sight of the view from the huge floor-to-ceiling picture window.

She gasped, walking toward it. It was four in the morning but the landscape was still alive with lights. Cars carried people home, a plane cruised past, lights blinking. Looking down, she was suddenly overwhelmed with a sense of detached wonder. There were so many people below, all with their own lives, going on with things as though everything was normal. But it wasn't normal. The world had tipped on its axis a few days ago. Nothing would ever be the same again. Didn't they know?

For just a moment, she was consumed with a longing to be one of those clueless people, riding through the night in a shiny car, going toward a future that didn't include as much heartbreak and tragedy as she knew was waiting for her once this adventure in Britain was over.

"Wow. You can see just about all of London from here, can't you?" She was practically pressing her nose to the glass.

"Not quite," he said, glancing out at the lights of the city. He liked this place better than most. It was close to the building where his offices were—centrally located and perfect for running the British branch of his foster father's multinational shipping business. "But it is a pretty spectacular view."

"I'll say." She was standing tall, both hands raised, fingertips pressed to the glass to hold her balance as she leaned forward, taking it all in. She looked almost poised to fly away over the city herself.

He started to suggest that she might want to keep her hands off the window, but as he watched her, he checked himself. With her long limbs and unusual way of holding her posture, she had an unselfconscious gawkiness, like a young girl, that was actually quite winsome. But she really wasn't all that young, and in that short skirt, her legs looked like they went on forever. So he kept quiet and enjoyed his own temporary view, until she tired of it and levered back away from the glass.

"Cities like this are kind of scary," she said, her tone almost whimsical. "You really get the feeling it's every man for himself."

He shrugged. "You're just not used to the place. It's unexplored territory to you." His wide mouth quirked. "As the song says, faces are ugly and people seem wicked."

She nodded as though pleased that he saw the connection. "That's the way I felt coming here tonight. A stranger in a very weird part of town."

He almost smiled but hadn't meant to. Didn't really want to. He needed to maintain an edgy sort of wariness with this woman. He still didn't know why she was here, and her reasons could be costly to him for all he knew.

Still, he found himself almost smiling. He bit it off quickly.

"This part of town is hardly weird," he said shortly. The real estate was high class and high-toned, and he was paying through the nose for that fact. "Maybe you miss the longhorns and Cadillacs."

She gave him a haughty look. She'd caught the ill-concealed snobbery in his tone. "I've been out of Texas before, you know," she said. "I spent a semester in Japan in my senior year."

"World traveler, are you?" he said wryly. But he rather regretted having been a little mean, and he turned away. He needed to be careful. The conversation had all the hallmarks of becoming too personal. He had to break it off. Time to get serious.

He led her on into his ultramodern, wide-open kitchen with its stainless-steel counters and green onyx walls. He got down two mugs, then put pods into the coffee machine, one at a time. In minutes it was ready and he handed her a steaming mug of coffee, then gazed at her levelly.

"Okay, let's have it."

She jumped in surprise. "What?" she asked, wide-eyed.

He searched her dark eyes. What he found there gave him a moment of unease. On the surface she seemed very open and almost naive, a carefree young woman ready to take on the world and go for whatever was out there. But her eyes held a more somber truth. There was tragedy in those eyes, fear, uncertainty. Whatever it was that she was hiding, he hoped it had nothing to do with him.

"Who are you and what are you doing here?" he asked again. "Why are you carrying around a very young baby in a strange city in the middle of the night? And most important, how did you even get in here?"

She stared at him for a moment, then tried to smile as she took a shallow sip of the hot coffee. "Wow. That's a lot to throw at a girl who's only half-awake," she noted evasively.

His grunt held no sympathy. "You threw a six-week-old baby at me," he reminded her. "So let's have it."

She took a deep breath, as though this really was an effort. "Okay. I think I already explained how I got in here. I hitched a ride with a party group and no one minded."

He groaned, thinking of some choice words he would have with the doorman later that day.

"As I told you, my name is Ayme Negri Sommers. I'm from Dallas, Texas. And…" She swallowed hard, then looked him in the eye. "And I'm looking for Cici's father."

That hit him like a fist in the stomach. He swallowed hard and searched her gaze again. He knew very well that he was now treading into a minefield and he had to watch his step very carefully.

"Oh, really?" he said, straining to maintain a light, casual tone. "So where did you lose him?"

She took it as a serious question. "That's just the trouble. I'm not really sure."

He stared at her. Was she joking? Nothing she said was making any sense.

"But I heard from a very reliable source," she went on, setting down her mug and putting her hands on her hips as she turned to look questioningly at him, "that you would be able to help me out."

Ah-ha. A very dangerous mine had appeared right in front of him with this one. Careful!

"Me?" he asked, trying not to let his voice rise with anxiety. "Why me?"

She started to say something, then stopped and looked down, uncomfortable and showing it. "See, this is why this is so hard. I don't really know. My source said that you would know where to find him." She looked back up into his face, waiting.

"So you think it's someone I know?" he asked, still at sea. "Obviously, it's not me."

She hesitated much too long over that one and he let out an exclamation, appalled. "You can't be serious. I think I would have noticed a little thing like that, and I know damn well I've never seen you before." He shook his head in disbelief.

She sighed. "I'm not accusing you of anything."

"Good. So why are you here?"

She took a deep breath. "Okay, the person who advised me to look you up is a man associated with the firm I work for."

"In Texas? And he thinks he knows who I know?" He shook his head, turning away and beginning to pace the floor in frustration. "This is absurd. How did he even know my name?"

"He told me you socialize in the same circles as Cici's dad. He said, 'Don't worry. He'll know how to find him.'"

"Oh, he did, did he?" For some reason this entire conversation was stoking a rage that was smoldering inside him. He stopped and confronted her. "So this person who's supposed to be Cici's father—this person I'm supposed to know where to find—what's his name?"

She half twisted away. This had all seemed so easy when she'd planned it out as she made her way to the airport in Dallas. She would dash off to London, find Cici's father, hand over the baby and head back home. She hadn't realized she would have to try to explain it all to someone in between. When you got right down to it, the bones of the story weren't making a lot of sense.

And she realized now that one element would sound really goofy to this man. She was hoping to keep that one under wraps for as long as possible.

She turned back with a heart-wrenching sigh and said dramatically, "Well…you see, that's the problem. I'm not sure what his actual name is."

He stared at her. The absurdity of the situation was becoming clear. She was looking for a man who had fathered her baby. She didn't know where he was. She didn't know his name. But she'd come here for help. And he was supposed to ride to the rescue? Why, exactly?

It was true that he had a reputation for knowing everyone who counted within a certain social strata. He'd made it his business to know them, for his own purposes. But he had to have something to go on. He couldn't just throw out possibilities.

"What are you going to do when you find him? Are you planning to marry the guy?"

"What?" She looked shocked, as though this very mundane idea was too exotic to contemplate. "No. Of course not."

"I see," he said, though he didn't.

She bit her lip and groaned silently. She was so tired. She couldn't think straight. She just wanted to go back to sleep. Maybe things would look clearer in the morning.

"How am I supposed to find someone if I don't know his name?"

She turned and gave him an exasperated look. "If this were easy, I could have done it on my own."

"I see. I'm your last resort, am I?"

She thought for a second, then nodded. "Pretty

much." She gazed at him earnestly, feeling weepy. "Do you think you can help me?"

He gazed at her, at her pretty face with those darkly smudged, sleepy eyes, at the mop of blond hair that settled wildly around her head as though it had been styled by gypsies, at her slightly trembling lower lip.

He had a small fantasy. In it, he told her flat out, "Hell, no. I'm not helping you. You give me nothing and ask for miracles. I've got better things to do with my time than to run all over London looking for someone I'm never going to find. This is insane."

As the fantasy began to fade, he saw himself reaching into his pocket and handing her money to go to a hotel. What a happy little dream it was.

But looking at her, he knew it wasn't going to happen. Right now, her eyes were filling with tears, as though she could read his mind and knew he wanted to get rid of her and her problems.

"Okay," he told her gruffly, clenching his fists to keep from following his instinct to reach out to comfort her. And then he added a touch of cynicism to his tone, just for good measure. "If all this is a little too overwhelming for you in your current state of hysteria…"

"I am not hysterical!" she cried indignantly.

He raised an eyebrow. "That's a matter of judgment and not even very relevant. Why don't we do this in a logical, methodical fashion? Then maybe we can get somewhere."

She moaned. "Like back to bed?" she suggested hopefully.

"Not yet." He was pacing again. "You need to fill in some of the blanks. Let's start with this. What exactly is your tie to Ambria? Give me the full story."

He'd given up wondering if she was here to harm him. The complete innocence she displayed wasn't very likely to be a put-on. And anyway, what sort of an incompetent murder master would send a young woman with a baby to do the dirty deed? It just didn't make sense.

"My parents were Ambrian," she began. "I was actually born there but that was just before the rebellion. My birth parents died in the fighting. I don't remember them at all. I was taken out with a lot of other refugee children and rushed to the States. I was adopted right away. I was only about eighteen months old, so as far as I'm concerned, my adoptive parents are my parents." She shrugged. "End of story."

"Are you kidding? We've barely begun." He stopped and looked down at her, arms folded over his chest. "Who told you about your Ambrian background?"

"Oh, the Sommerses had Ambrian roots, too. Second generation American, though. So they told me things, and there were some books around the house." She shook her head. "But it wasn't like I was immersed in the culture or anything like that."

"But you do know about the rebellion? You know about the Granvilli family and how they led an illegal coup that killed a lot of people and left them in charge of an ancient monarchy that should have been left alone?"

She blinked. "Uh…I guess."

"But you don't know much about it?"

She shook her head.

He gazed at her, speculation glowing in his silver-blue eyes. "So you don't have family still in Ambria?"

"Family?" She stared at him blankly. "Not that I know of."

"I guess they were all killed by the rebels?"

She blinked and shook her head. "I don't know if the rebels killed them."

He raised a cynical eyebrow. "Who do you think killed them?"

She ran her tongue nervously over her lower lip. "Well, to tell you the truth, I really don't know what side they were on."

That stunned him. The idea that someone decent might support the rebels who had killed his parents and taken over his country didn't really work for him. He dismissed it out of hand. But if she were around long enough, and he had a chance, he would find out who her parents were and what role they played. It seemed like something she ought to know.

"Now that we've established who you are, let's get to the real topic. Why are you really here?"

She sighed. "I told you."

But he was already shaking his head. "You told me a lot of nonsense. Do you really expect me to believe you had a baby and don't know the father? It doesn't add up, Ayme. How about giving me the real story?"

She felt like a bird caught in a trap. She hated lying. That was probably why she did it so badly. She had to tell him something. Something convincing. Had to be. She was beginning to see that she would really be in trouble if he refused to help her.

But before she could conjure up something good, a wail came from across the apartment. Ayme looked toward where the sound was coming from, uncertainty on her face. Why didn't this baby seem to want to sleep for more than an hour at a time, day or night?

"I just fed her an hour ago," she said, shaking her

head and thinking of her dwindling stash of formula bottles. "Do you think she really wants to eat again?"

"Of course," he told her. "They want to eat all the time. Surely you've noticed."

She bit her lip and looked at him. "But the book says four hours…."

He groaned. She was still using a book?

"Babies don't wear watches," he noted, feeling some sympathy for this new mother, but a lot of impatience, as well.

"True." She gave him a wry look as she turned to go. "But you'd think they could look at a clock now and then."

He grinned. He couldn't help it. If he really let himself go, he would start liking her and he knew it. And so he followed her into the room and watched as she stroked the little round head rather inefficiently. The baby was definitely crying, and the stroking was doing no good at all. From what he could tell, Ayme didn't seem to have a clue as to what to do to quiet her.

"Why don't you try changing her?" he suggested. "She's probably wet."

"You think so?" That seemed to be a new idea to her. "Okay, I'll try it."

She had a huge baby bag crammed full of things, but she didn't seem to know what she was looking for. He watched her rummage around in it for a few minutes, then stepped forward and pulled out a blanket which he spread out on the couch.

"I can do this," she said a bit defensively.

"I'm sure you can," he said. "I'm just trying to help."

She winced, feeling genuine regret for her tone. "I know. I'm sorry."

She pulled out a paper diaper and laid it on the blanket, then pulled Cici up out of the drawer.

"There you go little girl," she cooed to her. "We're going to get you nice and clean."

David stood back and watched, arms folded across his chest, mouth twisted cynically. She didn't seem very confident to him. Cici wasn't crying hard, only whimpering at this point, but he had the impression that she was looking up at the woman working over her with something close to apprehension.

"Don't you have someplace else you could be?" she muttered to him as she worked, and he could see that she was nervous to be doing this in front of him. Like someone who didn't really know what she was doing.

One thing he knew for sure—this woman didn't know the first thing about taking care of a baby. How crazy was that? And then it came to him. She wasn't the mother of the baby. Couldn't be. In six weeks time anyone would have learned more than she seemed to know.

"Alright Ayme Negri Sommers," he said firmly at last, "come clean. Whose baby is this?"

She looked up, a deer in the headlights.

"Mine."

"Liar."

She stared at him for a moment, degrees of uncertainty flashing across her pretty face. Finally, she threw her hands into the air. "Okay, you got me." She shrugged, looking defeated. "She's not really mine." She sighed. "What was your first clue?"

He grunted, stepping forward to take over. "The fact

that you don't know beans about taking care of a baby," he said, taking the diaper from her and beginning to do an expert job of it in her place. "The fact that you're still reading a book to figure out which end is up."

She heaved a heart-felt sigh. "I guess that was inevitable. It's really such a relief. I hated living a lie." She looked at him with more gratitude than resentment. "How come you know so much about babies, anyway?"

"I grew up in a big family. We all had to pitch in."

She sighed. "We didn't have any babies around while I was growing up. It was just me and Sam."

The baby was clean and in dry diapers. David put her up against his shoulder and she cuddled in, obviously comfortable as could be and happy to be with someone who knew what he was doing. He managed a reluctant smile. It was just like riding a bicycle. Once you knew how to hold a baby, you didn't forget.

He turned back to Ayme. "Who's this Sam you keep talking about?"

She swallowed, realizing the answer to that question was going to be tied to very different emotions from now on.

"My...my sister, Samantha. She was Cici's real mother."

And that was when the horror hit her for the first time since she'd left home. Her legs turned to rubber. Closing her eyes, she sank to the couch, fighting to hold back the blackness that threatened to overtake her whenever she let herself think, even for a moment, about Samantha. It was the same for her parents. The accident had taken them, too. Her whole family.

It was all too much to bear. If she let herself really

think about what had happened and about the emptiness that was waiting for her return to Dallas, the bubble she was living in would pop in an instant. She couldn't think about it and she couldn't tell him about it. Not yet. Maybe not ever. The pain was just too raw to manage.

Steeling herself, she forced out a quick explanation.

"Sam died in a car accident a few days ago." Her voice was shaking but she was going to get through this. "I…I was taking care of Cici when it happened. It was all so sudden. It…"

She took in a gasping breath, steadying herself. Then she cleared her throat and went on.

"Now I'm trying to get her to where she belongs. I'm trying to find her father." She looked up, surprised to find that she'd gone through it and was still coherent. "There. Now you know it all."

He stared at her. Her eyes looked like dark bruises marring her pretty face. The tragedy in her voice was mirrored by her body language, the tilt of her head, the pain in her voice. He didn't doubt for a minute that everything she'd just told him was absolutely true and it touched him in a way he hadn't expected.

The urge was strong to put down the baby and take the woman in his arms. If anyone needed a bit of comfort, Ayme did. But he stopped himself from making that move. He knew it wouldn't work out well. The last thing she wanted right now was compassion. The smallest hint of sympathy would very probably make her fall apart emotionally. He assumed that she didn't want that any more than he did. At least he hoped so. He looked away and grimaced.

But—back to basics—he still didn't understand why she'd come to him.

"Ayme, I'm not Cici's father," he said bluntly.

"Oh, I know. I know it's not you."

He shook his head, still at sea and searching for land-fall. "Then why are you here?"

She shrugged. "You're going to help me find him." She gazed at him earnestly. "You just have to. And since you're Ambrian…"

"I never said I was Ambrian," he broke in quickly. He had to make that clear. As far as the rest of the world knew, he was a citizen of the Netherlands, born and bred Dutch. That was the way it had been for twenty-five years and that was the way it had to be.

"Well, you know a lot about Ambria, which not a lot of people do."

Reluctantly, he admitted it. "True."

Rising from the couch, she began to pace much the way he had a few minutes earlier. She was exhausted and her emotions were spent. But she had more work to do. Glancing over at David, she noticed that Cici's downy head was tucked against his shoulder and the little eyes were closed. She was asleep. Ayme's sigh was from the depths of her wounded soul.

"If only I'd had you along on the flight over the Atlantic," she said.

"Don't try to change the subject," he said, turning to lay the baby down very carefully in her makeshift bed. "If you want my help, you've got to give me more. I can't do anything unless I understand the parameters I'm dealing with."

She nodded. He was right, of course. But what could she say to explain this crazy situation? She moved rest-lessly toward the doorway and leaned against the door-jamb. From there, she could see across the living room and out through the huge picture window surveying the city. The mass of city lights spread out below added a manic energy, despite the time of night.

That made her think—what if all those lights went out one night?

She nodded, realizing that the stars would take their place. And that would be a whole different dynamic. She wasn't sure which she would prefer at the moment— manic energy or soothing starlight. But her preference didn't mean a thing. She had to deal with what she had before her.

Throwing her head back, she began.

"Sam didn't tell me much about Cici's father. Actually, I hadn't seen her for almost a year when she showed up with a baby in her arms. I had no idea…" She put a hand to her forehead as she remembered the shock of Sam's return home. "Anyway, she didn't tell me much, but she did tell me that Cici's father was Ambrian. That she'd met him on a trip to London. And that she wanted nothing more in the world at that moment than to find him and show him his baby."

Of course, there were other moments, even hours, when Sam acted as though she didn't care at all—especially when she took off without her baby. But he didn't have to know about that.

She turned and came back into the room, watching David tuck a blanket in around Cici. It was unusual to see such a strong, handsome man doing something like that. At least it seemed unusual to her. But who knew? Maybe she should get out more.

That sweet little baby was finally getting the sort of care she deserved. She thought of how careless Sam had seemed with Cici. Their mother had been appalled.

But maybe that was because of her precarious circumstances. If she could have found Cici's father and they could have formed a real family, maybe things would have been different.

"Now she'll never get the chance," she murmured softly, then caught herself and frowned. None of that. She couldn't let herself drift off into that sort of sadness. They would never get anything done.

He'd finished with the baby and he came to stand in front of her, looking down. "But she didn't tell you this guy's name?"

She hesitated. "She told me a name, but…."

"Who? You've got to tell me, Ayme. I don't see how I can help you if you won't tell me."

She turned away again and he followed her out to the picture window. "Do you ever see the stars?" she asked.

"Not much," he said impatiently. "Will you stick to the point?"

She drew in a deep breath and looked up at him as though this was a hard thing to do.

"Do you know anything about the lost royals of Ambria?" she asked him.

CHAPTER THREE

FOR JUST a second, David thought he'd heard Ayme wrong. Then the implications of what she'd just said crashed in on him. He could hardly breathe.

"Uh, sure," he said, managing not to sound as choked as he felt. "I've heard of them, anyway. What about them?"

She shrugged and sounded apologetic. "Well, Sam claimed Cici's father was one of them."

"Interesting."

He coughed. He'd heard of sightings before. Mostly, they were nothing, led nowhere. But there had been one that had panned out, and when he'd followed up on it, he'd found his oldest brother, the crown prince. There might be more brothers out there. Could it happen again?

"Which one?" he asked, intrigued, emotionally touched, but not really expecting much.

She gazed up at him with those huge brown eyes. "She said he was the second born, and that his name was Darius."

The room seemed to grow and then contract, as though he'd taken a hallucinogenic of some sort. It took all his strength to stay balanced without reaching for support. She was still talking, telling him something more about her sister, but he couldn't concentrate on what she was saying.

Sam had named him…*him*…as the father of her baby. But that was impossible. Incredible. Wrong. Wasn't it?

He did some quick calculations. Where had he been ten to twelve months ago? Whom had he dated? It was true that he'd spent some time over the years finding love in all the wrong places. There had been a period of his younger life when he'd made conquests first and asked questions later—if at all. He wasn't proud of those times and he was sure he'd put them well behind him. But what had he been doing last year? Why was it that he couldn't really remember?

He thought of Cici's cute little face. Was there anything familiar in it? Had he felt a slight connection? Some magic sense of kinship? A tie? Anything?

He agonized for one long moment, searching his heart and soul for evidence. But he quickly decided there was none. No, he was sure there had been nothing like that. It was crazy to even think this way.

"Have you ever heard of him?" she was asking. "Do you know much about him? Any idea where we can even look to find him?"

"We"? He noted the question and realized what it meant. She really did think he was going to drop everything in his life and start helping her, didn't she? The problem was, he would have to do just the opposite. He needed to melt away and very quickly. She didn't realize how dangerous this could be for him. She was sort of like a grenade someone had pulled the pin on and rolled into his apartment. Things could explode at any moment. The smallest jolt could blow everything up.

"No," he said shortly. "What gave you the idea I would know these things, anyway?"

"I told you, I was given your name as someone who might be able to help me."

She was looking nervous. He hated to disappoint her. But this was serious and now it had his complete attention.

"Given my name?"

As the full implications of that began to come into focus, an icy finger made its way down his spine and all his instincts for survival began to stir.

"Who was this who gave you my name?"

"A man associated with my law firm. He deals with Ambrian things all the time and he knew who you were."

He took that in and considered it carefully. But wait. His Ambrian roots weren't known to more than three or four of his closest associates. To most of the world, he was Dutch. How in hell would someone in Texas know otherwise?

"His name?" he said quickly, staring at her intensely, as though he could draw the information out of her if he tried hard enough.

"Carl Heissman. Do you know him?"

Slowly, he shook his head. He'd never heard the name before, at least, not that he could remember.

She shrugged. "I really didn't know him until…"

"How did you get in touch with him? Did you go to him and ask for his help?"

"No, it wasn't like that." She shook her head. "No, not really. I went to the office and asked for a leave and explained about Cici…."

"So how did he contact you?"

"He must have heard about what I was doing from my boss, so he gave me a call."

His heart was thumping in his chest. "He told you my name over the phone?"

"No. Actually, he wanted to meet at a little wine bar downtown. We sat out on the patio."

"Where he couldn't be recorded," he muttered to himself.

"What?" she asked.

She was beginning to wonder why all this was such a big deal to him. Either he could help her or he couldn't. The man in Texas was a side issue as far as she was concerned. She frowned at him, just to let him know she thought he was going off down a blind alley and that wasn't very helpful.

But he wasn't paying any attention to that. He shook his head, his brow furled, obviously thinking things he wasn't sharing with her.

"Go on."

"Well, I thought he knew you from the way he talked. He gave me your name and address and then he even offered to pay for the trip."

David's eyes flared at that bit of information.

"Why would he do that?"

She shrugged. "I thought it was odd at the time, but I assumed it might have been the law firm that was offering to pay. I didn't take anything from him, but…"

"But you don't really know who he is or what his connection to your law firm is, do you? He just came at you out of the blue."

She gave him an exaggerated glare for the interruption, but she plowed ahead.

"I have a number where I'm supposed to call him

when I find Cici's father." She glanced around, looking for a phone. "Do you think I should give him a call?"

He held back the grunt of exasperation he was tempted to mete out. That was obviously the last thing he wanted her to do.

"You haven't called him yet?"

"No."

"Don't."

She blinked. "Why not?"

He hesitated, then shrugged. "You haven't found Cici's father, have you?"

"Maybe not." She eyed him speculatively, her chin high.

He groaned, turning away. He knew he couldn't let her call the number. That would pinpoint his exact location for sure. But how to convince her of that without giving away the entire background?

Whoever this Carl Heissman was, the man was playing games. Deadly games. He had to think fast and get back to basics and consider all possibilities.

He glanced at her again, studied her, tried to pick up on any details he might have missed so far. Why was she really here? Was this a ploy? A plot to coax him out of hiding?

Whatever. He had to get out of here right away and hope whoever was behind sending her here wasn't already on his trail—or worse, here as well and just hadn't revealed himself as yet. He heard a sound behind him and turned quickly, jumpy as a cat.

There was nothing there—this time. That wary buzz was back in full force. Ayme had invaded his space like the point guard of a small enemy army and he was going to have to be on alert every minute. He couldn't afford to trust her or anything about her. His eyes narrowed as he looked her over and considered every angle.

And then the house phone rang.

They stared into each other's eyes for a long moment as it rang once, twice….

Then David took three steps and picked up the receiver, staring down into the identifying screen. Nothing was there. It was blank.

His face turned to stone and his heart beat so hard he could hardly breath. It was never blank. It always said Private Caller if nothing else. But this time, it was blank.

He couldn't answer. That would give the caller absolute knowledge of where he was at this very moment. There wasn't a doubt in his mind that this person wasn't calling in the middle of the night for a friendly chat. This was the danger he'd always known would come his way—and until he understood the exact threat better, it was something he had to avoid at all costs.

And more than that, he had to get out of here.

He turned to look at Ayme, wondering if she'd caught the connotations of this late night call, if she might even know who it was and why he was calling. But her face was open and innocent and her gaze was shining with curiosity. He couldn't believe she could be an expert liar and con artist with eyes like that. No, she didn't know any more than he did. He would have bet anything on that.

"Okay, you've been begging for sleep," he told her, putting the phone back on its cradle. "Why don't you take the spare bedroom around the corner from where you were? Get a few hours sleep. You'll be better for it in the morning."

"Lovely," she said, pure gratitude shining from her eyes for a few seconds. She only hoped that Cici would have as much compassion and give her a chance to get in some real, sustained sleep. Small dozes had been the rule for days.

She glanced at David. His eyes were clouded with some problem he was obviously working through and his handsome face looked a bit tense. That made her all the more grateful.

She was lucky he was taking her presence with such equanimity. Most people would have kicked her out by now, or at least edged her toward the door. But he was ready to let her stay. Thank God. She wasn't sure she could think clearly enough right now to get herself a room in a hotel on her own, especially carrying a baby around. It was great of him to invite her in. She could hardly wait to throw herself on the bed and let sleep take over.

Then she had second thoughts. He hadn't said anything about getting sleep himself, had he?

"What are you going to do?" she asked suspiciously.

He shrugged rather absently, as though his mind were miles away. "I've got some business to wrap up."

She knew it was an excuse, but she didn't push it. She was just too tired to challenge him. The thought of sheets and a real pillow were totally seductive for the moment. So she followed him to the spare bedroom and waited while he carried Cici in, setting her little bed right beside the real bed without waking her at all. He seemed to have the magic touch.

She smiled, watching him tuck Cici in. So precious.

"I'll see you later," he said gruffly, and she nodded,

waiting just until he closed the door before slipping out of her skirt and sweater, leaving only her underclothes on, and sliding between the sheets. She dropped into sleep instantly, but for some reason, she began to dream right away, and her dreams were full of tall, dark-haired men who looked very much like David.

Meanwhile, David was moving fast, preparing to vacate the premises. He'd been planning for this day from the time he could think through the consequences of being found by the vicious Granvilli family who had taken over his country. He knew they wanted all remnants of the Royal House of Ambria wiped out, wherever they might be hiding. They wanted no lingering threats to their ugly reign of terror over the ancient island people.

And he and his older brother Monte were a threat, whether the Granvilli bunch knew it yet or not. At any rate, they were determined to be one. He was already committed to being in Italy by the end of the week to meet with other Ambrians and begin planning in earnest for a return to power. He might as well leave now. There was nothing keeping him here. He'd already made his office aware of the time off he planned to take. He could begin his journey a little early and make his way to Italy in a more careful trajectory. There was no telling what other obstacles he would find along the way.

"Nothing really worth having is easy." Someone had said that once, and right now it made perfect sense to him. The struggle to get his country back was going to be a rough one and he was ready to get started.

And he had to go on his own, he told himself. There was no way to take Ayme along, no reason to do it. Why should he feel this tug of responsibility toward her? He tried to brush it away. She would be okay here. He hadn't even known she existed two hours ago. Why should he feel he owed her anything?

He didn't. But he did owe the people of Ambria everything. Time to begin paying them back.

He had preparations that had to be dealt with, paperwork that had to be destroyed so that the wrong people wouldn't see things they shouldn't see. It took some time to do all that and he had an ear cocked toward the phone in case the interested party from a half hour before might try again. But the night moved relentlessly forward without any more interruptions. The sky was barely beginning to turn pink as he wrapped up his arrangements.

Completely focused, he pulled on a dark blue turtleneck cashmere sweater and finished dressing at warp speed, then glanced around his bedroom. He hesitated for half a second. Did he have time to grab some things and shove them into an overnight bag? What the hell— he had to have something with him, and he'd taken all this time already. Why not? It was all right there and it took no time at all.

He slid into his soft leather jacket as he headed for the door. Despite all the rationalizing he'd been doing, he felt pretty rotten about leaving Ayme behind this way. She was so all alone in the city. She didn't know anyone but him.

That gave him a quick, bitter laugh. She didn't really know him, did she? Which was what was so ridiculous about all this. Still, he hesitated in the open doorway. Maybe he would call the doorman from his car and ask that he look after her. Sure. He could do that. She would be okay.

Right. He took one more step and then stopped, head hanging forward, and uttered an ugly oath. He knew he couldn't leave her.

There was no telling who that had been on the phone There was no telling who was after him—except that he was rock-bottom sure it was an agent for the Granvillis. What if the assassin came into his apartment after he left? Who would protect her? Not the doorman. That was pure fantasy.

No, he couldn't leave her—even if she was the one who had brought all this down on him. He was almost certain that she didn't know anything about it herself. She was an innocent victim. He couldn't leave her behind.

Giving out a suppressed growl of rage, he turned and went back, opening the door to the spare bedroom and looking in.

"Ayme?" he said tersely. "I'm sorry to wake you, but I've got to go and I don't want to leave you here."

"Huh?" She stared up at him, startled, her eyes bleary. She'd had less than an hour of sleep—not nearly enough. "What?"

"Sorry, kiddo," he bit out. "You're going with me." He glanced around the room. "Do you have any other clothes?"

She blinked, trying to get her fuzzy mind to make sense of the question. "I left my bag in the corner." She nodded her head in its general direction.

He stuck out his hand to her. "Come on."

She took his hand in hers and stared at it as though it were a foreign object. "Where are we going?"

He gave her a little tug and she didn't resist, rising halfway out of bed.

"Away from here."

"Why?"

"Why?" He looked into her eyes, alert for any hint of guile. "Because it's too dangerous to stay."

"Oh."

That seemed to convince her. She tumbled out of bed like a sleepy child, pulled the sheet around herself and began to look for where she'd tossed her clothes. He'd started to turn away in order to leave her to it, but something about the picture she made with the fabric twisted around her torso, leaving one shoulder bare and most of both long, golden legs exposed, had him rooted to the spot. There was a fluid, graceful beauty to her that took his breath away and reminded him of something. What was it? Some picture from history, some long forgotten fable…

Ambria. The legend of the lake. It was the familiar story of loss and earned redemption. He could remember sitting in his mother's lap as she turned the pages of the picture book and read the story to him.

"Look, Darius. Isn't she beautiful?"

The lady sat on a large rock overlooking the lake, weeping into her cupped hands, and the flowing garment she wore was very like Ayme's sheet. Funny. He hadn't thought of that scene in years and yet it came back to him so clearly as he watched Ayme leaning over to retrieve her clothes. He'd felt the same tug of compassion as a boy as he felt now.

Well, not the same, exactly. He wasn't a boy anymore and the pang of sympathy was mixed with something else, something that had to do with how creamy her bare skin looked in the lamplight, especially where the sheet pulled low, exposing the soft curve of her breast just beneath a lacy strapless bra.

For some odd reason his heart was beating hard again, and this time it had nothing to do with a phone call.

Ayme looked up and caught the look. She gave him one of her own, but hers was cool and questioning.

"Where did you say we were going?"

"I didn't. Let it be a surprise."

She frowned, not sure she liked where this seemed to be headed. "I don't like surprises." She bit her lip, then tried another idea. "I could just stay here with Cici until you get back."

"I don't know when I'll be back. If ever."

That startled her. "Oh."

"And we don't know who might be coming for a visit. So you'd better come along with me."

"I see." The seriousness in the tone of his voice finally got through to her. "In that case, can you excuse me for a moment?" she asked, politely but firmly pointing out that she needed to drop the sheet and she darn well wasn't going to do it until he was out of the room.

He had the grace to look just a bit sheepish.

"Of course," he said as he began to walk out into the living area.

But then he stopped and looked at her again. What was he thinking? Too much about what she did to his libido and not enough about what she could do to the preservation of his life and limbs.

"Wait a minute," he said, turning on his heel and walking back. "Listen Ayme, I've got to know, and I've got to know right now. Are you wearing a wire or any kind of tracking device?"

That stunned her. She clutched the sheet against her chest. What was this, spy versus spy? In her groggy state of mind, it seemed very bizarre and she couldn't make heads nor tails of it.

"What? What are you talking about?"

"I'm serious. I'm going to have to check."

She backed away, her eyes huge as she realized what he was saying and what it actually meant. She held tightly to her fabric.

"Oh, no you're not."

"Hold on," he said gruffly. "I have to do this. I'm sorry. If you've got anything on you, we've got to get rid of it."

She shook her head firmly. "I swear I don't."

"That's not good enough." He gestured for her to come closer. "Come here."

"No!"

Her voice was strong but it was determination built on sand. She was struck by his demeanor and her will was beginning to crumble around the edges. He wasn't a pervert and he wasn't kidding around. She wasn't sure how she knew this with such certainty, but she did.

"You might be bugged and not even know it," he said earnestly, holding out his hand. "Let me see your mobile."

That she could deliver.

"Be my guest." She tossed it to him, but pulled the sheet even more tightly around her body and was very sure to stay out of his reach, frowning as fiercely as she could muster.

He slid open the little compartment, flipped out the battery and checked behind it. Nothing. He put the battery back and switched it off, then tossed it back to her.

"I'll have to ask you to leave it turned off," he told her. "A working mobile is a basic homing device."

Funny—and sad, but turning off her cell phone would have seemed like turning off her source of oxygen until very recently. But now it didn't really faze her. Most of the people she might expect a call from were gone. The people most important to her no longer existed in her life. With a shudder, she pushed that thought away.

But her mind was finally clearing and she was beginning to realize this whole security exercise was not the normal routine for overnight guests, at least, not in her experience. What the heck was he doing here?

She set the phone down and glared at him. "Would you like to explain just exactly why it's suddenly too dangerous here?" she asked crisply. "And why you feel the need to search for bugs and homing devices? Are you expecting some sort of home invasion? Or just being friendly?"

The corners of his mouth quirked but there was no hint of humor in his blue eyes. "Just being careful," he said evasively. "Crossing all the t's, dotting all the i's. As they say, better safe than sorry."

"Hmm," she said, cocking her head to the side as she gazed at him. "And yet, here I've been feeling safe for all these years without ever once submitting to a strip search. Just foolishly naive, I guess."

Her tone was mocking and he felt the sting. "Ayme, I don't like this any more than you do."

"Really?" Her tone was getting worse and she knew it, but, darn it all, he deserved it. He took a step forward and she took a corresponding step back, staying just out of reach.

"Can you tell me what exactly you're looking for?" she demanded. "Will you know it when you see it?"

"Yes, I'll know it when I see it," he said, nodding. "Now will you just stay put for a minute?"

"I don't think so." She made a sideways move that put even more distance between them.

"Ayme, be reasonable."

"Reasonable!" She laughed out loud. "Reasonable? You call searching me to see if I'm wearing a bug reasonable? I call it unacceptable. And I'm not going to accept it."

"You're going to have to accept it."

"Don't you think any bugs are more likely to be in my clothing or luggage?" she noted quickly.

He nodded his agreement. She was absolutely right. But there was another element to this situation. Now that he'd alerted her to his intentions, he had to follow through without giving her a chance to go behind his back to get rid of anything she might know about that she had on her. He'd started this train down the track and he had to follow it to the end if this was to be in any way effective.

"I'm planning to search your things. But first I need to search you."

He gave her a stern look as he followed her sideways move.

"Hold still."

Reaching out, she quickly dragged a chair between them and gazed defiantly over it.

"Why are you doing this, David? Who's after you? Whom do you suspect?"

He moved the chair aside and stepped closer.

"We don't have time to go into that."

"No, wait," she said, half rolling across the bed and landing on her feet without losing her sheet. Now she'd put the entire bed between them and she was feeling a bit smug about that.

Not that her success would hold up. She knew that. Still, she hoped it was getting through to him that she was not happy about all this and she was not about to give in.

"David, tell me what's changed," she challenged. "Something must have." She frowned at him questioningly. "When you first found me here, you were annoyed, sure, but now it's different. Now you're on guard in an edgier way." Her eyes narrowed. "It was that phone call, wasn't it?"

He hesitated, then nodded. "Yes," he admitted.

"Do you know who it was?"

He shook his head. "No, but it seemed like a wake-up call. It made me realize I was being too casual about you."

"Too casual! I beg to differ."

He stared at her and growled, "Ayme, enough. We need to get going. But first, we've got to check you out. Someone might have put a bug on you somewhere, somehow."

"Without me noticing?"

"That's what they do, Ayme. They're experts at attaching devices to your clothes or your purse or even your body in ways you wouldn't think of."

"Who? Who do you think would do that?"

"I don't know. Maybe this character who gave you my name."

She shook her head, thinking that one over. It didn't make any sense at all. "But he's the one who gave me your address. He already knows where you live. Why would he…?"

"Ayme, I don't know," he said impatiently. "And when you don't know things, it's best to cover all the bases. Will you stand still and let me look you over? I promise I won't…"

"No." Her voice was a little shaky, but adamant. "It won't do any good, anyway. I've seen those TV shows. They have gotten very inventive about hiding things on people. There's no way you can check it all. There's no way I would let you."

He sighed, shaking his head as he looked at her.

"You think I don't know that? I can only do so much, and probably only find something if it's pretty obvious. But I have to try. Look, Ayme, I'm really sorry, but…"

Her face lit up as she thought of a solution. She looked at him speculatively, wondering if he would go for it. With a shrug, she decided she had nothing to lose.

"*I'll* do it," she said firmly, shaking back her hair.

He stared at her. "You'll do it? You'll do what?"

Her smile was bemused. "I'll do it. Myself. Why not? Who knows my body better?" She gave him a grin that was almost mischievous. "You're going to have to trust me."

He stared. Trust her? But that wouldn't work. Would it?

Why not? asked a voice inside his head. *Look at that face. If you can't trust this woman, you can't trust anyone.*

Which was actually what he'd pledged from the

beginning—don't trust anyone. Still, there were times when you just had to make concessions to reality.

"Okay," he said at last. "Go for it. We'll see how you do."

"*I'll* see how I do," she corrected. "You'll be going over my bags and clothes. With your back to me. Got it?"

"Ayme," he began in exasperation, but she signaled that he should turn away. It was pretty apparent that following her orders was going to be the only way to move things along, and they really needed to get going. So, reluctantly, he did as she demanded.

He went through her things methodically. He'd had some training in this sort of search in some security classes he'd taken lately, so he didn't feel as strange handling her panties and bras as he might have under other circumstances. He had to take it on faith that she was doing her part. She chattered away throughout the entire exercise—and he didn't find a thing.

"I really understand, you know," she was saying. "And I want to do a good job at this because I figure, if I'm going with you, the danger is as much to me and Cici as it is to you."

"You got it," he said. "That's the whole point."

"So I just want you to know, I'm really being meticulous."

"Good."

"Searching every place I can think of."

That gave him pictures in his head he didn't want to dwell on and he shook off a delicious little shiver.

"Are you finished?" he asked at last, waiting for the okay to turn around.

"Just about," she said. "Listen, I saw this one show

on TV where they had these little homing signal things sort of stapled into a man's skin. What do you think? Is that really a possibility?"

"Sure."

She hesitated. "Okay then, I've been going over every inch of skin, feeling for any strange lumps, and I haven't found anything suspicious. But just to be safe…"

He turned and looked at her. She was standing just as before with the sheet pulled around her and clutched to her chest, watching him with those huge dark eyes.

"What?"

She sighed and looked sad. "I can't see my back. I can't reach it, either."

He stood very still, looking at her. "Oh."

She licked her lips, then tried to smile. "You're going to have to do it."

"Oh," he said again, and suddenly his mouth was dry and it felt like he hadn't taken a breath for too long.

"Okay, then."

He was willing.

CHAPTER FOUR

THIS was nuts.

David swore softly, trying to get a handle on this crazy reaction he was having. She was just a woman. He'd been with more women than he wanted to think about. He didn't get nervous around females anymore. He'd gotten over that years ago. He'd made successful passes at some international beauties in his day, film stars, rock singers, even a female bull fighter, without a qualm. So why was his heart thumping in his chest as he approached Ayme to check out her back?

She stood there so demurely, holding the sheet tightly to her chest so that it gaped in back, exposing everything down to the tailbone, but not much else. The entire back was there, interrupted only by the slender scrap of lace that was the band of her bra, but that might as well have been invisible. He didn't even notice it. He reached out to push her hair back off her neck, his fingers trailing across her warm skin, and the flesh beneath his hand seemed to glow.

"Okay, I'll do this as fast as I can," he said, then cleared his throat to try to stop the ridiculous quavering he could hear in his voice. "I'm just going to run my hand across your back a few times."

"Get it all," she said, head tilted up bravely. "I can take it." She drew in her breath as his fingers began to move.

"But don't linger," she warned softly.

Don't linger.

For some reason, those words echoed over and over in his head as he worked. Her skin was buttery smooth, summer-day hot, totally tempting, and every inch seemed to resonate to his touch. But he swore to himself that he wasn't going to notice anything, no matter how crazy it made him. He wasn't going to notice how good she smelled or how sweetly her curves seemed to fill his hand.

So why was his breath coming so fast? Why was his body tightening like a vise? This was insane. He was responding to her like he hadn't responded to a woman in ages. And all he was doing was checking for foreign objects on her back.

And being subtly seduced by her gorgeous body. He closed his eyes as he made a last pass down as low as he dared let himself go, and then drew back, saying, "We'd better check your underclothes, too," and heard his voice break in the middle of it.

He swore angrily, feeling his face turn as red as he'd ever felt it turn, but she didn't look back. She reached under the sheet and pulled off her bra and panties in two quick moves and checked them herself.

"They seem clear to me," she said without turning to look at him. "You can check too if you'd like."

"I'll take your word for it," he said gruffly.

This was unbelievable. He felt sixteen again. How had he ended up here? There was a tension in the room that was almost electric. Was he the only one who felt it, or did she feel it, too? It was probably best not to go there. He turned to leave the room without looking at her again.

"Wait," she said. "Do you think I'm clear?"

Reluctantly, he made a half turn back but didn't meet her gaze. "I didn't find any sign of anything, so I guess you are."

"Good. I'm glad. So now you don't suspect me any longer?"

He turned all the way and looked right into her dark eyes. "I suspect everyone, Ayme. Don't take it personally."

She made a small movement meant to be a shrug but almost more of a twitch. "I'm trying not to. But it's not easy."

His gaze was caught in hers and he couldn't seem to pull it away. There had been a quiver in her voice, a thread of emotion he couldn't quite identify, and it had touched him somehow. Looking at her, he felt suddenly confused, not sure how to respond to her.

"Go ahead and get dressed," he said gruffly as soon as he managed to turn away from her. Not looking her way again, he went through the doorway. "We'll get going in just a minute."

She didn't answer and he went into the kitchen, poured himself a glass of cold water and gulped it down, then took in a deep breath and tried to rationalize away what he'd just done.

It wasn't what it seemed, of course. How could it be? He didn't do things like that. His over-the-top reaction to her body was just a symptom of everything else going on around them—the muted fear, the preparations for running, the memories of his own tragic past. Just natural heightened apprehension. Hardly unusual. Nothing to be alarmed about.

She was just a girl.

Relieved and resolute, he went back into his more normal confident action state and returned to the bedroom with a spring in his step. Luckily, she appeared dressed and ready to go and when he looked into her face, there was nothing special there—no regrets, no resentment, no special emotions making him uncomfortable.

"Come on. We've got to get out of here." He slung his overnight bag over his shoulder and reached for the baby. "I'll get Cici. You bring your bags, okay?"

He led the way to the back steps, avoiding the elevator. It was a long, long climb down, but eventually they hit the ground floor, made their way to the parking garage and found his little racy sports car. He made Ayme and the baby wait against a far wall while he prepared for departure.

He'd done everything right. He'd switched out the license plates on the car. He'd checked under the hood and along the undercarriage for explosives. But even so, he winced as he started the engine with the remote, relieved when nothing went "boom."

Another day, another risky move, he thought to himself as he helped Ayme into the car and began packing baby supplies away in all the nooks and crannies. One of these times the click from the starter just might be the last thing he ever heard.

Now the next dilemma—should he head for a big city where they could get lost in the crowd, or for the countryside where no one would ever think to look? For once he chose the country.

But that was still a long way away. First, he headed into a direction directly opposed to where he actually wanted to go. After an hour of driving, he pulled into a protected area and hustled Ayme and Cici out of the car with all their belongings. Then he hailed a cab and they went in a totally different direction, stopping at a garage where he had arranged for another of his cars to be stored. This car was a complete contrast to his usual transportation, small and boxy and not eye-catching at all.

Ayme carefully maintained a pleasant expression. She didn't want to be a whiner. But she couldn't resist, as they squeezed into the small, cramped car, saying "I like the sports car better."

"So do I, believe me," he told her. "This is my incognito car."

"I can see why. You could probably join the Rose Parade unnoticed in this thing."

Glancing sideways, he threw her a quick smile that had actual warmth and humor in it, and she tingled a bit in response. It was nice to know he could do that. She'd been worried that he might be all scowls and furled brows with very little room for fun. But it looked like there was hope. It might not be all sex appeal with him.

She smiled to herself, enjoying her own little joke. She would love to tease him but she didn't quite dare, not yet. If he was right, they were running from danger here. Not a time for light-hearted humor.

Danger. She frowned out the window at the passing buildings. She wished she knew a little more about this "danger" element. Who was this dangerous person and why was he after David?

For just a moment, her mind went back to what had happened in the bedroom just before they left David's apartment. The way her pulse had surged in response to a few hot looks from the man was all the danger she could deal with right now. Clear and present danger. That's what he represented to a girl like she was.

Woman, she corrected herself silently. *You're a woman, darn it. So act like one!*

"You might as well relax," he said, glancing her way again. "It'll be a few hours before we get to our destination."

"I'm relaxed," she claimed. "Don't worry about me."

"Why don't you try to get some sleep while Cici is taking her nap?"

It was a sensible suggestion, but she wasn't in a sensible mood. Despite her bone-aching weariness, she was too full of adrenaline to sleep now.

"But I'll miss the sightseeing," she told him. "I want to see the countryside."

He glanced out at the gaunt, charred-looking buildings they were passing. "We're not going through a lot of countryside right now. More like an industrial wasteland."

She nodded, her eyes big as she peered out at everything, trying to take it all in. "I noticed that."

"Our route is circuitous and it's not going to take us through many of the nicest parts of England I'm afraid. I'm trying to keep it low key and stay away from places where I might see someone I know."

"It's smokestack city so far," she noted wistfully. "Oh, well. Maybe I will try to sleep a little."

"The views will be better in an hour or so," he promised.

"Okay." She snuggled down into the seat, closed her eyes and went out like a light.

He noted that with a sense of relief. As long as she slept, she couldn't ask questions.

He really had mixed feelings about Ayme. Why had he brought her along, anyway? He'd almost left her behind and it probably would have been the reasonable thing to do. But he felt a strange sense of responsibility toward her and of course he wanted to make sure that she was protected.

On the other hand, she probably wasn't going to thank him in the end for dragging her along on this wild-goose chase. She would be better off in a nice hotel in a touristy part of town where she could while away her time shopping or sightseeing or whatever. At the same time, he would have been free to slip in and out of various cities and countries without having to adjust for a baby. After a day hauling a child all over the landscape, she might be ready to accept a solution such as that.

It was a tempting proposition, but there was a major flaw in his thinking and it came to him pretty quickly. Someone out there in the world was fathering babies under his name. This was not helpful to the world situation or even to his own peace of mind. He had to find out who it was and he had to get it stopped. Until he'd managed that, it might be best to keep tabs on the young woman who'd dumped this particular problem in his lap.

Well, that was hardly fair. The problem had been there all the time. He just hadn't been aware of it until she'd arrived on his doorstep carrying the evidence.

But when you came right down to it, all that might be an excuse to keep her around, just because he liked looking at her. He glanced down at her. She was super adorable when she slept.

He had never been one to be bowled over by a pretty face. After all, there were so many pretty faces and he'd had his share of romantic adventures back when he was indulging in that sort of thing. He wasn't going to let a little fatal attraction get in the way of his plans.

He was hardheaded and pragmatic, as he had to be if he and his brother were going to succeed in getting their country back. Romance wouldn't work in times like these, and even a casual flirtation could cloud a man's mind and get in the way of the goal. What he and his brother planned to do was going to be hard, perilous and very possibly fatal.

Relationships were out. Period.

He wondered, and not for the first time, what Monte would think of what he was doing. He wanted to call him but this wasn't the place—nor the time. He had to be somewhere secure. Later—once they found a place near the coast to stay for the night, he would find a way to contact his brother.

She slept for two hours and then woke, stretching like a kitten and looking up at him as though she were surprised to see him.

"Hi," she said. "You're still here."

"Where would I go?" he asked, half amused.

She shrugged. "Since my life became a bad dream, I expect dreamlike things to happen all the time. Maybe a Mad Hatter at the wheel, or at the very least, an angry hedgehog."

"It's a dormouse," he muttered, making way for another car to merge onto the roadway in front of him.

"All right, an angry dormouse." She smiled, amused that he would know the finer points of the Alice in Wonderland story. "So you're neither?"

"Nope. But I have been accused of White Rabbit tendencies in the past." He gave her a sideways grin. "Always late for that important date."

"Ah." She nodded wisely. "Annoying trait, that."

"Yes. They say habitual lateness is a form of selfishness, but I think it's something else entirely."

"Like what?" She was curious since she was always late for everything herself and would like to find a good new excuse for it.

But he never got to the point of telling her. Cici intervened with a long, loud demand for attention from the backseat.

"Wow, she's hungry," Ayme noted, going up on her knees to tend to her over the back of the seat. She pulled a bottle of formula out of the baby bag, regretting that she couldn't warm it. But Cici wasn't picky at the moment. She sucked on the liquid as though someone had been starving her.

"Don't feel like the Lone Ranger, little girl," Ayme cooed at her. "There's a lot of that hunger thing going around."

"Subtle hint," he commented.

"I can get less subtle if it bothers you," she said, flicking a smile his way. "Do we have any food with us at all?"

"Not that I know of."

"Oh." His answer was disappointing, but pretty much what she'd expected. "Are we planning to rectify that anytime soon?" she asked, trying to be diplomatic about it.

He grunted. "I guess we could stop when we see something promising."

"Good. You don't want me to start wailing away like Cici does. It wouldn't be pretty."

She spent the next ten minutes feeding the baby, then pulled her up awkwardly and tried to burp her. David noted the lack of grace in her efforts, but he didn't say anything. She would learn, he figured. Either that, or she would find Cici's father and head back to Texas, free of burdens and swearing off children for all time. It seemed to be one of those either-or deals.

"We need a real car seat for her," he said as Ayme settled her back into the backseat. "If we get stopped by the police, this makeshift bed won't cut it. We'll probably both get carted away for child endangerment."

She plunked herself back into her seat and fastened the seat belt, then tensed, waiting for the inevitable complaints from the back. After a moment she began to relax. To her surprise, Cici wasn't crying. What a relief!

"When I was young," she told David, "my father would put me in a wash basket and strap me to the seat and carry me all over the Texas Panhandle on his daily route."

"Those were the days when you could do things like that." He nodded with regret. "Those days are gone."

"Pity."

He almost smiled thinking of her as a young sprout, peering over the edge of the basket at the world.

"What did he do on his route. Salesman?"

"No, he was a supervisor for the Department of

Agriculture. He checked out crops and stuff. Gave advice." She smiled, remembering.

"It was fun going along with him. My mother worked as a school secretary in those days, so my father was basically babysitting me and my sister." She laughed softly. Memories.

"Sam's basket was strapped right next to mine. As we got older, we got to play with a lot of great farm animals. Those were the best days." She sighed. "I always liked animals more than people, anyway."

"Hey."

"When I was a child, silly. Things have changed now."

The funny thing was he wasn't so sure all that much had changed with her. From the little bit she'd told him of her life, he had a pretty good idea of how hard she worked and how little she played. Someone ought to show her how to have a little fun.

Someone. Not him, of course, but someone.

They stopped at a small general store and he went in, leaving her in the car entertaining the baby. Minutes later he came out with a car seat in tow.

"This ought to do it," he said, and in no time at all they were back on the road, Cici officially ensconced in the proper equipment.

"She seems to like it fine," Ayme noted. "She's already falling back to sleep."

He handed her a couple of sandwiches he'd picked up in the store and she looked at them suspiciously.

"This isn't going to be one of those strange British things, is it?" she asked. "Vegemite or Marmite or whatever?"

He grinned. "Those are Australian and British, respectively. I'm Dutch. We eat kippers!"

"What's a kippers?"

"Kippers are canned herring, usually smoked."

"Fish?" She pulled back the paper. "Oh, no! What is that smell?"

"It's a great smell," he retorted. "A nice, sea-faring nation smell. Lots of protein. Eat up. You'll love it."

She was ravenously hungry, so she did eat up, but she complained the whole time. He ate his own kipper sandwich with relish.

"Good stuff," he remarked as he finished up. For some reason the fact that she was complaining so much about the food had put him in a marvelous mood. "That'll hold us until we get in later tonight."

She rolled her eyes, but more as a way to tease him than for real. Now that she'd had something to eat, she was sleepy again, but that made her feel guilty.

"Would you like me to drive?" she said. "You must be dead on your feet. You need some sleep."

He shook his head. "Do you have a license?" he noted.

"No," she said sadly. "Only for Texas."

"That won't work."

She sighed. "Sorry."

But in another few minutes, she was asleep again.

Just looking at her made him smile. He bit it off and tried to scowl instead. He wasn't going to let her get to him. He wasn't that easy. Was he?

When he couldn't resist glancing at her again he realized that maybe he was. But what the hell, it didn't mean a thing. It was just that she was so open and natural and so completely different from the women he was used to. For years now, he'd been hanging out with a pretty sophisticated crowd. And that was on purpose. He'd found out early that you could find out a lot if you hung with the right people and learned to listen. He had a very large hole in his life. He needed some very specialized information to fill it in.

Twenty-five years before, he'd been woken in the middle of a terrifying night, bundled up and raced out of the burning castle he'd lived in all six years of his young life. He knew now that his parents were being murdered at about the same time. It was likely that many of his brothers and sisters were killed as well. But one old man whose face still haunted his dreams had come to his room and saved his life that night.

Taken by people who were strangers to him from his island nation and smuggled into the Netherlands, he arrived the next day, a shaken and somewhat traumatized refugee, at the noisy, cheerful home of the Dykstra family. He was told this would be his new home, his new family, and that he must never speak of Ambria, never let anyone know anything about his past. The people who brought him there then melted away into the scenery and were never seen again—at least not by him. And there he was, suddenly a Dykstra, suddenly Dutch. And not allowed to ask any questions, ever.

The Dykstras were good to him. His new parents were actually quite affectionate, but there were so many children in the family, it was easy to get lost in the shuffle. Still, everyone had to pitch in and he did learn to take care of the younger ones. He also learned how to listen and quietly glean information. From the very beginning his purpose in life was to find out what had happened to his family and to find a way to connect with any of them who might still be alive. As he got older, he began to meet the right people and gain the trust of the powerful in many areas, and little by little, he began to piece things together.

At first the socializing had just been a natural inclination. But over time he began to realize that these people did move in circles close to the wealthy and the influential, elements that might prove helpful in his quest to find out what had happened to his family—and his country. Over the years various things half-heard or half-understood sent him on wild-goose chases across the continent, but finally, six months ago, he'd hit pay dirt.

He'd been playing a friendly set of tennis with Nico, the son of a French diplomat, when the young man had stopped his serve, and, ball in hand, had stared at him for a long moment.

"You know," he said, shaking his head, "I met someone at a dinner in Paris last week who could be your twin. It was a fancy banquet for the new foreign minister. He looked just like you."

"Who? The foreign minister?"

"No, idiot." Nico laughed. "This fellow I met. I can't remember his name, but I think he was with the British delegation. You don't have a brother in government?"

By now, David's heart was pounding in his chest as though he'd just run a four-minute mile. He knew this might be the break he'd been searching for. But he had to remain cool and pretend this was nothing but light banter. He took a swing into empty air with his racquet and tried to appear nonchalant.

"Not that I know of. All my brothers are happily ensconced in the business world, and spend most of their time in Amsterdam." He grinned across the net. "And none of them look much like me."

He was referring to his foster brothers, but the fact that he wasn't a real Dykstra was not common knowledge and he was happy to keep it that way.

"The ugly duckling of the family, are you?" teased Nico.

"That's me."

Nico served and it was all David could do to pay enough attention to return it in a long drive to the corner. Nico's response went into the net and that gave David a chance for another couple of questions, but Nico really didn't seem to know any more than what he'd said.

Still, it was a start, and the information breathed new life into his hopes and dreams of finding his family. He got to work researching, trying to find a list of the names of everyone who had attended that banquet. Once he had that, he began searching for pictures on the Internet. Finally, he thought he just might have his man.

Mark Stephols was his name. There were a couple of other possibilities, but the more he stared at the pictures of Mark, the more certain he became. Now, how to approach him and find out for sure?

He could find out where Mark was likely to be at certain public events, but he couldn't just walk up and say "Hi. Are you my brother?" And if he actually was, the last thing he could risk was standing side by side with the man, where everyone could immediately note the resemblance between them and begin to ask questions. So as he waited for the right chance, he began to color his hair a bit darker and grow a mustache. There was no point in making identification too easy.

His highly placed social intimates came in handy, and

very soon he obtained an invitation to a reception where
Mark Stephols could be approached. Despite the hair
dye, despite the mustache, the moment the introduction
was made—"Mr. Stephols, may I introduce Mr. David
Dyskstra of Dyskstra Shipping?"—their gazes met and
the connection was made. There was instant—though
silent—acknowledgment between the two of them that
they had to be related.

They shook hands and Monte leaned close to whisper,
"Meet me in the rose garden."

A few minutes later they came face-to-face without
any witnesses and stared at each other as though they
each weren't sure they were seeing what they thought
they were seeing.

David started to speak and Monte put a finger to his
lips. "The walls have ears," he said softly.

David grinned. He was fairly vibrating with excitement. "How about the shrubbery?"

"That's possible, too, of course. Don't trust anything
or anyone."

"Let's walk, then."

"Good idea."

They strolled along the edge of a small lake for a
few minutes, exchanging pleasantries, until they were
far enough from the house and from everyone else, to
feel somewhat safe. They looked at one another, then
both jockied comments back and forth for another few
minutes, neither knowing just what to say, neither wanting to give the game away, just in case what looked true
wasn't.

Finally, Monte said out of the blue, "Do you remember the words to the old folk song our mother would sing
when putting us to sleep for the night?"

David stopped where he was and concentrated, trying to remember. Did he? What had that been again?

And then he closed his eyes and began to murmur softly, as though channeling from another time, another place. In his head, he heard his mother's voice. From his mouth came the childhood bedtime song in Ambrian. When he finished and opened his eyes again, he turned to his brother. Mark had been still, but tears were coursing down his tanned cheeks. Reaching out, he took David's hand and held it tightly.

"At last," he whispered. "At last."

CHAPTER FIVE

AYME didn't sleep for long, and soon she was up and reacting to the beauty of the countryside.

"I don't know why I haven't come to Europe before," she said. "I've just been so wrapped up in law school and starting a new career and being there for my family."

Her voice faded on the last word and she had to swallow back her feelings. Every now and then it hit her hard. She had to hold it back. There would be a time to deal with sorrow and pain. The time wasn't now.

"And boyfriends?" David was saying. "I'm sure you've got a boyfriend back home."

She settled down, shaking away unhappiness and trying to live in the moment. "Actually, I don't," she admitted.

"Really."

"Really." She thought about it for a moment. She kept meaning to get a boyfriend. So far her life had just been too busy to have time for that sort of thing. "I've been going to college and going to law school and working, as well. There just hasn't been time for boyfriends."

"You're kidding." So it was just as he'd thought. She was a workaholic who needed to learn how to be young while she still had the chance. "Most women make time."

"Well, I didn't. I was so set on doing the very best I possibly could and succeeding and making my parents proud of me."

"Your adoptive parents, right?"

She nodded, biting her lip.

"Ah." He nodded, too. So it was a classic case of over-compensation. She probably spent all her time working frantically to prove it was a good decision for them to have chosen her. "You're the girl driven to bring home the As on her report card."

She smiled fleetingly, pleased he seemed to under-stand.

"And your sister Sam?"

"Sam not so much." She winced, wishing she hadn't said that. She didn't ever, ever want to say anything that even hinted at criticism of her adoptive sister ever again. She put her hand over her heart, as though she could push back the pain.

"I came over to Texas with a bunch of kids who'd lost their parents in the rebellion. We were all adopted out, mostly to American families with Ambrian roots."

"So it was an organized rescue operation."

"Sort of. I've told you all this, haven't I? I was adopted by the Sommers of Dallas, Texas, and I grew up like any other American kid." Her parents' faces swam into her mind and she felt a lump in her throat. They were such good people. They should have had another twenty or thirty years. It didn't pay to expect life to be fair.

"You don't remember Ambria at all?" he asked after a moment.

She gave him a look. "I was eighteen months old at the time I left."

"A little young to understand the political history of the place," he allowed with a quick, barely formed grin. "So what do you really know about Ambria?"

"Not much." She shrugged. "There were some books around the house." Her face lit up as an old memory came to her. "One time, an uncle stopped in to visit and he told Sam and me about how we were both really Ambrian, deep down, and he told us stories." She half smiled remembering how she and her sister had hung on his every word, thrilled to be a part of something that made them a little different from all their friends.

Ambrian. It sounded cool and sort of exotic, like being Italian or Lithuanian.

"Other than that, not much."

He thought that over for a moment. He'd had the advantage of being six years old, so he remembered a lot. But when you came right down to it, the rest he'd learned on his own, finding books, looking things up on the Internet. His foster parents had taken him in and assumed he was now one of the family and Dutch to boot. No need to delve into things like roots and backgrounds. That just made everyone uneasy. They had been very good to him in every other way, but as far as reminding him of who he was, they probably thought it was safer if he forgot, just like everyone else.

And if it hadn't been for one old man who had moved to Holland from Ambria years before and lived near their summer home, he might have done just that.

"Too bad your parents didn't tell you more," he mused, comparing her experience to his and wondering why such different circumstances still ended up being treated the same way by the principals involved.

"They were busy with their jobs and raising two little girls, getting us to our dance practices and violin lessons and all that sort of thing."

She moved restlessly. This was getting too close to the pain again. She hadn't told him about her parents yet and she wasn't sure she ever would. She knew she would never be able to get through it without breaking down, and she wanted to avoid that at all costs. Better to stick to the past.

"They were great parents," she said, knowing she sounded a little defensive. "They just didn't feel all that close to Ambria themselves, I guess." She brightened. "But being Ambrian got me a grant for law school and even my job once I passed the bar."

He remembered she'd mentioned something about that before but he hadn't really been listening. Now he realized this could be a factor. "Your law firm is Ambrian?"

"Well, a lot of the associates are of Ambrian background. It's not like we sit around speaking Ambrian or anything like that."

This was all very interesting. The Ambrian connection was going to turn out to be more relevant than she knew—he was sure of it. His jaw tightened as he remembered that he still didn't really know why she had shown up in his apartment or who had sent her.

But of course, there was a very possible explanation. She could, even unwittingly, be a stalking horse for a real assassin. Or she could merely be the one testing the territory for someone who meant to come in and make sure David never reached the strength to threaten the current Ambrian regime. It was hard to know and he was more and more convinced that she didn't know anything more than what she'd told him.

He remembered what she'd said about not knowing which side her parents had been on. Since she had no emotional identification with either side, she was pretty much an innocent in all this. If she was here because an enemy of his had sent her, she wasn't likely to be aware of it.

Still, he shouldn't have brought her along. It was a stupid, amateur thing to do. He should probably find a way to park her somewhere—if it wasn't already too late.

Because he couldn't keep her with him. He was due in Italy by the end of the week for the annual meeting of the Ambrian expatriate community. This would be the first time he'd ever attended. It was to be a gathering of the clan, a coming together of a lot of Ambrians who had been powers, or were related to those who had been, in the old days. He needed to be focused on the future of Ambria, not on Ayme and Cici. He couldn't take them along.

So—what to do with them in the meantime?

He'd promised he would help Ayme find Cici's father and he meant to keep that promise. It was bound to get a bit complicated, seeing as how his name had come into the picture, and he didn't have much time. But he had a few contacts. He would do what he could to help.

The only thing he could think of was Marjan, his adoptive sister who was married with two children and lived in a farming town in a northern area of Holland. It was a good, out of the way place where they could melt into the scenery. Maybe even he could slip in below the radar there.

It was odd how quickly he seemed to have slipped into the cloak-and-dagger mold. But then, he supposed he'd been training for it ever since he left Ambria, in attitude if not in action. It was true that he'd never felt he could fully open himself to others in his life. He always had to hide, not only his real identity, but also his feelings about things.

"So I guess you could say," he said, going on with their conversation, "bottom line, that you don't really care about who runs Ambria?"

"Care?" She looked at him blankly. "I've never given it a second thought."

"Of course not."

He turned away, feeling a surge of bitterness in his chest. Was it only he and his brother who still cared? If so, they were going to have a hard time rallying others to their cause. But it was hardly fair to lay this complaint on her. She couldn't help it that no one had bothered to educate her about her background.

And if he were honest with himself, he would have to admit that the strength of his own feelings had been greatly enhanced by his relationship with his brother. Before he knew Monte, his interest in Ambria was strong, even passionate, but diffused. It had taken an intensive experience with his brother to bring out the nuances.

It had been exciting and a fulfillment of a lifelong dream to find Monte the way he did. But it had been very difficult for the two of them to have any sort of relationship. They couldn't trust most forms of communication, they couldn't appear together anywhere because of how much alike they looked, they had to be aware of the possibility that someone was listening every time they spoke to each other. So Monte finally hit upon the perfect scheme—a six-week sailing trip in the South Pacific.

They met in Bali and proceeded from there, getting to know each other and hashing out the possibilities of being royals without a country to call their own. They had huge arguments, even huger reconciliations, they shared ideas, hopes and dreams and emotions, and they ended up as close as any two brothers could be. By the time the six weeks was up, they had both become impassioned with the goal of taking their country back, somehow, someday. To that end, they quickly become co-conspirators and developed a plan.

They decided to continue to go under their aliases. That was necessary for survival. Monte would travel in international circles he already had access to and try to gain information—and eventually supporters— and David would go undercover in the social jet-setting world he knew so well to glean what he could from business contacts on one side and the inebriated rich drones he partied with on the other. Their primary goal was to find their lost brothers and sisters and begin to work toward a restoration of their monarchy.

So he had a very large advantage over Ayme. He certainly couldn't expect her to share his goals when she'd never even heard of most of them and wouldn't know what to do with them if she had.

Their conversation had faded away by now and she spent some time watching the countryside roll past. Morning had come and gone and afternoon was sending long shadows across the land. The countryside was much more interesting now with its checkerboard fields and beautiful green hedgerows and the quaint little towns. This was more like the England she'd expected to see.

But the unanswered questions still haunted this trip as far as she was concerned. Where were they going? And why?

They stopped for petrol and David noticed a park nearby.

"Want to get out and stretch your legs?" he suggested as he maneuvered the car into the little parking lot next to a large tree. "I need to make a phone call."

They got out of the car and he strolled out of listening range. She let him go. There was no reason to resent his wanting privacy, after all.

He looked back as their paths diverged. He didn't want her to get too far away. But he needed to make contact with his brother.

Once he had Monte on the line, he filled him in on Ayme and the fact that he had her in tow. Monte was not enthusiastic.

"You're not bringing her to Italy, are you?"

"No, of course not. I'm taking her to my sister's. Marjan will take good care of her."

"Good."

"But in the meantime, I'd like you to do me a favor."

"Anything. You know that."

"Just information. First I need to know about a car accident outside of Dallas, Texas, sometime last week. A young woman named Samantha Sommers was killed. I'd like a brief rundown of the facts in the case, the survivors, etc."

"I'm jotting down your info as we speak."

"Good. Besides that I'd like anything you can find on Ayme. Her name is Ayme Sommers. She's an attorney for a law firm in Dallas that has a division which specializes in Ambrian immigration issues."

"Will do."

"And here's another one. There seems to be someone—probably in the greater London area—who is fathering babies under the guise of being Prince Darius."

That gave Monte pause. "Hmm. Not good."

"No. Do you think you can make inquiries?"

"I can do more than that. I can start a full-fledged investigation on that one."

"Without identifying your own interest in the case?"

"Exactly. Don't worry. I can do that easily."

"Good. I figure he's either found a way to make time with the ladies using the royalty dodge, or…"

"Or he's an agent trying to flush you out."

"You got it."

"I'm voting for the latter, but we'll see." Monte's voice lightened. "In the meantime, David…a bit of news. I've found the perfect wife for you."

David's head reared back. Despite his overwhelming respect for his brother, that hadn't sat well with him from the beginning.

"I don't need a wife right now," he shot back. "And if I did, I could find my own."

"You can find your own mistresses, Darius," Monte said, his tone containing just a hint of rebuke. "Your wife is a state affair."

David groaned softly, regretting his reaction. Where had his tart response come from, anyway? He and his brother had already discussed this and he knew very well that he needed a wife to help support the cause. The right wife. It was one of the obligations of royalty.

The two of them had pledged that everything they were going to do from now on was going to be for the benefit of Ambria. No self-serving ambitions or appetites would be allowed to get in the way. They were both ready to sacrifice their private lives—and even their actual lives if it came to that. He was firmly committed to achieving their goals. Nothing else mattered.

"Families are the building blocks of empires," Monte was saying blithely. "We need you to be married and to have a solid relationship. We've talked about this before. I thought you were on board."

"I am," David put in hastily. "Sorry, Monte. I'm just a little tired and short tempered right now. Don't pay any attention."

"Good. Wait until you meet her. She's beautiful. She's intelligent. And she's totally devoted to overturning the Granvilli clan's totalitarian regime. She'll fight by your side and rule there, too, when we achieve our goal." He chuckled. "I'm not worried about how you'll react. She'll knock you out when you see her."

"I'm sure she will."

But David grimaced, wondering if Monte wasn't perhaps overselling the case. He'd known a lot of bright, gorgeous and astonishing women in his time. So this was another one of them. Readiness to fight for the cause would be just the icing on the cake. He'd seen it all before.

But he couldn't completely discount Monte's opinion. He'd spent so many years adrift, not knowing where he was going or what he wanted to do with himself. He'd done well in his Dutch father's business, but his heart wasn't in it.

Once he and Monte had found each other, their future trajectory became clear. Now he knew what he was on earth to do. He had a new seriousness and a sense of purpose. His life had meaning after all. Finding the rest of his family and restoring them all to power was all he lived for.

"Keep me apprised as best you can. Let me know where you are if you can."

"I will."

Ringing off, he started back to join Ayme and the baby, stopping only to toss the cell phone into a trash can. You couldn't be too careful and he had a stock of extras, just in case.

The park was pretty and green and centered on a pond with a small bridge over it, creating a lovely vantage point for watching small silver fish swim by below.

"Look, Cici. Look at the fishies," Ayme was saying, holding the baby precariously at the rail and making David laugh. Still, he moved in quickly to avoid disaster.

"She's a little young for a swim," he commented. "Here, I'll take her."

And he did so easily. Ayme sighed. It seemed to come naturally to him and she was having such a hard time with it.

She watched him for a moment. He glanced up and caught her eye, but she looked away quickly, still uneasy, still not sure what the point of all this was. The questions just kept bubbling up inside her and she needed some answers.

"Okay, here's what I don't understand," she challenged him as they walked through the grass. "If you're Dutch, how come you care so much about Ambria? What is your tie to the place?"

He looked startled, then like a man trying to cover something up. "Who says I care so much about Ambria?"

"Oh, please! It resonates in everything you say."

Hmm. That wasn't good news. He was going to have to be a bit more guarded, wasn't he? Still, it did seem churlish to keep such basic information from her. It would all be common knowledge soon enough. Once he got to Italy, all would very likely be revealed anyway. He decided she deserved to be among the first to know. Just not quite yet.

"We can talk about this later," he said evasively.

"Wait a minute," she said, stopping in front of him and putting her hands on her hips. "I'm staging a small rebellion here."

Her dark eyes were flashing and her pretty face was set firmly. He knew better than to laugh at her, but it was tempting. She did look damn cute.

"What are you talking about?" he asked instead.

She sighed, shaking her head. "I don't get it. What the heck are we running from?"

"Danger."

"What danger? From whom?" She threw her hands up. "I don't see what I've done to put myself in danger. All I did was hop on a plane and come to England looking for Cici's father. How did that put me in danger?"

He raked fingers through his hair and looked uncomfortable. "It hasn't exactly. It's put *me* in danger." He took in a deep breath and let it out again, slowly. "And because you're currently attached to me, it's put you in danger, too."

Her chin rose and she watched him with a hint of defiance in her gaze. "Then maybe I should unattach myself."

She was just throwing that out there, waiting to see what his reaction would be. When you came right down to it, the thought of "unattaching" from him filled her with dread. At this point, she didn't have a clue what she would do without him. And she really didn't want to find out.

"Maybe you should," he said calmly, as though it didn't mean a thing to him. "It's a good idea, really. Why don't you do that? We can find you a nice hotel and get you a room…."

She observed the way he was holding the baby, so casual, so adept, and she looked at his handsome face, so attractive, so appealing. Did she really want to trade this in, danger and all, for the sterile walls of a hotel room on her own? Wouldn't she just end up trudging from place to place, trying to find someone who could help her?

Hmm. Good luck with that.

Maybe she ought to reconsider before this went too far. She wasn't going to detach herself from him until she had to. Who was she kidding, anyway? She was going to stick around and see what happened. She knew it. He probably knew it, too.

"On the other hand," she said in a more conciliatory tone, as they began to walk again, "if you would just let me know what's going on so I could understand and be prepared, it would be nice. I'd like to be able to make plans for myself once in a while." She searched his face hopefully. "It would be a big help."

His jaw tightened. "You want to know what's going on."

"Yes, I do."

He nodded. She was really a good sport. She deserved more information than he'd been giving her. He couldn't tell her everything. But he could do a better job than he'd been doing so far. He shifted the baby from one arm to the other, stood in one spot with his legs evenly spaced, like a fighter, and looked into her eyes. He was taking a risk in telling her. But what the hell—life was a risk. And despite everything, his gut feeling was that he could trust her.

"Okay Ayme, here's the deal. I am Ambrian. You guessed right from the beginning."

"I knew it!" Her eyes flared with happy sparks and she wanted to grab him around the neck and give him a triumphant kiss, but she restrained herself admirably.

"There's more."

He glanced at her, his intensity burning a hole in her skin and as she realized how seriously he was taking this, her victorious satisfaction faded.

"I've been working with other Ambrians determined to overthrow the usurpers and get our country back."

She gaped at him, suddenly feeling as though her bearings had been yanked away.

"No kidding," she said softly, feeling shaky. "No wonder there are people after you."

No wonder. That was a choice he'd made. But she hadn't made that choice, so what the heck was she doing putting herself and the baby in this sort of jeopardy?

Maybe she was going to have to tell him thanks, but no thanks, after all. Time to say goodbye?

His face was hard and serious and his tone was low and intense as he went on.

"The people who run Ambria right now have spies everywhere. They are very much interested in trying to destroy any opposition they see beginning to crop up. That's why I have to be careful and why I'm afraid of being tracked."

"Okay." She folded her arms across her chest and hugged herself worriedly. "Now I get it. Thank you for telling me that." She blinked up at him, her eyes wide, a picture of pure innocence. "Believe me, I won't betray your confidence."

He wanted to kiss her. Looking down, the urge swept over him. Her face was so fresh and honest, her lips full and slightly parted, her cheeks red from the outdoor air and he didn't think he'd ever seen anyone look prettier. The urge passed. He didn't act on it.

But it left behind another feeling—guilt.

She trusted him.

Ah, hell, he thought.

Guilt filled his throat. He was still lying to her, still leaving things out. She didn't know he was actually the man she was seeking. Well, that wasn't exactly the case, but close. If she knew who he really was, she would be able to focus better on finding the real father. On the other hand, maybe she would just believe he had fathered the child himself. Then what?

There would be no time for DNA tests. He had to be in Italy in less than a week. And he couldn't tell her about that—not yet. Probably not ever. After all, she wasn't going with him, so why did she have to know?

They went back to the car and packed everything away, including the now-sleeping baby, then climbed in themselves and started off. But all the while, he was thinking about their conversation.

There was still so much he couldn't tell her, but he could tell her a bit more than he had.

"Here's some more truth, Ayme," he told her after a few miles. "The truth is, I'm just like you."

"Like me?"

"Yes. I'm an Ambrian orphan, too. I was adopted by a Dutch family right after the rebellion. Just like you."

She thought about that for a moment. It seemed to fit the scheme of things nicely and it gave her a warm feeling of bonding with the man. Though when she glanced at his face, she didn't see any reciprocating on the bonding thing. He appeared as much as ever as though his profile had been hewn in stone.

So now she had some important information and she could use it to fill in the blanks. She knew why David was afraid someone was after him. And she knew why he felt such deep feelings for Ambria. And she knew why he might have connections in the Ambrian community that would help her find Cici's father. But she didn't know…

Turning to face him again, she confronted him with a steady gaze.

"Okay, mister," she said firmly. "Let's have it. More truth. I understand why you might have felt you had to take off from your apartment. And why you want to keep on the move. But what I don't understand is this— why did you bring me along?"

CHAPTER SIX

THAT was a very good question and David wasn't sure he had the guts to answer it, even to himself. He looked at Ayme.

He'd meant a quick glance, but something in her pretty face held him for a beat too long and he had to straighten the car into the proper lane when he put his attention back on the road.

That was a warning—don't do that again.

For some reason Ayme's allure seemed to catch him up every time. He didn't know why. She was pretty enough, sure, but it was something else, something in the basic man-woman dynamic that got to him, and he didn't seem to be able to turn it off.

"Come on, David," she was saying. "Tell me. Why did you bring me along?"

He shrugged and tried to look blasé. "Why do you think?"

She made a face. "My charm and beauty?" She managed to put a sarcastic spin on her tone that made him grin.

"Of course."

She rolled her eyes. "No, really. What was the deciding factor?"

He glanced at her, then looked back at the road and put both hands firmly at the top of the wheel.

"Okay, if you want me to be honest about this, I'll tell you." He hesitated and grimaced again. Since this seemed to be the time for truth why not go a little further? She could handle it.

"This won't be easy for you to understand. You'll think I'm overstating things. You might even think I'm a little nuts. But just hear me out and then decide."

"Of course."

"There are a couple of things going on here. First…" He took a deep breath and went on. "I've always had good reason to expect that someone would try to get to me and kill me someday and I'm not going to talk about why."

She sat very still, but she made a small grating noise, as though she were choking. He ignored it.

"When you arrived on my doorstep I had to consider the possibility that you, or someone who sent you, might be involved in something like that."

"David." Her voice was rough. "You thought I could be a killer?" The idea shocked her to her core.

He looked her full in the face and shrugged. "You bet. Why not?"

She sputtered and he went on.

"But it's more likely to be your Carl Heissman person. Don't you see that? And if I have you with me, you can't contact him and let him know where I am."

She made a gasping sound. "David, what have I done that would lead you to think—"

"Not a thing. And believe me, Ayme, I don't suspect you of anything at all. It's the people who sent you who have me on guard."

"Sent me?" She shook her head, at a loss. "Nobody sent me. I came on my own."

"Someone found out your plans, sought you out and gave you my name. Why?"

She stared at him, realizing he had a point. She remembered that she had been surprised when Carl Heissman contacted her and wanted to meet. He'd been friendly, concerned, charming and her doubts had quickly evaporated. But now that David brought them up again, she had to acknowledge them.

She could see that but, still, this all seemed crazy to her. People killing people was something she just wasn't used to. Assassinations. Killers. Spies. Those things were on TV and in movies, not in real life.

Was he for real or just some insane paranoid? But the more she studied his beautiful face, the more she was sure he believed every word he said.

Did that make it all true? Who knew?

"There's one little problem with that whole scenario," she pointed out right away. "If you left me behind, I wouldn't have known where you were within minutes of your leaving. So how could I tell anyone anything?"

His mouth twisted sardonically. This was obviously not a new thought to him. But all he said was, "True."

She waited a moment, but he didn't elaborate and she frowned.

"Anyway, I thought you were just protecting me from the bad guys, whoever they may be. Isn't that what you said?"

"I did say that, didn't I."

She frowned again, watching him as though she was beginning to have her doubts. "But we don't know who the bad guys are. Do we? I mean, we know they're these

Ambrian rebel types, but we don't know what they look like or what their names are. Right?"

"You're absolutely right. Rather a dilemma, don't you think?"

"Kind of nuts, that's what I think." She shook her head. "Maybe we should have stayed in the apartment. Maybe if we just stayed in one place and waited for them to show up, we'd find out who they are."

"We'd find out more than that. Not a good idea."

"Maybe. But you can't live your whole life just running all the time. Can you?"

"I don't know. I've only just begun."

She made a sound of exasperation and he grinned.

"We have a destination, Ayme. We're not just running for the fun of it."

"Oh. How about letting me in on where that destination is so I can share that feeling of comfort?"

"Not yet."

Her sigh had a touch of impatience to it. "In that case, I'm just useless baggage. So I still don't see why you brought me along."

"Because I feel some responsibility toward you. You came and you asked me for help. Isn't that enough?"

"So you're really planning to help me?" she asked as though surprised that such a thing might be the case.

"Of course. I told you I would."

She settled back and tried to think. What was the old expression, jumping from the frying pan into the fire? That was pretty much what she felt like. She'd been feeling vulnerable enough just searching for Cici's father. Now she was still searching for the man and being tracked by assassins, as well. And everyone knew what happened to people who hung out with people who were being tracked by assassins. Nothing good.

It was like reaching the next level in a video game. Suddenly the danger was ratcheted up a notch and you had to run that much harder.

From what she could gather going over the information he'd relayed, he was part of a revolt against the current regime in Ambria. Too bad she didn't know more about it so that she could decide if he was a good guy or not. From his point of view, he was obviously the "goodest" of the good guys, but that sort of thing tended to be a biased assessment. A strange thought came to her unbidden. What if he considered her a hostage?

The beginnings of a wail from the backseat interrupted her musings and gave notice that Cici was awake again.

"Uh-oh, here we go," Ayme said with apprehension.

David gave her a look. "You seem to live in dread of this baby waking up. She's barely announced her presence. And actually she's been quite good all day."

She sighed. She knew she shouldn't be taking it out on the baby. Still. "You don't know what it was like on that airplane crossing," she told him.

"Babies on planes." He nodded, thinking it over. "Yes, I have to admit that is not a pleasant prospect. But it was probably the pressurized cabin. It probably hurt her little ears."

"You think so?" That put Cici in the category of someone transgressed against instead of the transgressor. She looked back at the baby and gave her a thumbs-up.

"Sure," he said. "It's not likely she's going to cry that way all the time."

He was right. She hadn't been all that fussy lately. But Ayme attributed it to David's calming influence. It certainly had very little to do with her. She only wished she knew the secrets of how to reassure a baby and get it to stop howling.

Cici was awake but gurgling happily as they came into the seaside area where they were going to spend the night.

"Where are we going to stay?" Ayme asked, looking longingly at the Ritz as they cruised past it. Then there was the Grand with its long, sweeping driveway and uniformed attendants standing ready to help guests as they arrived at the huge glass doors. They zipped right by that one, too.

"It's just a little farther," he said, leaning forward to read a street sign.

She noticed that the farther they went from those elegant hotels, the farther they also went from the bright lights and sparkling entryways. Soon they were surrounded by gloom.

"Here we are," he said at last, pulling into a driveway that immediately plunged them down a dark tunnel and into a broken-down parking lot. "This is the Gremmerton."

She took note of the oily puddles and stained walls. "Might as well be the Grimmer-ton," she muttered softly to herself.

"What was that?" he asked, glancing at her as he parked and shut off the engine.

"Nothing," she said, feeling sulky and knowing she was being a brat. "Nothing at all."

He grimaced. He knew exactly what she was thinking but he didn't bother to explain why they were staying here. She would have to figure it out for herself. When you were trying to travel below the radar, you had to stay in places where people would never expect to find you. And at the same time, you had to be low key, so that people wouldn't look at you and sense the incongruity and say among themselves, "Hmm. What is someone like that doing here? You would think someone like that would be over at the Grand."

"We're running low on formula," he noted as they unloaded the car and prepared to carry things up into the room.

"I saw a small market on the corner when we drove up," she said. "If you'll watch her for a while, I'll run out and get some. After we get settled in."

"Good."

They climbed two flights of stairs and found their room. It wasn't really too bad, although it did have wall-paper peeling from one corner and a single light bulb hanging down from the ceiling.

It also had only one bed.

She stared at it for a long moment, then turned to look at him, perplexed. "What are we going to do?" she asked. "Maybe we can order in a rollaway."

"No," he said calmly. It was fascinating watching the sequence of emotions as they played across her face. "We're pretending to be a family. We'll share the bed."

Her eyes widened. "I don't know if we ought to do that," she said, gazing at him with huge eyes.

That one statement, along with her horrified look, told him everything he needed to know about the state of her innocence—as well as the state of her media-fed imagination. He bit back a grin and coughed a bit before he could respond.

"Ayme, do you think I'm not going to be able to control myself? Do you really think I'm going to attack you during the night?"

She looked very stern. Evidently that was exactly what she was worried about.

"Okay," she said. "Here's the honest truth. I've never slept in a bed with a man."

"No!" He pretended to be surprised, then wished he hadn't. He didn't want her to think he was mocking her. It was really very cute that she was so concerned. Compared to most of the women he'd become accustomed to, it was delightful.

"No, really," she was saying earnestly. "I don't know what will happen. I…I don't know men very well." She shook her head, eyes troubled. "You read things…"

"Ayme, don't pay any attention to what you read."

He reached for her. It seemed a natural enough instinct to comfort her. He took her pretty face between his hands and smiled down at her.

"Pay attention to what I tell you. I won't pretend I'm not attracted to you. I am. Any man would be. But it doesn't mean a thing. And anyway, I can handle it. I'm not going to go mad with lust in the middle of the night."

She nodded, but she still seemed doubtful. What he didn't realize was that she was reacting to only one of the things he'd mentioned: the fact that to him being attracted to her didn't mean a thing.

He'd realized by now that he shouldn't have touched her at all and he drew back and shoved his hands into the pockets of his jeans. Then he frowned, watching emotions play over her face and wishing he'd never started down this road.

But now she could add missing the wonderful feel of his warm hands on her face to the fact that to him, she didn't mean a thing. He'd actually said that. Any attraction between them was a biological urge, nothing more. She could have been any woman, it would have been the same.

Wow, she thought sadly. *Talk about crushing a girl's spirits. Didn't mean a thing.*

But what did she expect? She looked at him, at how large and beautiful he was. He was an exceptional man. He probably dated a lot of exceptional women. And he probably thought she was young and silly. Meanwhile, she'd begun to think that he was pretty wonderful.

He cleared his throat, wishing he understood women. She appeared unhappy and he didn't know if it was because of the bed situation or if something else was bothering her. "So let's just play this by ear, okay?" he tried hopefully.

"Okay," she said softly.

"You sleep on your side, I'll sleep on mine. If it would make you feel better, we can make a barrier down the middle with pillows."

Her smile was bright but wavering. "Like an old Puritan bundling board?" she said.

"If you want."

She seemed to be somewhat reassured, but he wasn't. He could still feel the softness of her face against his hands. He shouldn't have touched her.

"Where's the bathroom?" she asked, looking about the room.

"Down the hall," he said. "You can't miss it."

"What?" Ayme shuddered. This on top of everything. "Down the hall?"

"That's right."

"Oh, no, I can't share a public bathroom." She was shaking her head as though this were the last straw. "Are you crazy?"

"This is the way old hotels are set up," he told her. "You'll have to get used to it. You'll be okay."

"I won't," she cried dramatically, flopping down to sit on the edge of the bed. "Bring me a chamber pot. I'm not leaving the room."

She bit her lip. Deep inside, she was cringing. That hadn't really been her, had it? Couldn't be. She didn't play the drama queen, didn't believe in it. But it seemed a combination of circumstances had come against her all at once and for just a moment, she'd cracked.

She was tired, she was scared, she was exhausted, and she didn't know where she was going or what was going to happen once she got there. It was no wonder she was on edge.

But she didn't have to take it out on David. When you came right down to it, he was being very patient. In fact, he was a super guy. Which made it that much worse that she was having a silly tantrum. She could feel her cheeks redden.

Slowly she raised her gaze to his.

"Okay," she said. "I'm done."

"You sure?"

She nodded.

"I'm sorry," she said, trying not to cry. "I'll go check out that powder room now. I'm sure it will be lovely."

It took all his strength to keep from laughing at her

sweet, funny face. He pulled her to her feet by taking both hands in his.

"Come on. You can do it. Others have and lived to tell the tale."

He smiled down at her as she looked up. He was so close. For a fleeting second or two, she had a fantasy, just the flash of an image, of what it might be like if he would kiss her.

But that was ridiculous. There was no reason for him to kiss her. This was not a kissing situation, and anyway, they weren't in a kissing relationship. And never would be. Besides, any feeling between them didn't mean a thing. Hadn't he said so?

Get it out of your head, she scolded herself silently.

Sure, there had been a couple of hot looks between them when they had struggled over the body search incident. And certainly, his hands on her skin had sent her into some sort of sensual orbit for a moment or two. But that was just natural sexual attraction stuff. It might have happened with anyone.

Maybe.

She had to face facts here. She knew her own nature and was inclined to try to find a little romance in almost anything that happened. When she saw a film or a TV show and there was no love interest, her attention would wander. She wasn't a deep thinker. Speculative theories could hold her interest for just so long and no longer. What she wanted to see and to think about was people loving each other.

Maybe it was because she'd never had a real romance of her own. She kept hoping, but no one really wonderful had ever come her way.

Until David, a little voice inside was saying.

Well, she couldn't deny he was pretty darn good. Still, he could never be for her and she knew it. Right now they were thrown together. They were hiding. They were running from someone. They were both taking care of a baby. There wasn't much romantic in all that, but it did keep them involved. She was just going to have to learn to keep his theory in mind at all times.

No matter what happened, it didn't mean a thing.

And then, gritting her teeth, she made her way down the hall and found that the bathroom wasn't nearly as bad as she'd expected. In fact, it was rather cozy, with newer decorations and more accessories than the hotel room itself.

The worst thing was the huge mirror set over a vanity area with a chair and small table. There she was in living color, looking even more horrible and haggard than she'd thought. She was a mess. Her hair resembled a bird's nest. Her eyes were tired and the dark circles beneath them were epic. She groaned and immediately went to work, splashing water on her face and pinching her cheeks to get some color in them. As she tried to comb her hair into a more pleasing tangle, she realized what she was doing and why she was working so frantically to make herself look a bit better. She cared what David thought of her.

"Doggone-it," she whispered, staring into her own eyes in the mirror. There was no hope. He'd already seen the worst of her.

She made her way to the corner market and found a brand of formula that looked like it would do. She was standing in line at the cashier when it occurred to her that she didn't have the right money.

"Uh-oh." She made a pathetic face to the bored-looking young woman behind the counter. "All I have are American dollars. I don't suppose…"

The cashier shook her head, making all her many piercings jangle at the same time. "Nah. We've had some bad experiences. We don't accept American money after six."

Ayme stared at her wondering what difference the time made. "Uh…what if I…?"

"Sorry," the girl said dismissively, pursing her brightly painted lips and looking toward the customer behind her.

Ayme sighed, starting to turn away. She might as well go back, climb the two flights of stairs, get some proper money from David, and do this all over again. But before she could vacate the premises, someone else had intervened, stepping forward to stop the clerk from going on to the next customer.

"Allow me, madam," he said with a gracious nod of his head. In his hand was exact change. He gave it to the clerk with a flourish.

Ayme gasped.

"Oh. Oh, thank you so much." She smiled at him, thoroughly relieved. What a nice man. He looked like her idea of what a composer or conductor should look like—eyes brightly seeing something over the horizon, white hair flying about his head, seeming to explode out from under a smallish felt hat, a supernatural smile as though he could hear music from the heavens. All in all, she thought he looked delightful, and she was so grateful she was bubbling with it.

"You are so kind. This is incredible. I wouldn't accept it but I'm just so tired tonight and the baby is out. But

I do have the money. If you'd like to come with me to the hotel room where we're staying…"

Even as she said the words she realized this wasn't a good idea. They were supposed to be in hiding, not inviting in strangers. She made a quick amendment to her suggestion.

"Please, give me your name and address so I can make sure you get repaid."

He waved all her protestations away. "Don't think twice about it, my dear. It's not a problem." He tipped his hat to her and turned to go. "I hope you have a safe journey to the continent."

"Thank you so much."

She smiled, but as he disappeared into the crowd on the street, her smile faded. How did he know she was on her way to the continent? She barely knew that herself. But this seaside town was a bit of a launching location for trips across the channel. So maybe she was taking his words too seriously.

Still, it did give her pause.

"I assume we're going to the continent?" she said as she returned to the room and began to unpack the little bottles of formula. David already had Cici sound asleep in her new car seat, tilted back and rigged as a bed. "Is that our next move?"

"Yes. Tomorrow we'll be crossing the channel," he told her. He gave her a quick glance to make sure she was suffering no lasting damage from the earlier trip into a public facility, and the fact that she looked calm and pleasant seemed to confirm that all was okay.

"Heading for France?" she asked hopefully.

France! Paris! She would love to see it all.

But he gave her an enigmatic smile and avoided the issue.

"Possibly," he said.

"Or possibly not," she said mockingly, making a face.

He grinned.

"I almost didn't get the formula," she told him as she began to set up a feeding for Cici. She explained about the cashier and the white-haired man.

"It was so nice of him," she said.

Alarms went off in David's head but he quickly calmed himself. After all, she was a very attractive woman. Any man worth his salt would have stepped forward to help her in a moment of need. He would have done it himself. Hopefully that was all there was to it.

Still, he was wary.

"What did he say?" he quizzed her. "Tell me every detail."

"Oh, he was just a nice old man," she insisted, but she told him everything she could remember, and he couldn't really find anything extraordinary in it.

"Let me know if you see him again," he told her. He briefly considered changing hotels, but then he decided he was being a bit paranoid. There was really no reason to suspect the man of anything at all. "Right now I want you to lie down on that bed."

"What?" she said, startled.

His mouth twisted. She was so predictable on certain subjects.

"I want you to get some sleep. I'm going out for a while, but when I get back, I'll take care of Cici should she waken. We may have to take off at an odd hour. I want you to take this chance to get the rest you need."

She turned to look at him. He was handsome as ever, but his eyes did look tired.

"But what about you? You're the one who's been driving and you need some sleep yourself."

He gave her his long, slow smile that he only handed out on special occasions. "I never sleep."

She laughed, charmed by that roguish smile. "Oh, please. What are you, a Superhero?"

"Not quite. But close."

It occurred to her that she knew precisely what he was—wary and mistrustful of something. What exactly did he think was going to threaten them? What was it he was running from? He'd given her a brief sketch of his theories, but not many specifics. She wished he would tell her so she could worry, too.

"Ayme, do what I say," he said firmly when she still hadn't moved. "We don't have time for long, drawn-out discussions."

"Aye aye, sir," she said, sitting on the edge of the bed.

"That's the spirit," he said approvingly. "Consider this a quasi-military operation. I'm the superior officer. You do what I say without questioning anything."

She rolled her eyes dramatically. "Oh, that'll be the day!"

"Indeed." He shook his head and turned to go. "I have to go out to make a phone call."

"Why can't you do it from here? Don't you have your cell phone?"

"I've got my mobile," he responded. "But it's not the phone I want to use for this call."

"Oh." More likely, she thought, it was a call he didn't want her to overhear.

"I'll be back."

She didn't bother to ask again. It was confusing at times. For whole moments he would seem to warm to her, and that special connection would spark between them. Then, in an instant, it was gone again. She wished she knew how to extend it.

But she had other things to think about. She got up off the bed and puttered for a bit, putting clothes away in the closet and cleaning off the dresser of things David had thrown there. Cici still slept. Maybe she would be able to get that nap in as David had suggested she do.

Something drew her to the side window, and peering down into the gathering gloom, she could see the walkway along the front of the hotel. Suddenly, she caught sight of David. He had a cell phone to his ear and seemed to be carrying on an energetic conversation with someone. She could see him gesticulating with his free hand. As she watched, he ducked into the side alleyway beside the hotel and she lost sight of him. She wondered who he was talking to. Hopefully it was someone who knew Cici's father.

Funny how she always thought of him that way—Cici's father—instead of Darius, the Ambrian Prince, or the lost royal. Was that because, deep down, she was pretty sure that either Sam had been fooling her or someone had fooled Sam. The story didn't really seem to hold together. But maybe David would find out the truth.

It was interesting how she trusted him and she really didn't want to analyze why that was. She had a feeling it had something to do with a deep need for a sense of stability in her life. She wanted him to be good. Therefore, he had to be good. Simple as that.

She looked at Cici. Babies were so adorable when

they slept. She was starting to get a handle on how to care for a baby. At least, she thought she was. She was trying to copy everything that David did. It was obvious that a strong, steady hand, a soothing tone of voice and a sense of confidence made all the difference. Cici hadn't been crying much at all and that was certainly a relief.

"I'm a fast learner," she muttered to herself. "I will survive."

Turning from the window, she lay down on the bed and fell instantly to sleep.

CHAPTER SEVEN

DAVID had made a couple of calls, but now he was talking to his brother again. Monte had some information on the requests he'd made earlier. Ayme's background checked out perfectly. She did have an adoptive sister named Sam who had a few teenage arrests for petty crimes and who had died in a car accident just days ago. But that wasn't all. The girls' parents had died in the same accident.

"That's odd," David said almost to himself, reacting to the horror of what Ayme must have gone through. "I wonder why she would have held that back from me?"

"Never trust a woman, David. You aren't falling for her, are you?"

"Hell, no. Give me some credit, okay?"

"Sure, I'm only kidding. I have no doubt about your ability to hang tough. But on to other matters, there is nothing new on the impostor pretending to spread your love about the land. I'll let you know as soon as I hear anything."

"Thanks."

"In the meantime, there's news. Our Uncle Thaddeus has died."

"Oh, no." David felt real remorse. He was the last of

the old guard. "That's a shame. I was looking forward
to meeting him someday, and hopefully hearing stories
about our parents and the old days."

"Yes, so was I. It is not to be. But his funeral is another matter. We must go to it."

David frowned "Are you serious?"

"Yes. As luck would have it, the ceremony will be
held in Piasa during the clan reunion gathering. It will
be a huge affair. He's considered the patriarch of the
Ambrian expat community. Everyone who means anything to Ambria will be there. It's our chance to begin to
step forward and take the reins of the restoration movement. Whoever takes charge at the right time is going
to rule the future." He paused, letting the importance
sink in.

"Darius, you must come. I need you by my side."

"Of course. If you need me, I'll be there."

Monte gave him the details. "The town will turn
Ambrian for a few days, it seems."

"Our covers will be blown."

"Yes."

David smiled. "Thank God."

"Yes."

They both laughed.

"Don't forget. Italy. Be there or be square."

"You got it."

He rang off, bemused and filled with conflicting emotions. He was looking forward to Italy. It was bound to
be an exciting, important lesson about his own past, as
well as a chance to lay the foundations for a new future.
But as he turned back toward the hotel, it was Ayme and
the information he'd heard about her parents that filled
his thoughts.

He went back up to the room and opened the door quietly. Ayme and Cici were both sound asleep. There was only one light on in the room, in the far corner, and he left things that way, pulling off his sweater and unbuttoning his shirt but leaving it and his jeans on as he came to the bed he was going to share with Ayme.

Looking down, his gaze skimmed over her pretty face, her lovely bare shoulder, the outline of her leg beneath the sheet. She appealed to him, no doubt about it. He waited as the surge of desire swept through him. That he expected. But what surprised him was another feeling that came along with it, a tightening in his chest, a warmth, an unfamiliar urgency. It took a moment to understand what it was, and when it came to him, he closed his eyes and swore softly.

Everything in him wanted to protect her. Every instinct wanted to make sure no one could hurt her.

Where had that come from? He didn't think he'd ever felt that before. He'd spent so much of his life protecting himself, he hadn't had the capacity to worry about others. In other words, he was a selfish, self-centered jerk. And he could accept that. So where had this new soft-headed urge to nurture come from?

Maybe it was just because of the baby. Maybe he was blurring the lines between them in a visceral way he couldn't control. He knew he needed to watch that. It could put him in unnecessary trouble. He didn't want to go doing anything stupid.

More likely the facts that he'd just learned about Ayme's parents' fate had something to do with it. And maybe it was just that he was so damn tired. Could be. He knew he needed sleep. And there was a bed right in front of him. Too bad it was already occupied.

She'd been so shocked by the thought of them sleeping together this way, he sort of hated to spring it on her with no warning, no time for her to prepare. But he wasn't a predator. He was just a sleepy guy right now. And the bed was just too tempting to pass up. With a sigh, he began to prepare for getting some sleep.

Giving a half turn, Ayme gasped.

There was a man in her bed!

Luckily, it was David. This was just what she'd been afraid of. Could she really allow this? Didn't she have to make a stand or something?

But maybe not. He still had his jeans on, but his chest was bare. Still, he was fast asleep and completely nonthreatening. She relaxed and went up on one elbow to look at him in a way she hadn't been able to do before.

She'd been telling the truth when she'd said she'd never had a serious boyfriend. She'd done some dating in college, but it never seemed to come to much. Most men she'd met had either disappointed or annoyed her in some way. The type of man she attracted never turned out to be the sort of man she thought she wanted in her life.

So far David hadn't annoyed her. But he wasn't trying to hit on her, either. Her mouth quirked as she realized that if his disinterest went on too long, that in itself might get to be annoying.

"You're never satisfied," she accused herself, laughing at the paradox. "Picky, picky, picky."

No doubt about it, he was about the most handsome man she'd ever been this close to. She liked the way his lustrous coffee-colored hair fell over his forehead in a sophisticated wave that could only have come from a high-end salon. Then she laughed at herself for even thinking that way. This was no time to dilute her Dallas roots.

"Hey," she whispered to herself. "He's got a good haircut."

But the rest of him was purely natural and didn't depend on any artifice at all. His features were clear and even, his brows smooth, his nose Roman, his chin hard and newly covered with a coat of stubble that only enhanced his manliness. He looked strong and tough, but he also looked like a good guy.

And then there was the rest of him. He had a build to make any woman's heart beat a little faster—something between a Greek statue and an Olympic swimmer. His skin was smooth and golden and the tiny hairs that ran down from his beautiful navel gleamed in the lamplight. His jeans were the expensive kind and his shirt was crisp and smooth, despite all it had been through in the day. His hands were beautiful, strong but gentle. She leaned a little closer, taking in his clean, male scent and the heat that rose from his body, feeling a sudden yearning she didn't really understand. It was tempting to lean down and touch her lips to his skin. She leaned a little closer, fantasizing about doing just that, about touching that belly button with her tongue, about running her hand along those gorgeous muscles.

Then she looked back up into his face and found his blue eyes wide open and staring right at her.

"Oh!" she gasped, ready to jump back away from him, but his hand shot out and stopped her.

"Don't make any sudden moves," he whispered. "Cici is stirring."

She stayed right where she was, just inches from his face.

"So," he said softly, his eyes brimming with laughter. "I guess I caught you checking me out."

She gasped again and turned bright red on the spot.

"I was doing no such thing," she whispered rather loudly, her eyes huge with outrage.

"Oh, yes, you were." He was almost grinning now. "I saw you."

"No, I was just…" Her voice faded. She couldn't think of anything good to pretend she'd been doing.

"Hey, it's only human to be interested," he said softly, still teasing her. "Come on, admit it. You were interested."

"I'm not admitting anything," she whispered back. "You're not all that wonderful, you know. I mean, you may be tempting, but I can resist you."

Somehow that didn't come out quite the way she'd meant it and she was blushing again. His iron grip on her wrist meant she was trapped staying close. So close, in fact, that she could feel his breath on her cheek. It felt lovely and exciting and her mouth was dry. The laughter in his eyes was gone. Instead something new smoldered in his gaze, something that scared her just a bit. She couldn't stay here against him like this. She pulled back harder and this time he let her go.

She swung her legs off the bed and sat up, looking back at him. "I…I think I'll get up for now," she said. "I think you should get some sleep and…and…"

He pulled up and leaned on one elbow, watching her. "I think sleep is going to be hard to find for a while," he said dryly as Cici began to whimper. "We might as well both get up."

She rose and went to the baby and by the time she'd pulled her up and turned back, he was up and putting on his sweater.

"I'll go down and get some food," he said. "I'm sure you're hungry by now. Fish and chips okay for you?"

"More fish?" She wrinkled her nose.

"It's good for you." He hesitated. "I could probably find an American hamburger somewhere, if that's what you want."

"No, actually I like fish and chips just fine. As long as the fish isn't kippers."

He grinned. "Don't worry. They don't make them that way too often."

He left the room and she sighed, feeling a delicious sort of tension leave with him. He'd said it didn't mean a thing, but she was beginning to think he'd been fooling himself. For her, it was meaning more and more all the time.

The fish and chips were okay and so was the pint of ale he brought back with them. But now it was time to tend to Cici and hope to convince her to go back to sleep so that they could get some rest, as well. After a half hour of pacing back and forth with a baby softly sobbing against her shoulder, Ayme had a proclamation to make.

"I've decided I'm not going to have any children," she said with a flourish.

"Oh." David looked up from the evening paper he'd picked up with the fish. "Well, it might be best to hold off until you get married."

She glared at him. "I'm not going to do that, either."

He smiled. "Right."

"I'm serious about this," she insisted. "Babies take over your life. It's unbelievable how much work they are."

"It's true." He had some sympathy for her state of mind. He'd been there himself. "They do monopolize all your time. But that doesn't last forever."

"It certainly seems to last forever on the day you're doing it."

He leaned back. "That's just for the moment. Before you know it, they're heading out the door with their friends and don't need you at all anymore."

She gave him a long-suffering look. "How long do you have to wait for that lovely day?"

"It takes a while."

"I'd be marking off the days on my calendar."

He grinned. "It can be hard, but think of the rewards."

"What rewards?"

Cici stirred in her arms, stretching and making a kitten sound. He watched as Ayme's fierce look melted.

"You see?" he said softly.

She smiled up at him ruefully. "Yeah, but is it all really worth it?"

He shook his head. How the hell had he become the family practices guru here? Still, she seemed to need some sort of reassurance and he supposed he could do that at least.

"Once you have one of your own," he told her, "I think you'll figure that out for yourself."

He rose and took Cici from her, and as he did, he thought of what Monte had told him. He'd thought from the beginning that there was a sense of sorrow lingering in her gaze, something deeper than she was admitting to. Why hadn't she told him about her parents? She must have a reason. Or maybe, as Monte hinted, it was a sign that he shouldn't trust her.

But what the heck—he didn't trust anybody, did he?

"Ayme, you've said you don't know much about your birth parents and you don't know much about Ambria. What exactly do you know?"

She scrunched up her nose as she thought about it. "Just a few things I've picked up casually over the years."

"You should know more."

She looked at him and made a face. "How much do you know?"

"I don't know as much as I should, either. I should have learned more."

"So we're both babes in the woods, so to speak."

He nodded, though there was obviously a vast gulf between what he knew and what she did. "Why weren't you more curious?"

She didn't answer that one, but she had something else on her mind.

"You were adopted just like I was," she noted. "Didn't you ever feel like you had to…I don't know. To prove to your parents that they should be glad to have picked you?"

He stared at her. "Never," he said.

She shrugged. "Well, I did. I was always trying so hard to make them proud of me."

He could see that. He could picture her as a little girl in her starched dresses with patent leather mary janes on her little feet.

Cici had finally fallen asleep and he laid her down in her little car seat bed before he turned toward Ayme again.

"And were they?" he asked softly, his gaze taking in every detail of her pretty face. "Proud of you, I mean."

"Oh, yes. I was the perfect child. I made straight As and won awards and swam on the swim team and got scholarships. I…I think I did everything I possibly could." A picture swam into her head. She'd entered the school district Scholars' Challenge, even though she was the youngest competitor and she was sure she had no chance. Jerry, a boy that she liked, had tried out and hadn't made it. He mocked her, teased her, made her miserable for days, saying she'd only made it on a fluke, that she was going to be the laughing stock of the school.

By the time the night of the competition rolled around, she didn't like him much anymore, but he had succeeded in destroying her confidence. She went on stage shaking, her knees knocking together, and at first, she didn't think she could hear the questions. She panicked. Jerry was right. She wasn't good enough. She looked to the side of the stage, ready to make a run for it.

Then she looked out into the crowd. There was her mother, looking so sweet, and her father, holding a sign that said Ayme Rocks. They were clapping and laughing and throwing kisses her way. They believed in her. There was a lump in her throat, but she turned and suddenly she knew the answer to the question, even though she thought she hadn't heard it right. She was awarded ten points. She wasn't going to run after all. A feeling of great calm came over her. She would do this for her parents.

She won the trophy for her school. Her parents were on either side of her as they came up the walk at home. Suddenly, her mother stepped ahead. She threw open the doors to the house, and there inside were friends and neighbors tooting horns and throwing confetti—a surprise celebration of her win. It was only later that she realized the celebration had been planned before her parents knew she would win. They were going to celebrate her anyway.

Thinking of that night now, tears rose and filled her eyes and she bit her lip, forcing them back.

"I think I made them very happy. Didn't I?"

Her eyes were brimming as she looked up into his face as though trying to find affirmation in his eyes.

He couldn't answer that for her, but he took her hands in his and held them while he looked down at her and wished he knew what to say to help her find comfort.

She took in a shuddering breath, then said forcefully, holding his hands very tightly, "Yes. I know I did." She closed her eyes, made a small hiccupping sound and started to cry.

He pulled her into his arms, holding her, rocking her, murmuring sweet comforting things that didn't really have any meaning. She calmed herself quickly and began to pull back away from him as though she were embarrassed. He let her go reluctantly. She felt very good in his arms.

"Sorry," she murmured, half smiling through her

tears. "I don't know what made me fall apart like that. It's not like me to do that."

"You're tired," he said, and she nodded.

He waited, giving her time, wondering when she was going to tell him her parents had died in the accident, but she calmed down and began to talk about a dog she had found when she was young.

"And what about Sam?" he asked at last, to get her back on track.

Now that she had unburdened herself this far, he felt as though she might as well get as much out in the open as she could bear. A catharsis of sorts.

And she seemed to want to talk right now. There was a little couch in the room and they sat down side by side and she went on.

"See, that's the flip side of it," she said. "The dark side, I guess. The better I did, the worse Sam seemed to do." She tried to smile but her face didn't seem to be working right at the moment. "The more I seemed to shine, the more Sam rejected that path. She became the rebel, the one who didn't succeed, on purpose. She got tattoos against our father's orders and got her nose pierced and ran around with losers."

"That sounds pretty typical. I've seen it before."

"I guess so." She shrugged. "Funny, but I can see it so much more clearly now than I ever did then. I knew she resented me." She looked up quickly and managed half a smile. "Don't get me wrong. We shared a lot of good times, too. But the undercurrent was always resentment. I used to think if she would just try a little harder... But of course, she felt like I'd already taken all the love slots in the family. There was no room for her to be a success. I'd already filled that role. She had to find something else to be."

"That must have been hard on your parents."

"Oh, yes. But in some ways, they didn't help matters. They weren't shy about telling Sam what they thought of her."

"And comparing her to you?"

"Yes, unfortunately. Which didn't help our relationship as you can imagine."

"Of course."

"So Sam left home as soon as she could. By the time she showed up with Cici, she'd been mostly gone for years, off with some boyfriend or another and only coming back when she needed something. She broke our parents hearts time and time again. And then, suddenly, there she was with a baby in her arms. Of course, part of us was thrilled. A new member of the family. But at the same time, my parents were horrified. Where was Cici's father? Had there been a wedding? I'm sure you can guess the answer to that one."

"I think I can."

"She was penitent at first. I think she'd been under a lot of stress trying to deal with a baby on her own. But once she got some good sleep and some good food, she quickly became defiant again. And when Mom tried to get her to make some realistic plans she had a tantrum."

"That was helpful."

"Yes. It was later that night that she told me who Cici's father was. She came to my room to ask me to take care of Cici. She claimed she'd tried motherhood and it didn't agree with her. So she was taking off."

"Just like that."

"Just like that."

"What did you say?"

She turned to him. "What do you think I said? I got hysterical." She threw up her hands. "I couldn't take her baby. I…I refused and I yelled a lot. I told her either our parents would have to raise her…or we'd have to put her up for adoption."

"Ouch."

"Oh, yes. I said horrible things." She looked at the sleeping baby. Was she looking at the situation any differently now? "Things I didn't mean. But I was trying to get her to face reality. She had the responsibility. She couldn't just shrug it off."

"And yet, somehow that is the way it worked out."

She nodded.

"She took the keys to my mother's car and drove off into the rainy night."

"And your parents went after her?"

"Yes. And they found her quickly enough."

"And?"

She flashed him a stiff smile. "There was an accident. And Cici became my problem."

He watched her, puzzled. Why not take that next step and tell him her parents had died in that accident, too? What was holding her back? It was a horrible thing and she was probably still reeling from the shock of it. But surely it would be better to open up about it, work through it, put it in some sort of context with her life. Until she did that, he was afraid she would have that look of tragedy deep in her eyes. And what he wanted most for her—wanted with a deep, aching need—was happiness.

CHAPTER EIGHT

CICI was fussy during the night and Ayme and David took turns walking her. That way, they both got enough sleep and in the morning they were actually feeling rather refreshed and ready to face another day.

And it was a beautiful morning. They ate a quick breakfast and then went walking along the stone path that led to the marina, watching the morning sun glint over the silver sea and the breeze shuffle some puffy white clouds across a cerulean sky. Cici was good as gold, her big blue eyes wide as she looked out at the world, so new and fresh in her young gaze.

Ayme had found a little stash of cute clothes in the bag, things she hadn't packed and didn't remember, so she'd been able to dress the baby very stylishly for their morning walk.

"This is the fun part, putting them in cute clothes," she told David.

"I never knew that," he said doubtfully. "Somehow that never appealed to me."

"Live and learn," she advised him with a sassy smile.

He grinned. He liked her sassy smile. In fact, he was beginning to realize he liked a lot about this young woman. Too much, in fact. But he wasn't going to think about that this morning. He was going to enjoy the weather, the scenery—and her.

They watched ships and boats sail in and out of the harbor, watched the fishermen come in with a catch. They listened to the sounds, smelled the sea odors and breathed in the sea air. Then it was time to go back and they walked slowly toward the hotel. David felt a strange contentment he wasn't used to. Cici made a cute, gurgling sound and they both laughed at her. He smiled. What a cute kid.

But whose kid?

Was there really a chance that he could be Cici's father? He'd racked his brain trying to remember who he'd been dating almost a year ago. He was afraid it was rather emblematic of his lifestyle that he was having so much trouble. What did it prove? Maybe nothing. But it did mean he'd had encounters with women that meant nothing to him, didn't it? And that wasn't anything to be proud of.

He was virtually certain he couldn't be the baby's father. And yet, one tiny little doubt kept nagging at him. It was the kind of thing where you woke up in the middle of the night and stared at the ceiling as the thought whirled in your brain, larger than life. During the day, it faded into irrelevancy, hardly noticeable. And yet, it wouldn't fade completely away and leave him totally alone.

He was thinking about it when Ayme suddenly whirled and pointed toward a man disappearing around a building.

"Look! There's the man from the little store last night."

He turned and looked but the man had disappeared. "What man?"

"The white hair…didn't you see him?"

"No. Who is he?"

"I don't really know, but he was very sweet to me last night at the convenience store. Remember? I didn't have enough money and he paid for me. Actually, I owe him some money. Keep a look out, maybe we can flag him down and I can pay him back."

The entire incident put David on alert. In his current frame of mind, seeing anyone twice on their itinerary was seeing them too often. He swore softly.

"Damn," he said as reality flooded back. "We're going to have to go."

"Go?" She turned to look at him. "Go where? Why?"

There was no point in trying to explain to her. She would just ask more questions. Besides, they didn't have the time.

"Come on, hurry. We've got to get going."

"Okay, but tell me why."

"I wanted to wait until dark," he said instead. "Everything's easier in the dark."

"Or harder, as the case may be."

"True." He flashed her a quick grin. "Let's pack up and get out of here post haste."

Ayme was hurrying along, but rebellion was smoldering in her heart.

"David," she said softly. "Tell me what we plan to do."

"Get away from your white-haired man."

"What? Why? He was very nice."

"Most assassins are great guys to go bowling with,"

he told her from the side of his mouth. "You can look it up. It's in the statistics."

She looked at him and shook her head. He wasn't taking her request seriously and it was beginning to make her angry. Swinging around in front of him, she blocked his path into the hotel and confronted him, hands on her hips.

"You know what? You need to give me a reason for all this. I can't do things without a reason. I'm a methodical, logical thinker and I really need to know why I'm doing things."

He seemed annoyed but tried to be patient. "I will. I promise you. Just give me a little more time."

She threw up her hands. "For all I know, we could be on our way to rob a bank or knock over a candy store or kidnap a famous hockey star or…who knows?"

"None of the above," he assured her, though he knew she was just using those as examples. "Ayme, we don't have time for this. We'll talk once we're on the road."

She sighed. She knew she wasn't going to be able to stand her ground. Not yet. But if he kept this up…

"Oh, all right," she said, and they raced for the stairway.

They were able to get a slot on the service that packed cars in for the trip through the tunnel, and they made it in record time. A short time later, they were back on the highway, on the French side of the channel.

Ayme was excited. After all, this was part sightseeing trip for her. But when David made a left turn where she was expecting a right one, she protested.

"Hey, the sign says 'Paris, that way'."

He glanced at her warily. "But we're not going to Paris."

Her heart sank. "Where are we going?"

"You'll see."

She bit her tongue. She'd had just about enough of this "you'll see" stuff. If he didn't trust her enough to let her know their destination at this point, what was she doing with him?

And then she had a brief moment of self-awareness and she realized she really ought to stop and think about what she was doing, period. Why was she running around the countryside with this man she barely knew? It was bad enough that she'd dropped everything to race to London with Cici on a mere address and a whim. But what was she doing now? This was crazy. His apprehension of being in danger was obviously sincere or he wouldn't be taking these measures to stay hidden. And here she was going right along with him—as though she were meant to. Insanity!

But she knew very well why she was doing it. Of course, his being such a gorgeous hunk of male humanity didn't hurt. There was a spark between them; she wouldn't deny that.

But there was something more, something deeper, something worse. She was doing it to avoid reality.

Funny, that—she'd jumped headlong into a dangerous chase in order to avoid her real-world situation. It seemed a contradiction. But she knew it was pretty accurate. Anything beat sitting around and thinking about her life. The longer she stayed on this journey to nowhere, the longer she could put off dealing with what had happened to her sister and to her parents. And the longer she could put off facing what the rest of her life was going to be like.

Okay, so she knew why she was doing this. And she

knew why he was doing this—at least she had a good idea. But that didn't mean she had to sign on to this "you'll see" business any longer. Either she was a partner in crime, or she would bail out of this situation. Well, maybe not bail exactly. But she would let him know she wasn't happy and insist on better treatment.

She settled back and looked at him, at his beautiful profile and his sexy day's growth of dark beard, at the way his gorgeous, shiny hair fell over his forehead. He glanced her way and frowned.

"What?" he said. "What's the matter?"

She didn't answer. She just kept looking at him. He glanced her way a few more times, and finally, with an exclamation of exasperation, he pulled over to the side of the road and turned to face her.

"What's wrong?" he demanded crankily. "You're driving me crazy with this silent routine. Tell me what you want."

She stared hard into his starry blue eyes. "Trust," she said at last. "I want to be trusted."

From the puzzled look on his face, she could see he had no idea what she was talking about.

"I trust you," he protested.

"No, you don't. If you trusted me, you'd tell me the truth."

A wary look suddenly clouded his gaze.

"Ah-ha!" she thought. There was evidence of guilt if she'd ever seen it.

"The truth about what?" he asked carefully.

"Everything," she said firmly.

Everything. He let his head fall back against the headrest and chuckled softly. If she only knew how much more complicated that would make it all.

"Ayme, Ayme, what makes you think I actually know the truth about anything?"

"You know more than I do. And that's all I want." She moved closer, touching his arm with her hand, trying to make him understand just how important this was to her. "You see, this is what I hate—you knowing and me not knowing. You guiding and me following without a clue. I need to be in control of my own destiny. I can't just sit here and let you control my fate. I have to have some free choice in the matter." Her fingers tightened on his arm. "Give me facts, let me make my own decisions. Let me make my own mistakes. But don't treat me like a child, David. Please. Let me be your partner."

He looked into her earnest face and felt a wave of emotion different from anything he'd ever felt before. He liked her. He liked her a lot. Too much, in fact. But he didn't care. There was something so good and true and valuable in her. Reaching out, he cupped her cheek with the palm of his hand and smiled into her eyes. The urge to kiss her bubbled up in his chest. Another urge competed. He wanted her to have whatever she wanted in life and he wanted her to have it right now. He wanted to protect her and be there for her and, at the same time, to let her fly free.

But mostly, he wanted to kiss her. He was moving closer, looking at her pretty lips. He could already taste her....

But wait. Swearing softly, he pulled himself up short. Someone had to. Taking a deep breath, he slipped his hand from her face and looked away and pulled himself together. What the hell was he doing here?

Frowning fiercely, he got tough.

"You want some facts, Ayme? Okay, here you go. I've

had word that there definitely are people following me. It's not all in my mind after all."

An early morning call to Monte had given him that information.

"I think your white-haired man may be one of them."

"Oh."

"Right now I'm trying to think of a way to get us to a safe place I know of without the bad guys knowing for sure where we are. So we are headed for a nice Dutch farm area to the north. My sister lives there. If we make it there without something bad happening, we're going to stay with her for a bit."

She sighed. That was all she wanted, a little sign that he trusted her, at least a little.

"Thank you," she said earnestly. Then she smiled. "That sounds nice. I always like people's sisters."

He watched her face light up and he groaned inside. The temptation to kiss her was with him all the time now. Every time he looked at her, he could feel what her body would be like against his and all his male instincts came to life. He had to find a way to ratchet his libido down. The whole sexual attraction thing was a new way to complicate his life and he had to resist it.

"I'm sure she'll like you, too," he said gruffly.

She nodded happily. "Okay then. Lead on."

And he did.

But he knew very well that the information he'd given her would only be the beginning. It was human nature. Once you had a taste, you wanted more. They hadn't driven for half an hour before she was asking questions again.

"So who exactly are these people who are following you?"

He shrugged. "I assume they are agents of the regime in Ambria. But I don't know that for sure."

"Because they know you are working against them?"

He nodded. This was no time to get into the rest of the reason.

She frowned thoughtfully, biting her lip. "We need something to call them. The Bad Guys is too generic."

"You think?"

"Yes, I do." She thought for another minute or two. "I've got it. Let's call them the Lurkers."

He shrugged, amused by her urge to organize everything. "Sounds fair."

She smiled, obviously pleased with her choice.

And she was pleased with Holland, too.

"It's so beautiful here," she said after a few hours of watching the landscape roll by. "It's like a fairy tale. Everything is so cute and clean."

"That's the Netherlands," he agreed. "It's quite a nice place."

"And you grew up here."

"That I did."

"Did that make you into a nice person?"

He grinned at her. "It's good to see you've noticed," he told her.

She smiled back at him. That spark thing happened and they both looked away quickly. But Ayme was warmed to her toes and floating on a cloud.

By late afternoon, they had arrived at the outskirts of the town of Twee Beren where David's sister lived.

"Here's another news flash for you, Ayme," he said

as he began to navigate the tiny streets. "If my current plan works out, we'll be making our way to my sister's house in a farmer's hay wagon. How's that for local color?"

"Oh. That's interesting." Though she was a bit taken aback at the prospect.

"I thought you'd like that. Hope Cici can take all the straw."

"The straw?" Ayme blinked at him. "What straw?"

"We'll be in hay. Straw." He gave her a puzzled glance. "You do know what a hay wagon is, don't you?"

"I…I think so. In fact, I think I've been on one before when I was a little girl and going around to the different ranches with my father."

"There you go. You should be an old hand at this."

"Hmm."

"The thing is, I'm sure the people following us…."

"The Lurkers, you mean."

He nodded, his wide mouth twisted in a half grin. "The Lurkers. They have the license number on this car, so we have to ditch it somewhere unobtrusive in the town. Then we'll switch over to the hay wagon. That ought to throw them off."

"I know it does that to me," she muttered, shaking her head, wondering what on earth he was thinking.

He pulled into a parking space near a vacant lot, switched off the engine, and turned to her. "Okay, here we go. We have about two blocks to walk. I'll carry Cici. Try to look inconspicuous."

She gazed at him, wide-eyed. "How do I do that?"

He looked her over. She was right. She was gorgeous with the afternoon sun shining in her golden hair.

Everyone within a half mile would be craning their neck to see her.

"Think ugly," he said, knowing it was no use. "Here, wear this wool cap."

She put it on and now she resembled a ragtime street urchin. He smiled. He couldn't help it. She was so darn adorable.

But someone else walking by was smiling at the picture she made, too, and he frowned.

"Come on. We're becoming a spectacle just trying not to be one. It's no use. We'll have to hurry along and hope we blend in."

They gathered their things, packed in a sleeping Cici and made their way down the street and around the corner to where a rather mangy-looking horse stood hitched to a relatively flat farmer's wagon. Hay was piled on it high as a hay stack and it had been left right in front of a small, friendly seeming pub.

David nodded with satisfaction.

"Good. Some things never change. Old farmer Shoenhoeven has been stopping here for his afternoon drink for as long as I can remember. When he leaves for home, he goes right past my sister's farm." He grinned at his own memories. "It's been fifteen years since I last did this. And to think the old man is still going strong. How old must he be? He seemed ancient back when I was a kid."

"You know him? Do you think he'll give us a ride?"

"He'll give us a ride but he's not going to know about it," David said, scanning the street. There weren't many people out and about. "We can't sit up there with him for all to see. We're going to hide in the back of his wagon."

"We're going to do what?" She came to a screeching halt and whirled to face him, appalled. "Even in Texas we don't do stuff as goofy as that."

"Well, here in Holland, we do." He looked around the quiet street again. There was no one in sight.

"Come on. As you walk past, turn in a little. There's a place where you can climb up. See the foothold? Just swing yourself up and make a dive under the straw."

She turned to face him, horrified. "Are you kidding me?"

"Hurry, Ayme," he commanded in a tone that brooked no debate. "Before someone comes around the corner."

"But…"

"Now!"

She threw her hands into the air but she did as he said. He came right behind her, handing off the baby and pushing back the straw so that they would all fit beneath it. They scrunched in, lay side by side under the straw and stayed very still. Ayme was holding her breath, listening intently, but no one came along to challenge their right to jump aboard.

"Is Cici okay?" David asked in a low voice at last.

Ayme looked at the baby, then blew a small piece of straw out of her mouth before she answered. "She's still asleep. Can you believe it?"

Carefully, she laid the baby down on a blanket between two wooden boxes, making sure no straw was touching her face. Then she turned back to David. They'd made a little cave in the straw and it was actually rather cozy. The corners of her mouth quirked.

"This is really silly," she whispered to him. "I feel like my feet are sticking out the bottom. Like the witch in *The Wizard of Oz*."

He grinned at her, leaning on his elbow and looking incredibly handsome with his eyes dancing and hay in his hair.

"Do I look like a farm boy?" he asked her, chewing on the end of a long straw.

"Uh-huh."

"Hush," he told her. "Or we'll have people calling in to the police about checking out a talking hay stack."

She couldn't meet his gaze without giggling. "Here we are in the back of a hay wagon." She was laughing out loud. Then she hiccuped and laughed harder.

"Shh," he hushed warningly, reaching to quiet her.

"This is just so funny, it's so ridiculous," she said between hiccups. "I mean, what are we doing here?" She was laughing again.

"You're getting hysterical," he warned near her ear.

"I'm not hysterical. You're tickling me."

"I'm not tickling you."

"Your breath. It tickles my skin."

Somehow that very concept sent her into new gales of laughter that she tried to stifle, but couldn't. He was on the verge of laughing, too, just from watching her. But she had to be quiet and stop making the haystack move if they were going to get away with this. And she showed no inclination to do so.

So he kissed her. As far as he could see it was the only option, short of throttling her.

It was meant to be a quick shock to her system, a way to stop the laughter in its tracks. A warning. A suggestion. A way to keep her from harming them all. But it turned into much more than that.

When his mouth covered hers, her lips parted immediately and her tongue flickered out as though to coax him inside. He took that invitation and made his move and then everything began to blur. His senses went into red-velvet mode. Everything about her felt soft and plush and everything he touched seemed to melt before him. He'd never felt anything this wonderful before. He never wanted to stop.

And neither did she. Every other man she'd ever kissed had been a wary exercise in testing waters that she hadn't found very warm, nor very tempting. This was so different. She felt as though she'd reached for a ripe fruit and had fallen over a cliff just as she grabbed it. It was a fall that had her spiraling from one level of delicious sensation to the next. She never wanted to reach the bottom of that canyon. She wanted to fall forever, as long as she was in David's arms.

She stretched. She reached for him—she was begging for more. His embrace was such a comfort to her, such a warm, safe place to be. She sank into the kiss as though she'd finally found a place where she really belonged.

But not for long. He pulled back, cursing himself silently for being such an idiot. This was exactly what he'd been warning himself against. He couldn't do this. It was stupid, but most of all it wasn't fair to her.

"I'm sorry," he said, hair falling over his eyes as he looked down at her. "I didn't mean to do that."

"Shh," she said, eyes wide. "He's coming."

They listened, quiet as mice, while the man called out his goodbyes and started to sing as he came toward the wagon.

Ayme gasped. "David, he's drunk!"

"Nah."

"Yes, he is," she whispered near his ear. "Listen to him."

"He's not drunk-drunk. Just a little tipsy. He's had his evening Bols and he's floating a bit. That's all."

The farmer climbed up into the driver's seat and called the horse to attention, and they started off. The wagon creaked loudly. The horses hooves clanged against the pavement. And the farmer sang at the top of his lungs.

"He's definitely had too much to drink!" Ayme hissed at David.

"Yes," he admitted. "Yes, he has. But it's okay. This isn't like a car. The horse knows the way. He'll take over."

"The horse!" She shook her head at the concept.

"You can always count on the horse. Out here in the country, you can fall asleep at the wheel…or the reins, I guess it is…and the horse will still get you there."

She wasn't sure she bought that one. "How do you know all this?"

"I used to live out here. Every summer, we spent at least a month in the country."

The wooden wheels hit a rock and they all bounced into the air.

"Ouch. This is bumpier than I remember. I guess my bones are older now."

Ayme was laughing again, which made him laugh. She was right. This whole thing was crazy. But at least they might be losing the Lurkers, leaving them in the dust. He certainly hoped so. He didn't know for sure what they wanted, but he knew he didn't want to give it to them. And he had a feeling it probably had something to do with an effort to keep him from showing up in Italy at the end of the week. That only made sense.

He was glad he'd thought of going to Marjan's. She was the closest to him in age of all his adoptive siblings. They'd been quite close growing up. She was married now and living a mile or so outside the little village of Twee Beren. He hadn't been able to call ahead, but he knew she would be happy to see him. She always was. Hopefully, she would be happy to take in Ayme and Cici until he could find Cici's father. That would leave him free to maneuver, and free to meet Monte in Italy. And that would get him away from the temptation Ayme was beginning to represent. The sooner the better for that.

They didn't have to be as sneaky bailing out as they had been climbing in. The farmer was singing so loudly, he wouldn't have noticed a brass band piling out from under the straw.

And then the farmhouse was right before them. David rang the bell and a pleasant-looking, slightly plump woman answered, took one look at them and threw her arms around her brother's neck without a word.

Ayme watched, just a step away, and then she followed them into the large, comfortable house while Marjan explained that her family was away and she was alone.

"Hans takes the children to see his mother every year for her birthday, and usually I go, too. But this time I had promised to make pies for the cheese festival in town, so here I am, rolling out pie dough all day instead."

David was glad he only had one person to try to explain things to. He'd been wondering just what he was going to say to her about why he was on the run, and why he wanted Ayme to stay with her. But he got a reprieve while the women chatted happily with each other and Marjan fixed up a bedroom for Ayme and the baby. Cici was being fussy and his sister helped quiet her with a practiced touch.

"You do that as easily as David does," Ayme told her with admiration as she watched.

"Oh, we all grew up taking care of babies. I sometimes think my whole life has been nothing but babies, from beginning to end."

David coughed discreetly. "There were those years at the Sorbonne."

Marjan grinned "Yes, but we don't talk about those." She rolled her eyes. "Massive waste of time."

David raised an eyebrow. "Didn't you have fun?"

Marjan gave him a look. "Fun is overrated. It often leaves behind a large mess that is very hard to clean up." She turned to Ayme. "You'll want your baby with you, won't you?"

"Oh! Of course."

"We still have a little crib that will be perfect."

She gave them both some soup and sent Ayme, who looked dead on her feet, off to bed. Then she turned to her brother.

"It's not her baby, is it?"

David smiled, waving a soup spoon at her. "You could tell that quickly?"

She nodded. "It wasn't just the fact that she doesn't have a smooth way of caring for her. There was something in the way she looked at the child." she shrugged. "That total depth of feeling just wasn't there."

David nodded slowly. "You're right. But she's actually

a lot better at hiding it than she was when she first burst into my life."

"Oh?"

"At that point she was practically holding the poor thing by one leg."

Marjan laughed. "She was claiming the baby was hers?"

"Yes. But when she constantly referred to a book on child care I knew pretty quickly that she was a fraud."

Marjan frowned. "That's a harsh word to use, don't you think?"

"You're right," he said ruefully. "Fake is much more accurate."

Marjan laughed. "Are you going to tell me the story? Or do I just have to wait and read about it in the papers?"

He looked at her ruefully, not sure how much he should tell her.

"Maybe we could start with this—just tell me where you two are headed."

"We're not 'you two'," he said defensively. "We're not a couple."

"No?"

"No. I'm going to Italy. And she's…" He sighed. "I was hoping she could stay with you for a few days."

"Of course." She nodded wisely. "I just read in the paper about the last of the old Ambrian royal family dying. Thaddeus, isn't it? I saw that his memorial service is scheduled to be held in Italy."

David stared at her. "Interesting," he said carefully.

"Yes." Her smile was guileless. "Will you be going to that?" she asked.

David's heart was beating a little harder.

"Why do you ask?" he said.

"No reason." She rose. "Would you like some more soup?" she asked him with a smile.

He didn't answer. He stared at her for a long moment. "How did you know?" he asked at last.

CHAPTER NINE

"OH, DAVID." Marjan ruffled his hair affectionately. "I've long had my own ideas about who you are and why you came to live with us in the middle of the night so long ago."

He stared at her. He'd never known she knew. "I hope you keep those ideas to yourself."

"Oh, I will. I understand the danger." She sat down next to him and reached out to hold his hand. "I figured it out years ago. Remember the summer you were fifteen? Suddenly you were too busy reading to go for a nice bicycle ride by the canals as we used to. You were always with your nose in a book, like you were possessed. I couldn't understand why, so I looked into what you were reading. Ambria. That funny little island country almost nobody knows anything about. But you were crazy for the place, and I was jealous. My buddy was hooked on something new and leaving me behind."

He squeezed her hand and she smiled at him.

"So I started reading about it, too, and I found information about the lost princes. The dates matched the time when you came to live with us. Then I looked at pictures of the royal family." She shook her head, smiling at him. "Then I knew. It was such a great story. My brother, the prince."

He sighed. "Do the others know?"

She shook her head. "I don't think so. I don't think of any of them ever stopped to wonder why you were with us or where you came from, or why a family who already had five children and more on the way would want another one. They just assumed your family were close friends with our parents and we took you in when you needed us to." She laughed softly.

"Do you remember? We spent long summer evenings talking about what was and what could be. I knew there was something more to you than mere happenstance. Besides, I remembered that night you arrived, everyone whispering and acting like something very scary was about to happen." She nodded. "So when I read about that death, I thought you might be going to Italy for the memorial service. I would think it is time for you to take up the cause."

"Are we going to Italy?" Ayme's voice cut into the kitchen's warmth.

They both jumped, realizing Ayme had come into the room behind them. David quickly scanned her face, looking for evidence that she might have heard more than he would want her to. But her eyes were clear. He didn't think she'd heard anything much.

"I have to go to Italy," he told her. "Marjan has said that you can stay here until I get back."

Her eyes suddenly filled with tragedy, imploring him. "Oh, no," she said softly. "But we haven't found that Darius person yet."

He got up from his chair and went to her, reaching

out to take both her hands. She was dressed in a long white nightgown Marjan had loaned her and she looked like an angel. A lump rose in his throat. She was so beautiful, it made his heart hurt.

"We'll talk about it tomorrow," he told her. "Get some sleep. Your eyes are like bruises on your face, they're so dark."

She searched his eyes, then nodded. "All right," she said. "I just came out to get Cici's warmed bottle, but…"

"Here it is," Marjan said, handing it to her. "Good night, Ayme. Let me know if you need anything else."

Ayme gave her a wavering smile. "Good night. And thank you so much."

She gave David one last look and turned to go.

Marjan looked at David's face and her eyes got very round. She nodded knowingly. "Not a couple?" she murmured.

But he was watching Ayme leave and he didn't seem to hear her.

Ayme fed Cici, put her back into her cute little crib and slipped back into the huge fluffy bed. It felt warm and luxurious. Maybe if she just closed her eyes and let herself go limp she would fall asleep right away—and not have to think.

She tried it. It didn't work.

Her eyes shot open and she stared into the darkness. But she wasn't going to think about Sam or her parents. She would never sleep if she let that happen. Better to think about David. She snuggled down into the covers and closed her eyes and imagined David in the bed with her. She was asleep in no time.

* * *

The next day dawned a bit blustery. David made a careful survey of the area from his window on the second floor, but he didn't see any sign of surveillance activities anywhere in the neighborhood. Ayme and Cici came out looking fresh and rested and Marjan cooked them all a wonderful breakfast.

Ayme and David lingered over coffee.

David was trying once again to figure out what had started this race across the continent, and why he'd suddenly known he was in danger and had to flee. Was it really Ayme showing up the way she had? Or the phone call in the night? Or just that it was time to leave for Italy and the sense of a gathering storm had become his reality?

"Have you tried to call that man in Dallas?" he asked her.

She shook her head.

"Has anyone tried to call you?"

She gave him a crooked smile. "How would I know? You made me turn my phone off."

"Check your voice mail," he said.

She checked, but there was nothing. Just the absence of the usual cheery greeting she could expect daily from her mother—a lump formed in her throat, but she shook it off.

He pulled out a leather case that had four cell phones in neat pockets and took a moment to choose one.

"Why do you have so many phones?" she asked.

"Just in case. I like to be prepared." He set a phone up and looked at her. "Okay, give me the number."

"What number?"

"That Carl guy. I want to check him out."

She opened her own phone again and retrieved it,

reading it off to him while he clicked the numbers in. In a moment, there was a snap and a voice answered.

"You've reached the number for Euro Imports. Mr. Heissman is out at the moment. Please leave your name and number so that he may call you back. Thank you for calling Euro Imports."

"Euro Imports," he muttered, getting out his laptop and going on the Internet. There it was. It seemed to be legit.

He looked at Ayme who had been watching all this with interest.

"I guess your friend Carl is at least a real businessman in Dallas," he said. "So if that was him calling the other night, maybe it wasn't such a threatening call after all."

She nodded.

"Or maybe it was something else entirely." He gave her his best Humphrey Bogart impression. "You just never know. The problems of three little people like us don't matter a hill of beans in this crazy world."

She laughed, warmed to think he was talking about the very three people she was thinking of. It almost made it seem like they were a family of sorts.

They finished up their coffee and David asked his sister to watch Cici for an hour so that he could take Ayme along on a pilgrimage of sorts. He wanted to see if old Meneer Garvora, the man who had taught him some of the fundamentals about Ambria, still lived in the area.

They set off down the lane between hedgerows and David told her how the old man had caught him fishing in a landowner's fishpond one day when he was about ten, and as punishment, he'd made him read a book about Ambria and come by to give him a report.

"I have no idea how he knew about my ties to that country, or if he even did know. But he insisted I learn a lot about the place. I owe him a debt of gratitude for that."

He realized now how much the old man had husbanded the flame in him, making sure it didn't go out in the cold wind of international apathy. How had he known how important that would be to David's future?

"I wish someone had taught me a thing or two," Ayme said in response.

He looked over at her and smiled. "I'll teach you everything you need to know," he said.

But she gave him a baleful look and he realized she was brooding about his plan to leave her with his sister.

They reached the little cottage where David's mentor had lived, but the place seemed a bit deserted.

"This looks like a place where hobbits might live," Ayme noted. "Or maybe the seven dwarves."

David knocked on the door but there was no answer. Walking about in the garden, they found a stone bench and sat together on it, gazing into a small pond and enjoying the morning sunshine, and he told Ayme about some of the lessons the old man had given him when he was a boy.

Memory was a strange thing. Now that he'd opened his mind to that past, a lot came flooding in that he hadn't thought of in years. He especially remembered how lost and lonely he'd felt as he tried to make sense of his situation. He'd spent years wondering about his family, wondering what had happened to them.

At one point in his childhood, he'd asked his foster mother. Neither of this second set of parents ever brought up the fact that he was an addition to their thriving nest. They treated him as though he'd come the same way the others had come, and looking back now, he was grateful. But at the time, it made it hard to bring up the subject of his old life. He felt as though he was betraying their kindness in a way. Still, he had to find out whatever he could.

When he'd finally built up the courage to ask, his foster mother had looked sad and pulled him onto her lap and given him a hug. She told him how sorry she was for the tragedies in his life. She gave him sympathy and a tear or two. But what she didn't give him was the truth.

Maybe she didn't know anything else. He realized that now. But at the time, he'd resented the lack of information. He'd felt as though he had to operate blind in a seeing world. He wanted to know about his siblings. He wanted to know what his parents had been like. He had a thousand questions and his foster parents gave him sympathy but not much else.

As he grew older he tried doing research on his own, but he couldn't find much. Most of the world seemed to assume that his entire family had been wiped out in the rebellion, but since he knew different, he didn't take that seriously. He knew there was hope that more royals had survived. Still, he was always aware, just as he'd been aware that dark, stormy night, that the wrong move or a careless word could bring on disaster.

And then he had been found by Meneer Garvora. The old man, in his crusty way, had opened up the world of

Ambria to him. Looking back, he realized now what a resource he had been.

"So he gave you what your new parents just couldn't," Ayme noted. "How lucky that you had him in your life."

He nodded. "My adoptive parents were very nice to me. I thoroughly appreciate all they did for me. And I've had a nice career working for my father's company." His gaze clouded. "But they were never my real parents the way yours seem to have been with you—we never had that special closeness." He shrugged. "Maybe it was because I could still remember my birth parents, and that made it more difficult to attach to new ones. But it was also because there were just so darn many of us kids, it was pretty hard to get much individual attention."

Ayme sighed. "I had all the attention in the world. I was the fair-haired child and I enjoyed every moment of it. Analyzing it now, I can see that their joy in my accomplishments pushed Sam to the sidelines, and I regret it so much."

Tears shimmered in her eyes. David reached out and put an arm around her shoulders, pulling her close. She turned her face up to his and he kissed her softly on the lips.

She smiled. "I like you," she said softly.

He'd only meant to comfort her. He only wanted to shield her from pain. But when she looked up at him and said that so sweetly, he lost all sense of reality in one fell swoop.

He wanted to speak, but his throat was too choked for him to say anything. He more than liked her. He wanted her, needed her, felt an overpowering urge to take her in his arms and kiss her lips and kiss her breasts and make her feel his desire until she was ready to accept him, body and soul.

The thought of taking her body with his set up an ache and a throbbing in him that threatened to blow away all his inhibitions. He was all need, all desire, all urgent hunger. He felt, for just a moment, like a wolf who'd caught sight of the prey that destiny had been saving just for him—how could he be denied?

He took her face in his hands and saw acceptance in her eyes. He could hardly breathe, and his heart was beating so hard he didn't hear the sound of the back gate opening until a voice called out, "Who's here?"

He froze. His body rebelled. Closing his eyes, he forced himself back into a sense of calm, and as he did Ayme slipped from his hands, rising to meet the elderly woman coming around the corner.

"Well, hello," she said. "I've just come to pick up the mail from the box."

David rose as well, feeling like a man who had just avoided the pit of stark, raving madness. He was breathing hard, but he managed to smile and ask "Doesn't Meneer Garvora live here anymore?"

"Oh, certainly, he still lives here just as he has for thirty years," she responded in a kindly manner. "But he's gone on a trip right now. First time I've known him to go anywhere for years and years. He said he might be gone for quite some time." She waved an arm expansively. "I'm watering his pots for him while he's gone."

"I see. I'm sorry to have missed him." Turning, he looked down into Ayme's clear brown eyes. There was a question in them. And why not? What he'd almost done was insane and she was wondering whether he should be committed, no doubt. Internally he groaned. He was going to have to control himself better if he didn't want to bring down the whole house of cards on his own head.

Man up! he told himself silently. *Think of Ambria. Think of Monte.*

"Yes," the lady was saying. "Aren't you one of the Dykstra clan? I seem to remember seeing you visiting here years ago. Am I right?"

"You're right. Meneer Garvora gave me some important geography lessons in the old days. I just wanted to come by and thank him for that."

"I'll tell him you came by."

They started to go and David turned back. "By the way, did he say where he was going?"

"Yes, of course. He went to Italy."

David's eyebrows rose at that news. Thanking the woman, he nodded to Ayme and they started back down the path to the farmhouse.

"Hmm," Ayme said, noting his reaction to hearing his old mentor's destination. "Are we going to Italy, too?" she asked, just a bit archly.

He growled but didn't really answer.

"If I could just find this Darius person," she murmured.

He looked at her and frowned. "Listen, we need to talk about that." He hesitated, but there was no time like the present. "You do realize it is not very likely he was ever planning to marry your sister."

"Oh, I know that." She waved his statement away. "Knowing Sam, I doubt she was ever planning to marry him." She smiled sadly, remembering her sister. "Sam wasn't one to yearn for marriage. In fact, she wasn't one to stick with one man for more than a weekend."

He made a face. "Ouch."

"Well might you say that." She nodded, remembering the painful past. "I'm expecting him to be a sort of male version of Sam, if you know what I mean." She gazed at him earnestly as they walked along. "I just think he has a right to know about Cici and she has a right to the chance that her Dad might want her."

He winced. He was only just beginning to realize how hard this was all going to be. "I know. It's been bothering me, too."

"I don't know how much you can blame him. I mean I'm sure he's the sort of man who has women throwing themselves at him constantly. Being a handsome young and eligible prince and all."

He had to give her that. He nodded with a half smile he couldn't hold back. "Of course he does. But that doesn't mean he has to accept them, does it? Not if he has any integrity."

She gave him a bemused smile. "Celebrities with integrity? I'm sure there are a few, but…" She shrugged. "Hey, I've had men throw themselves at me all my life. Some seem to think I do have certain charms."

His sideways glance was warm. "I'll second that emotion."

She felt a glow of pleasure but she didn't want to lose her equilibrium. "But I would never let it go to my head. That way lies the pit, and once you fall over the edge, you're done for."

He grinned at her melodramatic tone. But then his grin faded as he remembered how he'd almost lost control just a half hour before. He hadn't even known it was possible. He'd never felt anything like that before, so strong, so overwhelming, so irresistible. It was almost scary—his own private "pit."

"So anyway, I think I should give him a chance to make a case for himself. Mostly for Cici's sake."

He had to admire her for that. If only he wasn't pretty sure that this guy was a rat, and maybe even needed exterminating.

Something stopped him just before they got back within sight of his sister's house. Some natural-born instinct for survival, perhaps. Whatever it was, it told him right away that danger lurked, and he had Ayme follow him as they stayed behind the bushes and traveled down along the hedge at the edge of the canal instead of walking in on the road. They kept out of sight and sneaked in through the back gate, surprising Marjan in the kitchen.

"Oh, I'm so glad you came in that way," she said as soon as she saw them. "I've just heard from my friend Tilly Weil that there is a man watching the house. He hangs out in that little stand of trees over there, across the way, pretending to be a bird watcher."

David went to the window, standing to the side. "How long has he been there?" he asked.

"Tilly thought he was there early this morning, then seemed to go have breakfast somewhere and is now back, binoculars in hand. So you see, you didn't get away with your ride in the hay wagon."

"Maybe," David said. "And maybe he's just watching my sister's house in case I might show up there. You can't tell." He looked at Ayme. "But I'd better go."

Ayme turned to look at him, her eyes huge. He felt

an ache in his heart. It was going to be hard to leave her behind.

"First of all," his sister said, "I know you're going to be anxious to go, but from what we've seen, I think you're right, that they don't know for sure whether you are here or not. And I say you wait until morning. If you do that, you'll have a place to stay tonight, and tomorrow I may have a way to get you out of here completely unseen by the outside world."

David thought for a moment. She had a point. If they left now, they would just have to find another place to stay for the night and it was getting late for that.

"All right," he said at last. "We'll go in the morning. Early."

"Ayme, I hope you'll be staying here with me," Marjan said, trying to help David do the right thing. She turned to him. "She'll be a big help, and at the same time I could teach her some practical things about babies."

He studied his sister's pleasant face for a moment, feeling a warmth for her he didn't feel for many other people. But he couldn't look at Ayme. He knew she was holding her breath, waiting to see what he would say.

Various and sundry thoughts ranged through his head as he stood there, thoughts about his brother's plan to match him up with the woman who was perfect princess material, about how his brother had warned him against getting entangled with Ayme, about how much easier it would be to sneak around on his own if she stayed behind. He had to keep his eye on the prize. He knew that. Ayme being with him tended to diffuse his focus at times.

His head knew all these things and agreed with them.

But his heart and soul had other ideas. He couldn't keep her with him forever, but he wanted her close right now. He needed her. Why? He wasn't ready to verbalize that just yet.

But he also wanted to make sure she was protected. For now. Not for always—that was impossible. But for now. For now.

He'd made up his mind. He was taking her to Italy with him. Monte wasn't going to like it, but he didn't care. Monte wasn't king yet.

"Thank you for your offer, Marjan. I appreciate it and love you for it. But I can't take you up on it. Ayme has to come with me."

Ayme's heart leaped in her chest. Yes!

Marjan's smile was understanding. "Well, then, how about the baby? You can leave her here. I'll take care of her. You need to be able to slide through the world without the baggage a baby entails."

Ayme's heart was beating as fast as a bird's, making her feel faint. She held her breath. Deep inside, she knew there was no way she would ever leave this helpless little baby behind. But what would David say?

He turned slowly. He looked at her and then he looked at Cici.

"That's up to Ayme," he said, then glanced at her. "She would be safe here," he suggested. "What do you say?"

She searched his gaze, looking for clues as to what he really thought. Did he want the freedom that being without the baby would bring? She could understand that he might. But she couldn't accept it. She needed Cici to come with them.

She drew in a deep breath. She was going to insist,

even if that meant David decided to have her stay instead of go. That was the way it had to be. She closed her eyes and said a little prayer.

Then she opened them and said, loud and clear, "Cici needs to go with us. That's where she belongs."

David smiled. "Good," he said firmly. "Thank you, Marjan, but we'll keep Cici with us."

Ayme felt a glow of happiness in her chest. It seemed to be settling right where her heart should be. She raced off to pack for the trip.

They had a lovely dinner. Ayme helped Marjan cook it, stopping to tend to Cici in between her duties. They ate heartily and laughed a lot. That night, they slept well.

When they were ready to go, they found that Marjan had set up a special plan for them.

"Okay, Mari. Tell me. What's your idea?" David asked her.

"Here's the scenario. You said you wanted to throw them off by going back to where you left the car and taking it."

"Yes."

Marjan frowned. "Won't they know?"

He shrugged. "I doubt it. They'll already have checked it out for any information they could use. There would be no reason for them to keep watch on it when they think we've abandoned it."

Marjan nodded, but suggested, "You could take my car."

"Thanks, Mari, but they probably have it pegged too, just in case. I think my idea is the best."

She nodded again, thinking. "All right then. Now, as for my plan, my friend Gretja takes her canal boat in to town every other morning. Today she is stopping by in half an hour to pick up my pies to take to the Cheese Fair. How would you like to ride back to town in a canal boat?"

David was all smiles. "That would be perfect."

"Good." She gave him a hug, then turned to Ayme and did the same. "I want you both to be safe and happy. So be careful!"

Forty minutes later they were on Gretja's canal boat, tucked away inside the little open cabin in a place where no one could see them from the shore. Gretja enjoyed the whole event more than anyone. As they were skimming along the waterway, the older woman grinned at them from above, her eyes sparkling as though she were carrying smugglers out of Kashmir.

"Oh, isn't this fun? I'm trying not to move my lips when I talk so they can't see me. Just in case anyone should be watching from the side, you know. I think I'll pretend to be singing. Yes, that should work just fine. Don't you think so?"

They humored her. The trip didn't take long, but it was fun while it lasted. They thanked her profusely when she dropped them off in town, choosing a crowded dock where they wouldn't be noticed. A few minutes later they were back in David's "incognito" car and driving toward France.

"I don't know how much more of this craziness I can take," Ayme said as she settled in and began to give Cici her bottle. "I'm just a stay-at-home girl from Dallas. I'm not used to all these shenanigans."

"Don't forget that semester in Japan," he reminded her sardonically.

"Well, yes, there was that." Her eyes narrowed as she

thought that over. "But we had escorts and chaperones everywhere we went. It was very controlled. Here I feel like I keep getting aboard a crazy train that's running wild. What if it goes off the tracks?"

He watched her, his eyes slightly hooded in a way she considered exceptionally sexy.

"Don't worry. You've got me to catch you if you fall off."

"Do I?"

He was kidding but she smiled at him anyway. At the same time, she wished she could ask him: *"But who are you?"*

She didn't ask it aloud, but it was always there in the back of her mind. She knew there was more to him than he was giving her. She just didn't know what it was.

She had caught a word or two between David and his sister, but she was in the dark. Bottom line, she didn't really care. She just wanted to be with David. She'd had to throw caution to the wind to go with him in the first place, and that was what she was doing again.

Was she falling in love with the man? How could she tell when she didn't really know who he was. She certainly had a pretty strong crush, stronger than any attachment she'd ever felt for any man—or boy— before. Was that love? She needed more information. Finally, she screwed up her courage and asked him the question.

"David, when are you going to tell me who you really are?" she asked, watching closely for his reaction.

His gaze flickered her way and she had the distinct impression he was looking to see just how much she thought she knew. What did that mean?

"I mean, I know most of the world thinks you're a

Dutchman named David Dykstra, but you're really not him at all. So who are you?"

"No, Ayme, you've got that wrong," he said with exaggerated patience. "I really am David Dykstra. It's just that I'm someone else, as well."

"Someone Ambrian."

"Right."

"And what is that someone's name?"

He shook his head and didn't look her way. "Later."

"Oh!" She growled. "I hate that answer."

"It's the only answer I can give right now."

"It's not acceptable." She waited and when he didn't elaborate, she added, "When is later, anyway?"

He glared at her, not smiling. "I'll let you know when I feel I can."

"Why can't you do it right now?"

"Ayme…"

She held up a hand. "I know, I know, it's too dangerous."

"Well, it is. I don't want you to get hurt because you know too much."

"Sure." Her mouth twisted cynically. "They could come and kidnap me. Where would I be then? They might put me on the rack and pull me apart until my bones snap." She punched a fist into the upholstery. "But I'll never talk. I'll say, 'No, you blackguards, you won't get anything out of me!'"

She sighed, dropping the phony accent. "Or I could tell them everything I know, which is more likely. So I understand why you won't tell me. You think I'll fold under pressure." She turned to give him a knowing look. "But what happens when I figure it out for myself? Then what? Huh?"

"You're making jokes, Ayme," he said calmly. "But your being tortured for information is no laughing matter. It could happen." He frowned. "Which makes me wonder why I let you come along."

"Okay," she said quickly. "Let's stop speculating. I won't beg for information anymore. I swear."

He looked at her earnest face and laughed. "Liar," he said softly.

"Okay, then how about this old chestnut? Where are we really going?"

"To Piasa, Italy. My uncle died. I need to attend his memorial service."

"Oh."

Wow. That was a lot more than she'd expected and it took her a moment of two to digest it.

"Your Ambrian uncle?" she asked.

He nodded.

She opened her mouth to ask more about that but he silenced her with a quick oath.

"No more, Ayme," he said. "That's enough for now."

"Okay." Suddenly, she remembered something.

"I forgot to tell you. I saw the white-haired man again."

His head turned quickly. "What? Where?"

"When we were transferring from the canal boat to the car. I couldn't warn you because we were sort of occupied at the time, the way we were sneaking around to find the car. But I saw him, or somebody who looked just like him, going into a store across the square. I don't think he saw us."

"Damn." He thought for a moment, then shook his head. "Okay, hang on."

Soon they were flying down the road at breakneck speed and Ayme was hanging on for dear life. She took a few minutes of this, then called out, "Hey, slow down. They can drive fast, too. You're not going to avoid them this way."

He let up a bit on the speed, but they were still going too fast. "You're right," he said. "I just wanted to feel like I was doing something, making some progress."

"With a little bit of luck, they don't know where we are and won't be coming up behind us," she said. "You never know." She sighed. "I never realized before how much of what happens to you in life is just based on dumb, blind luck."

He nodded, slowing even more. "Sure, to some extent. But there's also grit and determination and how much you're willing to put into life."

"One would hope. I've always used that as my template. Work hard and ye shall reap the rewards thereof, or something like that. But…" She threw up her hands. "Look at how much luck smoothed the way for me in life. I was adopted by a wonderful set of parents who adored me and did so well for me. What if I'd ended up with some other people? I was so lucky to get the Sommerses."

"So lucky, it almost balanced out the bad luck of losing your birth parents to begin with," he noted dryly.

"You're right." She frowned. "There's as much bad luck as there is good, isn't there?"

"At least as much."

She thought for a long moment, then ventured a look his way. "That last day in Dallas, I was alone with Cici. She slept all day. I was terrified she would wake up and

I would have to hold her. I had no clue what to do with babies. My parents had raced off to find Sam and bring her home without telling me anything except, 'take care of Cici.'" She sighed.

"If only Sam hadn't run away. If only my parents hadn't found out so quickly where she'd gone. If only… If only…" She closed her eyes for a moment, then opened them again.

"But when I opened the front door and found a policeman standing there, I knew. Right away, I knew. It was like the end of the world had come to my door. The end of my world, for sure."

He peered at her sideways, wondering if she was finally going to tell him about her parents' deaths.

"But consider this," she went on. "I was in shock, and it was just luck that I was so overcome that I didn't think to mention Cici to them. If I'd had her out at the time, or if she'd begun to cry, I would have remembered to tell them about her. They probably would have taken her away. Instead, there I was with Sam's baby and no family left."

There it was. He waited, poised. No family left. Maybe now she would go on and tell him about her parents. He looked at her, waiting for her to amplify. But she was staring out the window, brooding, so he coaxed her to continue.

"So that was bad luck?"

"No. No, not really. When I was able to think straight again, I realized Cici was now my responsibility. I couldn't let some social agency take her. I had to find her father."

He shrugged. "Perhaps if you'd told the authorities about her, *they* would have found her father."

"Maybe. But because of Sam's lifestyle and the crazy things she did, I have a feeling there would have been entanglements and problems. And delays. And red tape. No, I knew from the beginning it would be better if I could find a way to take care of it myself. Besides, I needed…" Her voice faded away.

He glanced at her. "Needed what?"

"Nothing." She cleared her throat. She'd needed to have something to do, somewhere to go, so that she wouldn't have to deal with her parents' deaths. "I was talking about Cici. At first, I didn't know anything about babies. My main concern was just to get her to someone who could take care of her and give her the love she needed. And that was why I dashed over here as soon as I found someone I could go to—and that was you."

"And here you are."

"Look at the blind dumb luck in you turning out to be the sort of man you are." She was looking at him with unabashed affection. "You actually cared. You gave me shelter from the storm."

"Some shelter," he said gruffly. "I threw you into a car and we've been racing across Europe ever since."

There was a quivering thread of passion in her voice when she said, "You made all the difference."

He looked away, steeling himself. He knew what was happening here. Her words were reaching into his heart and soul and touching his emotions like they'd never been touched before. If he wasn't careful, he was going to fall for it.

Not that she was trying to fool him. She wasn't. It was obvious that she was totally sincere. But Ayme's sincerity was already messing with his mind and he knew how much he already cared about her. He couldn't afford any more. If he let her into the secret places where his real feelings lay buried, he'd be done for.

CHAPTER TEN

DAVID had always known he was royal. He wasn't Monte. Monte would probably have been king right now if they were back in Ambria where they belonged. He was glad that responsibility was his older brother's and not his. Still, he knew if anything happened to Monte, he would be more than ready to take his place. It was the natural order of things.

Sometimes he wondered why he seemed to know this so instinctively. He hadn't had a family to pound these things into him, like most royals would have. He didn't have years and years of tutors teaching him about his place, years and years of servants treating him like he really was someone special. But he knew anyway. He knew it was both a special advantage and a special danger—as well as a responsibility.

"Uneasy lies the head that wears a crown," as Shakespeare wrote so long ago. He accepted that. It was part of the role as he'd always envisioned it. But that didn't mean it was a simple thing to deal with.

And romance certainly complicated matters. For a long time he'd assumed that casual romance came with the territory. It seemed all the royals he read about in the gossip papers were naturally promiscuous. He'd given that a try himself, but he hadn't really taken to it. Something in him seemed to be searching for that special someone who would complete his life.

Where he had gotten such a mundane, ordinary idea he wasn't sure. Maybe it had to do with the good, solid Dutch family that had raised him with morals and values that he couldn't seem to shake, even if he'd wanted to. Maybe it was something more basic. He wasn't sure, he only knew it made it hard to treat love as casually as people seemed to expect.

And now there was Ayme.

Wait. Why had he thought of that? What did this woman who had appeared out of nowhere and parked herself and her baby in his apartment have to do with anything? He wasn't falling in love with her. Of course he wasn't because that would be nuts.

"Where are we going next?"

He smiled. Her questions didn't even annoy him anymore. He expected them, like a parent expected the inevitable "Are we there yet?".

"As I told you, our ultimate destination is in Italy," he said to her.

"Are we going through Paris?" she asked hopefully.

"No. We're sticking to the back roads."

"Oh." Her disappointment was obvious. "I've always wanted to sip a glass of wine in a Parisian café," she said, her head tilted dreamily. "Preferably a sidewalk café. With a man playing an accordion and a woman singing torch songs in the background."

"Edith Piaf, no doubt."

"If possible." She grinned at him. "Why not?"

"I don't think she's around anymore."

"I know. Only in dreams."

He looked at her. More than anything, he wanted her to be happy.

"We'll do it," he said softly.

She looked at him in surprise. "But we're in a hurry."

He nodded. "We can't go to Paris. But don't worry. I'll find us a sidewalk café. Just have faith."

"I've got nothing but faith in you," she told him happily.

He took one look at her face and pulled over to the side of the road. In one smooth move, he had his arms around her and was kissing the heck out of her. She kissed him back once she was over her surprise. And when he pulled away, he touched her cheek and said, softly, "I thought you needed kissing."

She nodded. "You were right. I did."

He grinned and turned back to the wheel. They were back on the road in no time at all.

It was a couple of hours later when he turned onto a rutted road and told her what their next stop would be.

"We'll find you that sidewalk café very soon," he said. "But right now, I want you to see Ambria."

"Ambria!" She sat up straighter. Suddenly she was terrified.

"Yes. Ambria."

She swallowed a sudden lump in her throat. "How am I going to do that?"

"Under the right conditions, you can see her from the shore. I've done it. It's just a few miles ahead."

She pulled her arms in tightly around her chest and looked worried. "I'm not sure I want to see Ambria."

He gazed at her levelly. "Why not?"

"I…I don't know. I'm afraid it will change things."

He looked out the window and frowned, thinking. "You may be right," he said at last. "But I think you should see it, anyway."

She was silent for a long time and he didn't push her. Finally she said, "I'll do it, as long as you stay with me."

"Of course." He looked at her again. "Don't forget, you were born there. Deep down, you're Ambrian."

That didn't sit well with her. "I'm an American," she told him. "And I'm a Texan. And maybe I'm an Ambrian, too. But I don't feel it."

He nodded and his smile was pure affection. "That's why I'm taking you there."

She took in that affection like a flower took in sunshine. And in her own way, she bloomed a little. "Okay. I'll try to see what you want me to see. I'll try to like it."

"That's all I ask."

She gave a little hiccup of a laugh. "Just remember," she said. "In the immortal words of the Supremes, you can't hurry love."

He nodded. He knew what she meant. "Even love of country."

"Exactly."

They stopped along the way to get a couple of cold lemonades and then to let Ayme give Cici a bottle. The baby wanted to play so the stop took longer than they had expected. It was early afternoon by the time they got to the seashore.

What Ayme saw was unimpressive. If she looked carefully, she could just make out a sort of somber lump of land hidden behind a wall of melancholy fog. The entire aspect was grim and cheerless, like a prison off shore. She looked at David, hoping he couldn't read her disappointment in her face. But he was staring out at it, so she went back to staring, too.

As they watched, the clouds began to part above the gloomy, fog-shrouded island nation. Ayme reached out and took David's hand but she didn't meet his gaze. Instead, she was staring straight out to sea.

They watched for a long time. Eventually, the sun broke through and shafts of silver-gold sunlight shot down, illuminating the place. The fog lifted and there it was. And suddenly, she was transfixed. She'd never seen anything so beautiful before.

"That's Ambria?" she asked, breathless.

"That's Ambria," he said, satisfaction in his voice. "I haven't been there since I was six years old but it lives in my heart every day."

She shook her head and looked back. The vision was so brilliant, she almost had to shield her eyes.

"It's not in my heart yet," she said, "but it's knocking on the door."

David started talking in a low, vibrant voice. He talked about their Ambrian ancestors, about what it must have been like for their parents, about lives lost and dreams deferred. She listened and took in every word. She began to feel what had been lost. He spoke of how her parents had probably died there, and tears began to well in her eyes.

She wanted to tell him to stop, but somehow she couldn't. He went on and on and she listened, and soon her tears became sobs. He took her into his arms, but he didn't stop talking. And then he mentioned the loss of her sister, Samantha, and finally, of her adoptive parents.

She didn't even stop to wonder how he knew about that. He knew everything, it seemed. He was her everything. She trusted him and she loved him. And finally, the dam within her let go and she could mourn.

She had a lot to mourn about. Her birth parents, Sam, her Texas parents. It hardly seemed fair that one young woman should have to bear the weight of so much suffering on her slender shoulders. And she had avoided it for a long time. But finally, it was here, and she had David beside her. She could mourn.

He held her tightly and he rocked her and whispered comfort in her ear. She clung to him. She needed him. He was all that was keeping her from being swept away by a river of grief.

And when her crying was spent and the torrent was over, she told him about the accident—about how her parents had found Sam and how Sam had jumped into the car and driven off, and how her parents had given chase. And Sam had made a hard turn that had sent her skidding the wrong way, and her father, unable to stop in time, had smashed into Sam's car. All three dead from one stupid accident that shouldn't have happened. And at first she'd thought she might as well have died with them. Her life was over.

Things didn't look quite that way any longer, but still, it was a black cloud that might never leave her.

She wasn't sure what she wanted anymore. In some ways she felt like her emotions had been tugged in too many different directions in the past few days. She couldn't take much more. She'd had it. The only place she wanted to be right now was in a nice warm bath, with candles set around for good measure.

Back at the car, she drank the rest of the lemonade and kissed Cici and felt a bit revived, and then they were off. David was determined to find a nice sidewalk café for her, and he did just that in the next little town. It was as cute and quaint as she could have asked for and the three of them left the car and sat at a table, and David and Ayme drank wine and ate lovely biscuits. The torch songs were on the radio, but they did just fine. It was wonderful.

And then, Ayme saw the man again, riding past on a bicycle.

"Oh, David, look. The white-haired man."

David spun around. "The man from the first place we stayed?"

"Yes. Did you see him?"

"Yes." He stared down into his wine. "I've seen him before."

"Where? When?"

It was odd how he'd never really remarked on it before, but the man had popped up along the sidelines of his life in the past. Now that she'd pointed him out, he saw that clearly. Was he a threat? How could he take it any other way?

"We've got to get out of here," he said, rising. "We'd better go."

"The car?"

"No. We can't take the car. We'll have to do something else. Come on."

They left the table and began to walk quickly down the street. And then a van drove up beside them and two men jumped out and life became a jumbled, violent mess.

It all happened so fast. The men grabbed David. He struggled, but Ayme saw blood and knew he'd been hit with something. Her first impulse was to stand still and scream at the top of her lungs, but that wouldn't have helped anyone. There was another man getting out of the van and she was pretty sure he would be coming for her next.

David was hurt. She knew it. She couldn't do anything about it, but maybe she could save Cici. She turned and ran as she'd never run before, down between buildings, across railroad tracks, through a yard, over a fence, down an alley, into a field and back between buildings again.

She couldn't breathe. She felt as though there was a stone on her chest. And still she ran, holding Cici as tightly as she dared, adrenaline rushing through her veins. If she could just find some place to hide, a hole in the wall, a little cave, a wooden box, something.

But she ran out of luck before she found it. She was never sure if it was the blow to her head or the cloth soaked with chloroform under her nose that knocked her out, but suddenly there were people at both ends of the alley she'd run down.

"End of the line, little lady," said a burly man, just before they put the cloth over her face and something hit her just above the temple. She was out like a light.

She woke up in a hospital bed. There were voices all around but at first she couldn't focus on what they were saying. She drifted off and when she woke again, she was a bit more alert. A man was sitting beside her bed.

She turned her head to look at him. It was the white-haired man.

She gasped and looked for an escape, but he leaned over the bed with a sweet smile, shaking his head.

"I'm not one of the bad guys, Ayme," he told her. "Believe it or not, I was the one who rescued your little group before the Granvilli thugs could cart you off to Ambria, which seemed to be their objective."

She stared at him. Should she believe him? She scanned the room, which seemed to be a normal hospital room, not some dungeon or hideout. She began to relax.

"David is in a room down the hall. I'm sure you want to know how he is. Well, he's doing fairly well, though his injuries are much more extensive than yours. You have a lump on your head and will probably have a headache for a while, but the doctor says you're doing fine."

"Cici?" she asked, as she reached up to touch the lump he was referring to.

"Not hurt at all. They have her in a crib in the children's ward, but that's only because they don't know what else to do with her right now."

She narrowed her eyes, looking at him. He seemed nice. But then he always had. Could she trust him?

"Who are you?"

He smiled again. "My name doesn't matter. I'm allied with the Ambrian restoration team. We want to restore the royal family to its rightful place on the throne of our country."

"Then, why were you following David everywhere?"

He leaned closer and spoke as though in private.

"The truth is, I've been following David for years, trying to make sure nothing threatened him until he was ready."

"Ready?" She was getting confused again. "Ready for what?"

He smiled. "I see David needs to explain a few things to you. But I'll let him do that." He rose from his chair. "And now that you're awake, I'll go back to David, if you don't mind. Have the nurse contact me if you need anything, my dear." He nodded his head in her direction and left the room.

She stared after him, still not sure what was going on. When the team of men had driven up in the van and they'd been attacked, she'd thought it was exactly what David had been guarding against all this time. At least, from what he'd told her, that was what she assumed.

But the white-haired man had been a part of that threat—hadn't he? Now it seemed David had been wrong about that. But she really didn't understand. How had she let herself get involved, anyway?

She had to get out of here and she had to get Cici out. Rolling out of the bed, she clutched the hospital gown around herself and made her way to the door. She was dizzy, but it wasn't bad enough to stop her. She had to know how David and Cici really were, not just what someone she didn't really trust was telling her.

Up and down the hallway all seemed clear and she started toward the room across the hall. In the third room she checked, there was David. He had a big bandage on his head and appeared to be regaining consciousness. The white-haired man was there. But the strange thing was, he was bowed over from the waist and seemed to be kissing David's hand.

"Your Highness," he was saying. "I'm at your service, always."

She pulled back so that she couldn't be seen and tried to catch her breath.

Your highness? Your highness?

But hadn't she suspected this? Hadn't she known it all along? It all fell together. The pieces just fell into place. David was royal. Of course.

The white-haired man left the room, walking off down the hall without seeing where she was standing, half-hidden by a bank of oxygen tanks. She waited until he was out of sight, then slipped into David's room and approached him.

He looked as though he'd been through a meat grinder. Her heart flipped in her chest as she saw his most obvious wounds.

"Oh, David," she said, reaching for his hand.

He looked up and tried to smile around a swollen lip.

"Hi, Ayme," he said. "Hey, nice little frock you've got on there."

She ignored that. "Are you okay?" she asked anxiously.

"I'm okay. I'm still groggy from pain medication, but once I get that out of my system, I'll be good to go." His smile was bittersweet and his voice was rough. "I didn't protect you very well, did I?"

"What?" She shook her head, then grimaced. It hurt to do that. "I'm just so glad you're not badly injured," she said. "It all happened so fast."

"Yes. Thank God for Bernard and his men."

She looked at him questioningly. "The white-haired man?"

"Yes. He said he'd talked to you."

"Yes."

"Did he tell you how he and his men swooped in and saved my butt?"

"No."

He nodded slightly. "Let's reserve that story for later," he said, obviously starting to lag a bit. "Just be thankful they were there, keeping an eye on the situation. Without them, we'd be…" He let his voice trail off. He didn't really want to speculate right now.

"So, let me get this straight," she was saying. "There were bad guys following us. But there were also good guys following us?"

"That's about it."

And that left the question of why. But she knew that now, didn't she? She studied his face for a moment and then gave him a sad smile.

"You're one of them, aren't you?"

His eyes had been drifting shut, but they opened again. "One of whom?"

"The lost royals." Her heart was hammering in her chest. "Which one are you?"

He closed his eyes and turned away.

"Don't tell me you're Darius. Are you?" She wanted to grab him and shake him, but she knew she couldn't do that. "Are you Cici's father?" she asked, her voice strangled.

He opened his eyes again and looked at her. "No. That I am not."

She shook her head, feeling as though she were drowning in unhappiness. "How do you know?"

"Ayme, I never met Sam. Believe me, I've thought long and hard about it, just to make sure. It's not me."

"But you're Prince Darius. And at the same time, you're looking for him? I don't get it."

He tried to pull up to a seated position, but it was beyond him at this point. "Don't you see? I'm not looking for Darius. I know where he is. I'm looking for the man who's pretending to be me. That's the one we need to find."

"Why is he pretending?"

"Why not? If it helps him with the ladies, why not?"

She lowered her head and thought about that. She had to admit, Sam had been just crazy enough to fall for something like that.

"Of course, there's another theory. He might have been pretending to be Darius in order to try to lure me or any of my siblings who may have survived out of hiding. That's why we've got to find him."

"So either way, he's probably a jerk."

"Looks like."

Her sigh came from the depths of her soul. "And what if he wants Cici? Do I have to give her up to a jerk who might even be a criminal?" She searched his eyes, desperate for a good answer.

But he didn't have one for her. He could barely keep his eyes open. She gave up.

"I'm going to go see if I can get checked out of here," she told him. "I'll be back later."

He didn't answer. He was sound asleep.

A few minutes later she was dressed and ready to leave. Luckily, no one seemed to be paying much attention to her and she'd managed to prepare to check out without having to fill out any forms. All she had to do was find

Cici. She started down the hall, then hesitated. David's room was like a magnet. She wanted to see him one last time. Walking softly, she looked into the room. There was a man she didn't recognize talking to David.

"You've still got the Ambrian girl with you," he was saying.

"Ayme?" David asked groggily.

"Yes. What do you want me to do about her?"

"Do about her?"

"Your brother, the Crown Prince, has asked that you not bring her to Piasa. He has someone he thinks would make a perfect match for you waiting there to meet you and it would be…"

Pulling back, she began to walk on down the hall, pacing quickly, thinking, thinking. Her mind raced with plans. The pain of being cast aside would overwhelm her if she let it. She had to push it away and ignore it for now.

What was she going to do? She had to get out of here and she had to take Cici with her. It was obvious that she would never have David. She had to shut that off, not think about losing him. She had lost so much lately. And then, as though fate had lead her to the right place, there was Cici, alone in a room with only one little crib.

"Oh, my baby!" she cried as she rushed to hold her.

Was that a smile? Yes! Her heart filled with love as she held the child close and murmured sweet things to her. At the same time her mind whirred with ideas of how she could take her away before people asked questions and began to require official forms to be signed. If she could just get her back on a plane to Texas, she would be in a position to make a claim on her. Once she lost control of her here in Europe, there was no telling what would happen next. She might have no chance of ever getting her back.

At the same time, she knew what she was about to do was probably illegal. If she got caught, it could be all over for her. But if she just let Cici slip away, the last thing she loved in this world would be gone. Some choice she had. The pit or the pendulum.

She was going to risk it.

David was on the phone with Monte.

"We found him."

David had to concentrate and be sure he understood. His mind was still fuzzy. "Okay, you've got the guy who was pretending to be me? Is that right?"

"Well, in a manner of speaking. He's dead, has been for a few weeks, but we know who he is."

"Dead? How?"

Monte's voice lowered. "It looks like an assasination. He was shot by a sniper."

"Oh, my God."

"Yes. We assume whoever shot him thought he was you. He'd been using that story about being one of the lost royals to seduce young women off and on for a couple of years. It finally caught up with him."

They were both silent for a moment, taking that in.

Finally, Monte said, "You know what this means, don't you?"

"You tell me."

"This means that, however much we're tempted to say 'aw, forget about it, let's just go on and live our lives like everyone else,' that's not going to work. Because there are people out there who feel threatened by our very existence, and until we find a way to take back our country and get rid of those people, we're in danger. We'll never be safe, and neither will the ones we love."

He was right. David closed his eyes and swore softly. He didn't have a choice. He was Prince Darius of Ambria and he was going to have to deal with it.

"So, I guess I'll see you in Piasa on Friday? You're good to go?"

"Yes. I'll be there."

Monte hesitated. "About this Ayme person," he began.

David was fully awake now. "She'll be there, too," he said firmly. "She's with me."

There was a pause. "You do realize how important this is," Monte reminded him. "Every Ambrian who can make it will be there. This is our time to claim our heritage."

"I understand that, Monte, and I'll be there right beside you. I'll fight to the death for you and for our cause. For our place in history. But I'll be the one to decide on my private life, on what I need and what I don't."

Monte let his breath out in a long sigh. "Okay," he said. "That's your call. But I wish you'd reconsider."

David smiled, thinking of Ayme, thinking of Cici. There would be no problem with them keeping the baby now. "I've gone beyond the point of no return," he told his brother. "Take it or leave it."

"Okay. I'll take it. See you in Italy."

David was fully awake now. He looked around the sterile hospital room.

"Enough of this," he said, ripping the IV out of his arm and easing off the bed. He took it slowly. He was weak and he didn't want to end up on the floor. But he was going to find Ayme if it killed him.

He found his clothes and put them on, then headed out into the hallway. He knew that finding Cici would be the key to Ayme's location, and he knew where Cici had been put. He passed three separate nurses and a doctor, each of whom gave him curious looks, but didn't try to stop him. But when he arrived at his destination, the room was empty.

Alarm shot through him. If she'd already left, would he be able to find her again? He looked out the window. From the third story where he was, he could see Ayme heading down the walkway, Cici in her arms.

He couldn't run, but he moved faster than he would have thought possible and caught up to her before she got off the grounds.

"What are you doing?" he called to her as he got close.

She whirled, holding Cici to her chest. "Uh…uh…" Her eyes were huge and she looked guilty as hell.

"You're kidnapping Cici," he said, trying to keep the amusement hidden in his eyes. "Do you know you could be put in prison for something like that?"

"I'm not!" She gasped. "Oh, no. That's not what I'm doing." Her eyes filled with tears. "Oh, David," she wailed.

"Ayme, darling," he said, laughing as he pulled her into his arms. "Why are you running away?"

She gazed up at him, tears streaming down her face. "David, I've lost everything I ever loved. And now I've lost you. I can't bear to lose Cici, too."

He looked down into her pretty face. "Why do you think you've lost me?"

"You're royal. I…I'm not from that world."

"Neither am I. Not really. I didn't grow up preparing to be royal." He dropped a kiss on her nose. "Oh, Ayme, I want you with me. We can learn about being royal together."

"But, Cici…"

He pulled back and got serious. "They found Cici's father. I'm afraid he's dead."

Quickly, he told her what Monte had told him.

"So your search is over." He touched her cheek. "But I'm hoping our journey together has just begun."

She searched his gaze. "Do you mean that?"

"With all my heart."

"Oh, David!"

He kissed her, then pulled back.

"Come on. Let's get a cab and find a nice hotel."

"But, don't we need to tell the hospital?"

"Don't worry about it. This is the good side of being royal. We have people who take care of these little details for us."

"Like the white-haired man?"

"His name is Bernard. Get used to it. I have a feeling we'll be seeing a lot of him."

"Really?"

"And that Carl Heissman who first sent you to me? He's an associate of Bernard's. He wasn't sure if Sam's claim that Prince Darius was Cici's father would hold up, but he thought it best to send you to me to find out. You see, there are wheels within wheels. I'm sure we don't know the half of it yet."

He sobered.

"Do you understand?" he asked her. "I love you, Ayme. I want to marry you. But I don't want to sugarcoat this. It's something you're going to have to consider going forward. I want you with me, but you have to be willing to take the risks involved."

She shook her head, ready to be supremely happy, but warned against it by the tone of his voice. "What are you talking about?"

"We're about to start a major push on Ambria to win our country back. If we go ahead with it, there will likely be fighting. There will be danger. There may be dying. You will be risking a lot just by being associated with me. You must think this through and decide if it's worth it."

Reaching up, she flattened her hand against the plane of his handsome face. "David, my life was over until I met you. Now it's about to begin again. I'll risk it. I'll risk anything to be with you."

He kissed her again. After all these years of wondering what the big deal about love was, it seemed like a miracle that he had found a woman he couldn't live without, a woman he had to spend his life with.

"We'll be together."

"And Cici?"

As if on cue, the baby gurgled happily. They looked at each other and laughed.

"I think she'll probably be with us, too."

Ayme sighed with pure happiness, looking down at the child she'd come to love with all her heart.

"Good. Let's go to Italy."

SINGLE FATHER,
SURPRISE PRINCE!

BY
RAYE MORGAN

This book is dedicated to Julie in San Diego

CHAPTER ONE

SOMEONE WAS WATCHING him. Joe Tanner swore softly, tilted his face into the California sun and closed his eyes. A stalker. He could feel the eyes focused on the sun-baked skin right between his bare shoulder blades.

He'd spent enough time as an Army Ranger in the jungles of Southeast Asia avoiding contact with snipers to know when someone had him in his sites. When you'd developed a sixth sense like that just to keep yourself alive, you didn't forget how to use it.

"Just like riding a bicycle," he muttered to himself, opening his eyes and turning to see if he could filter out where the person was watching from.

He'd first noticed the interest he was getting from someone—someone possibly hostile—the day before, but he hadn't paid a lot of attention. Joe knew he was tall and tanned and reasonably good-looking, with thick brown hair tipped blond by the sun, and he seldom passed unnoticed by onlookers wherever he went. He'd assumed it was basically a casual surveillance. Living half his day wearing nothing but board shorts, he was used to having his half-naked body studied by strangers. He knew he had interesting scars.

Besides, he had other things on his mind. Someone was arriving tonight—someone from his old life, although he'd never met her. He was nervous. So he'd been thinking about important changes that were coming, and he'd ignored the lurker.

It wasn't until today that he began to get that creepy shiver of caution down his spine. When the hair on the back of his neck started to rise, he knew it was time to give this situation due diligence. Better safe than sorry, after all.

His gaze swept the San Diego beach. Though there was a fog bank threatening to come ashore, it was a fairly warm day and the usual suspects were flocking in for the waves and the atmosphere—the surfers, the moms chasing little children across the sand, the hobos hoping for a handout. The flirty beach girls were also out in full force—a curvaceous threesome of that variety were lingering close right now, giggling and smiling at him hopefully. There'd been a time when he would have smiled right back, but those days were long gone.

You could at least be friendly, a little voice inside his head complained. He ignored it. What was the point? It only encouraged them. And he had nothing for them, nothing at all.

He gave them a curt nod, but moved his attention on, searching the storefronts, the frozen-banana stand, the tourist shop with the slightly risqué T-shirts, the parking lot where a young, swimsuit-clad couple stood leaning against a sports car, wrapped in each other's fervent embrace, looking as though the world were about to end and they had to get a lifetime's worth of kissing in before it did.

Young love. He had a sudden urge to warn them, to tell them not to count on each other or anything else in this life. Everyone had to make it on his own. There were no promises, no guidelines to depend on. There was only Murphy's Law—anything that can go wrong will go wrong. You could count on that, at least. Be prepared.

But he wisely passed up the chance to give them the advantage of his unhappy experiences. Nobody ever listened, anyway. Everybody seemed to have to learn the hard way.

So who was it that was causing the hair on the back of his neck to bristle? The blind beggar in the faded Hawaiian shirt, sitting out in the sun on a little wooden stool next to his wise old collie? That hardly seemed likely. The cop making lazy passes down the meandering concrete walkway on his bicycle? No, he was watching everyone in a thoroughly professional manner, as he always did. The bag lady throwing out bread crusts to the raucous and ravenous sea gulls? The teenager practicing acrobatic tricks on his skateboard?

No. None of these.

As time ticked by, he began to settle on one lonely figure, and as he zeroed in, the way his pulse quickened told him he was right.

The person was lurking alongside the wall that separated the walkway from the sand. Joe pulled his sunglasses off the belt of his swim shorts and jammed them in front of his eyes so that he could watch the watcher without seeming to be looking in that direction. The culprit was wearing a thick sweatshirt with the hood pulled low, baggy jeans caked with wet sand around the feet, so it was difficult at first glance to see the gender he was dealing with. But it took only seconds of focused attention to realize the truth—this was a woman pretending to be a boy.

That only sharpened his sense of danger. His military experience had taught him that the most lethal threats often came wrapped in the most benign-looking packages. Never trust pretty women or adorable kids.

Turning as though scoping out the activity at the nearby marina, he watched from the corner of his eye as the woman slipped down to sit on the low wall, pulling a small notebook out of the front pocket of the sweatshirt and jotting something in it before stowing it away again.

Yup. It was her all right. And she was keeping notes. So what now?

He considered his alternatives. Direct confrontation was usually counterproductive. She would just deny that she had any interest in him at all, and slink away.

And then what? Very likely, whoever had sent her would just send someone else. Another case of treating the symptom instead of the cause. His curiosity had been aroused now. He wanted to know who was behind this and why.

The only way to make a real attempt at getting to the bottom of the situation would be to get to her somehow—earn her trust, maybe. Get her to talk. But first he would have to draw her out, force her into making a move that would prove her intent.

And why not? He had nothing better to do for the next hour or so of his life.

With a shrug, Joe leaned down to pick up his surfboard, and started toward the next pier. It was undergoing renovation and there were signs posted warning people to stay away. Nice and out of the way, with most of the beach crowd focused in another direction, it would be perfect.

He trudged through the sand, letting his natural inclination exaggerate the slight limp he still had from the leg that was only beginning to fully heal after almost a year of recuperation.

He didn't even turn to see if she was following. He just assumed she would be. The type who tried to mess with his life always followed the script to the letter, and he had no doubt she would do the same.

Kelly Vrosis bit her lip as she watched the man who called himself Joe Tanner start walking. She saw where he was headed—way off the beaten path. Her heart began to thump in her chest. Should she follow him? She was going to have to if she was going to do this thing right, wasn't she?

She only had one week, and she'd already wasted a day and a half not daring to get close enough to really do anything observant. Either she was going to document all Joe Tanner's activities and figure out if he was who she thought he was, or he wasn't, and she'd wasted a lot of time and credibility on a wild-goose chase. Taking a deep breath, she fingered the little digital camera hidden in her pocket, and rose slowly to her feet, ready to do what had to be done.

"Here goes," she muttered to herself, and then started off down the beach, staying higher, closer to the store-fronts, trying to be as invisible as possible, but still keep the tall, muscular figure of the man she was following in sight.

She was pretty sure he hadn't noticed her. She wasn't the sort who usually got noticed in crowds, and she'd worked hard on an outfit that would keep her anonymous.

Yesterday, after she'd driven out from the airport and checked into a motel room close to the address she'd found for Joe, she'd walked by his little beach house twice, so nervous she'd thought she couldn't breathe as she went quickly past his gate. She had no idea what she would do when she finally came face-to-face with the man she'd been researching for months now. The whole thing had become ridiculously emotional for her. Oh Lord, what if she passed out?

She didn't really expect that to happen, but it was true that there was something about him that sent her pulse racing—though she would never have admitted it to her coworkers, who had tried to talk her out of coming.

She worked as an analyst at a bureau in Cleveland, Ohio, the Ambrian News Agency. A child of Ambrian parents herself, she was fast becoming an expert in all things Ambrian. The little island nation of her ancestry wasn't well-known, especially under the current xenophobic regime. She'd taken as her special area of expertise the children of the monarchy that had been overthrown twenty-five years before.

It was recorded that they all had been killed that night of the coup, along with their parents, the king and queen. But now there was some question as to whether a few may have survived. And when she'd opened the national newsmagazine almost a year ago now and caught sight of a picture of Joe Tanner, returning war hero, she'd gasped in immediate recognition.

"Ohmigosh! He looks just like… Oh, it can't be! But he sure does look like…"

She knew it was nuts right from the beginning, and everyone she worked with agreed.

So she'd dug into the life of Joe Tanner and used all the resources available to her at the agency to find out all she could. Meanwhile, she became one of the top experts on the royal children. She knew everything about them that was to be known. And a few things that weren't. And she became more and more obsessed.

Now here she was, testing out her theory in real time. And scared to death to actually talk to the man.

It wasn't like her to be such a ninny. She'd grown up with two brothers and usually had an easy time dealing with men on the whole, but ever since she'd caught sight of Joe's face in that magazine article, she'd put him in a special category. She knew he was an extraordinary man, from what she'd read about him. He'd done things—and survived things—that no one she knew had ever done. What was he going to do when he realized that she was prying into his life?

"Kelly, you can't do this," Jim Hawker, the older man

who was her boss and office mate, had warned when she confided her plan to him. "You're letting a wacky obsession take over your common sense. You took one look at that picture and your overactive imagination created a huge conspiracy around it."

"But what if I'm right?" she'd insisted passionately. "I have to go to California and see what I can find out. I've got two weeks of vacation. I've got to see for myself."

Jim had grimaced. "Kelly, you're going to be annoying a man who has done things to people with his bare hands that you couldn't imagine in your worst nightmares. If he really is who you think he is, what makes you think he's going to be happy that you figured it out? Let it go. It's a crazy theory anyway."

"It's not crazy. It's way out, I'll admit. But it's not crazy. Just think how important it could be to the Ambrian community if I'm right."

"Even if you're right, you'll be poking a tiger with a stick. Without the blessings of the agency, you'll be all alone. No backup." He shook his head firmly. "No, Kelly. Don't do it. Go to Bermuda. Take a cruise. Just stay away from California."

But she couldn't stay away from California. She had to find out if she was right. She'd promised Jim she would be very careful. And she wouldn't approach the man himself until she was sure of how she would be received.

Of course, once she'd arrived it had all turned out to be a lot harder than she'd bargained for. She'd picked him out of a crowd right away, but she'd begun to realize she wasn't going to find out much just by observing him.

She needed more—and time was short. That morning she'd spent an hour watching him surf, all the while trying to map out a plan. She was going to have to interrogate people who knew him.

Well, maybe not "interrogate." More like "chat with." She'd already begun to make a list of likely contacts, including the man who ran the little produce store on the corner of his block. The two had seemed quite friendly as she'd caught sight of Joe buying a bag of fruit there on his way home the night before. Then there was the model-pretty girl who lived in the tiny beach cottage next door to his. She'd positioned herself to say hello to him twice already, and though he didn't seem to respond with a lot of enthusiasm, he did smile. She might know something. He didn't seem to throw those smiles around too freely.

And what a smile he had. It made Kelly shiver a little just to remember it, and it hadn't even been aimed at her.

There were also the neighbors on the other side of his house—two college students who shared an apartment in the two-story building. She'd seen him talking to them as they got their racing bikes out that morning, so they might know something. She'd worn shorts and a T-shirt and jogged slowly up and down his street early enough to be rewarded with that glimpse of his day. Then she'd watched as he walked off toward the beach, surfboard tucked under his arm, and she'd quickly donned her current baggy outfit to keep him from noticing that he might have seen her before.

This had been a lot of work, and so far, she'd reaped

very little in the way of rewards. Despite her trepidation, she was feeling a little grumpy. She'd hoped for more.

Kelly kept her distance, continuing to skirt the beach by staying up near the buildings. But she noticed they were mostly boarded up now. The stores had petered out into a semi-industrial area, and it looked as though this whole section of shore had been condemned for demolition and renovation. She glanced around, noting that no one seemed to be about.

And then she looked back at where Joe had been walking.

Wait a minute. She froze. She'd lost him.

She hesitated, realizing she'd last sighted him just before he'd gone behind an old fishing boat someone had hauled up onto the sand. She'd spent a moment of inattention gazing out at the ocean, then at the old buildings.

So where was he? He couldn't have stopped there.

Had he gone under the closed pier? There was more beach on the other side and she waited a moment, searching for him, expecting him to pop out and continue walking on across the empty sand, but he didn't.

There was no one on that side of the pier. The shore turned rocky there, and a fog was rolling in—a bad combination for surfers. Why was he carrying his board if he didn't plan to surf? To keep it safe, she supposed, but it seemed a long way around. Where was he going, anyway?

Glancing back at where she'd begun, she frowned. The sun still shone and people still swarmed the sidewalks, but they looked faraway now. The scene ahead seemed still and eerie.

What should she do now?

Kelly pressed her lips together. She had to keep going. She didn't want to have to waste a lot of time staking out his house again and hoping he'd appear, as she had the day before. Too boring and very little payoff. Now that she had a fix on him, it would be better to keep on the trail right here and now.

Except he'd disappeared behind a boat or under a pier.

With a sigh, she started off. She was going to have to find out which.

The wet sand felt cold against her bare feet. The fog was rolling in fast, and there was no longer any evidence that a sun existed at all. She walked quickly around the old boat, eyeing the peeling paint and barnacles. No sign of Joe. She was going to have to walk under the pier.

She wrinkled her nose. The place was hardly inviting. Dark and dank and creaking, it smelled bad and looked worse. Shadows hid too many angles from view. Crabs scurried from one piling to another. Even the water had a scummy look.

Kelly paused, peering toward the beach, wondering where he could have gone. The fog was too thick to see far. She was going to have to walk through to the other side to really see anything. An eerie foghorn sounded off the shore, completing the strange ocean feel.

Wasn't this the way most murder mysteries began?

She hesitated a moment longer. Did she really have to do this? Couldn't she just go back the way she'd come?

Anyone with any sense would be on her way already. But Kelly was still going. This was what she'd come for....

With another sigh, she stepped under the crumbling supports of the pier, walking quickly to get it over with. Each step took her farther from the light and sank her more deeply into the cold and clammy gloom. She tried to keep her attention on the hints of daylight ahead. Just a few more steps and she would be out....

When the hand came shooting out of nowhere and yanked her hood off her head, she gasped and stumbled in surprise.

"So you *are* a girl," a rough voice said. "What the hell do you want?"

The shock sent her reeling. She couldn't scream, and her legs weren't working right. She looked up frantically, her heart in her throat, trying to see who this was.

Joe Tanner, the man she'd been following? Or someone else, someone more sinister?

This wasn't how she'd planned it. She wasn't ready. She could hardly make him out in the gloom, and wasn't sure if this was the man she had spun her theories about or not. Whoever he was, he was just too big and too overwhelming. Everything in her rebelled, and mindlessly, Kelly turned and ran toward daylight.

Although she felt as if she was screaming, she didn't hear a sound. Only the crunch of sand under her feet, her breath coming fast, and finally, the grunt as he tackled her and threw her to the beach, his hard body coming down on top of hers.

A part of her felt complete outrage. How dare he do this to her?

Yet another part felt nothing but fear. The way the fog had closed in around them, she knew no one had seen what he'd done. She couldn't hope for help from a passerby—not even a cell phone call to the police. It was as though they were in their own world. Jim's warning flashed in her head: *You don't want to be alone with this guy when he realizes you're studying him.*

Her mind frantically searched for all the lost details of that women's survival course she'd taken three years ago. Where were those pressure points again?

"Who are you?" His hand was bunched in the fabric of her sweatshirt. "Why are you tailing me?"

She sighed and closed her eyes for a few seconds, catching her breath. At least he hadn't hurt her. For now, he wanted to talk, not wrestle. Straining to turn her head so that she could see around the edge of her hood, she looked at the man who had her pinned to the ground with the weight of his body, and she saw what she'd been hoping to see.

Yes, this was Joe Tanner. Relief flooded her and she began to relax, but then she remembered Jim's warning again. Kelly was in an odd situation. She knew Joe had no right to treat her like this—but what was she going to do about it?

"Could you let me up?" she asked hopefully.

"Not until I know why you've got me staked out."

"I don't," she protested, but her cheeks were flaming.

"Liar."

He hadn't hurt her and something told her he wasn't going to. She began to calm down. Now the major emotion she was feeling was embarrassment. She should have handled this in a more professional manner. Here she was, lying on the beach with the subject of her investigation. Not cool. She hoped Jim and the others at the office never found out about it.

"You see, Kelly," she could almost hear Jim saying, *"I told you to leave these things to people who know what they're doing."*

Of course, she always made the obvious argument. "How am I ever going to learn how to do this right if you never let me try?" But no one took her seriously.

So here she was, trying, and learning—and messing up a little bit. But she would get better. She gritted her teeth and promised herself that was what was happening here. She was getting better at this.

But she had to admit it wasn't easy to keep her mind on business with this man's incredible body pressed against hers, sending her pulse on a race. He was hard and smooth and golden—all things the perfect prince should be. Good thing she was covered from head to foot in sweatshirt material and denim, because he wasn't covered with much at all.

"Come on," he was saying now. "I want to know who put you up to this." He sounded cold and angry and forceful enough to wipe out any thoughts of sensuality she might be dreaming up. "Who are you working for?"

"N-nobody."

Which was technically true. Her office hadn't author-
ized this investigation. She was strictly on her own.

"Liar," he said again.

Reaching out, he pulled the hood all the way off
her head, exposing her matted blonde curls. She turned
her pretty face and large dark eyes his way and he
frowned.

"What the hell?"

This young woman was hardly the battle-hardened
little tough he'd expected. She was a greenhorn, no
doubt about it. No one in his right mind would have
sent her up against him.

A little alarm bell went off in the back of Joe's mind,
reminding him about lowering guards and being lulled
into complacency. But even that seemed ridiculous in
this case. She was too soft, too cute, too…amateur. His
quick survey of her nicely rounded body as he'd brought
her down had told him she wasn't carrying a weapon,
though she did have a couple of small, light objects in
the front pockets of her sweatshirt.

He'd had plenty of experience in fighting off threats.
He'd fought off hired guns, martial arts experts, Mata
Hari types with vials of poison hidden in their bras.
This little cutie didn't fit into any of those categories.
He would have staked his life on her being from outside
that world of intrigue he'd swum in for years. So what
the hell was she doing here?

"I'm not 'tailing' you and I don't have you 'staked
out,'" she insisted breathlessly.

He raised one sleek eyebrow, looking her over.

"Then it must be love," he said sarcastically. "Why

else would you be mooning around after me for days at a time?"

Shocked at the very suggestion, even though she knew he was just making fun of her, she opened her mouth to respond, but all that came out was a strangled sound.

"Never mind," he said in a kindly manner, though he was obviously still mocking her, and his mockery stung. "We'll just stay here this way until you remember what the answer is."

"To what?" she managed to choke out.

She tried to wriggle out from under him, but soon realized it was probably a mistake. She could see him better, but that only sent her nerves skittering like jumping beans on a hot plate.

He had hold of her sweatshirt and one strong leg was still thrown over hers. It was pretty clear he didn't like being followed. He was angry and he wanted the truth. Nothing amorous about it.

Still, he was just a little too gorgeous for comfort. She wasn't usually one to be tongue-tied, but being this close to him sent every sensible thought flying right out of her head. His huge blue eyes were gazing at her as though her skin were transparent and he could see everything—every thought, every feeling. She stared at him, spellbound, unable to move.

He began to look impatient.

"Let's cut to the chase," he said shortly. "I gave you your options. Pick one."

She licked her dry lips and had to try twice before she got out an actual word or two. "I…I can't."

"Why not?" he demanded. "I want the truth."

She shook her head, trying to clear it. What could she possibly say that he would understand at this point? All her explanations needed too much background. Despair began to creep into her thought processes.

"I have to get up," she told him. "If you don't release me, I'm going to get hysterical."

"Be serious," he scoffed. But then he looked at her a bit closer and what he saw seemed to convince him. Reluctantly, he rolled away.

"Women," he muttered darkly, but he let her get up, and he rose as well.

She took a deep breath and steadied herself. At least they were out from under that awful pier. The fog hid the sun, but the sand was still warm here and that was a bit comforting.

She looked up at him. He was all tanned skin and muscles, with sand sprinkled everywhere, even on his golden eyelashes. For a moment she was dazzled, but she quickly frowned and brought herself back down to earth. This was no time to let attraction take over. She had work to do.

"What's your name?" he demanded.

"Kelly Vrosis," she responded.

He almost smiled. That answer had been so quick, so automatic, he had no doubt it really was her name. What was going on here? Didn't she know she was supposed to lie about these things?

"Okay," he said. "I was nice to you. Your turn."

She opened her eyes wide, playing dumb. "What?"

she asked, shaking her head as though she didn't have a clue what he wanted from her.

He gave her a long-suffering look. "Okay, Kelly Vrosis. No more messing around. There are only three reasons people follow me. Some want information. Some want to stop me from doing something. But most want me dead." He pinned her with a direct stare. "So which is it?"

CHAPTER TWO

KELLY SHOOK HER HEAD, feeling a touch of panic. "None of those. Honest."

Joe's hard face looked almost contemptuous. "Then what?"

She glanced up at him and swallowed hard. She'd had a cover story ready when she'd started this. It had seemed a good one at the time—something about thinking he was her college roommate's brother—but now it just seemed lame. She had to admit this had turned out to be very different from what she'd expected or planned. Serious consequences loomed. This was scary.

"Uh, well…" she said, trying to buy time while she thought up something better. But then she stopped herself. There was no point in filling the air with nonsense just to give the impression she had something to say. He wasn't going to buy it, anyway.

Things were happening too quickly. She needed a moment to reflect, to stand back and look at this man and make a judgment call. Was he or was he not the man she theorized he had to be?

She'd put all of her credibility on the line, coming to

California and looking him up. Had she done something stupid? Or was she a genius?

Of course, she'd been crazy to get this close to him this early. She was on her own. If she got into trouble there would be no one to call.

Was she in trouble right now? Hard to tell. But it sure felt like it.

She looked him over. His blond-tipped hair was too long and sticking out at all angles. His skin was too tan. His body was too beautiful—and also too scarred to look at without wincing. He was barefoot and covered with sand. He didn't look like any prince she'd ever seen before.

Was she crazy? What if she was completely wrong? How could she have put herself and her career out on a limb like this? Maybe she should just pull back and rethink this whole thing.

"I saw you writing in a notebook," he said, moving toward her in a deliberate way that made her take a step backward. "It was about me, wasn't it?"

"What? No…" But she knew her face revealed the truth.

His clear blue eyes challenged her. "I want to see it."

Taking a deep breath, she tried for a bit of professionalism. She couldn't just roll over for this man.

"You have no right to see it. It's private property. My property."

"If it's about me, I think I have every right."

"No, you don't!"

"Hand it over."

"No."

"Never mind," he said impatiently, reaching for her. "We'll do it this way."

She wasn't certain what he had in mind, but was pretty sure she wasn't going to like it. She took another quick step backward.

"Wait." She put her hand to her mouth. "I think you chipped my tooth."

His first reaction was skepticism and she didn't blame him. It was a ploy, but she was desperate at this point.

"When?"

"When you tackled me."

To her surprise, he actually began to look concerned. "Here, let me see."

Moving forward and not giving her any room to maneuver, he took her face in his hands and looked down. This was a bit more than she'd bargained for. She wanted to protest, but after all, she'd set this up herself, hadn't she? And she really did feel a sharp edge on one of her upper fronts. Now she had to go through with it to prove her point. Tentatively, she opened her mouth.

"Here." She pointed at the place that felt sharp.

He leaned close, staring down. His hands were warm on her cheeks. His maleness overwhelmed her for a moment and she felt a bit light-headed. But his inspection didn't last long. He touched the tooth, then pulled back.

"As far as I can see, no tooth was injured during my expertly executed preemptive strike."

She gave him a look. "Cute," she said, exploring again with her tongue. "It feels chipped to me."

But while she was distracted, he was reaching to pull down the zipper of her sweatshirt, and that was another matter altogether.

"Hey," she cried, trying to jump away from his reach. "What do you think you're doing?"

"Checking," he said with calm confidence.

"Checking what?" She bristled with outrage.

"Don't worry. I've seen it all before." He gave her a sudden grin that just about knocked her backward on its own. "Just checking to see if you have a recorder on you. A bug. A mic."

She moved quickly to protect the little microcassette recorder tucked in the front pocket of her sweatshirt, but his hand was already sliding in there.

"Ah-hah." He pulled it out and waved it at her. "Just as I thought."

"Hey," she cried, truly indignant now, trying without success to snatch it back. "You can't do this."

He grinned again, eyes mocking as he dangled it just out of her reach. "Sue me."

And while she stretched to try to claim it, his other hand shot forward into her other pocket and snagged her notebook and her tiny digital camera.

"Give me back my things," she said, glaring at him, hands on her hips. A part of her was wincing, reminding her that she was reacting like any woman might, instead of like the intelligence agent she wanted to be. But she didn't have time to consider that. She couldn't let him do this!

"Okay now, this is just not fair."

"Not fair?" He set her items on a rock and stood in

front of them, so she knew she didn't have a chance to grab them unless he let her. "Life ain't fair, baby. Ya gotta learn to turn your lemons into lemonade."

Despite his obviously experience based advice, she wasn't ready to sign on to that attitude. She stuck her chin out and shot daggers at him with her eyes.

"You're bigger than I am. You're stronger than I am. You've got an unfair advantage. This isn't a fair fight."

He shrugged and took hold of the hood of her sweatshirt on either side of her face so she couldn't escape, pulling her closer and gazing down into her eyes. Strangely, his look went from mocking to dreamy in less time than it took to think it. As she gazed into his blue eyes, he grazed her cheek with one palm, touching her as though he liked the feel of her skin.

"Who says we're fighting?" he said, his voice suddenly low and sensual.

As humiliating as it was to know that he could turn her reactions on and off like a switch, she couldn't seem to stop them. The seduction in his voice washed over her like a wave, turning her outrage into a sense of longing she'd never known before. All the blood seemed to drain from her head, and for a moment, she actually thought she was going to faint.

Kelly closed her eyes and summoned all her strength. Whatever was going on, she wouldn't let it happen.

"Oh, no, you don't," she said, trying to make her shaky voice firm as she looked at Joe again. "You think you can manipulate me like a puppy dog, don't you?"

He dropped his hand from her face and gave her a

pained look. "I see," he said, turning from her. "What we've got here is a drama queen."

She took a step after him. "Look, you've taken everything I brought with me. You proved you could do it." She put out her hand. "So can I have them back now?"

He shook his head. "Not yet." He hesitated, gazing at her speculatively. He'd already been through her sweatshirt pockets. All that was left were the pockets in her jeans. "What I'd like to see is some ID. Where's your wallet?"

"Oh, no, you don't," she repeated, backing away again. "You're not coming anywhere near these pockets."

His mouth twisted. "I suppose that would be going a step too far," he said with obvious regret.

"Even for you," she added. "Besides, you have no right to do any of this."

He shrugged. "Okay. Come on back here and sit down." He gestured toward the rock. "Let's take a look at what you've found out about me."

He was going to look through her research notes. She frowned, not sure what to do. If she didn't have a real need to get along with him, she would certainly be treating this invasion of her space quite differently. In fact, she might be willing to swear out a warrant right now.

"Sit down," he said again.

"Sorry," she said crisply. "I don't have time. I have to go find a policeman to have you arrested."

He looked at her for a moment, then rubbed his eyes tiredly. "Kelly, sit down."

She gazed at him defiantly. "No."

He gave her a world-weary, heavy-lidded look. "Do I have to tackle you again?"

She hesitated, watching as he sat on the long black rock and began to go through her things.

"Hey, you can't look at that," she said, stepping closer.

"I thought you were going to see if you could find a cop to stop me," he noted casually as he flipped through the pages of her notebook. "This is quite a little document of my life for the last two days," he noted. "But pretty boring."

"The truth hurts," she quipped.

His mouth twisted. That wasn't the only thing that hurt. The leg that had taken a bullet almost a year ago still wasn't totally healed. It ached right now. He'd been standing on it for too long.

And yet he was probably better off than he'd had any reason to hope he would be when he'd returned from overseas. He'd been torn and wounded, in soul as well as in body, and the bitterness over what had happened that last day in the Philippines still consumed him. That had always been worse than the physical pain. The bullets that had torn through the jungle that day had shattered his life, but the woman he loved had died in his arms.

Was that it? Was that what Kelly was after? Was she just another writer looking for a story? He eyed her speculatively.

At first he'd thought she must have worse things in mind. There were plenty of people from his past who might want to take him out. But he was pretty sure that wasn't what she'd come for. She wasn't the right type. And all this note taking suggested she was looking for information, not trying to do him actual harm. At least not at the moment.

In the VA hospital, there'd been a reporter who had hung around, wanting to know details, fishing for angles. He'd seen the article about the "returning heroes" that had featured Joe as well as a group of other men, and he'd sensed there was something more there. He'd wanted to write up Joe's story, wanted to use his life as fodder for a piece of sensational journalism. He hadn't actually known about Angie, but he'd known there had to be something.

Joe hadn't cooperated. In fact, things had gotten downright nasty there for awhile. There was no way he would allow Angie to be grist for anyone's mill. And anyway, the last thing guys like him needed was publicity. Something like that could destroy your usefulness, wipe out your career. If people knew who you were and what your game was, you were dead. Incognito was the way to go.

He was confronting this issue right now. His body was pretty much healed, but his mind? Not hardly. Was he going to be able to go back to work?

That was the question haunting him. He wasn't in the military any longer, but there were plenty of contractors who were ready to pay him a lot of money to do what he was doing before, only privately. And—let's face it he didn't know much of anything else. But did he still have the heart for it? Had losing the woman he loved destroyed all that?

It hardly mattered. In just a few hours, his little girl—a little girl he'd never met—was arriving on a flight from the Philippines. He should be preparing for that. Once Mei was here, Joe had no idea what his life was going to be like. Everything had been on hold for months. Now he was about to see the future.

He still had no answers. But he knew one thing: he wasn't going to let anyone write about him. No way.

"So it *was* information you were aiming for after all," he said, paging through the notebook and feeling his annoyance begin to simmer into something else.

"Well, not really," she began, but he went on as though she hadn't spoken.

"Too bad you weren't around when I was smuggling contraband across the border," he said sardonically, looking up to where she was standing. "Or when I was inviting underaged girls over to my place for an orgy. Or hiding deserters in my rec room."

She finally slipped down to sit beside him in the rock. "I don't believe you ever did any of those things."

He winced. "Damn. I just can't get any respect anymore, can I?"

She gave him a baleful look. "You're wrong about me," she said calmly. "I'm not trying to dig up dirt on you."

His eyes were hooded and there was a hard line around his mouth. "No? Then what *are* you trying to do?"

She hesitated. What should she tell him? How much could she get away with and not let him know the truth? It was too soon to tell him everything. Much too soon.

And once he knew what she was here for, she had every reason to think that he would like her even less than he did now.

He was waving her notebook at her, his knuckles white. "This is me," he said, and to her surprise, his voice was throbbing with real anger. "You've taken a piece of me and you have no right to it."

She blinked, disconcerted that he was taking this so seriously. "But it's me, too. My writing."

"I don't care." He flipped the notebook open again and ripped the relevant pages out. Looking at her defiantly, he tore them into tiny pieces.

Her heart jumped but she held back her natural reaction. Something in the strength of his backlash warned her to let it be for now. Besides, she knew she hadn't written down anything very interesting as yet. It didn't really matter.

He dropped the scraps into her hand. "Let's see you try to put that back together again."

"Don't worry," she said brightly. "I don't need it. I can remember what I wrote."

"Really. Without this?" He held up her microcassette recorder. "And without this?" He added her tiny digital camera to the collection.

She bit her lip. Once again he was threatening to go too far. Tearing up some notes was one thing. Tampering with her electronics was another.

With a reluctant growl, he handed her back her things.

"Whatever," he said dismissively. "Do your thing. But just stay out of my way, okay?" He turned, running fingers through his thick hair and looking for his surf-board.

She quickly stashed her things away in her front pockets again, watching him anxiously. This seemed a lot like disaster in the making. He now knew who she was, so she couldn't very well follow him. If he found out she was questioning his neighbors, she wasn't sure what he would do, but she knew it wouldn't be pretty.

So she was stuck. Kelly couldn't do anything surreptitiously. Any new research would have to be done right out in the open and to his face. And for that she needed to have a civil relationship with him. That didn't seem to be in the cards, the way things were working out.

Without looking her way again, he began to stride off through the sand, his board under his arm.

She watched him go for a moment, watched the fog begin to swallow him up, her heart sinking. This couldn't be all there was. This couldn't be the end of her research. She might never know the truth now. Was he the prince or wasn't he? She had to find out. Gathering herself together, she ran after him.

"Wait!" she called. "Joe, wait a minute. I…I'll tell you everything."

He kept walking.

"Wait."

She caught up with him and managed to get him to glance at her again. "Have you ever heard of a little island country named Ambria?" she asked, searching his eyes for his reaction to her words.

He stopped in his tracks and turned, looking at her. And then he went very still. Everything about him seemed to be poised and waiting, like a cat in the jungle, preparing to strike.

"Ambria," he said slowly. Then he nodded, his eyes hooded. "Sure. I've heard of the place. What about it?"

There was something there. He'd reacted. She couldn't tell much, but there was a thread of interest in his gaze. Should she tell him what she thought she knew? She was trembling on the brink, but held back. The time wasn't right.

"Nothing," she said quickly, flushing and looking away to hide it. "I just…I'm Ambrian. Or I should say, my parents were. And I work for the Ambrian News Agency in Ohio."

He was searching her eyes, his own dark and clouded. "So?"

"I saw that article about the returning heroes six months ago where you were one of the soldiers featured."

He nodded, waiting.

"And…well, I got some information…. I'm following a lead that you might be Ambrian yourself. I'd like to talk to you about it and…"

He frowned. "Sorry." He turned from her again. "I'm not Ambrian. I'm American. You've got the wrong guy."

No. She didn't believe that. She'd seen the flicker behind his eyes.

"Wait," she said, hurrying after him again. "I really need your help."

She paused, realizing there was absolutely no reason

he should want to help her. She had to add something, something that would give him an excuse to get
involved.

"You see, what I'm doing is researching people who
were forced to leave Ambria by the revolution twenty-
five years ago. A lot of people were killed. A lot of the
royal family was killed."

He looked cynical. "Well, there you go. I wasn't
killed. And neither was my mother."

Kelly glanced up in surprise. "Who was your
mother?"

If he had a mother—a real mother—that could
change everything. Her entire investigation was riding
on a theory snatched out of thin air. At least that was
what they'd told her at headquarters.

Her mouth felt very dry. What if she'd come all the
way out here for nothing? Could she stand the ribbing
she would take when she went back to her office? Could
she hold her head up in meetings, or would she know
they were always thinking, *Don't pay any attention to
Kelly. She's the one who went on that wild-goose chase
after a lost prince who turned out to be not lost and not
a prince. Crazy woman.*

She cringed inside. But only for a moment.

Backbone, Kelly, she told herself silently. *Don't give
up without a fight.*

Holding her head high, she went back into attack
mode.

"Who was your mother?" she asked again, this
time almost accusingly, as though she was sure he was
making it up.

His mouth twisted and he looked at her as though he was beginning to wonder the same thing herself. "You know, I don't get it. What does this have to do with anything? It's all ancient history."

"Exactly. That's why I'm researching it. I'm trying to illuminate that ancient history and get some people reconnected with the background they've lost."

Meaning you, mister!

He was shaking his head. "I don't need any lost family. Family isn't really that important to me. It hasn't done me all that much good so far."

"But—"

Joe turned on her angrily. "Leave me alone, Kelly Vrosis. This is an important day for me and you've already wasted too much of it. Stay out of my way. I've got no time for this."

"Wow," she said, controlling herself, but letting her growing anger show. "And here I thought you were a good guy. The article I read made you sound like a hero."

He stared at her, his face dark and moody. "I'm no hero, Kelly. Believe me." He worked the muscles in his shoulders and grimaced painfully. "But I'm not a villain, either. As long as I'm not provoked."

"Oh, brother." She gave him a scathing look. "You can't call someone who's never been tempted a saint, can you?"

He studied her, his eyes cold. "I'm not really interested in your philosophy of life. And I still don't know who sent you here."

"I came on my own," she insisted.

He stared at her, then slowly shook his head. "I don't believe that."

He was striding off again, but this time she stayed where she was, blinking back the tears that threatened. There was no doubt about it, no tiny glimmer of hope. He'd closed the door. This investigation was over. There wasn't much more she could do.

CHAPTER THREE

JOE GLANCED AT his watch. It looked as if he still had a couple of hours to kill before heading to the airport. He knew he should be home preparing the place for the arrival of his little girl, and preparing his own psyche for how he was going to deal with her, but he was too rattled, too restless to stay in one place for long. He turned into his favorite coffee bar a couple blocks from his house and got into the line at the counter.

Yeah, coffee. Just the thing to settle his jangled nerves. What was he thinking? A good stiff shot of whiskey would have been better.

But he wasn't going to be drinking the hard stuff anymore, not while he had his daughter living with him. Everything was going to be different.

It had been hard enough just getting her here. Angie's mother, Coreline, had been against their marriage from the beginning, and she'd done all she could to keep Joe from bringing his baby home after Angie died. He'd been prepared, now that he was mostly healed, to go to the Philippines and fight for custody, but word had come suddenly that Coreline had died, and that baby

Mei would be sent to him right away, along with her nanny.

Thank God for the nanny! Without her, Joe would be in a panic right now. But luckily, she would stay for six months to help him adjust. In the meantime, he would make arrangements for the future.

His baby was coming to be with him. It was all he could think about.

The only thing that had threatened to distract him had been his strange encounter with Kelly Vrosis earlier that morning. Hopefully, his demeanor had discouraged her enough that he wouldn't see her again.

He took his drink from the counter and turned, sweeping his gaze through the crowded café, and there she was, sitting in the shadowy back corner. She'd cleaned up pretty well. Instead of the baggy clothes, she was wearing a snug yellow tank top and dark green cropped pants with tiny pink lizards embroidered all over them. His own crisp button-up shirt and nicely creased slacks added to the contrast of the way they had both looked that morning.

As his gaze met hers, she smiled and raised her hand in a friendly salute.

"Hi," she said as he came closer. Her smile looked a little shaky, but determined.

He grimaced and went over to her table, slumping down into the seat across from her.

"What are you having?" she asked, just to be polite. "A nice latte?"

He held up his cardboard cup. "A Kona blend, black. Extra bold."

She raised her eyebrows. "I should have known."

He didn't smile. "You're doing it again," he said wearily.

She looked as innocent as possible, under the circumstances. "Doing what?"

"Following me."

She pretended shock. "Of all the egos in the world! I was here first."

He gave her a look. "Come on, you know you are."

"Hey, I'm allowed to inhabit all the public spaces you inhabit until you get a court order to stop me."

He groaned. "Is it really going to take that?"

She stared at him frankly, pretending to be all confidence, but inside she was trembling. She'd almost given up a bit earlier, but it hadn't taken long to talk herself into giving it another try. Now here she was, trying hard, but it seemed he still wasn't buying.

"Kelly, don't make me get tough on you."

Was that a threat? She supposed it was, but she was ready to let that go as long as she had a chance to turn his mind around. She leaned forward earnestly. "You know how you could take care of this? Make it all go away like magic?"

He looked skeptical. "Maybe I could have you kidnapped and dropped off on an uninhabited South Pacific island," he suggested.

"No. All you have to do is sit down for an interview and let me ask you a few questions."

That hard line was back around his mouth and dark clouds filled his blue eyes. "So you *are* a writer."

"No, I'm not." She was aching with the need to find

a way to convince him. "I'm not interested in writing about you. I *wouldn't* write about you. I know it would be dangerous for you if I did, and I would never do anything to hurt you."

He studied her, uncertain what the hell she was talking about. She was pretty and utterly appealing, and he wasn't used to being mean to pretty girls. But did he have any choice? He needed to be rid of her.

"Listen, I came all the way from Ohio to find you. Let me talk to you for, say…one hour," she suggested quickly. "Just one."

He frowned at her suspiciously. "What about? What is it that you want to know?"

She brightened. "About you. About where you come from. Your background."

He shook his head. This didn't make any sense at all. "Why? What do you care about those things? I thought you were finding places for refugees from your island to go or something. What does all that have to do with me?"

"Because I think…" She took a deep breath. "Because there's plenty of evidence that you might be…"

"What?"

She coughed roughly and he resisted the urge to give her a good pat on the back. When she stopped, she still looked as though she didn't know what to say to him.

"What could it be?" he said, half teasing, half sarcastic. "Maybe Elvis's love child?"

"No." She licked her dry lips and forced herself onward. "Have you…have you ever heard of…the lost royals of Ambria?"

That damn island again. This was the second time she'd mentioned Ambria and she was the second person this week to bring up that little country. What the heck was going on? He stared at her for a long moment, then shrugged. "What about them?"

"I think you're one of them."

His brows came together for a second. "No kidding? Which one?" he added, though he didn't really know a thing about any of them, not even their names.

She took a deep breath. "I don't know that for sure. But I think Prince Cassius would be the right age."

Joe shook his head, an incredulous look on his face. "I want to understand this. You came to California just so you could follow me around and decide if you thought I was this prince?"

"Yes."

"Do you know how nutty that sounds?"

"Yes, I know exactly how nutty it sounds. Everyone I know has been telling me that ever since I got the idea."

He stared at her for a few seconds longer, and then he threw back his head and laughed aloud. "You're insane," he said, still laughing.

"No. I'm serious."

He shook his head again, rising and grabbing his cup. "I should have known better than to stop and talk to you," he muttered as he turned to go. Looking back, he laughed again.

"Now that I know you're unstable, I feel vindicated in not wanting to have anything to do with you and your crazy theories." He raised a hand in warning. "Stay out of my way, Kelly Vrosis. I mean it. Don't waste any more of my time."

She sat very still as she watched him walk away, and the realization hit her hard: he didn't know.

How amazing was that? If he really was one of the princes, he didn't know about it. It seemed almost unbelievable, and yet, somehow it fit with the way he'd been living his life. No one would have thought he was a prince.

No one but her.

She'd lived sith the story of the lost royals for months now. Twenty-five years ago, the mysterious little country of Ambria had been invaded by the Granvilli clan. The king and queen were killed, the castle was burned and the royal children—five sons and two daughters—had disappeared. For years it was assumed they had been murdered, too. But lately a new theory had surfaced. What if some of them had been spirited away and hidden all these years? What if the lost royal children of Ambria still existed?

That was the question that had filled her ever since she'd read about them. And once she saw the pictures of Joe in the magazine article, she'd been sure he was one of them.

And was she right? Could this ex-Army Ranger, this California surfer boy, really be one of the lost royals of Ambria? Could he really be a prince? He didn't act like it. But then, if he hadn't been raised to know how a prince was supposed to act, why would he?

Despite all that, the more she saw of him, the more confident she was in her instincts. The DeAngelis family that had ruled Ambria for over five hundred years had the reputation of being the most attractive royals ever. Her opinion? He fit right in.

"Mr. Tanner? This is Gayle Hannon at the customer service desk at the airport. There's been some sort of mix-up. A little girl has arrived designated for your reception, but—"

Joe gripped the receiver tightly. "She's here already? She wasn't supposed to arrive until tonight."

"As I say, there's been a mix-up. She was diverted to a different flight, and it seems the required child caretaker has disappeared. She's…" The woman's voice deepened with new emotion. "Mr. Tanner, she's all alone. Poor little thing. I think you had better come quickly."

"She's hardly more than one year old," he said, stunned. How had she ended up arriving alone on an international flight? "I'll be right there."

All alone. The words echoed in his mind as he searched for his keys and dashed for his car. This wasn't good. He had to get there, fast.

Kelly was out on the sidewalk in front of Joe's house, waiting for him. She'd spent the last few minutes giving herself a pep talk, and she was ready to hang tough this time. As he started his car out, she bent forward and knocked on the half-open passenger side window.

"Joe, listen, I've really got to talk to you. There is something you should know."

He looked at her blankly. "Huh?" he said. "What?"

She hesitated, sensing an opening. "Where are you going?"

"The airport," he said distractedly.

"Can I come with you? I just need to…"

He shook his head, not even listening. "Whatever," he muttered, pulling on his seat belt.

"Oh."

She took that as pure encouragement. Reaching out, she tugged on the door handle. Miraculously, it sprang right open and she jumped in.

"Great."

"Hey." He glared at her, finally seeming to realize who she was and why she was sitting beside him in his car. "Listen, I don't have time for this."

She smiled. "Okay," she said agreeably. "Let's go then."

He hesitated only a moment, then shook his head and swore. "What the hell." He grunted, stepping on the accelerator. "Hang on and keep quiet," he told her firmly. "I'm in a hurry."

She did as he said. He took the city streets too fast and then turned onto the freeway. Once he'd settled into a place in the flow of traffic, she turned and smiled brightly at him.

"So, the airport?" she said. "Are you meeting someone?"

He didn't even glance her way. "Yeah," he said, concentrating on his driving. Then he shook his head and muttered, "She's all alone in the middle of the airport and she's hardly more than one year old."

Kelly waited for a moment, and when he didn't elaborate, she asked, "Who is?"

He glanced at her sideways. "My little girl."

Kelly's jaw dropped. In all her time researching Joe Tanner, she'd never seen a shred of evidence that he had a child.

"Your little girl? What's her name?"

"Mei. Her mother named her. I wasn't there to help with it." He swore softly, shaking his head. "I was never there. Damn it. Some husband, huh?"

This was all news to Kelly. "You're married?" she asked, stunned.

He took in a deep breath and let it out. "I was married. Angie died in a firefight in the Luzon jungle a year ago. And now I'm finally going to meet our baby."

Kelly sat staring out at the landscape as they raced along. The enormity of what she'd thrown herself into finally registered, and it was like hitting a brick wall. She thought she knew so much, and now to find out she knew so little… Had she made a terrible mistake? All those months of researching this man and she didn't have a clue. He'd been married and had a baby? Stunning.

What else didn't she know? If she was so clueless about so much, could she possibly be right about his royal background? It didn't seem very likely at the moment. Heat filled her cheeks and she scrunched down in the seat, wishing she was somewhere else.

Traffic slowed to a crawl. Joe drummed his fingers on the steering wheel, mumbling to himself and looking pained. "What am I going to do with her?"

Kelly sat up straighter. He was obviously talking about his daughter. Why did he sound so lost, so troubled?

"Didn't you have a plan when you sent for her?" she asked.

He raised a hand and gestured in frustration. "There was supposed to be a nursemaid with her. Someone who knows her and can help take care of her."

There was anger in his voice, but also so much more. Kelly heard anxiety she would never have expected from such a strong personality. He'd obviously come up against something he didn't really understand, something he wasn't sure he could deal with. Despite everything, her heart went out to him.

"What happened?" she asked.

He shook his head. "I don't know. They called and said Mei had come in early and she was all alone." He turned and glanced at Kelly, and swore softly, obviously regretting that he'd let her into the car in a distracted moment.

"Why are you here?" he demanded, looking very annoyed. "This has nothing to do with you. And if you think you're going to write about this… Listen, I'm going to drop you off at a pay phone as soon as we get off this freeway."

"No." All thoughts of disappearing from the scene had flown right out of her mind. His dilemma had touched her. She wanted to help. "I swear to God, Joe, I will not write anything about you and your baby. I'm not a journalist. I'm not a writer." She took a deep breath. "And I'm coming with you."

"The hell you are!"

"Joe, don't you see? You need help. You can't handle a baby all by yourself."

"Sure I can. I bought a car seat." He nodded toward the back, and she turned and saw a state-of-the-art monstrosity sitting there, ready to go. Evidently he was ready to buy anything necessary for his child and pay for the best. That should be a good sign, she supposed. Still, he didn't seem to understand what taking care of a young child entailed.

"By handling a baby, I mean more than just putting her body someplace and telling her everything is okay." Kelly bit her lip and then appealed to his common sense. "She's going to be scared. You'll be driving. She'll need more attention than you can give her on the ride home. Face it. You're going to need help."

Kelly took his sullen silence to mean he saw her point, and she breathed in relief. As she studied his profile, her confidence began to creep back. Maybe she hadn't been so wrong about everything, after all. He was so handsome. Handsome and quite royal looking, if she did say so herself.

Joe spotted Mei as soon as he walked into the building. Just seeing her hit him like a thunderbolt.

She was sitting on a chair behind the airline check-in counter, her little legs out straight, her feet in their white socks and black Mary Janes barely reaching the edge. Her dark hair was cut off at ear length, with a thick fringe of bangs that almost covered her almond-shaped eyes. His heart flipped in his chest and suddenly he was out of breath.

Once he'd caught sight of her, he didn't see anything else. The rest of the world faded into a bothersome mist. There were people talking all around him, but he didn't hear a thing. She sat there as though there was a spotlight shining down on her, and he went straight for her.

Joe stopped in front of her, and for a moment he couldn't speak. His heart was full. He hadn't expected this. He was always the tough guy, the one who didn't get caught up in emotions. But from the moment he'd seen this little girl, he knew he was in love. She was so gorgeous, so adorable, he could hardly stand it.

"Mei?" he said at last, his voice rough.

She looked up and stared into his eyes, her little round face expressionless.

"Hi, Mei," he said. "I'm…I'm your daddy."

There was no change, no response. For a second, he wondered if she hadn't heard him.

"I'm taking you home," Joe said. His voice broke on that last word.

Gazing up at him, she shook her head. "No," she said, looking worried.

He stared at her, hardly hearing her or noticing her mood. For so long she'd been a dream in his heart, and now she was here.

And suddenly, the past came flooding in on him. He saw his beautiful Angie again, saw her trembling smile. Saw the love in her eyes as she greeted him, the delight as she told him of the new baby he'd never seen, the fear as their hiding place was discovered by the rebels…the gunfire… Saw the peace and acceptance on her lovely face as she died in his arms. He remembered the agonizing cry ripped from his chest as he'd realized he'd lost her forever, remembered the gut-wrenching fury as he'd taken off through the jungle after her murderers. Felt again the searing pain as their bullets hit his flesh, the aching frustration as he fell to the ground, helpless.

It all came back in a flash, and Joe tried to shake it away just as quickly. He couldn't let this precious child, this gift of love between him and Angie, be hurt by the ugly past.

Still, the past was what it was. He couldn't change it. It had made him into the bitter recluse he was today. But he wasn't going to inflict that on the child. Looking at her now, he knew he was going to do everything he could for her in every way. His heart seemed to swell in his chest. She would be his life from now on. But why did it hurt so much?

"For you, Angie," he murmured softly, his voice choking, his vision blurring with tears.

Kelly looked at Joe in surprise. All she'd seen so far was his tough side, the sarcasm, the arrogance, the disdain. She'd never dreamed such a very small girl could bring a man like this to tears.

Kelly had come in right behind him, but was trying to stay to the side and out of the way. She didn't want to intrude, didn't want to push in where she didn't belong, but he was just standing there, paralyzed with emotion. If she didn't do something, he was going to scare the poor kid to death. There was really no choice. She stepped forward.

"Hi, sweetie," she said with a cheery smile, bending down. "My name's Kelly. I'm your daddy's friend. I'm going to help take you home. Okay?"

The huge dark eyes stared at her solemnly. For a moment, Kelly thought there would be no response. The child's gaze seemed flat, emotionless. Her little features didn't move at all.

Kelly glanced at Joe for guidance, but the look on his face told her he wouldn't even hear her right now.

"Mei?" Kelly said, smiling hopefully. "You want to come with me?"

As though a veil was lifted, Mei's eyes lit with interest and her little head nodded.

Flooded with relief, Kelly put out her arms and Mei went to her willingly, then clung to her. And that was that. Mei seemed to think she belonged with Kelly. No room for other options.

They waited for a required interview with a supervisor, then Joe began to make his way through the paperwork, while Kelly tried to keep the baby entertained as best she could. The bustle of people all around them helped. Whenever Mei felt anxious, Kelly was there to soothe away her fears. At the same time she kept one ear open to the questions Joe was answering, hoping to glean something that would help with her identification. She didn't get much there, but she did hear the name Angie repeated often enough to realize that had to be Mei's mother, and Joe's wife. One look at his face was all she needed to understand the tragedy involved in his losing her.

Kelly noticed that Joe was very carefully avoiding

glancing at Mei. She thought she knew why. He was protecting himself, just getting through the bureaucratic formalities with all due speed. This child had power over him, and he had to wait until they were out of here before he could begin learning how to deal with it.

They were almost done when Joe visibly steeled himself and turned to smile at his daughter.

"Okay, Mei," he said, holding out his arms. "Why don't you let me carry you for awhile?"

The baby shrank away, and as his hands touched her, she let out a shriek that could probably be heard all the way back to Manila. Joe jerked back, his face like stone. He glanced at Kelly, who was at a loss as to how to fix this situation, and then he turned and walked back to the airline counter, where he had a bit more business to complete.

Kelly held Mei closely, knowing this was not good, and feeling a surge of compassion for Joe that almost brought her to tears. But what could she do?

Once all the paperwork was done and they were heading for the parking lot, little Mei's arms went around Kelly's neck and she snuggled in tightly. But whenever Joe turned to look at her, she stiffened, and Kelly began to realize there might be more problems ahead than he had ever anticipated.

CHAPTER FOUR

JOE WAS SILENT on the drive home from the airport.
He was the sort of man who liked to be in command of
every situation, understanding what was needed, hitting all the bases. The problem was, right now he didn't
have a clue. He felt like a swimmer who couldn't touch
bottom and had lost sight of the beach. What was he
supposed to do now?

The idea of a baby daughter had seemed vaguely
pleasant. A little girl to call his own. A miniature version of Angie, maybe—sweet, pretty, a blessing in his
life. She was his child and his responsibility.

He'd pictured a friendly meeting at the airport. The
nanny would be in charge. After all, he'd been told the
woman had been taking care of Mei ever since she was
born. He would drive them home, and that would be
that. A child in his life—but a child with a caretaker,
someone who knew what she was doing.

That was the plan. Reality had caught him unprepared and hit him like a blow to the gut.

No nanny. No caretaker. No safety net.

That wasn't going to work. He didn't know the first

thing about taking care of a kid this age. Or any age, really.

But even worse had been his own emotional reaction to seeing little Mei in the flesh for the first time. He hadn't expected to have the pain flood in that way. His stomach turned again just thinking about it. If he'd known that was going to happen…

Traffic was light, but his headlights bounced against the fog and he had to pay close attention, peering into the darkness as though he might find some answers there. Kelly was sitting next to Mei in the back, talking to her softly, helping her play with a toy attached to the car seat.

He listened for a moment, craning to hear, as though she were speaking in a foreign language he didn't understand. And he didn't. What was he doing here? What was he going to do with this child?

"Did you find out what happened to the nanny?" Kelly asked him as he turned off the freeway and stopped at a red light.

He hesitated, reluctant to tell her anything. She shouldn't even be here. Still, if she wasn't, he would be in even bigger trouble. He supposed he owed her a bit of civility, if nothing else.

"They said she was seen with Mei right up until they went through customs here at the airport, and then she disappeared." He shook his head in disbelief. "They found her sitting there in one of those plastic chairs. She had a tag around her neck with her papers and my name and all that. They gave me the address the nanny used as a contact point, but something tells me that's going to be useless."

He glanced in the rearview mirror. He couldn't see Mei, but that was okay. Right now he didn't want to.

"They said it happens all the time. She'll probably blend right into the immigrant community and it will be hard to ever find her."

Kelly nodded. "That's what I was afraid of."

He frowned and didn't speak again as he turned onto his street and pulled into the driveway.

"You're lucky," Kelly said softly. "She's asleep. I'll bet you can carry her in without waking her."

"Good."

"Do you have a bed for her?"

He turned off the engine and looked back. "Of course I have a bed for her. I've got a whole room ready."

"Oh. Good."

He got out and held the rear door open. He was still avoiding taking a look at Mei. Instead, he studied Kelly, noting that she'd pulled her curly blonde hair back and tied it with a band, though strands were escaping and making a halo effect around her face. She had a sweet, pretty face. She looked nice. His baby needed somebody nice. What if he asked her to stay and…

Grimacing, he turned and looked into the fog that surrounded his house. What was he thinking? He didn't need a woman like this hanging around, distracting him from the work he had to do creating a family for this baby. He should tell Kelly to take a hike. She had no business being here with them. He didn't know her. And she was all wrong for this job. The last thing he wanted for a nanny was a woman this appealing to the senses. She had to go.

Still, the thought of being alone with Mei struck a certain level of terror in his heart. He needed help. Who was he going to get to come at this time of night?

"What are you going to do?" Kelly asked softly, standing in front of him.

He shrugged. "Try to hire a nanny, I guess," he said gruffly.

"You won't be able to do that until morning."

He nodded.

"I'll stay," she said. It was less an offer than a firm statement of intent.

"You?" He looked at her with a scowl. Suspicions flooded back. He may have just been considering asking her to stay, but why was she offering? "Why would you do that? You're not going to get a story out of me."

She threw up her hands in exasperation. "I told you, I'm not looking for a story. I'm not a writer."

She'd said that again and again. But if she wasn't trying to get a story, what was her angle? Everybody had one.

"Then what *do* you want, Kelly?" he asked.

She gazed up into his troubled eyes. She wasn't sure why this was all so upsetting to him, but she could see that it was. He was fairly bristling with tension. Was it just that he didn't know how to take care of a baby and was nervous about it?

No, she was pretty sure it was something more. Something deeper and more painful. Everything in her yearned to help him, human to human. This had nothing to do with her quest for his real identity.

"What I want is to help you. To help the baby."

She saw the doubt in his face, and reached out and touched his arm. "Seriously, Joe. Right now that's all I care about."

He searched her eyes. "I'm telling you straight out, I don't trust you," he said gruffly. "But at the moment, I feel I don't really have a choice. With the nanny gone…" He shrugged, not needing to complete the sentence. His blue eyes were clouded. "You've seen the way Mei reacts to me."

Kelly bit her lip and nodded. She'd been wondering if he'd really noticed, wondering if that was what was hurting him. An unexpected feeling of tenderness toward him flooded her. There was no way she was going to leave him alone with his baby until…well, she didn't know. But not yet.

He looked at her and saw the softening in her face. Suddenly he was breathless. That halo effect her hair had was working again. She looked like an angel.

He didn't want to need her. He wanted to pick up his little girl and carry her into the house and live happily ever after, without Kelly Vrosis being involved in any way. But that wasn't going to happen.

He didn't want to need this woman, but he did.

"Do you have any real experience?" he asked, as though interviewing her for the job. "Any children?"

She shook her head. "I'm not married," she told him. "But I do have two brothers, and they both have kids. I've spent plenty of time caring for my nieces and nephews. I'll be okay."

He stared at her a moment longer, then shrugged.

"You want to bring in her stuff?" he asked shortly, nodding toward the baggage that had come across the Pacific with Mei as he leaned in to unbuckle the baby seat from the car.

"Sure," Kelly said, working hard on looking non-threatening, efficient and cheerful as she gathered the things together. "Lead the way."

He took her through a nice, ordinary living room, down a hallway and into an enchanting little girl's paradise. Kelly gazed around in wonder. The carpet was like walking on marshmallows and it was shiny clean. A beautiful wooden crib stood against one wall, an elaborate changing table beside it. A large, overstuffed recliner sat in one corner. The closet doors opened to reveal exquisitely organized baby clothes on shelves and hangers, along with row upon row of adorable toys.

"Joe, this is perfect. I can't believe you did this on your own."

"I didn't. I hired a consultant to help me."

She almost laughed at the thought. "A consultant?"

"From Dory's Baby Boutique in the village. The woman who runs it knows someone who does these things, and she set me up with a meeting." He put the car seat down and picked up a business card left on top of the changing table. "Sonja Smith, Baby Decorator," he read.

Kelly looked around the room in admiration, her gaze

caught by the framed pictures of cartoon elephants in tutus and walruses in tights. "She does a great job."

Standing in the middle of the room, looming over a sleeping Mei in her car seat, he raised one dark eyebrow and looked at Kelly speculatively. "Maybe you know her?"

She glanced at him in surprise. "No. Why would I know her?"

He shrugged again. "She was sort of pushing me about this whole Ambrian thing, too."

Kelly's eyes widened and her heart lurched in her chest. "What?"

"So you thought you were my first?" he said, showing amusement at her reaction.

Kelly's imagination began to churn out crisis scenarios like ravioli out of a pasta machine, but she held back. She knew better than to pursue it now. The focus had to be on Mei.

Joe moved the car seat closer to the bed, obviously wondering how he was going to make the transfer to the crib without waking his little girl. Kelly started to give him some suggestions, but he did a great job on his own, laying her gently on the mattress. Kelly pulled a soft blanket over her and they both stood looking down at her.

"She's adorable," Kelly said softly.

He closed his eyes and leaned on the rail, his knuckles white. His reaction worried her.

"Joe, what is it?"

He turned toward her, his eyes dark and haunted. He stared at her for a moment, then shook his head.

"Nothing," he said gruffly. "But listen, I really appreciate that you offered to stay. I'm going to need the help."

"Of course you are."

And then she realized he didn't only mean with the care and feeding of a small girl. There was something else tearing him apart. For a man like this, one usually so strong and so confident, to admit he needed help was a big step. She wasn't even thinking about the whole prince thing any longer. She was thinking about the man standing here, looking so lost, racked with some kind of pain that she couldn't begin to analyze.

"I'll sleep right here in the room," Kelly said quickly.

He looked around. "There's no bed."

"The chair reclines. With a pillow and a blanket, I'll be fine."

He frowned. "You won't be comfortable there."

"Sure I will. And I want to be right here in case she wakes up. She'll be scared. She'll need someone at least a little bit familiar."

He moved restlessly, then looked at Kelly sideways. "Okay. I don't have any women's clothes hanging around, but I can give you a T-shirt to sleep in."

She smiled at him. Despite everything, he looked very appealing with his hair tousled and falling over his forehead, and his eyes heavy and sleepy and his mouth so wide and inviting.

Whoa. She pulled herself up short. Where the heck did she think she was going with that thought?

"Uh…a T-shirt would be perfect," she said quickly, her cheeks heating as she turned away.

"Okay."

He didn't seem to notice her embarrassment. Without another word, he left the room.

She let her breath out slowly, fanning her cheeks. She had to remember who he was. Or at least, who she thought he was. She wasn't getting very far on that project—but there would be time. Hopefully.

Joe returned with pillows, a comforter and a bright blue T-shirt that looked big enough to be a small dress on Kelly. She began to set up the chair for sleeping.

He frowned, watching her. "I should be the one to do that. I should sleep in here tonight."

"No," she said firmly. "If she wakes up, you might scare her."

For just a moment, he looked stricken, and Kelly regretted her quick words.

"This is ridiculous," he said, his voice gravelly with emotion. "She's my baby. I've got to find a way…"

"Joe." Kelly felt the ache in him and could hardly stand it. Reaching out, she took his hand, as though to convey by touch what her words couldn't really express. "Joe, it's not time yet. Don't you see? She's probably been raised by only women so far, and to her, you're big and male and scary. She's not sure what to do with you yet. You've barely met at this point. You've got to give her a little time."

"Time," he echoed softly, staring down at Kelly, his gaze hooded. He didn't seem receptive, but he wasn't pulling away from her grip on his hand.

"Yes. She's clueless right now. The one person she depended on, the nanny, deserted her. Mei doesn't know what you might do. Let her get to know you gradually."

"You're probably right." He said it reluctantly, but turned the tables so that he was holding *her* hand, and slowly raised it to his lips, kissing her fingers softly.

Kelly held her breath. She hadn't expected anything like that. But he didn't look into her eyes as he did it, and he didn't say anything more, so when he dropped her hand again, she felt almost as though he'd done it anonymously. Or maybe it was a sort of thank-you for her assistance.

Maybe she'd imagined the whole thing. Or maybe he was just distracted. He was definitely confusing her.

"Uh...thanks, Kelly," Joe said as he turned to go. "Thanks for staying."

She sent a radiant smile his way. "No problem. See you in the morning."

He stared back at her for a long moment, then nodded and left the room.

She shivered. What was it about haunted handsome men that was so compelling?

Sighing, she turned back to the crib. Looking down at the sleeping child, she wanted to brush the hair off her forehead, but was afraid that would waken her. What a beautiful little girl!

"Well," Kelly murmured to herself, "what have you gotten yourself involved in now?"

And then she remembered what he'd said about the designer and Ambria. Alarm bells were still ringing in her head over that one. She wanted to know more. She *had* to know more. But right now he wasn't going to be interested in anything that had to do with the obscure island nation, not until things were a bit more settled in his life.

Kelly only hoped they had the time to wait.

Sleeping in a recliner quickly lost its charm, but she got in a few dozing sessions before Mei stirred. When she heard her, she got up quickly and went to the crib, talking to the baby softly and patting her back until she fell asleep again.

By then Kelly was wide awake and thinking about what she might need the next time Mei woke up. Moving quietly, she opened the door and went silently through the darkened house to the kitchen, to see what Joe had done with the baby bottles and other supplies they had brought from the airport.

The layout of the house was simple, but she'd never been there before, so she was feeling her way when a movement caught her eye, stopping her cold. Someone was on the deck. She could see a dark form through the French doors. Her heart jumped into her throat and she shrank back against the wall, where she wouldn't be seen.

But even as she did so, she realized it had to be Joe. Kelly breathed a sigh of relief and went to the doors. Yes, there he was, leaning on the railing and gazing out toward the ocean—and looking like a man going through hell. Compassion flooded her and she sighed, wishing she knew what she could do to help him.

* * *

Joe tried to pull himself together. "Hell" had been watching the woman he loved die. This wasn't fun, but it was a piece of cake compared to that.

Not to say that it was easy. Seeing Mei reminded him of losing Angie, and that had opened up the past in a bad way. He had earned his agony, but he didn't have a right to take it out on anyone else. He'd gone through a lot a year ago. He'd hated life for awhile, hated his fate, his luck and everything else he could think of. But that was over.

He thought he'd mostly taken care of this already, during all the hours of therapy in the veterans hospital, the long nights of soul searching. He'd finally come to terms with what had happened, and said goodbye to Angie. Hadn't he?

But that was before he'd seen Mei.

That same old deadly agony was lurking. If he let it all flood back over him, he was going to drown. He couldn't go through that again. His eyes were stinging, and suddenly he realized why. Tears. What the hell? He never cried. This was ridiculous. Now, twice in one night… Leaning against the railing, he swore at himself, softly and obscenely. No more tears.

His head jerked up as he heard the door to the deck open. There Kelly stood, lighting up the gloom with her wild golden hair. How could this be hell if he had his own personal angel?

"Hi," she said. "You can't sleep, either?"

He turned slowly to face her, and she peered at him. It was too dark for her to see if his expression was welcoming, or if he wished she'd just go away. That wouldn't be so unusual. He usually seemed to want her gone.

But she wasn't going to go. She had a feeling he was out here brooding, and she didn't think that was a good thing.

"Are you okay?" she asked as she approached.

He didn't answer. He was dressed in jeans and a huge, baggy dark blue sweatshirt with a hood pulled up over his head, while she stood before him in nothing but his bright blue T-shirt. A cool breeze brought in a touch of chill, reminding her of her skimpy nightgown, and she hugged herself, giving thanks that the slip of a moon wasn't giving much light.

Looking up at him for a moment, she still couldn't read his eyes. In fact, she could barely make out the features of his face, hiding there in the shadows of his hoodie. Her heart was beginning to thump again. Why didn't he say anything? Was he angry? Did he think she was meddling? She couldn't tell and she was getting nervous.

She stepped past him and leaned on the rail next to him, looking out at what moonlight there was shimmering on the distant ocean. She could hear the waves, but couldn't see them. Too many houses blocked the view.

"I can tell you're upset," she said tentatively. "Do you want to talk about it?"

"Talk about it!" He coughed and cleared his throat. "You like guys who spill their guts, do you?"

Kelly was glad he'd finally spoken. Still, she could tell that something was bothering him. She could see it, feel it. And if talking it out could soften that sense of turmoil in him, it would be best to do it.

And not just for his sake. If he wasn't careful, his vibes were going to scare the baby. He needed to grapple with it, get rid of it, before he attempted to deal with the new little girl in his life. Kelly sighed, hardly believing what she was thinking. What made her so sure of these things, anyway? She didn't usually walk around claiming to have all the answers, and she knew very well she was groping in the dark as much as anyone.

But there was a child at stake here. For the sake of the baby, she had to do what she could.

"I know you don't really know me," she told him earnestly, "but that might make it easier. In a few days, I'll be gone and you'll never see me again." She gave him an apologetic smile. "Honest. I don't plan to stay in California any longer than that. So if you want to…I don't know…vent or something, feel free."

He looked at her and didn't know whether to laugh or hang his head. So this was what he'd come to—women volunteering to let him cry on their shoulders. How pathetic was that?

Well, he wasn't ready to open his heart to her, probably never would be. But he wouldn't mind another perspective on what he was torturing himself with at the moment. For some unknown reason, he felt as though he could talk to Kelly in ways he seldom did with other women.

Maybe, he thought cynically, it was the same quality in her that made Mei think she was a safe harbor in a scary world. Whatever it was, he supposed it wouldn't hurt to try.

"Okay, Kelly, you asked for it." He turned toward her. "Here's what I'm thinking." He hesitated, taking a deep breath before going on. "I'm thinking this whole thing was a very bad idea."

Just hearing that said out loud made him cringe inside.

She frowned at him, confused. "What was a bad idea?"

"To bring Mei here."

She gasped. "What are you talking about? She's your baby."

"Yeah." He turned and leaned on the railing. "But it was selfish. I was thinking about having an adorable little girl of my own, like she was a doll or something." He looked at her, despising himself a little. "A pet. A kitten."

"Oh, Joe."

"I know better, of course. She's a real human being." He shook his head. Thinking of Mei and her cute little face, he couldn't help but smile. "A beautiful, perfect little human being. And she…she deserves the best of everything."

Turning from Kelly, he began to pace the wooden deck, his hands shoved deep into his pockets. "I didn't think…I didn't realize… I can't really give her what she deserves. Maybe I should have left her with Angie's family. Maybe she would have been better off."

Kelly stepped forward and blocked his way, grabbing

handfuls of sweatshirt fabric at chest level to stop him in his tracks.

"No," she told him forcefully, her eyes blazing.

He stopped and looked down at her in surprise. "No?"

"No. You're wrong."

He bit back the grin that threatened to take over his face. She looked so fierce. And then it came to him—she really did care about this.

"What makes you so sure about that?" he asked her.

"Common sense." She tried to shake him with the grip she had on his sweatshirt. She didn't manage to move his body, but got her point across. "She's your responsibility."

He winced, his gaze traveling over the planes of Kelly's pretty face. She had good cheekbones and beautiful eyelashes. But her mouth was where his attention settled. Nice lips. White teeth. And a sexy pout that could start to get to him if he let it.

"You're right," he told her at last. "You're absolutely right." Then he added softly, "How'd you get to be so right about things?"

She released his shirt, pretty sure she'd convinced him, then lifted her chin and gazed into his eyes. He was so handsome and so troubled, and she wanted so badly to help him, but she couldn't resist teasing him a little.

"I'm an objective observer. You should take my advice on everything."

"Fat chance." He chucked her under the chin and

made a face. "You're the one who wants me to start chasing royal moonbeams, aren't you?"

She caught her breath, wanting to argue, wanting to tell him he was going to be surprised once she'd really explained things. But she stopped herself. It still wasn't time.

She needed more information before she jumped in with both feet. She wouldn't want to raise false hopes. She shivered, as much with that thought as with the cold.

"I'm no prince. Look at me." His voice took on a bitter edge. "My baby's even scared of me."

"That won't last. Give her time."

He nodded, a distant look in his eyes. "My head says you're right, but my heart…" He shrugged. "Like Shakespeare wrote, 'there's the rub.'"

She smiled. A man who quoted Shakespeare. "Where did you get so literary?" she asked him. "I didn't think you went to university."

"I didn't. I signed up for the army as soon as I graduated from high school. But I read a lot."

"In the army?" That didn't fit her preconception.

"Sure. Once you get deployed overseas you have a lot of downtime."

"I thought army guys usually filled that with wine, women and song."

He nodded. "Okay, you got me there. I did my share of blowing off steam. But that gets old pretty fast, and our base had a great library. Plus, the master sergeant was a real scholar, and he introduced me to what I should be reading."

Joe frowned when he saw her shivering. "You're cold."

She nodded. "I should go in."

"Here, this will take care of it."

In one swoop, he loosened the neck of his sweatshirt, then lifted the hem, capturing her under it. Before she knew what was happening, he'd pulled her in to join him.

"What are you doing?" she cried, shocked.

"Shhh." His arms came around her, holding her close, and he whispered next to her ear,"You're going to wake up the neighbors."

The thought of anyone seeing them this way sent her into giggles. "Joe, this is crazy."

Was he just close so that he could whisper to her, or was he snuggling in behind her ear?

"Warm enough?" he asked.

"Oh, yes. Definitely warm."

Though she had to admit *hot* might be a better word. The darkness and the fact that her face was half hidden in the neck of the shirt saved her from having him see how red her cheeks had turned. His skin was bare under the sweatshirt, and now she was pressed against his fantastic, muscular chest. If it hadn't been for her thick T-shirt…

It doesn't mean a thing, she warned herself, and knew that was right. But how could she resist the warmth and the wonderful smoothness of his rounded muscles against her face? She closed her eyes, just for a moment. His arms held her loosely, and since they were outside, wrapped in fabric, it was okay. She knew he was purposely trying to keep this nonthreatening, and she appreciated it. But no matter how casual he tried to make this, she was trapped in an enclosed space against his bare upper body. Her heart was beating like a drum and her head was feeling light. If she'd been a Victorian miss, she would be crying out for the smelling salts about now.

But she wasn't Victorian. She was up-to-date and full of contemporary attitudes. Wasn't she? She'd had sex and provocative bodies and scandalous talk thrown at her by the media all her life. She could handle this. Never mind that her knees seemed to be buckling and her pulse was racing so fast she couldn't catch her breath. This was worth it. This was heavenly. It was a moment she would never forget.

And then she remembered that he was supposed to be a prince of Ambria. She had no right to trifle with him this way. That thought made her laugh again.

"Joe, let me go," she said, pushing away. "I've got to go in and check on Mei."

"And leave me out here all alone in this sweat-shirt?"

"I think you'll be able to manage it." She wriggled free, then shook her head in mock despair as she looked at him. "I feel like I was highjacked by the moon-light bandit," she grumbled, straightening her T-shirt nightdress.

His grin was crooked. "Think of me as the prince of dreams," he said, and then his mouth twisted. "Bad dreams," he added cynically.

"Stop agonizing out here in the dark and go get some sleep," she advised as she turned to leave. "Mei is going to need you in the morning."

CHAPTER FIVE

KELLY SLEPT LATER than she'd planned, and when she opened her eyes, sunlight was streaming into the room. She turned her head and found a pair of gorgeous dark eyes considering her from the crib. Mei was standing at the railing, surveying the situation.

"Good morning, beautiful," Kelly said, stretching. "Did you have a good sleep?"

The cute little face didn't change, but the baby reached down to pick up a stuffed monkey that had been in her bed, and threw it over the nail as though it were a gift. Kelly laughed, but wondered how long she'd been awake, just standing there, looking around the unfamiliar room, wondering where she was and who was going to take care of her. Poor little thing.

Rising quickly, Kelly went to her. "I'll bet you need a change, don't you?"

She didn't wait for an answer, and Mei didn't resist, going willingly into her arms. Kelly held her for a moment, feeling the life that beat in her, feeling her sweetness. There was no way Joe was sending her back. No way at all.

* * *

Joe was waiting for them when they came into the kitchen. He had coffee brewed and cinnamon buns warmed and sitting on the table. He'd set two places and poured out two little glasses of orange juice. Kelly was carrying Mei and she smiled at how inviting everything looked. Including Joe, who'd made the effort to dress in fresh slacks and a baby-blue polo shirt just snug enough to show off his muscular chest and bulging biceps.

He caught her assessing look and smiled. She quickly glanced away, but in doing so, her gaze fell on where he'd tossed the big blue sweatshirt over the back of a chair. Memories of how it had felt inside that shirt the night before crashed in on her like a wave, and suddenly her cheeks were hot again. She glanced at him. His smile had turned into a full grin.

He was just too darn aware of things.

"Here's your baby," she said, presenting his child for inspection. "Isn't she beautiful in her little corduroy dress?"

"She is indeed," he said brightly, looking warmly at his child. "Good morning, Mei. Can you give me a smile today?"

Evidently not. His daughter shrank back, hiding her face in Kelly's hair and wrapping her chubby arms tightly around her neck.

Kelly sent Joe an anxious glance, wishing she knew what to do to make this better. His smile hadn't faded, though his eyes showed some strain. She approved of the effort he was making. He met her gaze and nodded cheerfully.

"New attitude," he told her.

"Oh. Good." She managed to smile back. "I guess."

"I'm going to take your advice and learn to roll with the punches."

"Did I advise that?" she murmured, gratified that he was at least thinking about what she'd said.

He moved into position so that Mei couldn't avoid looking at him.

"Tell me," he asked her, "what does a little girl your age like to eat?"

Mei scrunched up her face as though she'd just tasted spinach for the first time.

Kelly sighed, but decided to try ignoring the baby's reactions for awhile and hope they faded on their own. Chastising her would do no good. She was a little young for a heart-to-heart talk, so that pretty much left patience. Kelly just hoped she didn't run out of it.

"I know when my niece was this age, she was all about finger food. She loved cut up bananas and avocados, and for awhile she seemed to live on cheese cut up into little squares."

He nodded. "I'll have to make a store run. I'd pretty much counted on the nanny to be the expert in this sort of thing."

"We can wing it for now," Kelly assured him. "And for the moment, I'll bet she would like one of those yogurts I saw in the refrigerator."

"You think so?" He pulled one out and held it up. "How about it, Mei? Ready for some yummy yogurt?"

Her gaze was tracking the yogurt cup as though she

hadn't eaten in days, but when he moved close with it, she hid her face again.

"I guess you'll have to give it to her," he said drily. "She's pretty sure I'm the serpent with the apple at this point."

Mei went into the high chair willingly enough after Kelly let her toddle around on her little chubby legs for a few minutes, but she kept her eye on Joe, reacting when he came too close.

"Don't worry," Kelly told him, smiling as they sat down at the table and she began to feed Mei from her yogurt cup with a plastic spoon shaped like a dolphin. "She'll come around."

He smiled back, but it wasn't easy. They talked inconsequentially for a few moments. Mei ate her yogurt lustily, then played with some cheese Kelly cut up for her. Joe offered Mei a bite of cinnamon roll, but she shook her head and looked at him suspiciously.

"You've gotten over those doubts you had last night, haven't you?" Kelly asked at one point, needing reassurance.

"Sure," he said, dismissing it with a shrug. "Funny how the middle of the night makes everything look so impossible." He gave her a sideways smile. "And yet makes doing things like snuggling in a sweatshirt suddenly seem utterly rational."

"You dreamer," she murmured, holding back her smile and giving Mei her last bite of yogurt. Then Kelly looked at him sharply. "But you aren't still thinking of…" She couldn't finish that sentence without saying things she didn't want to say in front of the child.

He shrugged again. "I know what I have to do. I think I understand my responsibilities."

She frowned. She would have been happier if he'd sounded more enthusiastic, but she had to admit she understood. In the face of so much rejection, it was pretty hard to get very excited. She wanted to tell him not to worry, that surely things would get better soon. There was no way he could stand a lifetime like this—no one could. But he wouldn't have to.

And you know this…how? her inner voice mocked her.

Kelly wasn't sure about that, but knew it had to be true.

"Are you going to be calling an agency to find a new nanny?" It was sad to think of someone else coming in and taking over, but it had to be done. She couldn't stay forever.

"I already have."

"Already? You're fast."

"Well, I called and left a message on a machine. They weren't open yet. But I have no doubt we'll get someone out here by this afternoon at the latest."

"Well, there's no hurry," Kelly told him. "I'll stay until you get someone else."

His eyes darkened and he gazed at her for a moment as though trying to figure out what made her tick.

"Don't you have someplace you need to be?" he asked at last.

"Not at all. My week is wide open."

He looked as though he didn't get her at all. "So you really did come here to California just to find me?"

She nodded.

He shook his head as though she must be crazy. She braced herself for questions, but he didn't seem to want to deal with it yet. Rising from his place, he took his plate to the sink.

Watching him in profile, she was struck once again by how much he looked like a member of the royal family of Ambria. She was going to have to bring that up again soon. But in the meantime, there was another issue to deal with.

"Joe, tell me something," she said as he put the orange juice in the refrigerator. "This designer person who brought up Ambria…"

He turned to face her, then sank back into his chair at the table. "Sonja Smith? What about her?"

Kelly wasn't sure how to go about this delicately, so she just jumped in. "What exactly did she say to you?"

He thought for a second. "She didn't say anything much. She said that Dory at the Baby Boutique had told her she thought I might be from Ambria. That's all."

"Why did the Baby Boutique person think you were Ambrian?"

He shook his head. "I don't know. I went in a week ago and talked to her about needing some advice on stocking a baby's room, and she told me about Sonja and had her call me." He grimaced. "I don't know where she got the idea for the Ambrian connection. I never said anything to Dory about that. I'm sure Ambria never came up. In fact, the existence of Ambria hadn't entered my mind in…oh, I'd say a year or two. As far as countries go, it's not high on my list." He shrugged. "The point is, Ambria isn't a favorite of mine. And I have no idea why anyone would think I was interested."

"Hmm." Kelly gazed at him thoughtfully.

"Sonja came over, did a great job, and that was it. End of story."

"That's all?"

He made a face. "Well, not really. She wasn't just a designer decorator. Turns out she also tries to rustle up customers for tours she arranges. She works at a travel agency and was putting together a tour to Europe, including Ambria, in the summer. She said if I was interested I should give her a call. She thought I'd enjoy it."

Kelly didn't know what to think about that. It seemed a bit strange. Of course, there could be any number of reasons someone of Ambrian heritage might find his face appealing—and familiar, just as she had. It might be completely innocent, just a businesswoman trying to drum up sales for her tour.

On the other hand, it might be someone allied with the usurper Ambrian regime, the Granvillis. And from everything she'd learned lately, if the Granvillis were after you, you were in big trouble. Joe was taking all this lightly, but she was afraid he didn't know the background the way she did. If he had, he might have been more on guard.

That meant she'd better tell him soon. It was only fair to warn him. The fact that she knew he would scoff at her warnings didn't encourage her, but she knew it had to be done. And that somehow she was going to have to convince him.

"Well? Are you interested in the tour?"

He gave her an amused look, then rose to take the rest of the plates to the sink. "No. I've never had a yen to travel to a place like that. In fact, I've done enough foreign travel for awhile. I think I'll stay put."

She nodded. "Are you going to see her again?"

"Maybe. She might come by to meet Mei. I suggested it. I thought she might like to see what the child she did all this for looked like in the midst of it." He frowned, turning to face Kelly. "Listen, what's with the third degree? Does this somehow impinge upon your royal dreams?"

She shook her head. He was teasing her, but she wasn't in a teasing mood. Until she found out what this designer person was up to, she was going to be very uneasy. "Not a bit," she claimed cheerfully. Glancing up, she saw that he was looking at Mei, his face set and unhappy. It broke her heart, and she immediately had the urge to do something about it.

Rising and moving to stand close to him at the sink, she leaned in so she could speak softly and not be overheard by Mei. She'd been thinking about different schemes for getting the child to accept Joe. She could hardly stand to see the obvious pain in his face when his little girl rejected him.

"Here's a thought," Kelly said, very near his ear. "Why don't you just go over and sit by Mei and talk Don't even talk to her at first, just near her. You could talk about your past with her mother. Maybe tell her how you met. Or anything else you can think of. Her name was Angie, right?"

He turned on her as though she'd suggested he sing an aria from La Bohème. "What? Why would I do any of that?"

Kelly blinked up at him, surprised at his vehemence. "Okay, if you don't want to do it directly, why don't you tell *me* about Angie in front of Mei. About where you met her, what your wedding was like, things like that."

His complete rejection of her idea was written all over his face. In fact, he was very close to anger.

"Why would I be telling you about Angie? Who *are* you?"

Kelly stared at him, her first impulse being to take offense at what he'd said. But she stopped herself. This was an agonizing situation. That was why she was trying to fix things. Didn't he see that? But maybe not. Maybe she was intruding and she ought to back off. Still…

She sighed, wishing she knew how to defuse the emotion he was feeling.

"I'm your friend, Joe. I care." Shaking her head, she looked into his eyes. "And I'd like to hear about it." She put a hand on his forearm, trying to calm him. "Just talk about it. I don't have to be there at all. Let her hear you."

The look on his face was stubborn and not at all friendly. "She's too young to understand what the heck I'd be talking about."

"That doesn't matter. And you never know how much children absorb."

He backed away, not accepting her touch. "No, Kelly. It's just not a good idea."

She searched his eyes. Anger was simmering in him just below the surface. She really wasn't sure why this should make him angry. He'd loved Angie. Angie was Mei's mother. What could be more natural than to tell her what her mother was like?

"It's your call, of course, but it just seems to me that talking about her mother, talking with open affection, would help draw her in, help make her feel like this is part of a continuum and not such a strange place, after all."

He shook his head, eyes stormy. "I think you're nuts."

"But Joe…"

"I'm not going to…to talk about…Angie," he said, his voice rough. "I can't."

Kelly's heart twisted and she licked her dry lips. He couldn't? She felt a surge of compassion, but still, that didn't seem right. He was the sort of man who could do anything. Was there more here than she knew? Obviously.

But there was also more at stake. Mei came first.

Still, Kelly couldn't ignore his outrage. What was she doing here? The last thing she wanted to do was torture him more. And yet she couldn't help feeling that he was going at this all wrong. Avoiding pain was often the best way to bring it on at the worst possible time. Her instinct was to try to nudge him out of the self-indulgence of his grief.

Wow, had she really thought that? Pretty tough stuff.

And yet she stood by it. After all, his comfort wasn't what was important anymore. He had a child to think of. He had to do what was best for Mei.

"Okay." Kelly turned back toward the high chair. "As I said, it's your call. If you can't get beyond the pain, there's no point, I guess."

He didn't answer and he didn't meet her gaze. She spent the next few minutes cleaning up Mei's tray and taking her out of the chair, talking softly to her all the time. He stood with his back against the counter, arms folded, looking out through the French doors toward the sliver of ocean visible in the distance. As she walked out, holding Mei's hand while she toddled alongside her, he didn't say a word.

He knew he'd hurt Kelly by his abrupt response, but it couldn't be helped. He felt angry, though not at her. He was pretty damn bitter at life in general. Self-pity wasn't his usual mode, but sometimes the enormity of it all came down on him and he couldn't shake it until it had worked its way through his system. This was one of those times.

Of course, Kelly had no way of knowing that every time he looked at Mei, he saw Angie. And right now, every time he saw Angie in his mind, he saw her dying right in front of him. He knew he had to get over it. He had to wipe the pain and shock and ugliness from his soul so that he could deal with this bright, new, wonderful child.

Kelly thought Mei's obvious rejection of him hurt. And of course, it wasn't fun to be rebuffed by a sweet little child like that. But he didn't blame Mei at all. She sensed his ambivalence, the way he felt torn and twisted inside, the way he almost winced every time he looked at her, and she reacted to it, as any sensitive, intelligent child would. It was going to take time for both of them.

Meanwhile he had Kelly's strange little project of convincing him that he was a prince of a funny little country he couldn't care less about to deal with. The whole thing could have been genuinely annoying if she weren't such a sweetheart. He had to admit, she wasn't exactly hard to look at, either. In fact, he was learning to like her quite a lot.

Moving restlessly, he gave himself a quick lecture on his attitude, ending with a resolution to be nicer to Kelly. Funny thing was, he knew right away it wouldn't be hard at all.

Kelly played with the little girl in her room for the next hour, helping her try out all the toys, and reading to her from a couple of the soft, padded books. Every few minutes, Mei would get up and run around the room, whooping to her own little tune, as though she had untapped energy that needed using up. She was bright, quick and interested in everything. So far she wasn't saying much, but Kelly had a feeling once the floodgates opened, words would come pouring out, even if they weren't understandable to anyone but the child herself.

Kelly spent some time reorganizing the shelves and finding interesting things packed away there, including some pictures and souvenirs that told a story better than Joe had been doing so far.

When Mei fell asleep over her book, Kelly wasn't surprised. She was still very tired from her long trip the day before. Kelly tucked her into bed, picked up a couple of items and went back out.

Joe was taking care of some bills on the Internet, and she waited until he logged off.

"What's up?" he asked, and she was pleased to see his eyes had lost the sheen of vague hostility they'd had when she'd seen him last.

"Mei fell asleep, but she won't be out long. I thought this would be a good time to plan a walk down to the beach."

"Do you think she's ready for that?"

"Sure. I think it would be really exciting for her." She gave him a smile. "Just think of your first time seeing the ocean."

"Kelly, she just came in on a plane over the Pacific," he reminded her.

"But that's not the same as up close and personal."

"No. You're right." He frowned, looking at her. "Will you be able to carry her? You know she still won't let me do it."

"Why would I carry her," she asked with an impish look, "when you've got that huge baby stroller?" She'd seen it standing in the hallway. "It would be a crime to let it go to waste. Like having a Porsche and letting it sit in the driveway."

"Oh." He grinned at the analogy. "That's right. I forgot all about it." His blue eyes softened as he looked at her, his gaze traveling over her face and taking in the whole of her. "Did anybody ever tell you that you brighten a room just by being in it?" he asked softly.

"No," she said, but felt a certain glow at that.

He shook his head, obviously liking what he saw. "I wonder why not."

She liked this man. How could she not? But liking him too much would be fraught with all sorts of dangers, she knew. She had to be very careful to keep things light and impersonal as much as possible.

"Probably because the whole concept is pure fantasy on your part," she said, trying to stick to her intentions with a little good-natured teasing.

But for once, he wasn't really cooperating. Instead of joining in the mockery, his look became more intense.

"No, it's not." Reaching out, he touched her curly hair, and his smile was wistful for a moment. "Tell me why you came looking for me, Kelly. Why you spent so much time watching me. I still don't understand it."

She looked up into his eyes. How could she explain? Did he really want to hear about her work at the Ambrian News Agency, about how her parents had raised her with a love of Ambria, how she'd studied the royal family for over a year before she saw his picture and knew instantly that he looked remarkably like one of the missing Ambrian princes would at this age? About how she'd fought everyone in her agency for this assignment, and then finally decided to come out on her own time, on her own money, to see for herself if what her intuition had told her was really true?

She might as well cut right to the chase.

"I work for an agency that gathers intelligence."

"What kind of intelligence?"

"Information. Things of interest to the exiled Ambrian community."

He frowned. "Why are they exiled?"

"Because of the people who took over Ambria twenty-five years ago. The coup was pretty bloody, but a lot of people escaped. There's a rather large group of us living in this country. More are scattered all over Europe."

He nodded, seeming to think that over. "So these folks who took over—are they some sort of oppressive regime?"

"Absolutely."

"Hmm. So what do you do at this agency? Don't tell me you're a secret agent—an undercover operative, perhaps?"

She glared at him. "What if I am?"

He grinned. "Well, there's really nothing I can say that wouldn't get me into trouble on that one. So I'll just keep my thoughts to myself."

"Don't worry. I'm not an agent. I'm an analyst."

"That's a relief." He paused. "So what does an analyst do?"

"I pretty much sit in a room and read articles in newspapers and magazines, and try to figure out what is actually going on in Ambria. I analyze information and write reports for policy makers."

"Sounds like a great job. But what does this have to do with me?"

She gave him a wise look. "Over time, I've developed a theory about you."

"You're not the first."

She hid her smile. "I'm sure I'm not."

He looked at her quizzically. "How about a short wrap-up on this theory thing? I've got to get going on some more paperwork, and I don't have time for anything long and involved."

She shook her head. "Never mind. You'll just laugh. Again."

"Laugh at you? Never."

Enough people had already laughed about her theory. For some reason, Kelly couldn't stand mockery from him right now. She had to be on firmer ground with her ideas of his being Ambrian royalty before she told him the whole story. He'd already told her she was crazy to think he might be an Ambrian prince. She wasn't going to go into that again right now. But she could try to get him to understand why she wanted so much to unravel this mystery.

"Do you ever do crossword puzzles?" she asked him.

He nodded. "There was a period of time during my recuperation when I felt like I was a prisoner in that hospital bed. But I had my crossword puzzles, and that was all I did, night and day."

She smiled. "So you know what it's like when you're almost finished with a puzzle, all except for one block of words. You look the hints up, you try different things, nothing works right. You try to put it aside and forget it, but you can't. No matter what you do or where you go that day, you keep fooling with that puzzle, trying different answers out in your mind. And then, suddenly, a piece of the tangle becomes clear and you think you have the key to the whole thing." She looked at him expectantly. "Has that ever happened to you?"

"Sure. All the time."

"You're so certain you have the correct answer," she went on, driving home her point, "but you can't prove it until you go back and find the puzzle and write in the words and see for yourself. Right?"

"Sure."

She threw out her hands. "That's what I'm doing here. I'm trying to prove I found the right answer to the puzzle."

He nodded, frowning thoughtfully at the same time. "So tell me, am I the answer or the puzzle?"

She grinned at him. "Both right now."

Their gazes met and held, and she felt her pulse begin to race in her veins. There was something between them. She could feel it. All her stern warnings to herself about not getting involved melted away. She wanted to kiss him. That desire grew in her quickly and was stronger than she'd ever felt it. Every part of her wanted to reach out to him, to come closer, to hold on and feel the heat. Attraction was evolving into compulsion. Her brain was closing off and her senses were sharpening. His warm, beautiful mouth was becoming her only focus.

Joe looked down at her eyes, her skin, her lips, and he was suddenly overwhelmed with the urge to kiss her. Would she stop him? It wouldn't be that unusual if he were to try to lose this lingering unhappiness in a woman's love.

Well, "love" would be asking a bit much at this stage.

How about losing it in a woman's warm, soft body? Not unusual—it happened all the time. What if he took her in his arms and held her close and let his male instincts come back to life…?

He looked into her eyes again and saw the questions there, but also saw the hint of acceptance. Reaching out, he slipped his hand behind her head, his fingers in her hair, and began to pull her toward him. Her eyes widened, but she didn't resist. His gaze settled on her mouth, and he felt a quick, strong pulse of desire, taking his breath away.

For the moment, she was his for the asking. But what gave him the right to be asking? This wasn't the way it should be. She deserved better. She deserved real love, and that was something he couldn't give her.

What the hell was he doing? Had he lost all sense of decency and self-control? He pulled his hand back and, instead of kissing her, turned away without a word. He felt nothing but self-loathing.

Kelly stood very still, watching him go, feeling such a deep, empty sense of loss that she ached with it. He'd been about to kiss her. What had stopped him? She knew very well what ought to keep *her* from kissing *him*. But what was his excuse?

Taking a deep, cleansing breath, she turned back toward Mei's room and tried to calm her emotions, settle her jumping nerves. If kissing was out, she might as well start preparing for their walk.

CHAPTER SIX

THE SUN SHONE on everything. There wasn't a hint of fog. The sky was blue and the ocean was even bluer. It was a beautiful day.

"I see why they call it the Golden State," Kelly noted. "Everything seems to shimmer with gold on a day like this."

Joe nodded, gazing out to sea and pulling fresh sea air deep into his lungs. He loved the beach. Turning, he glanced at Kelly. She looked good here, as if she belonged.

"I called Angie's family in the Philippines," he told her. "They say they have no idea what happened to the nanny. I got the impression that they couldn't care less."

"You'd think they would want to know Mei was okay."

He sighed. "It's a long story, Kelly. Angie's family didn't ever like me much, and they act like they've written Mei off now that she's with me." He shrugged. "But that's a problem for another time."

Kelly couldn't imagine how anyone could see Mei

and want to forget her. But she quickly pushed that aside. Mei took up all her attention at the moment.

As they strolled down the promenade, Mei sat like a little princess, watching everything with huge eyes. She didn't cringe when Joe came near anymore, but she definitely wanted Kelly to be in her range of vision at all times, and would call out if she lost sight of her. She loved the ocean. When they took her close enough to see the waves, she bounced up and down with excitement and clapped her hands.

Mei was a treat to watch, and Kelly glanced at Joe every so often to make sure he was enjoying it, too. He gave every indication of growing pride in his adorable child.

"Look at how smart she is," he kept saying. "See how she knows what that is? See how she called the dog over? See how she stops and thinks before she calls you?"

She did all those things. The trouble was, she didn't call *him*. And Kelly knew that was breaking his heart.

They bought tacos at a food stand for lunch, then stopped by a viewing platform to sit down and eat them. Kelly had brought along some baby food in a jar for Mei. The child took the food willingly enough, but then would forget to swallow. There was just too much to look at. She didn't have time for the distractions.

They finished eating, and when they weren't staring at the wild and beautiful surf, they sat back and watched Mei watch the people strolling by.

"I've never been to Ambria," Kelly told Joe. "But

from the pictures I've seen, the beaches look a lot like this."

He turned to glance at her, then sighed and leaned back as though getting ready for a long ordeal.

"Okay, Kelly," he said, as if giving in on something he'd been fighting. "Lay it on me. Tell me all about Ambria. I'm going to need the basics. I really don't know a thing."

She gazed at him, suddenly hit by the awesome responsibility he'd given her. If he really was the prince and she was going to be the person who introduced him to his country, she'd better get this right.

Clearing her throat, she searched her memory wildly, trying to think of the best way to approach this.

"Nothing fancy," he warned. "And don't take forever. Just the facts, ma'am."

She took a deep breath and decided to start at the beginning. "Okay. Here goes." She put on a serious face. "You know where Ambria is located. And you know it's a relatively isolated island nation. The DeAngelis family ruled the country for hundreds of years, starting in the days of the Holy Roman Empire, when the Crusades were just beginning. Their monarchy was one of the longest standing ever. Until twenty-five years ago, when it ended."

"And why did it end?" he asked, sounding interested despite himself.

"The vicious Granvilli clan had been their rivals for years and years. Most of their plots had failed, but finally, they got lucky. They invaded under the guise of popular liberation, gained a foothold and burned the castle. The royal family had to flee for their lives."

"Yikes," he murmured, frowning.

"Yikes, indeed," she responded, leaning forward. "They sent their children into hiding with other families sworn to secrecy. The king and queen…" She paused, realizing she might be talking about his parents. "They were killed, but only after having arranged for it to be widely believed that all their children had been killed, as well."

"So as to keep them safe from the Granvillis," he said softly, absorbing it all.

"Yes. If the Granvillis knew they were still alive, they would have tried to find them and kill them, to wipe out any natural opposition to their rule. That's why the children are called the lost princes."

"How many are there?"

"There were five sons and two daughters, but no one knows how many might have survived."

"If any did," he reminded her.

"Of course. Remnants of the old ruling order do exist, but none of them know for sure what happened to the royal children. There are refugee communities of Ambrians in many parts of Europe and the U.S.A. Reunions are held periodically in the old Roman town of Piasa, high in the northern mountains, where they say the oldsters talk and drink and dream about what might have been." She paused for a moment, her eyes dreamy as she pictured the scene. "Meanwhile, most of the younger generation have gone on with their lives and are modern, integrated Europeans and Americans, many quite successful in international trade and commerce."

He nodded, taking it all in with a faraway look in his eyes, just as she had—almost as though he was sharing her vision.

"So what about these lost princes?" he ventured. "What's happened to them?"

"Lately, rumors have surfaced that some of them did survive. These rumors have become all the rage. They've really ignited the memories of the oldsters and put a spark in the speculative ideas of the younger generation. Ambria has been a dark place, shrouded in mystery and set apart from modern life, for twenty-five years. It's a tragedy for history and for our people. Ambrians burn to get their nation back."

He laughed shortly. "Sure, the older ones want a return to the old ways, no doubt, and the younger ones want the romance of a revolution. Human nature."

She frowned. She didn't much like his reducing it to something so ordinary.

"Every Ambrian I know is passionately devoted to getting rid of the usurper regime," she said stoutly.

He grunted. "Mainly the oldsters, I'll bet."

"Sure. Don't they count?"

He shrugged. "Go on."

"Different factions have been vying for power and followers, each with their own ideas of how an invasion might be launched. The conviction has grown that this can only happen if we can find one of the lost royals still alive. Believe me, the ex-pat community is buzzing with speculation."

"Like honeybees," he murmured.

That put her back up a little. "You can make fun of it if you want to, but people are ready to move. The Granvillis have ruled the country badly. They're really considered terrible despots. They've got to go."

Her voice rose a bit as she tried to convince him, and he turned and grinned. "A regular Joan of Arc, aren't you?" he commented.

She colored. "No, of course not. But I don't think you understand how passionate a lot of exiled Ambrians are about this."

He sat up straighter and looked cynical. "Yeah, sure. People are totally passionate in the talking and threatening phase. It's when you put a gun in their hand and say, 'Okay, go do it,' that they suddenly remember something they have to take care of at home."

She swallowed back her first response. After all, he'd actually been one of the ones doing the fighting. He knew a whole heck of a lot more about that than she did.

"Maybe so," she said. "But something has happened that is threatening to put a lot of Ambrians in one place at one time, and if one of the princes shows up…" She shrugged.

He looked up at that, curious in spite of himself. "What are you talking about?"

"Here's what's going on." She leaned forward almost conspiratorially. "The old duke, Nathanilius, has died. He was the brother of the king who was killed during the invasion, and was considered the titular head of the family. The funeral is being planned in Piasa, and it threatens to be chaotic—no one knows who will show up, but they expect a lot of people who haven't been seen in years." Kelly gazed at Joe significantly. "The question is, who will try to seize the mantle of the old regime? Will the Granvillis try to disrupt the ceremony or even assassinate any of the DeAngelis loyaltists who will come out of hiding for the event? It's a pretty exciting time." She smiled. "Dangerous, too."

Some of his cynicism melted away. "Wow. Interesting."

"Yes."

He frowned, thinking. "Twenty-five years ago."

"You would have been about four, right?"

He merely nodded, looking out at the ocean. Memories—yeah, he had a few. He wasn't about to tell her, but he did have some pictures in his head from when he was very young. He remembered a fire. He remembered fear. He remembered being in a boat in the dark. The sound of oars splashing in inky water.

But were they really his own memories? That was the trouble with these things. How much was from tales he'd been told and how much from stories he'd made up himself when he was a boy? He had a feeling he knew what she would say about them. But he wasn't ready to surrender to her royal dreams.

He wasn't sure he wanted to be a prince.

Besides, he had other things on his mind, the most important of which was finding a way to get his daughter to like him. He was getting better at looking at her without feeling Angie's tragic presence. That should help.

He had no doubt she'd sensed that from the beginning, and that had helped fuel her reaction to him.

In some ways he was torn. Anything that reminded him of Angie should be good, shouldn't it? And yet it didn't quite work out that way. He'd loved her so much. Losing her had been hard. But that was hardly Mei's problem.

When you came right down to it, he himself was probably the roadblock to happiness there. He was pretty sure Kelly thought so. The baby was getting vibes from him, a sense of his pain, and she didn't like it. Who could blame her? The thing was, how to get it to stop before it became a habit she wouldn't ever shake? She couldn't distrust him forever.

They walked slowly home, enjoying the adorable things Mei did. People stopped them to say how cute she was. Dogs came up wagging their tails. Even the seagulls that swooped overhead seemed to be screaming her name. When one came especially close, then wheeled and almost lost its balance, Joe and Kelly looked at each other and laughed.

This was real life. This was pretty good.

But Joe's smile faded as he thought of Angie and how she'd never had a chance to live this way with her baby. On impulse, he reached for Mei's hand, hoping she would curl it around his finger. For just a second, she seemed about to try.

But then she realized it was his, and she pulled back and began to cry. Huge, rolling tears sprang instantly into her eyes. Kelly bent over to quiet her, but nothing was going to work this time.

"She's tired." Kelly looked up at Joe apologetically as she lifted Mei out of the stroller. "Don't take it to heart."

"Don't take it to heart?" Had she really said that? A dark sense of despair filled him and he turned away. How could he not take it to heart?

"Joe, I need to give her a bath. Then I'll read her a book and let her play before I put her down for a nap. Maybe you could come in and watch her play? Or maybe even read to her?"

"Yeah, sure," he said. "Maybe."

Kelly watched Joe walk away, and knew he had no intention of doing either of those things. Her heart ached for him, but she went ahead with her plans. Mei loved her bath and liked pointing out the animals in her books while Kelly read to her. She was ready for sleep by the time Kelly put her down. And just as she'd foreseen, Joe never showed up.

She searched until she found him in the garage, waxing down his surfboard.

"You didn't come in to see Mei playing," she said, trying not to make it come out like an accusation, but failing utterly.

He glanced up at her with haunted eyes and looked completely guilty. "I know. What's she doing right now?"

"She's asleep."

He threw down his cloth. "Okay. I'll go in and watch her for awhile a bit later."

Kelly frowned, not convinced he really meant it. This did not bode well. But she had no hold over him. She couldn't make him do something he didn't want to do, could she?

"I'm going to take this opportunity, while she's asleep, to run over to my motel and get a few things. Okay?"

"Sure." He took another swipe at his board. "Do you need my car?"

"No. It's only a couple of blocks away. And anyway, I've got my rental car there. I guess I might as well drive back in it."

Kelly hesitated for a moment, then pulled one of the items she'd found in the room out of a shopping bag she'd brought along. It was the framed photograph of a lovely young woman.

"Is this Angie?" she asked bluntly, holding up the picture.

His head snapped back and his eyes narrowed. "Where did you find that?" he demanded gruffly.

"In Mei's room, packed away on a shelf."

He stared at it, nodding slowly. "Yes. That's Angie."

"I thought so. When I showed it to Mei, she said, 'Mama.' And she smiled. So she obviously knew who it was."

Joe grunted. He didn't have to ask what her point was. He knew.

"She's lovely," Kelly said, looking at the photo. "She looks like a wonderful person."

He nodded. "She was," he said softly.

Kelly looked into his face with real determination. "She deserves to be talked about and treated like a real woman, not an icon on a pedestal. Can't you see that, Joe?"

He nodded again, clearly a little surprised by her vehemence. "Of course."

She drew in a deep breath, then stepped closer.

"You know, Joe, I've had bad things happen. I've had periods of unhappiness when I wondered 'Why me?' I've spent some time drowning in depression."

She looked up to see if he was listening. He seemed to be.

"But I began to read about a psychologist who has a theory that we very much make our own happiness and our own unhappiness. One thing he suggests doing is to act like you're happy, even when you're not. Go through the motions. Pretend. It can seem awkward at first, but the more you do it, the more it begins to come true. Reality follows the form. In a way, you're teaching yourself happiness. And if you work hard enough at it, it can become a part of you, a part of your being."

He was looking skeptical, but he was listening.

"I'm sure it doesn't always work, but it worked pretty well for me."

He peered into her eyes for a moment, then went back to rubbing the surface of his board. "That sounds like a lot of new age garbage."

"Fine. Call it names if it makes you feel better. But it made a real difference in my life." Kelly started toward the door and said flippantly, over her shoulder, "Just sayin'."

Joe kept pretending to work until he heard her go out the front door, then he slumped against the wall and closed his eyes. Why the hell had he let this woman into his life to challenge all his attitudes and assumptions? He'd been thinking about almost nothing else since she'd made her crazy suggestion that morning in the kitchen that he talk about Angie.

He'd been angry with Kelly at first, but deep down, he knew it was inevitable that he do it at some point. After all, he had Angie's baby here. Someday she would want to know all about her mother. Was he going to be able to tell her everything?

Kelly wanted him to get started right away, but she didn't know about what had happened in that jungle. How did you explain to a little girl about how her mother had died and why? Would Mei learn to blame him?

He blamed himself, so why not?

But of course Kelly was right. What was he thinking? It wasn't all about death. It wasn't all about pain and unhappy endings. He'd had many full, rich, happy experiences with Angie that had had nothing to do with the painful part. There'd been love and affection and music and flowers and boat rides on the lake and swimming to the waterfall. It was way past time he let himself dwell on that part of the past, not the horror at the end.

He finished up his work on the surfboard whistling a tune he didn't recognize at first. He knew it was an old song, but where had it come from? And then the words spilled out in his head. "Pretend you're happy when you're blue," it began. Then something about it not being hard to do. He groaned. Even his own brain was against him.

* * *

Kelly wasn't gone long, though she stopped at the market for some baby supplies. But when she got back, something felt wrong. She stopped and listened. Nothing. At least Mei wasn't awake and crying.

She started toward the bedroom, but something stopped her. There was a rustling. There, she heard it again. The sound was coming from a room she assumed was a den, and something about it seemed downright furtive.

Setting down the bags she'd brought, Kelly walked toward the room as quietly as she could and gave the unlatched door a little push. It opened without a creak, and she saw a tall, curvaceous, platinum-blonde woman with a superstar tan going through a large wooden file cabinet. She had her cell phone to her ear at the same time and was talking softly.

"I'm telling you, there's not even a picture book about Ambria around here. Nothing. I can't find one little hint that he even knows what the country is."

Suddenly the woman realized someone was in the doorway, and she whirled to face Kelly, staring into her astonished eyes.

"Uh, talk to you later," she said into the phone. "I've gotta go." She snapped it shut.

"What are you doing?" Kelly demanded.

"Well, hello." The woman said with a smile. She was quite attractive in a tight-bodiced, bleached-blonde, fire-engine-red lipstick sort of way. But somehow, Kelly missed the appeal.

"Why are you going through Joe's things?" she demanded. She was pretty sure she already knew who this was, but it would be nice to have confirmation.

"Oh!" The woman looked stunned that she might be suspected of doing anything wrong. Her eyes widened in faux innocence. "I'm not. Not really. I just wanted to see how Joe had his files set up, because I'm going to be giving him a bid on renovating this den, doing a little decorating, and I wanted to see—" she waved a hand majestically "—I wanted to see how he works."

Kelly didn't buy it for a minute. Frowning, she balanced on the balls of her feet, feeling fierce and protective. "You were going through his files."

The woman was beginning to lose some of that overweening self-confidence she exuded. She actually looked a little worried.

"No. Oh no. I was checking things over so that…"

"Hey, Kelly. You made it back."

It was probably a good thing that Joe appeared at this point. Kelly was not in a forgiving mood. He came into the room carrying a large screwdriver and looking from one woman to the other.

"I was just putting up a growth chart for Mei in the bathroom," he explained, then frowned. "What's the problem?"

Kelly pointed accusingly in the woman's direction. "She was going through your files."

Joe appeared bemused. "Was she? But Kelly, I basically told her to." He gave her an indulgent smile, as though she were a little kid who just didn't get it. "This is Sonja. The woman who did such a great job on Mei's room. She's just looking around, trying to get the lay of the land in case I hire her to redecorate my living areas."

Oh no, she wasn't. Joe hadn't seen what Kelly had seen, heard what she'd heard. She had caught Sonja going through the files, and now she wanted to know exactly what she'd been looking for.

"This was a lot more than merely surveying the work space," she began.

He didn't want to hear it. "Listen, I'm sure it's a mis-understanding. She's okay. I knew she was going to be snooping around, getting ideas."

Sonja sensed victory and she smiled like the Cheshire cat. Kelly bit her lip in frustration. She couldn't understand why Joe didn't see that.

"Sonja, this is Kelly," he was saying, as though introducing two women he was sure would be fast friends. "She's helping me out with Mei, since the nanny didn't show up."

"I'm so glad you got someone." The tall, beautiful woman tossed her hair back and turned her dazzling smile on Joe. "I'd volunteer myself, but you know how it is. I'm good at kiddy decorating but I don't know a thing about actually taking care of the little darlings." She glanced Kelly's way. "I leave that to nannies like your friend here."

"I'm not a nanny," Kelly stated.

"Well, you're doing nanny work, aren't you?" she noted, never taking her eyes off Joe.

"What's wrong with child care?" Kelly asked, at a loss as to why the woman would be saying that with just a hint of disdain. "Every mother on earth does it."

Sonja had obviously grown bored with the conversation. She rolled her eyes in Joe's direction, then sighed. "Well, I'm going to have to get going. Places to go, promises to keep. You know how it is." Her slick smile was all for Joe. "But don't forget, we need to get together and go over my ideas. And talk about my tour plans—plans I'm hoping to rope you into." She gave him a flirtatious smile. "In the meantime, don't forget you owe me a dinner." She tapped her index finger on his chest. "You promised."

Joe was grinning back, basking in all this obvious admiration. It made Kelly's blood boil to see how easily he seemed to fall for it.

"Sure," he said happily. "We'll have to see what we can do to keep that promise."

"I'm looking forward to it."

To Kelly's shock, the woman leaned close and gave Joe a kiss on the cheek, then turned and winked insolently in Kelly's direction. Her attitude very plainly said, *Don't think you've got this one on the line yet, sister. I've got skills you can only dream of.*

She started out, and Joe gave Kelly a happy shrug, then turned back to his carpentry job in the bathroom. Kelly hesitated a moment, then decided to go after Sonja. That woman had some explaining to do.

CHAPTER SEVEN

"WAIT A MINUTE," Kelly said from the curb as Sonja reached for her car door.

The woman turned back with a frown, and Kelly hesitated again. She wanted to accuse her, wanted to question her, but didn't want to do anything that would make Sonja think she was right to suspect Joe had a connection to Ambria. Kelly had to be very careful here.

"No matter what Joe thinks, you and I both know you were searching for information in his files."

She shrugged, putting on her huge dark sunglasses. "Like he said, you misunderstood."

"No. I heard you on the phone, talking about some sort of evidence of a connection you were looking for. If you want to know something about Joe, why can't you just ask him to his face?"

"My dear, once again, you've misunderstood."

"Have I?"

"Yes. Don't you worry your little head about all this. Just take good care of that baby." And she slipped into the car and drove off.

Kelly drew a deep breath. This wasn't good. She was sure of what she'd heard when she'd entered into that room. If Sonja wasn't after Joe because she thought he was Ambrian, she was after him for something else. At any rate, he had to be prepared for whatever was going to be coming down the pike.

Kelly went back into the house and slipped into Mei's room to check on her. The precious child was sound asleep, and Kelly watched her for a moment, wondering what her life would be like. Surely she would warm to Joe soon. He would hire a good nanny and their life together would develop over time. Something inside Kelly yearned to know the outcome, but she knew she probably never would. That was all in the future, however. She was more concerned with keeping them both—Joe and Mei—safe right now. And that was really beginning to worry her.

She had to convince Joe that his friend Sonja was not on the up and up. Slipping back out of Mei's room, Kelly searched for Joe and finally found him just finishing up.

Not giving him time to distract her with jokes, she quickly told him about what she'd heard Sonja say on the phone, and when she'd confronted her a few minutes later. He listened, nodding and looking interested, but he didn't act like a man ready to jump in the car and head for higher ground.

"She was sent here for a reason. I'm sure of it, Joe. She suspects something. She was hunting for evidence of an Ambrian connection."

He was picking up his tools and looking rather proud of the new wooden measuring chart he'd affixed to the wall. Instead of being concerned about what she was saying, he stood back and admired it.

"Well, since I don't have any evidence of an Ambrian connection," he said casually, making a tiny adjustment to the way the chart was hanging, "she's out of luck, isn't she?"

"But don't you see? Just the fact that there are suspicions shows the danger you're in."

He raised one dark eyebrow as he gazed at her cynically. "As a matter of fact, Kelly, the only evidence of an Ambrian connection around here is you."

She opened her mouth but no words came out. What could she say to that? In a way, he was right.

"I hope you were discreet," he added with a hint of laughter in his blue eyes.

"Yes, Joe. I was very discreet." She shook her head as she thought of the last person who had warned her of that. "So discreet, Jim would have been proud of me."

He frowned. "Who's Jim?"

She sighed. "My boss. The one who told me not to come looking for you."

His flash of a grin was electric. "I'm glad you're such a disobedient worker."

She looked up in surprise and her gaze met his and held. That electricity was still there and it sparked between them for just a second, making her nerves tingle and her heart beat a little faster.

She turned away. She didn't want to feel this sort of spicy provocation. This wasn't why she was here.

But she needed to make some things clear to him, and she wasn't sure how she was going to do it. She had to explain more firmly to Joe what this was all about—that he might just have that elusive Ambrian connection, and if he did, he had to face the consequences of that fact. Because those consequences could be lethal.

Turning back, she steeled herself and looked at him sternly. "Joe, you need to listen to me, and you need to take what I say seriously. No kidding around."

The humor drained from his eyes and he waited, poised. She blinked at him in wonder. He was actually receptive to what she had to say. She felt a rush of affection for him and that only made it all so much harder.

Kelly sucked in a deep breath. "I think you have to get out of here. I think you have to go."

His face hardened. "What are you talking about?"

"They've found you," she said earnestly, trying to convince him. "These people—Sonja and whoever she was talking to on the phone—must be either representatives of the Granvilli clan or someone in sympathy with them. Joe, you can't stay here. You can't risk it."

He was frowning. "Risk what? Kelly, I'm not your prince. I'm not *their* prince, either."

"But you see…" She stopped, tortured and not sure how she was going to convince him. "It doesn't even matter if you are or you aren't. If the Granvillis think you're one of the princes, it's the same as if you are. And they'll probably try to kill you."

There. The words were out. She gazed at him, hardly believing she'd actually said it. He stared back, his eyes cold as ice. She couldn't tell what he was thinking, but he took his time giving her an answer, so she knew he had to be considering what she'd said.

"Listen, Kelly," he replied at last, "I've got a few skills in the hopper. I think I can take care of any threat of that kind." He smiled, but there was no humor in it. "I'm not exactly a sitting duck."

She shook her head. She had no doubt he could hold his own in a fair fight. She knew he was a trained warrior. But that didn't mean he could guard against everything. Why did he refuse to understand?

"You can't fight off the secret service of a whole country on your own," she told him ardently.

He looked pained. "Now you're being melodramatic. Slow down. Take it easy. I'm not going anywhere."

"You can't just think of yourself now, you know," she added, trying to drive her fears home to him. "You have Mei to consider."

"Of course." A slight frown wrinkled the skin between his brows. "I'm very aware of that."

"Are you?" She felt tears prickling her eyelids. Why wasn't she better at expressing just how serious this was?

Joe took her by the shoulders and looked down into her face. "You want me to run off and hide somewhere because a woman I hired to decorate my baby's room looks at me and thinks of Ambria." He shook his head as though he just couldn't buy it. "How do you know she isn't one of the good guys? Why are you so sure she didn't emigrate as a refugee, just like your parents and you? How do you know she doesn't want to recruit me into fighting the Granvillis just like you do?"

He had her there. Kelly had no idea, no evidence at all. But she had a very strong feeling. Still, held here in his grip, she could only look up at his beautiful face and wonder why he wouldn't let her save him.

"I'm not getting into anyone else's wars," he told her, searching her eyes as though he thought he might find something to reassure him there. "I've had enough of that. Enough for a lifetime."

"Joe, I…I understand…I…" She was babbling. What else could she do? He was so close Kelly could feel the heat from his body. Her head was full of his clean, masculine scent and her heart was beating like a drum. She couldn't think straight, couldn't manage a coherent sentence. All she could do was stare at the beautiful smooth and tanned skin revealed by the opening in his shirt. Her head felt light and she was afraid she was going to pass out.

Suddenly, as though he'd realized he was holding her shoulders and wasn't sure why, he pulled his hands away and she swayed before him, blinking rapidly and trying to catch her breath.

"Are you okay?" he asked.

She nodded, embarrassed beyond belief. "Yes," she managed to say. "I'm okay. Really."

"I'm sorry to be so adamant about this, Kelly," he told her, his brow still furrowed. "I've got my own problems, and I'm not in the mood for more."

"Of course not," she murmured, but he was already turning away. She watched him go, and slowly began to regain equilibrium, glad he had been too wrapped up in their argument to notice what a fool she was making of herself. She'd never realized she could be such an easy mark for a sexy man. She was going to have to be more careful.

Inhaling another deep breath, she got back with the program. Something had to be done to convince Joe to take the threat of harm more seriously. Kelly thought for a moment, then nodded and went straight for her cell phone. Time to call in the cavalry on this one.

When her boss answered, she smiled, glad to hear his voice again.

"So, Kelly, how's it going, anyway? Found any more princes out there in sunny California?" He chuckled.

She had to bite her lip to keep from reacting sharply. She was so tired of being the focus of all their joking at the agency. "Princes, princesses, earls, dukes. They're a dime a dozen out here, Jim. You ought to come out and find one for yourself."

"Hey, I thought you were going to San Diego. Not Hollywood."

"Cute." She sighed. "Actually, I think Joe is the real deal. I just haven't been able to convince him of it yet."

There was a pause, then Jim said, "You mean he doesn't know if he is or isn't?"

"Nope."

"Wow. That's a new one."

"Yes, it is. And pretty frustrating."

"Hmm." Jim seemed to agree. "But tell me this. If he doesn't know the truth, who does?"

"I do. And apparently someone else suspects as well. Jim, can you do a little research for me? I need some background on a woman calling herself Sonja Smith."

She heard him choke on his cup of coffee, and sighed. "Yes, I know. It's not likely to be her real name. But she's affiliated with a baby boutique here in San Diego." She gave him the rest of what she knew, and he agreed, reluctantly, to look into it for her.

"Don't expect too much," he said in his droll way. "In my experience, every Madame Smith tends to evaporate as soon as you shine a light on her."

"I know. But she's been prodding Joe about Ambria. Now how many people without ulterior motives are likely to be doing that?"

"Not many," he agreed. "Of course, there's you."

She groaned. "Spare me the lecture. I've already heard it."

He snickered and Kelly felt her face go hot. How she would love to prove all the naysayers she worked with wrong!

"Okay, now here's a question for you," Jim said. "When are you coming back?"

"Back?" Her hand tightened on her phone. "I'll be in on Monday. Why?"

"Because it turns out half the office will be going to the funeral in Piasa. We're going to need you here to cover."

Kelly frowned. "What's going on?"

"It looks like one of your lost princes really has shown up."

"What?" Her heart leaped.

"There are rumors that Prince Darius has been seen."

"No!"

"Seems he was living with a family in Holland for many years, then he was a businessman in London."

This was fantastic news. All these months, ever since she'd presented the people she worked for with an outline of her theory on what might have happened to the lost princes, she'd had nothing but doubt and ridicule thrown her way. If they began to show up, her vindication would be sweet.

"And all the time, no one knew."

"That seems to be the case." Jim cleared his throat. "And now he's on his way to Piasa, as is just about everyone in the Ambrian universe."

"Except me." She knew she had no hope of getting the assignment. She was the lowest level employee there, and would be left behind to cover for everyone else. That went without saying. But she could dream, couldn't she?

"I'm not going, either. We'll be here analyzing the dispatches. You know the drill."

"Indeed."

"So, when can you get back?"

"Saturday is the very soonest I can manage."

"Make it early on Saturday. This isn't a joke, Kelly. We're really going to need you."

This news was so exciting, Kelly wanted to dance all the way back to Mei's room. She wanted to tell Joe, but she stopped herself. Not yet. First, she had to show him that there was really a reason he should care.

Mei was still asleep, so Kelly went out to the entryway to pick up some of the packages she'd brought. First she changed out of the clothes she'd worn for two days now, and put on a pair of snug jeans and a cropped seersucker top that showed off a bit of belly button. She spent a few minutes putting baby food into a cupboard, then went out on the deck, where Joe was reading a newspaper.

"What have you heard about the nanny?" Kelly asked him.

He turned and smiled in a way that let her know he liked how she looked out here in the late afternoon sun.

"She'll be here tomorrow afternoon."

"Oh. Good. I hope I'll have time to train her on what Mei likes."

He gave her a lopsided grin. "You've already become an expert on that, have you?"

She answered with a jaunty tilt of her chin. "Sort of."

The truth was, she was falling in love with the child. But since doing so was crazy and would only lead to more heartbreak, she kept quiet about it. Why tell him, anyway?

"Mrs. Gomez is her name. A good friend of mine runs this agency. She'll make sure she's completely vetted. I trust her judgment."

Kelly nodded, biting her lower lip. If she was really honest, she would admit that she didn't relish the prospect of someone else taking over Mei's care.

"The first thing to notice is if she starts asking any questions about Ambria," she pointed out as she made her way to the railing and leaned against it, looking toward the ocean.

"You got it. We don't trust those Ambria-asking people."

She turned her head to glare at him. "This is serious, Joe. Your friend Sonja might just use her influence to stick a ringer in, someone who would spy for the regime. You never know."

"Ah, come on," he said, rising to join her at the railing. The sun was low in the sky and a beautiful sunset was promising to develop. "Even Sonja has her good points."

From the thread of amusement in his voice, Kelly knew he was goading her just for the fun of it. She could either challenge him or play along. She gave him a sideways look and impulsively decided on the latter.

"Wow, you were bowled over by her beauty, weren't you?" she said accusingly.

He shrugged, his eyelids heavy as he looked at her. "You've got to admit she's pretty nice to look at."

"Right." Kelly made a face. "No wonder the Mata Hari types succeed so well with the dopey gender. Men are totally blinded by beauty. To the point where they ignore danger."

He managed to look innocent as the driven snow. "Well, yes. What's wrong with that?"

If only he was as innocent as he looked. She forced back a smile. "Men are just clueless. Babes in the woods. Easy prey for the machinations of the fairer sex."

"Is that how you see me?"

She threw out her hands. "If the shoe fits…"

His eyes narrowed cynically. "Well, Kelly, my dear,

look who's talking. I mean, you've clearly got a crush on me."

Her mouth dropped at that outrageous statement. "I do not!"

"Really? Why not?"

His expression was endearingly surprised and woe-begone, and she had to laugh, knowing he was teasing her.

"You're crazy," she told him. "I'm just trying to warn you to beware of Sonja."

"Sure. That comes through loud and clear." He moved a little closer so that their shoulders were touching. "Are you sure you're not jealous?" he asked softly, as though it was a secret he was sharing with her.

"Jealous?" she practically squealed. "Why would I be jealous?"

He looked at her for a long moment, smiling, then shrugged. "You got me there."

She cleared her throat, a bit relieved. "Exactly."

They stayed there for a few minutes, side by side, neither speaking. The sun touched to the ocean, turning the water red and painting the sky in peaches and crimson. Kelly had a wild fantasy of turning to look into Joe's eyes and curling into his arms. The thought almost stopped her heart cold. She bit her lip and wished it away.

Whether he believed it or not, he was a prince of the Ambrian realm. He wasn't for the taking. She had to keep her thoughts away from such things.

Finding out the truth about his heritage and making sure he knew how to make the most of it—that was what she was really here for. The fact that he was about the handsomest man she'd ever seen beyond the silver screen had nothing to do with it. Nothing at all.

She sighed and turned to go in and check on Mei, but he stopped her with a hand on her upper arm.

"Kelly, tell me why," he said, and as she looked into his eyes, it seemed to her they were haunted by some lingering emotion she couldn't quite identify.

"Why what?" she asked, though she knew.

He swept his arm in a wide arch. "Why all this? Why you're here. Why you want to do this." He shook his head, his gaze searching hers. "But most of all, why you're so intent on putting me up as royalty on a tiny little godforsaken island no one goes to."

She licked her dry lips and searched for the words to explain, words that would convince him what he had to do.

"I told you I'm an analyst for the Ambrian News Agency. I'm the newest, youngest employee, even though I've been there almost two years now. Everybody treats me like a kid."

He pulled back his hand and she returned to leaning on the rail next to him.

"Everything interesting goes to one of the men. Every time a juicy assignment comes up, it's the usual, 'Sorry, dear, we need someone with experience for this one.' And when I ask how I'm supposed to get experience if no one lets me try, all I get are blank stares."

He nodded. "The old Catch 22."

"Exactly. So I decided to pick something no one else was working on, and make it my special field of expertise." She turned to look directly into his eyes. "I picked you."

He laughed and shook his head.

"I'd already been reading a lot about Ambria, and when I picked up a book about the possibility that there were lost children from the old regime who might still be alive, I knew right away this was it. I started finding out everything I could about them. About you."

He looked skeptical. "Did you find any evidence that they really exist?"

She hesitated. "Well, nothing solid. Not then. But I've read everything I could find on the speculation and the rumors. And I've interviewed a few people who think it's possible. And.. ."

She stopped. She wasn't ready to tell him about his brother Darius being sighted yet.

"But no one who's actually seen one?" Joe asked when she paused.

She winced. It was a sore point, she had to admit. "No."

"And then you saw my picture in that article last year?"

"Yes." She perked up as she remembered her excitement that day. "I'd been working on a montage of photos from the old monarchy, and I'd gotten so familiar with the faces. When I saw yours, it was like a bolt of lightning hit me. I just knew."

"Whoa. Not so fast." He held up a hand as though he were stopping a train. "You still don't really know anything."

"But I strongly suspect. Don't you?"

He didn't seem happy with that question. "I don't know," he muttered.

"There are ways to find out."

He looked uncomfortable and turned his gaze out toward the ocean.

"What if I don't want to find out?" he asked softly, then he swung back and faced her. "Tell me, how is being one of these royal guys who everyone wants to kill going to enhance my life?"

CHAPTER EIGHT

KELLY BLINKED AT Joe. This was quite a revelation. It had never occurred to her that anyone would want to pass up a chance to be a prince, especially of Ambria. It was an honor. Why didn't he get that?

"Do it for history," she suggested.

"For history?" He raised one eyebrow and looked amused.

"Why not? What have you done for history lately?"

He thought about that for a few seconds, and then started to laugh. "What's history done for me?" he countered.

"We don't know yet." She hesitated, then admitted, "Let's put it this way. In all honesty, if you are one of them, it could do a lot for me."

He nodded. "Your reputation?"

"Yes. I'd finally get a little respect at the agency."

He smiled, admiring the light of ambition in her eyes. She had spirit. He liked a woman with spirit. "Does your work mean that much to you?"

"Sure."

The sound of Mei's voice cut off anything else she

might have been about to say. Once Kelly knew the baby was awake, that was her first priority.

"Want to come help me change her?" she asked him hopefully.

He paused a moment, then shook his head. "I'll get dinner ready."

Disappointed, she went in by herself. Mei was standing at the crib railing and calling out, not crying yet, just letting people know she was ready to get out and join the world again. Kelly laughed and held out her arms. Mei threw out her own arms and laughed, too. Kelly held her tightly, murmuring loving words, and wished with all her heart that she would see this sort of interaction between Mei and her daddy soon. Very, very soon.

What they'd been doing so far wasn't working, and there wasn't much time left. She had to start training Mei to deal with Joe in a good, loving way. In another forty-eight hours, she wasn't going to be here for this little girl. Or for Joe, either.

Having Mei acting this way toward Joe complicated things as far as getting him to accept his place as a prince of Ambria. But in some ways, it was all part of the same challenge. Mei had to accept Joe, Joe had to accept his heritage. And what did Kelly have to accept? The fact that she was starting to fall for him in a big way?

No! Where had that thought come from? Nothing of the sort. She was okay. She'd be leaving soon. This was nothing but an assignment, even if she had assigned it to herself. It was a job she had to do. Falling for Joe was not part of the plan.

The main problem wasn't romance, however. The main problem was getting him to realize how important his position was. She had to back off, calm down and think this through. Why wasn't it working? Why wasn't he sharing her concerns? What was she doing wrong in the way she was presenting it to him? Most of all, why didn't he believe that he was the prince?

Quickly, she went back over what had happened since she'd come face-to-face with him. Of course, at first she'd assumed he knew. She'd never dreamed that he would think she was crazy when she brought up the subject. He had no idea who he really was, and at first he'd taken it as a joke.

But what had she really done to convince him? Why should he believe it? She hadn't presented any evidence to him. That was what was missing. She had to lay the foundation or it wasn't going to work.

Kelly changed Mei, played with her for a few minutes, then got her ready for her dinner. She brought her out and put her in the high chair, then got down a jar of baby food and a long plastic spoon. Meanwhile, she chatted with Joe, who was serving up a frozen lasagna he'd warmed in the oven. He'd also whipped up a couple of delicious salads to go with it.

"Hey," she said in admiration. "This looks great. You can cook for me anytime."

"Is that a promise?" he teased.

But when she met his gaze, she stopped smiling. There was something serious lurking behind his humor. What did it mean? She looked away again.

They sat down and ate, laughing companionably

together over things Mei did. The baby didn't seem to pay much attention to her father now, but at least she wasn't screaming every time he came near her.

"She's getting better, don't you think?" Joe asked hopefully, after he'd handed Mei a sippy cup of milk and she'd hesitated only a moment before taking it and drinking.

"Oh yes. I'm sure of it."

Kelly wasn't sure at all, but she wanted to keep his spirits up.

He looked at her and smiled, and she wondered if he could read her mind.

"So when do you think they'll invade?" Joe asked innocently as they leaned back from their meal.

"Who?" Kelly asked blankly.

"The nefarious Granvilli clan, of course. Tell me, what's their modus operandi? Do they like to sneak in at night when their targets are sleeping? Or do they prefer a full frontal confrontation in broad daylight?"

She groaned. "Now you're just making fun of me." Her eyes flashed. "You'll see. Something very bad will happen and then you'll find I was right."

He tossed down his napkin and laughed. "That's reassuring."

"Sorry," she said, rising to take Mei from her high chair. "I'm trying to be pragmatic and realistic. Too much optimism leaves you unprepared for whatever might be coming next."

Joe stayed where he was while she took Mei off to clean her up and change her. He wasn't sure what he thought about this royalty business. It seemed like a red herring to him. If Kelly wasn't so cute and fun to have around, he would be dismissing the whole thing out of hand. But the longer she helped him with Mei and the more she tried to get him to understand how important she thought this all was, the more he understood just how adorable and sweet *she* was, and the more he wanted to do whatever it took to make her happy. So here he sat, contemplating being a prince.

What the hell?

She came back, baby in tow, and he got up to clear the table and wash the dishes. She didn't say anything, but she had a portfolio with her and she took Mei into the living room. He knew she was up to something. He went on cleaning up from dinner, then went out to the living room to join her.

Kelly stood holding Mei on one hip. As he entered the room, she turned and gave him a tremulous smile. She'd arranged eight-by-ten-inch photographs in groups over every flat surface in the room.

"Meet the royal family," she told him with a flourish.

Joe stared at the pictures, and his heart began to beat faster.

"Where did you get these?" he asked her.

"This is my area of research. I brought them along to show to you."

Taking a deep breath, he began to walk the length of the room, looking at them all, one by one. His mouth was dry and he could tell his hands were shaking. He could tell right away that there was something about these people that he connected with, something familiar that resonated in the core of his being. These pictures were going to change his life.

"Well, what do you think?" Kelly asked, after he'd had a good long time to soak it all in.

He turned and looked at her with troubled eyes. "Tell me exactly who these people are," he said.

She pursed her lips. "I warn you, I'm going to talk about them as though they were your family."

He nodded impatiently. "Whatever. Let's just do this. Let's get it done."

She stopped before the first picture, of a very handsome couple dressed quite formally. "This is King Grandor and Queen Elineas, your father and your mother," she said quietly. "This is their official portrait."

She picked up two enlarged snapshots, one of them just after a tennis game, another of them sitting before a fire, both showing an engaging, happy pair. "And here are pictures of them in more casual settings."

He nodded again. His throat was too tight to speak.

"Here is your uncle Lord Gustav. Your uncle the Archduke Nathanilius—the one who just died. Your aunt, Lady Henrika. Your grandmother, also named Henrika."

Kelly paused, giving Joe time to take it all in. He went over each picture slowly as she named the subject, examining the eyes, studying the faces. She put Mei down in her play chair with all its attached toys and turned back to him. As she watched, she could see that his emotions were calming.

"Are you okay?" she asked him at last.

He looked up, his eyes hooded, as though he wasn't comfortable letting her see just how moving this was to him. "Yes. Why wouldn't I be?"

She shrugged. "For a minute there I thought you were freaking out."

He gave her a smile that was quickly gone. "Not me," he said, going on to the next. "Who are these charming children?"

"These are pictures of your sisters and a couple of your brothers. They were taken just a few weeks before the coup."

Joe lingered, studying each face as if trying to learn as much as he could about that individual. His expression had gone from shock and pure reaction to great interest. The pictures might even be said to be doing what she'd wanted them to.

She pointed to the last one. "And here is a picture of you as a four-year-old."

He stared at that one a long, long time. Did he see himself in it? She wasn't sure. She knew darn well *she* saw him in the adorable little blond boy playing with a pail and shovel in the sand.

Joe felt like a man riding a hang glider over a storm. A part of him was clinging hard to the reality that had been his all his life. The other part was catching a thrilling ride on a rainbow. Which one would he end up with? Was he even allowed to choose, or had these things already been chosen for him?

He'd grown up in a working-class family, learning working-class behavior. His goals had been those of the salt-of-the-earth types he saw around him. He'd always known he had a bright, inquiring mind that wanted to go a bit further than most of those around him cared to venture. He'd certainly taken enough ribbing for it in his past. But once he'd become an adult, he'd lived his own life and followed his own dreams. Still, they'd had nothing to do with royalty.

Royalty only happened in fairy tales. He wasn't a fairy-tale sort of guy. Everything in him wanted to reject this crazy idea. It just wasn't him.

And yet, as he looked at this picture of a little prince playing in the sand, something deep inside him resonated with it just a little. As he stared into the faces of the royals Kelly had put around the room, something in each one caught at a place in his emotional makeup that he wouldn't have dreamed of before she had dropped into his life. But he couldn't admit it to her, not yet.

Finally he looked up and smiled at her. "Thanks, Kelly," he said calmly. "This really does help me get a fix on what this is all about."

She waited, hoping to hear more, but he wasn't forthcoming so she shrugged and went on to the next subject.

"I called my office a few hours ago," she told him significantly. "There's news."

He frowned. "What sort of news?"

"There are rumors that one of your brothers has been sighted on his way to the funeral in Piasa."

Joe's mouth quirked. He didn't bother to remind her there was no proof that any of these were his brothers. Not yet. "Which one?"

"Prince Darius." She pointed to his picture. "He would be almost two years older than you."

Joe nodded, looking at the picture and frowning uncertainly. "More rumors," he murmured. "I'd like to hear some substantiated eyewitness reports."

"Of course. We all would." She searched his face. "So what do you think?" she asked again. "Does seeing these pictures stir any memories? Do you feel a connection to these people on any sort of visceral level?"

She was so eager, so hopeful. He turned away and didn't answer for a long time, gazing at the pictures of his brothers. Finally he gave her a lopsided smile.

"Sure, Kelly. They look like a great bunch. Who wouldn't want to be related to people like this?" Joe raked his fingers through his hair, making it stand up in crazy patches like it did right after surfing. "But just because they and their lifestyle of the time are very attractive, that doesn't mean anything, does it?"

"But what if you are related to them? Wouldn't that be wonderful?"

He gave her a glance that said *Not so fast.* "How can I ever know for sure?"

"DNA testing," she answered quickly. "It will take a while to get the results, but it will be worth it. You'll have the facts."

He stared at her for a long moment in a way that made her think he wasn't really seeing her at all. He was seeing something else—something in the past, something in his future.

"But do I really want them?" He looked tortured as he turned away. "Would knowing mean I would suddenly have a whole new area of responsibility? What would I have to do? And what the hell do I care, anyway?"

She swallowed, surprised and somewhat dismayed at his reaction. "Are you saying you really *don't* care? That you don't want to know?"

"Kelly…" He turned and stared at her again. Then his expression softened and he took her face in his hands and tilted it up. "Kelly, I know you care so much. You've been living with this, trying to get the answer to this puzzle, for so long. You have your own life invested in it. But I don't. Until I see more than this…"

She was breathless, not sure why he was holding her face this way, as though she was someone he treasured. But she liked it—she really liked it. Her body felt as though it were made of liquid, as if she could float away on a magical stream of happiness if she let herself. He was so close and his touch felt so good.

He seemed to be studying her face, but she hardly noticed. She was caught up in a wave of feeling—feeling his hands on her face, feeling his breath on her lips, feeling his affection, even his desire. Was that right? Wasn't that the flicker of something hot and raw that she saw in the depths of his eyes? Was she imagining it?

As if to answer that question, he dropped a quick, soft kiss on her lips, and then reluctantly—she could swear it was reluctantly—drew away.

"I've already got a life planned out, Kelly," he told her. "I don't need a major change. I'm not sure I could handle it."

Her face felt cool where his palms had been, and now her heart was chilled by what he was saying.

"I...I think you could handle just about anything," she said, working to regain her equilibrium. "I've seen you surf."

His quick flash of a grin reassured her, but he still looked as though he wanted to go. Maybe he needed to. Maybe he needed to assimilate the information he'd taken in here. Still, *she* needed more from *him*. She had only a short time left and she had to get all she could from it.

"Wait," she said, afraid he would leave the room entirely. "Please, Joe. Do one more thing for me."

He looked into her eyes with a tenderness that confused her. "Anything," he replied.

She took in a deep breath. "Sit down here on the couch with me for a few minutes. Tell me about what you remember of your childhood. Help me fill in some of the blanks."

"Sure." He shrugged, then glanced at Mei. "Is she going to last?"

Kelly hesitated. "I think so. She's still tired from her flight, I think. Baby jet lag. So she'll probably go down soon. But we'll hope for the best."

Kelly sat and so did he.

"The information I have on your background is really sketchy," she began. "I know you spent your early years in London. The woman listed as your mother died, and you were adopted by your aunt and uncle, and they brought you to New York. By the time you were a teenager, the family had moved here to San Diego."

He gazed at her in wonder. "How do you know all this stuff?"

She shrugged. "I know where to look. It's all in public records, and not that hard to get when you know what to ask for." She gave him a quick smile. "It's my job, remember?"

He began to look at her as though he wasn't sure if she was the same Kelly he thought he knew. "Are you some kind of private eye?"

"I've told you all about it before. I'm an analyst. An investigator of sorts. But really just an analyst."

He was still looking at her as though he wasn't too sure, but she was ready to move on.

"Listen, I know about your service with the Army Rangers in Southeast Asia. And I know a little bit about what you went through in the Philippines."

He glanced at her and bit his tongue. There were things he could say, but he wasn't going to say them. She might think she knew, but there was no way she could know the half of it.

"I know about how you were wounded. In fact, it was that article in a local newspaper I just happened to see, all about your wounds and how you were recuperating. That's how I first found out about you. What I don't know is all the connections in between. Tell me why you went into the army instead of going to college. Tell me how you ended up being adopted by those people." She put her hands out, palms up. "Tell me the story from your point of view."

He watched Mei playing with a stuffed clown for a moment, then took a deep breath. "Okay, here goes. Here's what the woman I called 'Mum' always told me."

"Your, uh, mother?"

"No. My mother was a maid who actually did work for the royal family of some country. Mum never seemed to be sure what one, but it could have been Ambria, I suppose. My mother's name was Sally Tanner. She wasn't married and no one knows who my father was. She brought me back to England when I was four, but she died when I was five. I actually remember her a bit. Just a little bit."

He paused for a moment, recalling it all. Yes, he remembered her. But he didn't remember loving her. And that had bothered him all his life.

"I got passed around from one relative to another for a few years and finally got adopted by a sister of Sally's. Martha and Ned Tanner. Martha is the one I called Mum. They brought me along when they emigrated to New York, and we moved to California when I was twelve."

"So you have a family," she noted, relieved to hear it.

He shrugged. "I *had* a family," he corrected. "A family of sorts. I never felt like I was any more than an afterthought, though. I never knew why they decided to adopt me. There was never any real closeness."

He stopped. What the hell was he doing, opening up old wounds to a woman he'd only just met? A woman he knew was fishing for exactly this type of information. Was he crazy? This was the sort of garbage that stirred up old resentments and made them fester. He never told anyone this stuff. Why was he telling her? He was going to stop. Let her find out what she wanted to know by going to these sources she seemed to be so good at finding.

Incredibly, despite his determination, he heard himself talking again. He was telling her more. Unbelievable.

"I grew up pretty much like any other American kid, playing baseball and football and living a typical suburban American life. Ned and Martha got divorced and things got a lot worse financially after that. My so-called brother and sister both began to get into trouble. Things just generally fell apart. So when I graduated high school, I wanted to get as far away from them all as possible. I joined the army. And I guess you know most of the rest."

She nodded, touched and saddened by what he'd gone through as a child. She was so sure he was royal, and yet he'd grown up in hard circumstances, the hardest being not having anyone to really love him. She wanted to put her arms around him and tell him it was okay, but she knew he wouldn't welcome something like that. Besides, what could she promise him? That life would be better from now on? That was something she really couldn't manipulate for him. Better to keep quiet.

By now, Mei was fussing and needed attention. Kelly rose, put a hand on his shoulder and said softly, "Thank you for telling me that, Joe. I know it's an intrusion to even ask you, so I really do appreciate it."

He caught her hand and brought it to his lips, kissing the palm in a way that startled her.

"Isn't it obvious I'll do just about anything for you?" he said, pretending to be teasing, but coming across as serious as she'd ever seen him. He let her go tend to the baby, but her heart was thumping.

She'd spent a lifetime finding all the men she met and dated completely inadequate. And now she'd turned around and fallen in love with a prince.

Mei, who had been so good for the last two days, fell apart when Kelly took her to her room. She cried and she wailed and she sobbed, and nothing could console her. Kelly rocked her and walked her and tried every trick she'd seen her sister-in-law employ. Nothing worked.

Joe looked in on them. "Anything I can do?" he asked.

Kelly shook her head. "She's just so tired, but she can't fall asleep," she told him. "I may have to put her down and let her cry herself to sleep, but I hate to do it. That can take hours."

He groaned. "Oh, well. You're a better man than I am, Gunga Din," he said as he walked back to the other room.

Kelly wasn't sure what that meant, but she knew it was a compliment, so took it in good spirits. But she was getting desperate as far as this baby was concerned.

She held Mei and rocked her and hummed a tune or two, trying to think of something she could sing besides "Rock-a-bye Baby," which she'd already done to death.

And suddenly one came to her. She hummed it for a moment and then began to sing. It was in a foreign tongue, but the words came naturally to her, and she realized after a moment that it was in Ambrian.

She didn't remember ever singing this song before, and yet she seemed to know all the words. She sang it more softly, again and again, and Mei finally began to quiet. It was the only thing that seemed to please the child. In a few minutes, she was asleep.

Kelly kept singing. She knew how easily babies came awake again and she was going to make sure this one was out. At the same time, she was marveling at the mind's ability to pull things from the past, things one didn't even know one possessed. She was singing a song in Ambrian that she was sure her mother must have sung to her when she was a baby. It was all there, sounds more than words, but nevertheless, complete. It felt like a miracle.

Joe heard the whole thing. He sat in the living room and listened to Kelly singing a song in a language he didn't understand, and suddenly he found he had tears streaming down his cheeks. He knew that song. Not consciously, not overtly, but his heart knew it. His soul had been nurtured by it years ago. It was a part of his heritage. He could never lose it.

And now he knew the truth. He was Ambrian. There was no denying it any longer.

CHAPTER NINE

RISING SLOWLY FROM his chair, Joe went to the garage and rummaged around until he found his old army duffel bag. Deep inside, down at the bottom, he found an old cigar box wrapped in rubber bands, and pulled it out. Most of the bands disintegrated as he tried to remove them, and the box opened easily. Inside were artifacts of a life he didn't really remember, and a place he didn't really know. He'd never understood what they were. Maybe Kelly would be able to interpret them for him. He tucked the box under his arm and went back into the house.

She had just put Mei down and was coming out of the room when she met Joe in the hall. He showed her the box.

"Come on into the living room. I want you to take a look at this," he said.

He spread the items out on the coffee table, under the light, and the two of them looked at them. Kelly's heart was beating out of her chest. There were three gold buttons with lion heads carved in them, such as might have been on a little boy's dress jacket. There was a small child's prayer book, a small signet ring, and a brightly colored ribbon with a tin medal dangling from it.

Kelly picked up the prayer book. There was an inscription in the front, written in Ambrian. She wasn't great at the language, but she knew enough to translate, "To my most adorable little son. Say your prayers! Your Mama."

Kelly could hardly breathe. She looked at Joe. "Where did you get these things?"

He shook his head. "I don't know. I've always had them. I assumed my mother, Sally Tanner, had collected them for me. I've never really paid any attention to them. I'm not sure why I've even kept them."

Kelly nodded, her eyes shining. "You understand what this means, don't you?"

He groaned and tipped his head back. "Probably."

"You are almost certainly…" she swallowed hard and forced herself to say it "…Prince Cassius."

"But what if I don't want to be?" he asked.

"Joe…"

He put up a hand to stop her and give himself space to explain his current thinking. "What I'm going to say now may sound like blasphemy to you. I'm a simple guy. I was raised by simple people. I've lived a simple life."

She was shaking her head. "I don't think what you've done with your life is simple at all."

"But it's not an upper-class, royal life. Kelly, once you get to my age, I don't think there's any turning back. I am what I am and what I'll always be."

She pressed her lips together, thinking. She understood

his argument, but didn't believe it was valid, and she was trying to figure out how to counter it successfully.

"I think you have a skewed idea of what royalty is really like," she said at last. "As people, they're not necessarily all that special. These days a lot of them seem pretty much like everyone else."

Joe made a face. "You mean like that prince of that little country I saw on the news the other day—the one who photographers caught with about twenty naked ladies running around on his yacht with him?"

Kelly laughed. "Those were not ladies."

"Probably not." He rubbed his head and grimaced. "Now, I'm not going to claim that such a thing wouldn't appeal to the male animal in me, but they said this prince had a wife and a baby at home. What normal man would think it was okay to do that?"

She sighed. "Sure, there are some royalty who take advantage of their opportunities in a rotten way. But there are plenty that don't."

"Name one."

She hesitated. "I don't have to name one," she said evasively. "And anyway, if there weren't any, you could be the first." Her smile was triumphant. "You haven't grown up being overindulged. You've got your own brand of honesty and integrity. You won't go bad."

His own smile was crooked but his eyes were still sad. "Your faith in me is touching," he said.

"Why not? You deserve it." She picked up the little gold buttons. "I'll bet these were on the jacket you wore the night you escaped."

He gave her a startled look. "What makes you so sure I escaped?"

She put them down and sat back. "Okay, here's what I see as what probably happened—based on a lot of research I've done on the subject and a lot of memoirs I've read. The castle was attacked. Your parents had already set up an elaborate set of instructions to certain servants, each of whom was assigned a different royal child, to smuggle you out if the worst happened."

"And you know this how?"

She shrugged. "People who knew about it wrote explanations later. Anyway, the worst did happen. The Granvillis began to burn the castle. Your mother's favorite lady-in-waiting was supposed to take care of you—she wrote about that in her book on the coup. But something went wrong and you ended up being whisked away by one of the kitchen maids instead, an English girl named Sally Tanner. Here's what I think happened after that. Sally catches a ride to the mainland in a rowboat. The trip takes most of the night, and it becomes impossible to hide you from the others escaping as well. She doesn't want them to know you are one of the royals, so she claims you as her own secret love child, and as no one else on the boat actually knows her, this is accepted."

His face was white. She stopped. "Joe, what is it?"

"I remember that boat ride," he said hoarsely. "The feeling of terror on that trip has stayed with me ever since."

Reaching out, she took his hand in hers. "Now Sally has you and doesn't know what to do with you. She didn't get the special instructions the others are following. She just grabbed a kid she saw needed help, and saved him. Now what?"

Joe laced fingers with Kelly's. "This is all sounding so right to me," he told her. "I can't believe you know this much."

"It's partly speculation, but speculation built on facts," she said. "Anyway, she doesn't know what to do. Should she try to contact someone? But that might be certain death for you. She knows, by now, what happened to your parents. She can't see any alternative. She might as well take you with her and hope something happens that makes it possible to find out what to do with you. She takes you to London to stay with her family, who aren't really sure who you are or what to make of you. They suspect you really are Sally's, a secret child she hadn't told them about. She tells them your name is Joe. Before Sally can contact anyone to find out what to do with you, she dies in an accident."

He nodded. "And that's why they tell me she's my mother." His half smile was sad. "And that's why I can't remember loving her the way a son should. When she died, I was probably still waiting for my real mom to show up and take me home."

"There you go."

He sat brooding for a few minutes. Kelly was still holding his hand, and she smiled at him.

"Joe, I'm sure this is all hard to hear, but you needed to know. Not only so you can decide if you want to take your rightful place in Ambrian society, but also so you can protect yourself. You need to be careful of people like Sonja. Or anyone who might come from the current regime."

He frowned, still trying to assimilate it all. "Tell me again what is so bad about the current regime?"

"They killed your parents."

His eyebrows rose. "There is that." He thought of those beautiful people in the photographs. To think of his parents a king and queen still seemed utterly ridiculous. But that couple had looked right to him. He liked them. He had to admit there was a crack in his heart when he thought of what might have been—if only the coup hadn't happened.

Joe looked at Kelly, enjoying the way her blonde curls were rioting around her pretty face. She was so gracious and decent and caring. And basically happy. How was he going to make sure that Mei turned out that way?

"Kelly, you said something earlier about some bad things that had happened in your life. I feel like I'm hogging all the emotion around here. Let's hear your story."

"Oh gosh, it was nothing like what happened to you. I'm embarrassed to even bring it up. It's nothing at all. It's just everyday life disappointments. You know how that is…."

"Come on." He tugged on her hand. "I told you about myself. Your turn. Don't hold out on me."

"Joe…"

"You told me about your family, and that there was a time when you were all very close."

"Yes." She went still. "That's true. Actually, I had a wonderful childhood. I tend to forget that sometimes."

"You see, that's what I want for Mei. Somehow I want to create that warm, safe, nurturing ideal, like the Norman Rockwell pictures, for her. Everything's got to be perfect."

Unspoken were the words *like I never had* and she heard them loud and clear. She often felt the same way.

"So come on. What about your family?"

"What about it? I've had one. It's pretty much gone now."

Funny, but this was an area where they had some things in common. No real family around. Not anymore.

"But your brothers and those nieces and nephews."

She nodded. "I see them at Thanksgiving and Christmas. The rest of the year they forget I exist."

Joe looked surprised and somewhat shocked. "Kelly, I didn't realize…"

"Oh, I don't mean to sound bitter. Really. But they're young professionals with young families, and they have very full lives, lives I don't fit into very easily."

He looked puzzled. "What happened to your parents?"

"My mother died when I was eighteen. When she was alive, I definitely had a family. She was the glue that kept us all together. And she was my biggest booster, my best friend. So her death was a major blow to me. It really threw me for a loop for months." And it still gave her a horrible, hollow feeling in the pit of her stomach whenever she thought of it.

"And your father?"

"My father." She took a deep breath and thought about him. A tall, handsome man with distinguished gray hair at his temples, he'd been a prime target for hungry females of a certain age as soon as her mother had died. They'd swarmed around him like bees, and he didn't last long. Kelly remembered with chagrin how she'd vowed to dedicate her life to taking care of the man, only to turn around and find him carrying on with a woman in tight T-shirts and short shorts, the sort of floozy her mother wouldn't have given the time of day to.

"My sixty-five-year-old father married a woman in her late thirties who wanted to pretend I didn't exist," she said, not even trying to hide the bitterness she felt this time. "They live in Florida. I never see them."

"Wow. I'm sorry."

He was looking at her as though he wasn't sure who she was. From the beginning, she'd fit his image of the perfect daughter in the perfect family full of people who loved each other and made sure things went right. Lots of presents at birthdays. A huge turkey at Thanksgiving. All the things he'd never had. And now to find out she was as lonely as he was… What a revelation. Joe had a hard time dealing with it.

Where, after all, was happiness in the world? Maybe you just had to make your own.

"So you see, we're alike," she said with a wistful smile. "We both had great families, and then we blew it."

"We didn't blow it," he countered. "Somebody blew it for us."

"Regardless, it was blown."

"So that's the goal," he said, holding her hand in his and moving in closer. "Don't blow it for the next generation."

She smiled at him. He was going to kiss her soon and she was ready for it. In fact, she could hardly wait. "You got it."

"We need to concentrate on finding good people to marry," he said, his brow furrowed as he thought about this. At the same time, he was cupping her cheek with his hand and studying her lips. Anticipation—what a sweet thing it was.

She nodded, feeling breathless. "Of course, that won't be any problem for you," she noted drily.

"What are you talking about?" he asked as he widened his hand and raked his fingers into the hair behind her head, taking her into his temporary possession.

She made a sound of derision. "You are the type of beautiful man that women swoon over all the time," she said, swooning a little bit herself.

He frowned. "So?" He pulled her closer.

She pushed his hand away. "I refuse to swoon," she claimed, but her words were a little slurred. His attentions were already having their effect.

A smile began to form in his eyes. "So you're an anti-swooner, huh?"

"You could say that. I'm anti feeding your oversize ego any more than absolutely necessary."

He dropped a soft kiss on her lips, then drew back so that he could look at her. "At least you admit my ego deserves a bit of nutrition."

"Hah!" She rolled her eyes. "Not really. I think it needs a strict diet." She smiled, checking out his reaction. "And maybe a few hard truths to help it get over itself."

"Hard truths, huh?" He began to pull her into his arms. "And you're just the person to give them to me. Right?"

She pretended to be challenging him at every turn. "Why not?"

He gave her that helpless look he put on when he was teasing. "Can I help it if women love me?"

"Yes." Kelly tried to pull out of his embrace and failed miserably. "Yes, you can. You cannot be quite so accessible. You walk around so free and easy with that lascivious grin…."

He stopped and looked thoroughly insulted. "What lascivious grin?"

"The one you've got on." She tapped his lips with her forefinger. "Right there on your face."

"You mean this one?" He leaned over her, finding the way to her mouth and kissing her with passion and conviction. "See?" he murmured against her cheek. "Women can't help but kiss me."

Kelly didn't answer. She was too busy doing exactly that.

The morning dawned brilliantly. The sun was shining in glorious celebration and the ocean gleamed like a trove of diamonds. They ate breakfast on the deck, watching the day begin. Joe had made a trayful of scrambled eggs and a pile of English muffins and honey, and Kelly fed

Mei from a small jar of baby oatmeal, then gave her some of the eggs as well. They talked and laughed as the seagulls swooped around, hoping for a handout. Kelly couldn't remember a more wonderful breakfast at any time in her life. This was the best.

A little later, after changing Mei and cleaning up from breakfast, she carried the baby out to find Joe sitting on the deck, looking a bit forlorn.

He'd decided to ignore all this royalty talk for now. He needed time to let it sink in. Today, he was all about Mei and doing what he could to change her mind about him.

"Hi," Kelly said. "What are you doing?"

"Sitting here feeling sorry for myself."

Reality was a bummer. He thought back to the dreams he used to have about what it was going to be like once Mei arrived. Father and daughter. He was already running little clips in his head of himself teaching her how to throw a ball. When he explained that to Kelly, she laughed at him.

"She's a girl. She might not be into sports."

"What are you, some kind of chauvinist?"

"No." Kelly looked lovingly into Mei's small cute face. "What about it, little girl? Want to play ball? Or take ballet lessons?"

Joe shook his head, enjoying how the two of them interacted. Mei was such a darling child. If only she liked him.

"Whatever she wants to do, we'll do," he said firmly "She's in the driver's seat on that one. It's just that…" He sighed. It didn't pay to get your hopes up.

"I've got an idea," he said, smiling at Mei, who studiously looked away without reciprocating. "I want to take her on a boat ride before the nanny gets here this afternoon."

"You think she's ready for that?" Kelly asked anxiously.

"Sure. There are some boats that go out from the pier. Just small, one hour trips. I think she'll like it."

Actually, it sounded like fun. "Let's go," Kelly said.

A few preparations had to be made. Joe went out shopping to find a little sweat suit for Mei, as her supplies from the Philippines had included nothing for cool weather.

"It will get cold out there on the bay, and this way we'll know she's warm as toast," Joe explained.

Kelly had to admit he was thinking ahead better than she was.

As they stood in line at the dock, Kelly noticed their reflection in the glass at the ticket office. They looked like a beautiful family. It warmed her heart, until she stopped herself.

Now, why had she thought that? What a crazy idea. They could never be a family. Joe was a true image of the prince she was convinced he was, and Mei looked like a little princess. But Kelly looked like an ordinary person. A nice, fairly pretty, ordinary person. There wasn't a hint of royalty in her demeanor.

The boat ride started out well. The captain was full of odd stories and funny anecdotes, and he kept up a running dialogue that had them in stitches half the time.

He showed them where huge sea lions had taken over a small boat dock, yelling like crazy when anyone came near. Then he drove on to an area where sea otters infested a kelp bed, some lying on their backs and opening oysters against rocks held on their bellies. There was a seabird rookery and an island made of an old buoy and a lot of barnacles that housed a family of pelicans. And then they headed toward open sea to find dolphins and possibly a whale or two.

They caught sight of a dolphin scampering through the water, but were out of luck with the whales, despite the fact that Kelly kept urging Mei to "look for whales, sweetie. Keep looking!"

Mei looked very hard, but there was no sign of a whale. She seemed disappointed, so it was time for Joe to pull out his surprise.

He'd gone into the shop at the dock and picked up a present for her, and now he took it from his jacket pocket and held it out. It was a stuffed killer whale, just the right size for a toddler.

"Here you are, honey," he said to his beloved daughter. "I bought you a present. Here's your whale."

Mei looked at him and looked at the whale, then held out her hand to take it. He gave it to her, and without a second of hesitation, she threw it overboard, right into the water. It tumbled in the wake for a second or two, then sank like a stone.

They sat for a moment, staring after it, stunned. Kelly couldn't believe Mei had actually done that. This was too much, a step too far. It couldn't be allowed. To overlook such shenanigans would be no good for Mei, and criminal toward Joe. Kelly glanced at the child, who looked pleased as punch.

"Mei," she said tersely, "No! Your daddy gave you that whale as a gift. You don't treat people that way. You don't throw away presents that people give you out of love."

Joe felt as though someone had just hit him in the head with a brick. It was no use. None of this was going to work. His little girl hated him. In a way, it almost felt as though a small part of Angie had just rejected him for good. How did he come back from that one? What more could he do about it? He really didn't have a clue.

All this garbage about being a prince didn't mean a thing to him. All he really wanted was for his little girl to accept him. Was that never going to happen?

"Mei, you hurt your daddy's feelings," Kelly was saying, keeping her voice calm but firm. "Tell your daddy that you're sorry."

Kelly knew very well that Mei couldn't even say the word *sorry*, but she wanted to get the emotional injury through to her at least. The concept was in that little brain, somewhere. She just wanted Mei to know that people had taken notice.

Mei's huge dark eyes were unreadable, but Kelly could tell her strong words were having an effect, so she stopped. She didn't want to overwhelm her with emotions. Pulling her close, she hugged her tightly and whispered in her ear, "Daddy loves you. And you love your daddy. You just don't know it yet."

The walk home wasn't as filled with fun as the walk to the pier had been, but they returned in time to greet the new nanny. Mrs. Gomez was a warm and lovely older woman, and Kelly could tell right away she was going to work out fine. It was a relief to have someone else to help with the burden of caring for Mei every day. That couldn't go on forever. But for now, it was the way things had to be.

Once Kelly had met Mrs. Gomez, she had no more doubts about her possibly being a spy sent by Sonja. The woman was an open book, a wonderful lady who loved children. But after a couple of hours, Kelly began to wonder what her own purpose here was.

She said as much to Joe. "I guess I could go back to my hotel," she offered, as she helped him wash dishes after lunch.

He looked at her in horror. "What are you talking about?

"I…well, with Mrs. Gomez here, I thought…"

It hit him like a thunderbolt—Kelly might leave. For some reason he'd just assumed she was going to be around as long as he needed her. That was foolish, wasn't it?

He frowned, his gaze traveling over every inch of her, really seeing her, really feeling how empty it would be around here without her. He liked her. He liked her a lot. Maybe too much.

Now why would he think a thing like that? Because of Angie?

He waited a second or two for the pain to grip his heart. There it was, but not quite as sharp as usual. And not quite as anguished.

He turned away, disturbed. A tiny thread of panic

hit him for a moment. Was he losing his feelings about Angie? Were they going to fade?

He remembered when they had racked him with such torture he'd almost thought about ending it all. Life hadn't seemed worth living without her. He didn't think he could go on with such pain wrapped around him like a straitjacket. And then, little by little, the pain had become a part of him.

Was it going to fade if he let himself fall for Kelly? Without it, would he still be the man he thought he was?

He looked at her again and knew it didn't matter. He liked her. He wanted her around. She made him happy in a totally different way than Angie had. But happy was happy. He didn't want Kelly to leave.

"You thought you wouldn't have anything to do here?" he challenged with a smile. "You're nuts." He gave a one-shouldered shrug. "There's always me to satisfy."

She couldn't keep from smiling at that one. "You want me to stay?"

"Heck, yes."

"Are you sure?"

He turned and held her by the shoulders. "Let's put it this way—you're not going anywhere."

She shivered with a feeling very close to delight. His hands felt warm and protective, and he was leaning closer, looking at her mouth. He just might kiss her.

"I'm going somewhere on Saturday," she reminded him. "I have to go home."

"Not if we think of a way to keep you here," he said

huskily, and his mouth took hers gently, and then with more urgency, kissing her again and again, until her lips parted and she invited him in. His arms came around her and she arched into his embrace.

"Kelly, Kelly," he murmured against her ear. "You've got to stay. I can't do without you."

Mrs. Gomez was coming down the hall with Mei, and they pulled apart, but Kelly carried the warmth of his words and the thrill of his kiss with her for the rest of the afternoon. It didn't mean a thing, she knew, but it sure was nice. While it lasted.

Despite the teasing and the kissing, it was quite evident that Joe was troubled by all the changes in his life. When he announced he was taking some time off to go surfing, Kelly knew he really needed space alone to think. She watched him walk away in his cutoff shorts, with his board under his arm and his wet suit over his shoulder and sighed. He was so gorgeous. But he had so much on his mind, and she hoped he found some peace in the cold California waters.

She called her office to see if there was any news, or if Jim had found out anything about Sonja Smith. She hadn't expected much on that score, and sure enough, he hadn't found anything.

"I did find that there are a number of small enclaves of Ambrian exiles we didn't have in the database before, all centered around the San Diego area. So she is probably a member of one of those."

"But you don't know much about them."

"Nope. Still working on that."

"Okay, Jim. Here goes. I got a pretty good confirmation. Joe is almost certainly Prince Cassius."

"So you think he's the real deal."

"Yes, I do."

"Only DNA testing can prove it. Is he willing?"

"He will be. Can you work on getting him a liaison to the current wise men involved? I think someone ought to contact him about going to the funeral."

"You got it. I know who to call."

"Thanks."

"Shall I have him phone you?"

She sighed. "No. I won't be here much longer. Better call Joe directly."

"Okay. And Kelly?"

"Yes?"

"Good work."

She smiled. "Thanks, Jim." And as she hung up she realized he hadn't made one joke at her expense.

CHAPTER TEN

KELLY TOOK MEI down to the strand where the best surfing was, looking for Joe. They found him just as he was coming out of the water. He was wearing his wet suit now and at first Mei looked at this monster in black neoprene coming toward them in horror. When he got close she realized who it was, and Kelly noticed that although she didn't react in a friendly manner, she wasn't stiff with resentment as she'd been before. And when he shook his head, spraying water all over her, Mei actually laughed and clapped her hands together. And then she turned away when he smiled at her.

Joe didn't care right now. The moment was too good to let little things spoil it. He'd had a good workout and thought some things through, and he'd seen his two fa-vorite women in the world standing in the sand, waiting for him as he came out of the ocean.

Good times. His heart was full.

They walked back to the house, enjoying the after-noon sun as it slanted against the neighborhood win-dows. It wasn't until they were back at the house that Joe told her he was going out in a half hour.

"I've got an appointment, believe it or not. I need a shower and then I'll be gone for about an hour or so."

"Oh," she said. "Okay. Well, I have some things to do. I guess I'll see you later."

He looked at her quizzically. "So you're not going to ask me who the appointment is with?" he teased, as she started to turn away.

She gazed at him, wide eyed. "It's really none of my business. But if you want to tell me…"

He shook his head and waved his hand dismissively. "No, not really. It'll just get you all riled up."

Now, of course, she had to know.

"Okay, Joe. You're dying to tell me. So tell me already. Who's your appointment with?"

He grinned at her. "Sonja. I'm meeting her at the coffee place."

Kelly put one hand on her hip and glared at him. "What?"

"I saw her this morning when I went to the Baby Boutique to find the sweatsuit for Mei. She wants to go over some of her ideas with me."

"What sort of ideas?" Kelly asked suspiciously.

"I guess I'll find out when we meet," he said cheerfully. "I'd ask you to come along, but something tells me we wouldn't get much accomplished that way."

He was right about that. Kelly fumed a bit, then told him, "Joe, you have to be very careful what you say around her. I really think she could be trouble."

"Really?"

"Don't let your guard down. And especially don't tell her about last night."

He pretended to look innocent. "You mean about how you were all over me on the couch?" he said, looking dreamy. "Frankly, I don't think she'd be interested."

"No, you know what I mean. About the things from your childhood. About our new determination about you. Things like that. It would be better if she didn't know."

He nodded, basically agreeing with her. "Despite the way I kid around, Kelly, I do understand where you're coming from. I'll be careful."

"I wish you wouldn't go at all," she fretted as the time came. "What if she—?"

"Hush." Joe put a finger to her lips. "I'll be back in an hour. You stay here and keep the home fires burning. Okay?"

Joe left for the coffee shop and Kelly began to pace. Every "what if?" possible was tumbling through her brain. Sonja was up to something. Kelly didn't trust her an inch. Why was he so easily taken in by her flirtatious act? He thought he was invincible, didn't he? He was going to get blindsided. If only Kelly was there to help him!

That was it. She *had* to be there to help him. Why hadn't she thought of that before? But she couldn't just walk in and stomp up to their table and flop down and join them. Though it would be fun to start needling Sonja, that wouldn't work out well.

No. She had to go incognito.

Racing to the room where she was storing her clothes, she pulled out the baggy sweatpants and hoodie sweatshirt she'd worn the day she first came face-to-face with Joe. It was the only disguise she had, so it would have to do. She asked Mrs. Gomez to listen for Mei, who was taking her nap, and she set off for the coffee shop.

She saw them right away, but they didn't even look up, so she wasn't afraid of being spotted. She ordered her drink, then took a table on the other side of the room and slipped into the chair, keeping her hood down over her eyes.

She could see them quite well, but couldn't hear a word. They were talking animatedly. Sonja seemed to be trying to convince him of something. He was shaking his head and generally doing what Joe did best—resisting joining in with female plans.

Sonja begged. Sonja pleaded. Sonja flirted and tried to persuade. Her body language told it all. And Joe deflected every bit of her proposal with humor and a shrug.

Which was all very well. But what else did Sonja have on her agenda for later? What was she planning to do to Joe? That was what was worrying Kelly.

For a moment, he seemed to get angry. He was making his own points rather forcefully. Kelly strained her ears, but she still couldn't hear a thing.

Then Sonja grabbed his hand and leaned toward him, pleading for something. Joe was looking long-suffering. He shifted away from Sonja. She leaned in closer. He turned his head away—and his eyes met Kelly's. He went completely still.

It was as though an electric charge ignited the air

between them. Kelly glanced around quickly, sure others must have seen it. He stared at her and she stared back. And slowly, a grin began to spread across his handsome face.

What was he going to do? She tensed, ready to run if she had to. He was still talking to Sonja, but he was looking at Kelly. In fact, he was making faces at her! She pretended to sip on the straw in her frappuccino, but her cheeks were flaming, she knew. No matter how much she pulled her hoodie down, she couldn't cover that up.

Finally Joe seemed to tell one too many jokes, and Sonja got up and left in a huff, leaving him behind at the table. He rose slowly and walked across the room to where Kelly was sitting, stopping at her table and waiting. Finally she couldn't stand it anymore and looked up into his face.

"What do you think you're doing here?" he demanded.

"I...I came to get a drink, of course." She straightened and tried to look cool, calm and collected. But he didn't buy it for a moment.

"Kelly."

"Well, I had to make sure. I don't trust her and I kept thinking about all the horrible things she might do."

"Uh-huh." He sank down into the chair across the table. "You thought she might get me into a hammerlock and force me into her car?"

Kelly pretended to consider it. "She's a big lady," she pointed out.

"Kelly." Reaching out, he took her hand in his.

"Listen, I think you take these people much too lightly," she told him earnestly. "They're dangerous." She searched his eyes. "So what did she do? Did she try to find out if you *are* Prince Cassius?"

"Yes. She did."

"I knew it!"

"Actually, she and Dory had pretty much decided I must be one of the princes, but they didn't know which one. They made the association from pictures just like you did."

Kelly snapped her fingers and murmured, "Shazam," under her breath.

"But she's not trying to get me to go back and sign up for my patriotic duty like you are. She wants me to help her make money. In fact, she offered me a job, paying twice as much if I really could prove I was the prince."

Kelly's mouth dropped open in reluctant admiration. "Oh, wow. Good move on her part."

"Yes, I thought so. Clever way to get me to confess." He grinned. "And nonviolent."

Kelly made a face at him. "You can never be too careful," she reminded him.

"Did you really think you were going to defend me from harm?" he asked, with laughter in his eyes and in his voice. "What were you going to do if she started to threaten me?"

"I assumed she really wouldn't do anything like that, at least not in public. But if she had a weapon…"

"You were prepared to throw yourself in front of me? Guard my life with your body?"

Kelly shook her head, all sweet innocence. "Whatever it takes."

"Hmm." He pursed his lips. "What about seduction?"

She frowned. "What about it?"

"If she'd tried it, would you be ready to guard me from that, too?"

She met his gaze and couldn't help but smile. "Maybe."

He held both her hands in his and looked at her across the table with so much affection she had to turn away.

"Don't worry, Kelly. I'll always be true. True to you."

That made her heart turn over in her chest. He might even mean that in the moment. But he didn't mean it the way she wished he would.

"Oh, Joe, stop it."

"You don't think I'm serious?"

She looked at him, loving him, regretting him. Didn't he get it yet? He was no longer free to decide whom he wanted to be true to. He was a prince of the realm. All his romances now belonged to the royal order. He didn't get to pick and choose.

Joe thought he was still in charge of his own destiny. He was a tough guy used to making his own decisions, fighting his own wars, making his own compromises when he chose to. He thought he could decide whether to go along with this royal gig or not, as his mood dictated. He was wrong.

And in some ways, it was all her fault. If she'd left him alone…

But no. That wouldn't have saved him. The Sonjas of the world were already seeking him out. If Kelly hadn't found him, someone else would have. The best, safest path would be for him to join his brothers and be a part of the fight for his homeland. She was convinced of that. Joe was going to have to come to that conclusion himself, though.

"Come on," she said to him, smiling with tears in her eyes. "Let's go back."

Mrs. Gomez went home at six in the evening, but first she made them a set of delicious quesadillas and a huge green salad to go with it. They had an intimate dinner after she left, talking softly, laughing a lot. Mei woke as they finished up, and Kelly brought her out and put her in the high chair to eat while Joe cleaned up the dishes.

He was thinking while he worked, remembering what Kelly had done for him the night before, with the pictures of the royal family, and it gave him an idea. He finished up and went to his room, opening a drawer where he kept most of his pictures of Angie. Just seeing her beloved face again made him smile, and that stopped him in his tracks. A smile instead of agony? Maybe things really were changing.

He took the pictures with him to the living room and invited Kelly to bring Mei to join him.

"What's up?" she asked curiously.

"I'm going to try it your way," he said. "I'm going to tell her about how I met her mother."

Kelly's dark eyes widened. "Oh, Joe," she said, and

a smile brightened her face. "I'll bring her in right away."

Joe set up pictures all around the room, and when Kelly came in, she put Mei down to play, and came over to sit by Joe on the couch. Joe looked at the little girl and felt his heart swell. He loved her so much and he was desperate to have at least a bit of that love returned.

"Mei, I want you to listen to me," he began, hoping this wasn't all for nothing. He was trying to keep his voice low and pleasant so as not to put her off, but so far, he might as well have been speaking pig latin. She made no sign that she heard a thing. This wasn't going to be easy.

"I'm not sure why you decided you had to make me pay like this. I think it probably has something to do with the fact that it was my fault you don't have your mother. I don't know how you could know that on a conscious level, but you feel it. Somehow, you feel it. And I accept it. I can't bring your mother back in the flesh. But I'm going to do as much as I can to show you what she was like. And how much she loved you. How much she still loves you. And how you came to be."

He rose from the couch and began to hold up photographs so that Mei might notice.

"These are pictures of your mother, Angie."

Mei seemed to be playing with her ring of plastic keys and completely ignoring everything Joe was saying and doing, but that didn't stop him. He began putting the pictures of Angie in more prominent places, not laying them on flat surfaces as Kelly had with the royals, but propping them up where Mei couldn't help but see them anytime she looked up from her toys.

"Here is the way your mother looked when I first met her. And now I'll tell you all about that."

He paused, and Mei glanced up as though she couldn't help herself. Joe smiled. Mei looked away quickly, but he met Kelly's gaze and they shared a grin. Mei could pretend all she wanted, but it was clear she was listening. How much she understood was another story, but at least she seemed to have some sense of what was going on here.

"I met Angie at a fiesta," he said softly. "I was stationed in the Philippines. We were out doing some cleanup work about a day's ride from Manila."

He held up some pictures and Kelly nodded. She was so impressed with Joe, so glad he'd decided to try this, although it didn't seem to be having much effect yet. So impressed that he could take advice, change his mind, do something because it might work. He was adaptable. You had to admire that in a guy.

Leaning forward, she asked, "By 'cleanup,' I assume you mean taking care of the bad guys?"

He favored her with a lopsided grin. "You catch on fast." He showed her a picture of himself and some of his army buddies riding in a Jeep. "Anyway, it was one of those huge Philippines parties that last for days. Everybody comes. There's singing and dancing and karaoke. And food—tables set up everywhere overflowing with food. Pancit and lumpia and roast pig."

Mei looked up at the familiar words. Joe smiled at her. She quickly looked down again.

"I caught sight of her right away. She was wearing a long skirt and a Philippines blouse with those high starched, gauzy sleeves. She looked like a butterfly about to take off over the trees. So pretty." He sighed. "Her mother didn't like me from the start. But Angie did, and for the moment, that was all that mattered. We got married and everyone had a wonderful time at our wedding. We didn't have a lot of time together, though. I had to go back to Manila and then, suddenly, I got shipped out to Thailand. She had you, Mei, while I was gone. By the time I finally got back there, rebels had taken over the whole area, killing most of the men."

Kelly gave a start, glancing at Mei. "Joe, do you really think you should…"

He took her hand and held it tightly. "Kelly, she lived with this all around her. She's seen things you wouldn't want a baby to see. And it wouldn't be honest to leave out the ugly parts." He gave Kelly a bittersweet smile. "The truth will set you free," he said almost mockingly.

"I'm not so sure that's always true," she retorted, but she saw his point. "Just don't get too graphic, okay?"

"Don't worry." He took a deep breath and continued. "The family was on the run. They had to leave their beautiful plantation behind and hide in the jungle, finding relatives who would take them in. I searched for Angie for days. When I finally found her, we only had a few minutes before—"

His voice caught and he didn't go on, but Kelly thought she understood. She'd read about how he'd been shot. Angie must have been killed at the same time. Kelly's heart broke for him.

"The rebels were pushed out and Angie's family got their plantation back. But Angie's mother blamed me for her daughter's death. I suppose she was right. It was my fault. If she hadn't come out to meet me that day…" Tears filled his eyes.

"Joe."

Kelly reached out to comfort him, but before her hand could grasp his, she realized Mei had come over, too. Toddling on her little chubby legs, she looked at him for a moment, then leaned forward and patted his leg with her hand. Two pats, and she turned and went back to her toys.

Kelly and Joe looked at each other in astonishment, hardly believing what she'd just done. Joe moved as though to go to her, but Kelly held him back.

"Later," she whispered. "Give her time to get used to this."

He nodded, took a deep breath and went on, talking about things he and Angie had done, about what life was like in the Philippines. As he talked, Mei played with her toys, then lay down on the floor and closed her eyes.

"Do you really think any of this is getting through to her?" Joe asked softly.

"Not the way it would to an adult." Kelly sighed. "But I think it's done a lot of good. It's all in the vibes."

He rose and walked over to where his daughter was lying. "There you go, I bored her to death. She's out cold."

"She's asleep." Kelly smiled. "And with babies, that's

usually a good thing." She rose as well. "Come on. Help me put her down in her crib."

"I'll do it," he said, and he bent down and slipped his hands under her neck and her legs. She woke as he lifted her, and her first reaction was to scrunch up her face and try to wrestle free. But Joe didn't let her. He pulled her against his chest and held her tenderly, rocking her and murmuring sweet words. In a moment, she stilled, and then her eyes closed again and she was limp as a noodle. Joe looked at Kelly and grinned.

Kelly was dancing with happiness—but very quietly. Together, they put the baby in her crib and pulled the blanket over her.

"It's going to be okay," Kelly whispered as they tiptoed out of the room. "You'll see. You've done it. Congrats."

"No, you've done it." He stopped, closed the door to the room and pulled her into his arms. "Thank God for you," he said, his voice low and husky. And then he kissed her.

She'd heard of kisses that took you to heaven, and she'd always scorned such talk.

But that was then. This was now.

And now was very different. Maybe it was the powerful maleness of him that did it. Suddenly everything was all senses—touch and smell and taste—and her brain seemed to go to sleep. His mouth on hers felt as hot and lush as black velvet looked, and it wasn't just touching—it was stroking and coaxing and plunging and drawing her out as she'd never been before. She seemed to be floating, and she couldn't feel her legs anymore.

Everything was focused on the kiss. She was living in this incredible sensation, and she never wanted it to stop.

His body was hard and lean and delicious, and she pressed herself against him, hungry to feel him against her breasts, wanting more of him and wanting it harder.

Vaguely, she realized he was saying something, and then he was drawing back. She didn't want him to go. She clung to him with an urgency she didn't know she had in her.

"Whoa, hold on," he said softly, taking her head in his hands and laughing down into her face. "Kelly, Kelly, if we keep this up, we'll be sorry, sweetheart. Let's take it easy for now. Okay?"

"Oh!" Her face turned bright red. "Oh, Joe, I've never…I mean I didn't…"

"Darling, it's quite obvious 'you've never.' And I don't think you're ready yet, either. No matter what that eager body of yours tells you."

She put her hand over her mouth. She'd never been so embarrassed in her life. "Oh Joe, I didn't mean to…"

"I know." He laced fingers with her, smiling at her with a sweet and lingering tenderness. "It's my fault. I got that train started down the track. I didn't know you didn't have any brakes."

"Joe!"

He laughed. "I'm kidding. Come on. Let's go out on the deck and cool off."

She went with him. The moon was out, the sound of the waves a calming backdrop. She looked into the night sky and sighed. If she hadn't already been pretty sure she was in love with him, she knew for sure now.

Kelly changed her plane reservations in the morning, but could add only one day. There was no getting out of going home on Sunday. After all, her job was worth saving.

Mei was beginning to respond to Joe. It was going to take time for her to be as natural with him as he would like, but it was coming along. They spent Saturday at the beach with her and then took her to a kiddie park where she could play on the equipment. They all three seemed to grow closer every minute they spent together.

Joe couldn't believe how happy it made him just to be with Kelly and Mei. But lurking in the background were the decisions he was going to have to make. Was he really a prince? And if so, was he ready to pick up that mantle?

This was a complicated problem. It wasn't as though there was a nice, placid life waiting for him in Ambria. If he wanted to claim his heritage, he was going to have to fight for it. There was a war waiting to be fought. Was he going to feel strongly enough about all this to be a part of that?

He'd been a fighter all his life. His career was based on the warrior creed. He'd assumed that was the only work he was trained in and the only work he would get. He'd had plenty of offers and he thought he'd take one soon.

But what if he could do something better? Something tied to his own heritage, his own destiny? Getting his country back from the evil clan who'd stolen it, the villains who had murdered his parents, the force that cursed his native land.

Wasn't that what his entire career, his entire life, had prepared him for? If he was a prince—and he was becoming more and more certain that he was—it was his duty, wasn't it?

Kelly seemed to think so.

"I've got my boss setting up some meetings for you," she told him that afternoon. "He'll arrange for your DNA test and—"

"Whoa," Joe said, shocked at how quickly this was coming at him. "I haven't said I would do that yet."

"No." She smiled at him sweetly. "But you will. Won't you?"

He melted. It was that smile that did it. This was not good. She could just about get him to do anything, couldn't she?

"I guess it wouldn't hurt to get the facts," he said grudgingly. "But what are these meetings you're talking about?"

"Different officials will be calling to discuss the possibilities with you." She hesitated, then smiled again, taking his hand in hers. "They'll want you to come to Italy."

"How am I going to do that? I can't leave Mei behind."

"Take her with you, of course. They'll find someone to help with that. Don't worry. Very soon, there will be people popping out of the woodwork to help you with everything. Get ready to feel overwhelmed."

He wasn't sure if he liked that prospect, and his eyes were troubled as he looked down at her. "I haven't said I'd do all this yet, you know," he reminded her.

She nodded. "But you will. You have to."

He had to? His natural sense of rebellion was rising up.

"I don't *have* to do anything," he claimed, feeling grumpy. Reaching out, he brushed back the hair from her face and looked at her lips. "Except kiss you. A lot."

She smiled up at him. "Of course," she murmured. "That goes without saying."

So he did.

On Sunday morning, Kelly was preparing to go, and it broke her heart. How was she going to say goodbye to the child who still clung to her neck every time she got the chance? How many mothers and mother surrogates did this baby have to lose in one lifetime?

And then there was Joe. Kelly couldn't even think about that.

Mei was asleep, and she wasn't going to go in and look at her once more. It was time. She turned to Joe.

He came toward her and pulled her into his arms, rocking her and holding her against him.

"Kelly," he said, his voice rough, "I want you to stay."

She closed her eyes. This was so hard. "Joe, you know I can't. I've thought about it long and hard. But I can't."

"Is it your job?"

She nodded, pulling her head back so she could look in his face. "You are Prince Cassius of Ambria and you have to take your place in that system. No matter how much you try to fight it, you belong there. I don't. I would have no place there, no tie, no claim. And anyway, I would lose my job." She shook her head sadly. "I have to look out for my own future."

He groaned. "If you get on that plane, we'll probably never see each other again."

She knew he was right. But it had to be. She stayed with him until she was already behind schedule, and then she finally tore herself away.

"I don't want you to come to the airport," she told him when he offered.

"Why not?"

She looked at him with tragic eyes. "I need to take my rental car back, anyway. I'd rather cut it off here and try to get back into my normal patterns right away. It'll…it'll be easier if I just…"

Her eyes filled with tears and she turned away. "Goodbye, Joe," she said, her voice choked. "Good luck."

"Kelly, wait."

Shaking her head, she kept walking, fighting back the tears.

She heard him coming up behind her, but she was startled when he put his hand on her elbow, pulled her around and took her into his arms.

"Kelly," he said roughly, looking down into her face. "Don't you know that I love you?"

"Joe…"

His mouth on hers was sweet and urgent all at once. She kissed him back, loving him, longing for him, wishing things were different. But they were what they were.

"Oh, Joe," she said brokenly as she clung to him. "I love you, too. But it doesn't matter. We can't…"

"Why can't we?" he said, wiping away her tears with his finger and gazing at her lovingly. "I don't have to be a prince. I don't even want to be one. I'd rather be with you."

"No." Drawing back, she shook her head. "No, Joe. You have to go to Italy. You have to explore your destiny. I couldn't live with myself if I kept you from that. You know you have to do it."

Reaching up, she pressed her fingertips to his lips in one last gesture of affection. "Goodbye," she whispered again. And she turned and left him there.

He didn't say anything at all as he watched her walk to the car. This wasn't like watching Angie die. Not anything close to that. But it hurt almost as badly.

To be or not to be. A prince, that was.

Did he really want to do this thing? Joe wasn't sure. He had now talked to the liaison people Kelly had set up for him, and they wanted him in Italy right away. They claimed they had accommodations ready for him, including servants and child care for Mei. It sounded kind of cushy—one might almost say royal.

Of course, they were expecting him to take a DNA test first thing. That was only reasonable. And he had no doubt what it would show. He was Prince Cassius. He knew that now.

Prince Cassius of the DeAngelis family who had ruled Ambria for hundreds of years. Wow. That was a real kick in the head.

Did he feel royal? Not really. He felt like the same Army Ranger he'd been since he left school. He'd grown up in a working-class household without any thoughts of privilege, and those early lessons would stay with him all his life. Admittedly, this was going to be quite an adjustment for him. Did he want to make it? Was he sure?

He wasn't sure of much of anything right now. His life was in flux and he was caught in the rapids. But there was one truth that he would never waver on—Mei was going to be with him wherever he went, whatever he did. His first priority would always be her. And Angie would always have a central place in his heart.

But there was something else that was becoming more and more important to him, and it centered around a woman with a mop of curly blonde hair and an irrepressible smile—the very woman who had brought all this royal stuff crashing down on him. Kelly. He missed her every minute. How could you miss someone so much who you hadn't even known two weeks ago? Something about her had worked for him from the very beginning. If he had Kelly with him right now, he'd be a lot more sure of what he was doing.

Was he in love with her? He thought back to how it had been with Angie, how he'd fallen hard from the moment he first saw her, how she'd swept up his life into days of passion, weeks of torture when he was away from her, moments of high drama and the awful, final act of destruction. It had been a wild ride, but—except for the ending—he wouldn't have missed a moment of it. Angie was part of him now, and she had left him with Mei, the best present of his life.

The way he felt about Kelly was different, and yet in some ways it was stronger even and more life-changing. She saw into his soul in ways no one else ever had. She could tell him more with a simple glance than anyone else, as well. In the short time she'd been with him, she'd made a lasting impact on them all. Kelly could have been his angel for the long haul, the center of something big and important. If only they'd had a little longer together…

But life didn't stand still and let you take time with decisions. It came at you quickly and you had to be ready to take it on. They wanted him to be a prince. Okay. He'd give it a try. He'd go to the funeral in Piasa. He'd meet the others and check the lay of the land and decide from there.

There was one missing ingredient, though. Something he was going to have to have. He sat down and looked up some numbers on his cell phone. He had a few people to call.

Kelly had been back to work for three days. California seemed like a dream. Had she really been there? Had she really fallen in love with a prince?

Yes, she had. But it was all over now. She had to get back to real life, even though there was a big, black hole in the middle of her soul.

She'd never been in love before. She hadn't realized

how much it was going to hurt to know she could never have Joe, no matter what she did. For the first two days, she'd felt as though her life was over. She was getting better now. She had finally slept the night before, and was actually able to force down some toast for breakfast before coming in. Now she was just trying to retrain herself to focus on her work and not dream all day about a certain golden surfer who was far, far away.

She was typing up a report when Jim came in waving a piece of paper.

"Guess who's going to the funeral?" he said, looking acerbic.

"Oh. Did you get an assignment?"

"No." He waved the paper at her. "You did."

"What?" She frowned. That couldn't be right.

"It says so right here. Better pack your things. They want you in Italy right away."

"Oh my gosh!"

The whole situation was crazy. How had she been chosen? But she didn't want to ask too many questions. She was afraid someone would say, "Hey, why are we sending her, anyway?" and it would be all over. So she kept her head down and made quick preparations, and before she knew it, she was on the plane to Italy.

And all she could think about was Joe. Would she see him? Would she get a glimpse of Mei? Maybe she'd see them at a fancy restaurant, or maybe there would be a parade and they would be in it. If she waved, would they wave back? How hard would that be—to see them passing and have them look right through her? She didn't know if she would be able to stand it.

But she was going. What would be would be. Piasa wasn't a very big town. Surely she would see them somewhere, at some point.

She landed at the airport and took a five-hour taxi ride into the mountains. The town of Piasa looked as if it belonged in the Swiss Alps. It was very quaint and adorable, with chalets and wildflowers everywhere. She almost expected to see Julie Andrews bursting into song every time she looked at the mountains.

Kelly spent the first day getting acclimatized, checking into her hotel, learning where she needed to go to get information, meeting some of the townsfolk. And asking discreetly if anyone knew anything about the lost princes. No one did.

But all in all, it was pretty exciting meeting Ambrians everywhere. The feeling of kinship was strong and there seemed to be a festive spirit in the air. Something was up, that was for sure.

When she finally got back to her hotel room that first night, there was a message from her home office of the Ambrian News Agency, asking why she hadn't contacted her client yet, and giving a number for doing so.

Client? What client? No one had told her there was a specific client involved. But she supposed that must be why she'd received the last-minute assignment, and no one had completed briefing her on what she was expected to do here.

She looked at the clock. It was too late to do anything about it tonight. She would call the number in the morning. With a sigh, she began to get ready for bed.

And then she heard a strange sound. She stopped, holding her breath. Something brushed against her door, and then there was whispering. And finally, a firm knock.

Her heart began to pound. This was an idyllic, picturesque little town, but she knew behind the pretty pictures lurked a perpetual menace. The Granvillis were behind most of the ugly incidents that happened to expatriot Ambrians. Everywhere she'd gone today, people had warned her to be careful.

She went to the door and listened. There was still whispering, but she couldn't make it out.

"Who is it?" she called.

A voice spoke—what sounded almost like a child's voice.

A child's voice. But it couldn't be….

"Mei?" she said, almost whispering herself. Throwing caution to the wind, she ripped the door open.

"Mei!"

There was the darling little girl, high up in Joe's arms, and now shrieking with laughter and clapping her hands. Kelly was so surprised she stood in shocked paralysis, her mouth open.

"Hey, better let us in," Joe advised, his grin wide and his eyes filled with affection. "You'll have your neighbors up in arms at all the noise soon."

"Joe!" She stepped back and herded them in. "I can't believe this. I was hoping I would find you somewhere, and here you are."

"Darn right," he said. "We've been trying to catch

up with you all afternoon. You were supposed to check in as soon as you got here."

She shook her head. "What are you talking about?"

"Didn't you guess? We're your clients—me and Mei. I got your agency to send you. I told them I needed to hire you as my communications director for awhile."

She stared at him, at a loss. Things were happening too fast.

"Hey." He pointed his thumb at his chest. "Meet the new boss. You're all mine now."

As if she hadn't been all along. Kelly started to laugh, and then she stopped herself, afraid she might lapse into hysteria. This was all so crazy.

Then she took a good look at them. Joe was dressed in a gray sweatshirt with a hood, and so was Mei. They looked like versions of how she'd appeared on the beach when Joe had first noticed her.

"Yeah, we're running around town undercover," he told her cheerfully. "Did you bring your sweats with you? You can join us. That'll keep you incognito as we make our way back to the Marbella House, where we're staying." He glanced at his watch. "Mei is up way past her bedtime, but she wanted to help me find you, so here she is."

Kelly shook her head in wonder. "So you two are okay now?" she asked, though she really didn't have to.

"Sure. Look at this." He set Mei down in a chair and knelt before her.

"Okay, Mei. We need to show Kelly your new talents. Show her. What does the pig say?"

Mei wiggled her nose and made a very cute grunting noise.

"What does the doggie say?"

She scrunched up her face and woofed heartily.

"What does the Mei say?"

She threw her arms out and wrapped them around Joe's neck. "Dada!" she cried happily.

Kelly watched with tears in her eyes. "That is the best present I could ever have," she told Joe, snuffling a bit as he stood and wrapped his arms around her.

"Okay," he said, lifting her chin and dropping a sweet kiss on her lips. "Then I guess I'll have to try to better it."

She blinked up at him. "What do you mean?"

He shrugged. "How would you like a royal wedding?"

"But…I'm not getting married."

He looked surprised. "Oh. Funny. I thought you were."

She was frowning. He was teasing her again, wasn't he? "No, I'm not, and it's not funny at all. In fact, I think you're—"

She stopped dead. He had a diamond ring in his hand. As she gaped at him, he went down on one knee and presented it to her. "Kelly Vrosis, would you be my wife?" he asked, his eyes shining with something that looked very much like love.

"Oh!"

He raised one eyebrow. "I was hoping for a yes."

"But…but—" She was utterly flabbergasted. Never in a million years had she expected anything like this.

"I need you with me, Kelly. Mei needs you, too. And the only way I can guarantee that is to marry you."

She laughed. "So what you're proposing is a marriage of convenience. Your convenience."

"You might say that. I'd rather say we were meant for each other and there is no point in delaying the inevitable."

Her smile could have warmed the room. "I like that kind of talk."

"And your answer is?"

"Yes! Oh, yes!"

"Dada!" Mei chimed in, clapping her hands.

Joe scooped her up and they had a three-way hug, a family at last.

* * * * *

CROWN PRINCE, PREGNANT BRIDE!

BY
RAYE MORGAN

This book is dedicated to Baby Kate

CHAPTER ONE

THOUGH MONTE COULDN'T see her, Pellea Marallis
passed so close to the Crown Prince's hiding place, he
easily caught a hint of her intoxicating perfume. That
gave him an unexpected jolt. It brought back a panoply of
memories, like flipping through the pages of a book—a
vision of sunlight shining through a gauzy white dress,
silhouetting a slim, beautifully rounded female form, a
flashing picture of drops of water cascading like a thousand diamonds onto creamy silken skin, a sense of cool
satin sheets and caresses that set his flesh on fire.

He bit down hard on his lower lip to stop the wave of
sensuality that threatened to wash over him. He wasn't
here to renew the romance. He was here to kidnap her.
And he wasn't about to let that beguiling man-woman
thing get in the way this time.

She passed close again and he could hear the rustle of
her long skirt as it brushed against the wall he was leaning on. She was pacing back and forth in her courtyard,
a garden retreat built right into this side of the castle,
giving her a small lush forest where she spent most of her
time. The surrounding rooms—a huge closet filled with

clothes and a small sitting room, a neighboring compact office stacked to the ceiling with books, a sumptuously decorated bedroom—each opened onto the courtyard with French doors, making her living space a mixture of indoors and outdoors in an enchanting maze of exciting colors and provocative scents.

She was living like a princess.

Did he resent it all? Of course. How could he not?

But this was not the side of the castle where his family had lived before the overthrow of their royal rule. That area had been burned the night his parents were murdered by the Granvillis, the thugs who still ruled Ambria, this small island country that had once been home to his family. He understood that part of the castle was only now being renovated, twenty-five years later.

And that he resented.

But Pellea had nothing to do with the way his family had been robbed of their birthright. He had no intention of holding her accountable. Her father was another matter. His long-time status as the Grand Counselor to the Granvillis was what gave Pellea the right to live in this luxury—and his treachery twenty-five years ago was considered a subject of dusty history.

Not to Monte. But that was a matter for another time.

He hadn't seen her yet. He'd slipped into the dressing room as soon as he'd emerged from the secret passageway. And now he was just biding his time before he revealed his presence.

He was taking this slowly, because no matter what

he'd told himself, she affected him in ways no other woman ever had. In fact, she'd been known to send his restraint reeling, and he knew he had to take this at a cautious pace if he didn't want things to spin out of control again.

He heard her voice and his head rose. Listening hard, he tried to figure out if she had someone with her. No. She was talking on her mobile, and when she turned in his direction, he could just make out what she was saying.

"Seed pearls of course. And little pink rosebuds. I think that ought to do it."

He wasn't really listening to the words. Just the sound of her had him mesmerized. He'd never noticed before how appealing her voice was, just as an instrument. He hadn't heard it for some time, and it caught the ear the way a lilting acoustic guitar solo might, each note crisp, crystal clear and sweet in a way that touched the soul.

As she talked, he listened to the sound and smiled. He wanted to see her and the need was growing in him.

But to do that, he would have to move to a riskier position so that he could see out through the open French doors. Though he'd slipped easily into her huge dressing room, he needed to move to a niche beside a tall wardrobe where he could see everything without being seen himself. Carefully, he made his move.

And there she was. His heart was thudding so hard, he could barely breathe.

The thing about Pellea, and part of the reason she so completely captivated him, was that she seemed to embody a sense of royal command even though there wasn't a royal bone in her body. She was classically beautiful, like a Greek statue, only slimmer, like an angel in a Renaissance painting, only earthier, like a dancer drawn by Toulouse-Lautrec, only more graceful, like a thirties-era film star, only more mysteriously luminescent. She was all a woman could be and still be of this earth.

Barely.

To a casual glance, she looked like a normal woman. Her face was exceptionally pretty, but there were others with dark eyes as almond-shaped, with long, lustrous lashes that seemed to sweep the air. Her hair floated about her face like a misty cloud of spun gold and her form was trim and nicely rounded. Her lips were red and full and inviting. Perfection.

But there were others who had much the same advantages. Others had caught his eye through the years, but not many had filled his mind and touched off the sense of longing that she had.

There was something more to Pellea, something in the dignity with which she held herself, an inner fire that burned behind a certain sadness in her eyes, an inner drive, a sense of purpose, that set her apart. She could be playful as a kitten one minute, then smoldering with a provocative allure, and just as suddenly, aflame with righteous anger.

From the moment he'd first seen her, he'd known she was special. And for a few days two months ago, she'd been his.

"Didn't I give you my sketches?" she was saying into the phone. "I tend to lean a little more toward traditional. Not too modern. No off-the-shoulder stuff. Not for this."

He frowned, wondering what on earth she was talking about. Designing a ball gown maybe? He could see her on the dance floor, drawing all eyes. Would he ever get the chance to dance with her? Not in a ballroom, but maybe here, in her courtyard. Why not?

It was a beautiful setting. When he'd been here before, it had been winter and everything had been lifeless and stark. But spring was here now, and the space was a riot of color.

A fountain spilled water in the center of the area, making music that was a pleasant, tinkling background. Tiled pathways meandered through the area, weaving in among rosebushes and tropical plants, palms and a small bamboo forest.

Yes, they would have to turn on some music and dance. He could almost feel her in his arms. He stole another glance at her, at the way she held her long, graceful neck, at the way her free hand fluttered like a bird as she made her point, at the way her dressing gown gaped open, revealing the lacy shift she wore underneath.

"Diamonds?" she was saying into the phone. "Oh, no. No diamonds. Just the one, of course. That's customary. I'm not really a shower-me-with-diamonds sort of girl, you know what I mean?"

He reached out and just barely touched the fluttering hem of her flowing sleeve as she passed. She turned quickly, as though she'd sensed something, but he'd pulled back just in time and she didn't see him. He smiled, pleased with himself. He would let her know he was here when he was good and ready.

"As I remember it, the veil is more of an ivory shade. There are seed pearls scattered all over the crown area, and then down along the edges on both sides. I think that will be enough."

Veil? Monte frowned. Finally, a picture swam into stark relief and he realized what she must be talking about. It sounded like a wedding. She was planning her wedding ensemble.

She was getting married.

He stared at her, appalled. What business did she have getting married? Had she forgotten all about him so quickly? Anger curled through him like smoke and he only barely held back the impulse to stride out and confront her.

She couldn't get married. He wouldn't allow it.

And yet, he realized with a twinge of conscience, it wasn't as though he was planning to marry her himself. Of course not. He had bigger fish to fry. He had an invasion to orchestrate and manage. Besides, there was no way he would ever marry the daughter of the biggest betrayer still alive of his family—the DeAngelis Royalty.

And yet, to think she was planning to marry someone else so soon after their time together burned like a scorpion's sting.

What the hell!

A muted gong sounded, making him jerk in surprise. That was new. There had been a brass knocker a few weeks ago. What else had she changed since he'd been here before?

Getting married—hah! It was a good thing he'd shown up to kidnap her just in time.

Pellea had just rung off with her clothing designer, and she raised her head at the sound of her new entry gong. She sighed, shoulders drooping. The last thing she wanted was company, and she was afraid she knew who this was anyway. Her husband-to-be. Oh, joy.

"Enter," she called out.

There was a heavy metal clang as the gate was pulled open and then the sound of boots on the tile. A tall man entered, his neatly trimmed hair too short to identify the color, but cut close to his perfectly formed head. His shoulders were wide, his body neatly proportioned and very fit-looking. His long face would have been handsome if he could have trained himself to get rid of the perpetual sneer he wore like a mark of superiority at all times.

Leonardo Granvilli was the oldest son of Georges Granvilli, leader of the rebellion that had taken over this island nation twenty-five years before, the man who now ruled as *The General*, a term that somewhat softened the edges of his relatively despotic regime.

"My darling," Leonardo said coolly in a deep, sonorous voice. "You're radiant as the dawn on this beautiful day."

"Oh, spare me, Leonardo," she said dismissively. Her tone held casual disregard but wasn't in any way meant to offend. "No need for empty words of praise. We've known each other since we were children. I think by now we've taken the measure, each of the other. I don't need a daily snow job."

Leonardo made a guttural sound in his throat and threw a hand up to cover his forehead in annoyance. "Pellea, why can't you be like other women and just accept the phony flattery for what it is? It's nothing but form, darling. A way to get through the awkward moments. A little sugar to help the medicine go down."

Pellea laughed shortly, but cut it off almost before it had begun. Pretending to be obedient, she went into mock royal mode for him.

"Pray tell me, kind sir, what brings my noble knight to my private chambers on such a day as this?"

He actually smiled. "That's more like it."

She curtsied low and long and his smile widened.

"Bravo. This marriage may just work out after all."

Her glare shot daggers his way, as though to say, *In your dreams*, but he ignored that.

"I came with news. We may have to postpone our wedding."

"What?" Involuntarily, her hands went to her belly—and the moment she realized what she'd done, she snatched them away again. "Why?"

"That old fool, the last duke of the DeAngelis clan, has finally died. This means a certain level of upheaval is probable in the expatriate Ambrian community. They will have to buzz about and try to find a new patriarch, it seems. We need to be alert and ready to move on any sort of threat that might occur to our regime."

"Do you expect anything specific?"

He shook his head. "Not really. Just the usual gnashing of teeth and bellowing of threats. We can easily handle it."

She frowned, shaking her head. "Then why postpone? Why not move the date up instead?"

He reached out and tousled her hair. "Ah, my little buttercup. So eager to be wed."

She pushed his hand away, then turned toward the fountain in the middle of the courtyard and shrugged elaborately. "'If it were done when 'tis done, then 'twere well it were done quickly,'" she muttered darkly.

"What's that my sweet?" he said, following into the sunshine.

"Nothing." She turned back to face him. "I will, of course, comply with your wishes. But for my own purposes, a quick wedding would be best."

He nodded, though his eyes were hooded. "I understand. Your father's condition and all that." He shrugged. "I'll talk to my father and we'll hit upon a date, I'm sure." His gaze flickered over her and he smiled. "To think that after all this time, and all the effort you've always gone to in putting me off, I'm finally going to end up with the woman of my dreams." He almost seemed to tear up a bit. "It restores one's faith, doesn't it?"

"Absolutely." She couldn't help but smile back at him, though she was shaking her head at the same time. "Oh,

Leonardo, I sometimes think it would be better if you found someone to love."

He looked shocked. "What are you talking about? You know very well you've always been my choice."

"I said *love*," she retorted. "Not *desire to possess*."

He shrugged. "To each his own."

Pellea sighed but she was still smiling.

Monte watched this exchange while cold anger spread through him like a spell, turning him from a normal man into something akin to a raging monster. And yet, he didn't move a muscle. He stood frozen, as though cast in stone. Only his mind and his emotions were alive.

And his hatred. He hated Leonardo, hated Leonardo's father, hated his entire family.

Bit by bit, the anger was banked and set aside to smolder. He was experienced enough to know white-hot emotional ire led to mistakes every time. He wouldn't make any mistakes. He needed to keep his head clear and his emotions in check.

All of them, good and bad.

One step at a time, he made himself relax. His body control was exceptional and he used it now. He wanted to keep cool so that he would catch the exact right time to strike. It wouldn't be now. That would be foolish. But it would be soon.

He hadn't been prepared for something like this. The time he and Pellea had spent together just a few weeks before had been magical. He'd been hungry to see her again, aching to touch her, eager to catch her lips with his and feel that soaring sense of wonder again. He had promised himself there would be no lovemaking to distract him this time—but he'd been kidding himself. The moment he saw her he knew he had to have her in his arms again.

That was all. Nothing serious, nothing permanent. A part of him had known she would have to marry someone—eventually. But still, to think that she would marry this…this…

Words failed him.

"I'd like you to come down to the library. We need to look at the plans for the route to the retreat in the gilded carriage after we are joined as one," Leonardo was saying.

"No honeymoon," she said emphatically, raising both hands as though to emphasize her words. "I told you that from the beginning."

He looked startled, but before he could protest, she went on.

"As long as my father is ill, I won't leave Ambria."

He sighed, making a face but seemingly reconciled to her decision. "People will think it strange," he noted.

"Let them."

She knew that disappointed him but it couldn't be helped. Right now her father was everything to her. He had been her rock all her life, the only human being in this world she could fully trust and believe in and she wasn't about to abandon him now.

Still, she needed this marriage. Leonardo understood

why and was willing to accept the terms she'd agreed to this on. Everything was ready, the wheels had begun to turn, the path was set. As long as nothing got in the way, she should be married within the next week. Until then, she could only hope that nothing would happen to upset the apple cart.

"I'll come with you," she said. "Just give me a minute to do a quick change into something more suitable."

She turned and stepped into her dressing room, pulling the door closed behind her. Moving quickly, she opened her gown and began unbuttoning her lacy dress from the neck down. And then she caught sight of his boots. Her fingers froze on the buttons as she stared at the boots. Her head snapped up and her dark eyes met Monte's brilliant blue gaze. Every sinew constructing her body went numb.

She was much more than shocked. She was horrified. As the implications of this visit came into focus, she had to clasp her free hand over her mouth to keep from letting out a shriek. For just a moment, she went into a tailspin and could barely keep her balance.

Eyes wide, she stared at him. A thousand thoughts ricocheted through her, bouncing like ping-pong balls against her emotions. Anger, remorse, resentment, joy—even love—they were all there and all aimed straight into those gorgeous blue eyes, rapid-fire. If looks could kill, he would be lying on the floor, shot through the heart.

A part of her was tempted to turn on her heel, summon Leonardo and be done with it. Because she knew as sure as she knew her own name that this would all end badly.

Monte couldn't be a part of her life. There was no way she could even admit to anyone here in the castle that she knew him. All she had to do was have Leonardo call the guard, and it would be over. They would dispose of him. She would never see him again—never have to think about him again, never again have to cry into her pillow until it was a soggy sponge.

But she knew that was all just bravado. She would never, ever do anything to hurt him if she could help it.

He gave her a crooked grin as though to say, "Didn't you know I'd be back?"

No, she didn't know. She hadn't known. And she still didn't want to believe it. She didn't say a word.

Quickly, she turned and looked out into the courtyard. Leonardo was waiting patiently, humming a little tune as he looked at the fountain. Biting her lower lip, she turned and managed to stagger out of the dressing room towards him, stumbling a bit and panting for breath.

"What is it?" he said in alarm, stepping forward to catch her by the shoulders. He'd obviously noted that she was uncharacteristically disheveled. "Are you all right?"

"No." She flickered a glance his way, thinking fast, then took a deep breath and shook her head. "No. Migraine."

"Oh, no." He looked puzzled, but concerned.

She pulled away from his grip on her shoulders, regaining her equilibrium with effort.

"I…I'm sorry, but I don't think I can come with you right now. I can hardly even think straight."

"But you were fine thirty seconds ago," he noted, completely at sea.

"Migraines come on fast," she told him, putting a hand to the side of her head and wincing. "But a good lie-down will fix me up. How about…after tea?" She looked at him earnestly. "I'll meet you then. Say, five o'clock?"

Leonardo frowned, but he nodded. "All right. I've got a tennis match at three, so that will work out fine." He looked at her with real concern, but just a touch of wariness.

"I hope this won't affect your ability to go to the ball tonight."

"Oh, no, of course not."

"Everyone is expecting our announcement to be made there. And you will be wearing the tiara, won't you?"

She waved him away. "Leonardo, don't worry. I'll be wearing the tiara and all will be as planned. I should be fine by tonight."

"Good." He still seemed wary. "But you should see Dr. Dracken. I'll send him up."

"No!" She shook her head. "I just need to rest. Give me a few hours. I'll be good as new."

He studied her for a moment, then shrugged. "As you wish." He bent over her hand like a true suitor. "Until we meet again, my beloved betrothed."

She nodded, almost pushing him toward the gate. "Likewise, I'm sure," she said out of the corner of her mouth.

"Pip pip." And he was off.

She waited until she heard the outer gate clang, then turned like a fury and marched back into the dressing room. She ripped open the door and glared at Monte with a look in her eyes that should have frozen the blood in his veins.

"How dare you? How dare you do this?"

Her vehemence was actually throwing him off his game a bit. He had expected a little more joy at seeing him again. He was enjoying the sight of her. Why couldn't she feel the same?

She really was a feast for the senses. Her eyes were bright—even if that seemed to be anger for the moment—and her cheeks were smudged pink.

"How dare you do this to me again?" she demanded.

"This isn't like before," he protested. "This is totally different."

"Really? Here you are, sneaking into my country, just like before. Here you are, hiding in my chambers again. Just like before."

His smile was meant to be beguiling. "But this time, when I leave, you're going with me."

She stared at him, hating him and loving him at the same time. Going with him! What a dream that was. She could no more go with him than she could swim the channel. If only…

For just a split second, she allowed herself to give in to her emotions. If only things were different. How she would love to throw herself into his arms and hold him tight, to feel his hard face against hers, to sense his heart pound as his interest quickened…

But she couldn't do that. She couldn't even think about it. She'd spent too many nights dreaming of him, dreaming of his tender touch. She had to forget all that. Too many lives depended on her. She couldn't let him see the slightest crack in her armor.

And most of all, she couldn't let him know about the baby.

"How did you get in here?" she demanded coldly. "Oh, wait. Don't even try to tell me. You'll just lie."

The provocative expression in his eyes changed to ice in an instant.

"Pellea, I'm not a liar," he said in a low, urgent tone. "I'll tell you or I won't, but what I say will be the truth as I know it every time. Count on it."

Their gazes locked in mutual indignation. Pellea was truly angry with him for showing up like this, for complicating her life and endangering them both, and yet she knew she was using that anger as a shield. If he touched her, she would surely melt. Just looking at him did enough damage to her determined stance.

Why did he have to be so beautiful? With his dark hair and shocking blue eyes, he had film-star looks, but that wasn't all. He was tall, muscular, strong in a way that would make any woman swoon. He looked tough, capable of holding his own in a fight, and yet there was nothing cocky about him. He had a quiet confidence that made any form of showing off unnecessary. You just knew by looking at him that he was ready for any challenge—physical or intellectual.

But how about emotional? Despite all his strength, there was a certain sensitivity deep in his blue eyes. The sort of hint of vulnerability only a woman might notice. Or was that just hopeful dreaming on her part?

"Never mind all that," she said firmly. "We've got to get you out of here."

His anger drifted away like morning fog and his eyes were smiling again. "After I've gone to so much trouble to get in?"

Oh, please don't smile at me! she begged silently. This was difficult enough without this charm offensive clouding her mind. She glared back.

"You are going. This very moment would be a good time to do it."

His gaze caressed her cheek. "How can I leave now that I've found you again?"

She gritted her teeth. "You're not going to mesmerize me like you did last time. You're not staying here at all." She pointed toward the gate. "I want you to go."

He raised one dark eyebrow and made no move toward the door. "You going to call the guard?"

Her eyes blazed at him. "If I have to."

He looked pained. "Actually, I'd rather you didn't."

"Then you'd better go, hadn't you?"

He sighed and managed to look as though he regretted all this. "I can't leave yet. Not without what I came for."

She threw up her hands. "That has nothing to do with me."

His smile was back. "That's where you're wrong. You see, it's you that I came for. How do you feel about a good old-fashioned kidnapping?"

CHAPTER TWO

PELLEA BLINKED QUICKLY, but that was the only sign she allowed to show his words had shocked her—rocked her, actually, to the point where she almost needed to reach out and hold on to something to keep from falling over.

Monte had come to kidnap her? Was he joking? Or was he crazy?

"Really?" With effort, she managed to fill her look with mock disdain. "How do you propose to get me past all the guards and barriers? How do you think you'll manage that without someone noticing? Especially when I'll be fighting you every step of the way and creating a scene and doing everything else I can think of to ruin your silly kidnapping scheme?"

"I've got a plan." He favored her with a knowing grin.

"Oh, I see." Eyes wide, she turned with a shrug, as though asking the world to judge him. "He's got a plan. Say no more."

He followed her. "You scoff, Pellea. But you'll soon see things my way."

She whirled to face him and her gaze sharpened as she remembered his last visit. "How do you get in here, anyway? You've never explained that." She shook her head, considering him from another angle. "There are guards everywhere. How do you get past them?"

His grin widened. "Secrets of the trade, my dear."

"And just what is your trade these days?" she asked archly. "Second-story man?"

"No, Pellea." His grin faded. Now they were talking about serious things. "Actually, I still consider myself the royal heir to the Ambrian throne."

She rolled her eyes. "Good luck with that one."

He turned and met her gaze with an intensity that burned. "I'm the Crown Prince of Ambria. Hadn't you heard? I thought you understood that."

She stared back at him. "That's over," she said softly, searching his eyes. "Long over."

He shook his head slowly, his blue eyes burning with a surreal light. "No. It's real and it's now. And very soon, the world will know it."

Fear gripped her heart. What he was suggesting was war. People she loved would be hurt. And yet…

Reaching out, she touched him, forgetting her vow not to. She flattened her palm against his chest and felt his heartbeat, felt the heat and the flesh of him.

"Oh, please, Monte," she whispered, her eyes filled with the sadness of a long future of suffering. "Please, don't…"

He took her hand and brought it to his lips, kissing the center of her palm without losing his hold on her gaze for a moment. "I won't let anything hurt you," he promised, though he knew he might as well whistle into the wind. Once his operation went into action, all bets would be off. "You know that."

She shook her head, rejecting what he'd said. "No, Monte, I don't know that. You plan to come in here and rip our lives apart. Once you start a revolution, you start a fire in the people and you can't control where that fire will burn. There will be pain and agony on all sides. There always is."

His shrug was elaborate on purpose. "There was pain and agony that night twenty-five years ago when my mother and my father were killed by the Granvillis. When I and my brothers and sisters were spirited off into the night and told to forget we were royal. In one fire-ravaged night, we lost our home, our kingdom, our destiny and our parents." His head went back and he winced as though the pain was still fresh. "What do you want me to do? Forgive those who did that to me and mine?"

A look of pure determination froze his face into the mask of a warrior. "I'll never do that. They need to pay."

She winced. Fear gripped her heart. She knew what this meant. Her own beloved father was counted among Monte's enemies. But she also knew that he was strong and determined, and he meant what he threatened. Wasn't there any way she could stop this from happening?

The entry gong sounded, making them both jump.

"Yes?" she called out, hiding her alarm.

"Excuse me, Miss Marallis," a voice called in. "It's Sergeant Fromer. I just wanted to check what time you wanted us to bring the tiara by."

"The guard," she whispered, looking at Monte sharply. "I should ask him in right now."

He held her gaze. "But you won't," he said softly.

She stared at him for a long moment. She wanted with all her heart to prove him wrong. She should do it. It would be so easy, wouldn't it?

"Miss?" the guard called in again.

"Uh, sorry, Sergeant Fromer." She looked at Monte again and knew she wouldn't do it. She shook her head, ashamed of herself. "About seven would be best," she called to him. "The hairdresser should be here by then."

"Will do. Thank you, miss."

And he was gone, carrying with him all hope for sanity. She stared at the area of the gate.

There it was—another chance to do the right thing and rid herself of this menace to her peace of mind forever. Why couldn't she follow through? She turned and looked at Monte, her heart sinking. Was she doomed? Not if she stayed strong. This couldn't be like it was before. She'd been vulnerable the last time. She'd just had the horrible fight with her father that she had been dreading for years, and when Monte had jumped into her life, she was in the mood to do dangerous things.

The first time she'd seen him, he'd appeared seemingly out of nowhere and found her sobbing beside her fountain. She'd just come back to her chambers from that fight and she'd been sick at heart, hating that she'd hurt the man she loved most in the world—her father. And so afraid that she would have to do what he wanted her to do anyway.

Her father's health had begun to fade at that point, but he wasn't bedridden yet, as he was now. He'd summoned her to his room and told her in no uncertain terms that he expected her to marry Leonardo. And she'd told him in similar fashion that she would have to be dragged kicking and screaming to the altar. No other way would work. He'd called her an ungrateful child and had brought up the fact that she was looking to be an old maid soon if she didn't get herself a husband. She'd called him an overbearing parent and threatened to marry the gardener.

That certainly got a response, but it was mainly negative and she regretted having said such a thing now. But he'd been passionate, almost obsessive about the need for her to marry Leonardo.

"Marry the man. You've known him all your life. You get along fine. He wants you, and as his wife, you'll have so much power…"

"Power!" she'd responded with disdain. "All you care about is power."

His face had gone white. "Power is important," he told her in a clipped, hard voice. "As much as you may try to pretend otherwise, it rules our lives." And then, haltingly, he'd told her the story of what had happened to her mother—the real story this time, not the one she'd grown up believing.

"Victor Halma wanted her," he said, naming the man who had been the Granvillis' top enforcer when Pellea was a very small child.

"Wha-what do you mean?" she'd stammered. There was a sick feeling in the pit of her stomach and she was afraid she understood only too well.

"He was always searching her out in the halls, showing up unexpectedly whenever she thought she was safe. He wouldn't leave her alone. She was in a panic."

She closed her eyes and murmured, "My poor mother."

"There was still a lot of hostility toward me because I had worked with the DeAngelis royal family before the revolution," he went on. "I wasn't trusted then as I am now. I tried to fight him, but it was soon apparent I had no one on my side." He drew in a deep breath. "I was sent on a business trip to Paris. He made his move while I was gone."

"Father…"

"You see, I had no power." His face, already pale, took on a haggard look. "I couldn't refuse to go. And once I was gone, he forced her to go to his quarters."

Pellea gasped, shivering as though an icy blast had swept into the room.

"She tried to run away, but he had the guard drag her into his chamber and lock her in. And there, while she was waiting, she found a knife and killed herself before he could…" His voice trailed off.

Pellea's hands clutched her throat. "You always told me she died during an influenza epidemic," she choked out. She was overwhelmed with this news, and yet, deep down, she'd always known there was something she wasn't being told.

He nodded. "That was what I told you. That was what I told everyone. And there was an epidemic at the time. But she didn't die of influenza. She died of shame."

Pellea swayed. The room seemed to dip and swerve around her. "And the man?" she asked hoarsely.

"He had an unfortunate accident soon after," her father said dryly, making it clear he wasn't about to go into details. "But you understand me, don't you? You see the position we were in? That's what happens when you don't have power."

"Or when you work for horrible people," she shot back passionately.

Shaking his head, he almost smiled. "The strange thing was, the Granvillis started to trust me after that. I moved up in the ranks. I gained power." He looked at his daughter sternly. "Today, nothing like that could happen to me. And what I want for you is that same sort of immunity from harm."

She understood what he wanted for her. She ached with love for him, ached for what he'd gone through, ached for what her own mother had endured. Her heart broke for them all.

But she still hadn't been able to contemplate marrying Leonardo. Not then.

To some degree, she could relate to his obsession to get and hold power. Still, it was his obsession, not hers and she had no interest in making the sort of down payment on a sense of control that marrying Leonardo would entail.

But this had been the condition she'd been in when she'd first looked up and found Monte standing in her courtyard. She knew she'd never seen him before, and that was unusual. This was a small country and most in the castle had been there for years. You tended to know everyone you ran into, at least by sight. She'd jumped up and looked toward the gate, as though to run.

But he'd smiled. Something in that smile captivated her every time, and it had all begun that afternoon.

"Hi," he'd said. "I'm running from some castle guards. Mind if I hide in here?"

Even as he spoke, she heard the guards at the gate. And just that quickly, she became a renegade.

"Hurry, hide in there," she'd said, pointing to her bedroom. "Behind the bookcase." She'd turned toward the gate. "I'll deal with the guards."

And so began her life as an accomplice to a criminal—and so also her infatuation with the most wrong man she could have fallen in love with.

Monte didn't really appreciate the effort all this had cost her. He'd taken it for granted that she would send the guard away. She'd done the same thing the last time he was here—and that had been more dangerous for them both—because they'd already seen him in the halls at that point. The whole castle was turned upside down for the next two days as they hunted for him. And the entire time, she'd had him hidden in her bedroom.

No one knew he was here now except Pellea—so far.

"Was that the DeAngelis tiara you were talking about just now?" he asked her. "I thought I heard Leonardo bring it up."

She glared at him. "How long have you been here spying on me? What else did you hear?"

He raised an eyebrow. "What else didn't you want me to hear?"

She threw her hands up.

"Don't worry," he said. "The wedding-dress-design discussion and your talk with Leonardo were about it."

They both turned to look at the beautiful gown hanging against a tall, mahogany wardrobe. "Is this the gown you're wearing to the ball tonight?"

"Yes."

It was stunning. Black velvet swirled against deep green satin. It hung before him looking as though it was already filled with a warm, womanly body. Reaching out, he spanned the waist of it with his hands and imagined dancing with her.

"The DeAngelis tiara will look spectacular with this," he told her.

"Do you remember what it looks like?" she asked in surprise.

"Not in great detail. But I've seen pictures." He gave her a sideways look of irony. "My mother's tiara."

She shivered, pulling her arms in close about her. "It hasn't been your mother's tiara for a long, long time," she said, wishing she didn't sound so defensive.

He nodded slowly. "My mother's and that of every

other queen of Ambria going back at least three centuries," he added softly, almost to himself.

She shivered again. "I'm sure you're right."

His smile was humorless. "To the victor go the spoils."

"I didn't make the rules." Inside, she groaned. Still defensive. But she did feel the guilt of the past. How could she not?

"And yet, it will take more than twenty-five years to erase the memories that are centuries old. Memories of what my family accomplished here."

She bit her lip, then looked at him, looked at the sense of tragedy in his beautiful blue eyes, and felt the tug on her heart.

"I'm sorry," she said quickly, reaching for him and putting a hand on his upper arm. "I'm sorry that I have to wear your mother's tiara. They've asked me to do it and I said yes."

He covered her hand with his own and turned toward her. She recognized the light in his eyes and knew he wanted to kiss her. Her pulse raced, but she couldn't let it happen. Quickly, she pulled away.

He sighed, shaking his head in regret, but his mind was still on something else.

"Where is it?" he asked, looking around the wardrobe. "Where do you keep it?"

"The tiara?" She searched his eyes. What was he thinking? "It's in its case in the museum room, where it always is. Didn't you hear Sergeant Fromer? The guards will bring it to me just before I leave for the ball. And they will accompany me to the ballroom. The tiara is under guard at all times."

He nodded, eyeing her speculatively. "And so shall you be, once you put it on."

"I imagine so."

He nodded again, looking thoughtful. "I was just reading an article about it the other day," he said, half musing. "Diamonds, rubies, emeralds, all huge and of superior quality. Not to mention the wonderful craftsmanship of the tiara itself. It's estimated to be worth more than some small countries are."

Suddenly she drew her breath in. She hadn't known him long, but she was pretty sure she knew a certain side of him all too well.

"Oh, no you don't!" she cried, all outrage.

He looked at her in surprise. "What?"

She glared at him. "You're thinking about grabbing it, aren't you?"

"The tiara?" He stared at her for a moment and then he threw his head back and laughed. That was actually a fabulous idea. He liked the way she thought.

"Pellea," he said, taking her by the shoulders and dropping a kiss on her forehead. "You are perfection itself. You can't marry Leonardo."

She shivered. She couldn't help it. His touch was like agony and ecstasy, all rolled into one. But she kept her head about her.

"Who shall I marry then?" she responded quickly. "Are you ready to give me an offer?"

He stared at her, not responding. How could he say

anything? He couldn't make her an offer. He couldn't marry her. And anyway, he might be dead by the end of the summer.

Besides, there was another factor. If he was going to be ruler of Ambria, could he marry the daughter of his family's biggest betrayer? Not likely.

"I think kidnapping will work out better," he told her, and he wasn't joking.

She'd known he would say that, or something similar. She knew he was attracted to her. That, he couldn't hide. But she was a realist and she also knew he hated her father and the current regime with which she was allied. How could it be any other way? He could talk about taking her with him all he wanted, she knew there was no future for her there.

"I'll fight you all the way," she said flatly.

He smiled down into her fierce eyes. "There's always the best option, of course."

"And what is that?"

"That you come with me willingly."

She snorted. "Right. Before or after I marry Leonardo?"

He looked pained. "I can't believe you're serious."

She raised her chin and glared at him. "I am marrying Leonardo in four days. I hope."

He brushed the stray hairs back off her cheek and his fingers lingered, caressing her silken skin. "But why?" he asked softly.

"Because I want to," she responded stoutly. "I've promised I will do it and I mean to keep that promise."

Resolutely, she turned away from him and began searching through a clothes rack, looking for the clothes she meant to change into.

He came up behind her. "Is it because of your father?"

She whirled and stared at him. "Leave my father out of this."

"Ah-hah. So it is your father."

She turned back to searching through the hangers. He watched her for a moment, thinking that he'd never known a woman whose movements were so fluid. Every move she made was almost a part of a dance. And watching her turned him on in ways that were bound to cripple his ability to think clearly. He shook his head. He couldn't let that happen, not if he wanted to succeed here.

"Leonardo," he scoffed. "Please. Why Leonardo?"

Unconsciously, she cupped her hand over her belly. There was a tiny baby growing inside. He must never know that. He was the last person she could tell—ever. "It's my father's fondest wish."

"Because he might become ruler of Ambria?"

"Yes." How could she deny it? "And because he asked."

That set him back a moment. "What if I asked?" he ventured.

She turned to him, but his eyes showed nothing that could give her any hope. "Ah, but you won't, will you?"

He looked away. "Probably not."

"There's your answer."

"Where is Georges?" he asked, naming the Granvilli who had killed his parents. "What does he say about all this?"

She hesitated, choosing her words carefully. "The General seems to be unwell right now. I'm not sure what the specific problem is, but he's resting in the seaside villa at Grapevine Bay. Leonardo has been taking over more and more of the responsibilities of power himself." She raised her head and looked him squarely in the eye. "And the work seems to suit him."

"Does it? I hope he's enjoying himself. He won't have much longer to do that, as I intend to take that job away from him shortly."

She threw up her hands, not sure if he meant it or if this was just typical male bombast. "What exactly do you mean to do?" she asked, trying to pin him down.

He looked at her and smiled, coming closer, touching her hair with one hand.

"Nothing that you need to worry about."

But his thoughts were not nearly as sanguine as he pretended. She really had no conception of how deep his anger lay and how his hatred had eaten away at him for most of his life. Ever since that night when the castle had burned and his parents were murdered by the Granvilli clan. Payment was due. Retribution was pending.

"Is your father really very ill?" he asked quietly.

"Yes." She found the shirt she wanted and pulled it down.

"And you want to make him happy before he…"

He swallowed his next words even before she snapped her head around and ordered curtly, "Don't say it!"

He bit his tongue. That was a stupid thing to have thought, even if he never actually got the words out. He didn't mind annoying her about things he didn't think she should care so much about, but to annoy her about her father was just plain counterproductive.

"Well, he would like to see you become the future first lady of the land, wouldn't he?" he amended lamely.

He tried to think of what he knew about her father. Marallis had been considered an up-and-coming advisor in his own father's regime. From what he'd been able to glean, the king had recognized his superior abilities and planned to place him in a top job. And then the rebellion had swept over them, and it turned out Vaneck Marallis had signed on with the other side. Was it any wonder he should feel betrayed by the man? He was the enemy. He very likely gave the rebels the inside information they needed to win the day. There was no little corner of his heart that had any intention of working on forgiveness for the man.

"Okay, it's getting late," she said impatiently. "I have to go check on my father."

"Because he's ill?"

"Because he's very ill." She knew she needed to elaborate, but when she tried to speak, her throat choked and she had to pause, waiting for her voice to clear again. "I always go in to see him for a few minutes at this time in the afternoon." She looked at him. "When I get back, we'll have to decide what I'm going to do with you."

"Will we?" His grin was ample evidence of his opinion on the matter, but she turned away and didn't bother to challenge him.

Going to her clothes rack, she pulled out a trim, cream-colored linen suit with slacks and a crisp jacket and slipped behind a privacy screen to change into them. He watched as she emerged, looking quietly efficient and good at whatever job she might be attempting. And ravishingly beautiful at the same time. He'd never known another woman who impressed him as much as this one did. Once again he had a pressing urge to find a way to take her with him.

It wouldn't be impossible. She thought he would have to get her past the guards, but she was wrong. He had his own way into the castle and he could easily get her out. But only if she was at least halfway cooperative. It was up to him to convince her to be.

"I don't have time to decide what to do with you right now," she told him, her gaze hooded as she met his eyes. "I have to go check on my father, and it's getting late. You stay here and hold down the fort. I'll be back in about half an hour."

"I may be here," he offered casually. "Or not."

She hesitated. She didn't like that answer. "Tell me now, are you going to stay here and wait, or are you going to go looking for Leonardo and get killed?" she demanded of him.

He laughed shortly. "I think I can handle myself around your so-called fiancé," he said dismissively

Her gaze sharpened and she looked seriously into his

eyes. "Watch out for Leonardo. He'll kill you without batting an eye."

"Are you serious? That prancing prig?"

She shook her head. "Don't be fooled by his veneer of urbanity. He's hard as nails. When I suggested you might be killed, I meant it."

He searched her eyes for evidence that she really cared. It was there, much as she tried to hide it. He smiled.

"I'm not too keen on the 'killed' part. But as for the rest…"

She glanced at her watch. Time was fleeting. "I'm running out of time," she told him. "Go out and wait in the courtyard. I just have one last thing to check."

"What's that?" he asked.

She looked pained. "None of your business. I do have my privacy to maintain. Now go out and wait."

He walked out into the lush courtyard and heard the door click shut behind him. Turning, he could see her through the glass door, walking back into her closet again. Probably changed her mind on what to wear, he thought to himself. And he had a twinge of regret. He didn't have all that much time here and he hated to think of missing a moment with her.

Did that mean he'd given up on the kidnapping? No. Not at all. Still, there was more to this trip than just seeing Pellea.

He scanned the courtyard and breathed in the atmosphere. The castle of his ancestors was all around him.

For a few minutes, he thought about his place in history. Would he be able to restore the monarchy? Would he bring his family back to their rightful place, where they should have been all along?

Of course he would. He didn't allow doubts. His family belonged here and he would see that it happened. He'd already found two of his brothers, part of the group of "Lost Royals" who had escaped when the castle was burned and had hidden from the wrath of the Granvillis ever since. There were two more brothers and two sisters he hadn't found yet. But he hoped to. He hoped to bring them all back here to Ambria by the end of the summer.

He turned and looked through the French doors into her bedroom and saw the huge, soft bed where he'd spent most of the two and a half days when he'd been here before. Memories flooded back. He remembered her and her luscious body and he groaned softly, feeling the surge of desire again.

Pellea was special. He couldn't remember another woman who had ever stuck in his mind the way she did. She'd embedded herself into his heart, his soul, his imagination, and he didn't even want to be free of her. And that was a revelation.

If he survived this summer…

No, he couldn't promise anything, not even to himself. After all, her father was the man who had betrayed his family. He couldn't let himself forget that.

But where was she? She'd been gone a long time. He turned back and looked at the closed doors to her dressing room, then moved to them and called softly, "Pellea."

There was no response.

"Pellea?"

Still nothing. He didn't want to make his call any louder. You never knew who might be at the gate or near enough to it to hear his voice. He tried the knob instead, pushing the door open a bit and calling again, "Pellea?"

There was no answer. It was quite apparent she wasn't there.

CHAPTER THREE

ALARM BELLS RANG IN Monte's head and adrenaline flooded his system. Where had she gone? How had she escaped without him seeing her? What was she doing? Had he overestimated his ability to charm, compared to Leonardo's ability to hand out a power position? Was she a traitor, just like her father?

All that flashed through his mind, sending him reeling. But that only lasted seconds before he'd dismissed it out of hand. She wouldn't do that. There had to be a reason.

The last he'd seen of her she was heading into her large, walk-in closet at the far side of the dressing room. He was there in two strides, and that is when he saw, behind a clothing bar loaded with fluffy gowns, the glimmer of something electronic just beyond a door that had been left slightly ajar.

A secret room behind the clothing storage. Who knew? He certainly hadn't known anything about it when he'd been here before.

Reaching in through the gowns, he pushed the door fully open. And there was Pellea, sitting before a large computer screen that was displaying a number of windows, all showing places in the castle itself. She had a whole command center in here.

"Why you little vixen," he said, astounded. "What do you have here? You've tapped into a gold mine."

She looked up at him, startled, and then resigned.

"I knew I should have closed that door all the way," she muttered to herself.

But he was still captured by the computer screen. "This is the castle security system, isn't it?"

She sighed. "Yes. You caught me."

He shook his head, staring at the screen. "How did you do that?" he asked in wonder.

She shrugged. "My father had this secret room installed years ago. Whenever he wanted to take a look at what was going on, he came to me for a visit. I didn't use it myself at first. I didn't see any need for it. But lately, I've found it quite handy."

"And you can keep things running properly on your own?"

"I've got a certain amount of IT talent. I've read a few books."

He looked at her and smiled. "My admiration grows."

She colored a bit and looked away.

"So you can see what's going on at all the major interior intersections, and a few of the outside venues as well. How convenient." His mind was racing with possibilities.

She pushed away from the desk and sighed again. "Monte, I shouldn't have let you see this."

"You didn't let me. I did it all on my own." He shook his head, still impressed. "Are you going to tell me why?"

She sighed again. "There are times when one might want to do things without being observed. Here in the castle, someone is always watching." She shrugged. "I like a little anonymity in my life. This way I can get a pretty good idea of who is doing what and I can bide my time."

"I see."

She rose and turned toward the door. "And now I really am late." She looked back. He followed her out reluctantly and she closed the door carefully. It seemed to disappear into the background of paneling and molding strips that surrounded it.

"See you later," she said, leading him away from the area. "And stay out of that room."

He frowned as she started off. He didn't want her to leave, and he also didn't want to miss out on anything he didn't have to. On impulse, he called after her, "I want to go with you."

She whirled and stared at him. "What?"

"I'd like to see your father."

She came back towards him, shocked and looking for a way to refuse. "But you can't. He's bedridden. He's in no condition…"

"I won't show myself to him. I won't hurt him." He shook his head and frowned. "But, Pellea, he's one of the few remaining ties to my parents left alive. He's from their generation. He knew them, worked with them. He was close to them at one time." He shrugged, looking oddly vulnerable in his emotional reactions. "I just want to see him, hear his voice. I promise I won't do anything to jeopardize his health—or even his emotional well-being in any way."

She studied him and wondered what she really knew about him. The way he felt about her father had been clear almost from the first. He was wrong about her father. She'd spent a lot of time agonizing over that, wondering how she could make him understand that her father was just a part of his time and place, that he had only done what he had to do, that he was really a man of great compassion and honesty. Maybe this would be a chance to do just that.

"You won't confront him about anything?"

"No. I swear." He half smiled. "I swear on my parents' memories. Do you trust me?"

She groaned. "God help me, I do." She searched his eyes. "All right. But you'll have to be careful. If you're caught, I'll claim you forced me to take you with me."

He smiled at her sideways, knowing she was lying. If he were caught, she would do her best to free him. She talked a good game, but deep down, she had a lot of integrity. And she was at least half in love with him. That gave him a twinge. More the fool was she.

"I only go when no one else is there," she was telling him. "I know when the nurse goes on her break and how long she takes."

He nodded. He'd always known she was quick and

sure at everything she did. He would have expected as much from her.

"Keep your eyes downcast," she lectured as they prepared to head into the hallway. "I try to go at a quiet time of day, but there might be someone in the halls. Don't make eye contact with anyone or you'll surely blow your cover. You can't help but look regal, can you? Take smaller steps. Try to slump your shoulders a little. A little more." She made a face. "Here." She whacked one shoulder to make it droop, and then the other, a tiny smile on her lips. "That's better," she said with satisfaction.

He was suspicious. She hadn't held back much. "You enjoyed that, didn't you?"

"Giving you a whack?" She allowed herself a tight smile. "Certainly not. I don't believe in corporal punishment."

"Liar." He was laughing at her. "Are you going to try to convince me that it hurt you more than it hurt me?"

She didn't bother to respond. Giving him a look, she stepped out into the hallway, wondering if she was crazy to do this. But she was being honest when she said she trusted him to come along and see her father with her. Was she letting her heart rule her head? Probably. But she'd made her decision and she would stick to it.

Still, that didn't mean she was sanguine about it all. Why had he come back? Why now, just when she had everything set the way it had to be?

And why was her heart beating like a caged bird inside her chest? It didn't matter that she loved him. She couldn't ever be with him again. She had a baby to think about. And no time to indulge in emotions. Taking Monte with her was a risk, but she didn't really have a lot of choice—unless she wanted to turn him in to the guard.

She thought about doing exactly that for a few seconds, a smile playing on her lips. That would take them back full circle, wouldn't it? But it wasn't going to happen.

Don't worry, sweet baby, she said silently to her child. *I won't let anything hurt your father.* She said a tiny prayer and added, *I hope.*

Monte wasn't often haunted by self-doubt. In fact, his opinions and decisions were usually rock-solid. Once made, no wavering. But watching Pellea with her father gave him a sense that the earth might not be quite as firm under his feet as he'd assumed.

In the first place, he wasn't really sure why she'd let him come with her. She knew how the need for retribution burned in him and yet she'd let him come here where he would have a full view of the man, his enemy, lying there, helpless. Didn't she know how dangerous that was?

It would be easy to harm the old man. He was still handsome in an aged, fragile way, like a relic of past power. His face was drawn and lined, his color pale, his thin hair silver. Blue veins stood out in his slender hands. He was so vulnerable, so completely defenseless. Someone who moved on pure gut reaction would have done him in by now. Luckily, that wasn't Monte's style.

He would never do such a thing, but she didn't really know that. She'd taken a risk. But for what?

He watched as the object of his long, deep hatred struggled to talk to the daughter he obviously loved more than life itself, and he found his emotions tangling a bit. Could he really feel pity for a man who had helped ruin his family?

No. That couldn't happen.

Still, an element confused the issue. And to be this close to someone who had lived with and worked with his parents gave him a special sense of his own history. He couldn't deny that.

And there was something else, a certain primal longing that he couldn't control. He'd had it ever since that day twenty-five years ago when he'd been rushed out of the burning castle, and he had forever lost his parents. He'd grown up with all the privileges of his class: the schools, the high life, the international relationships. But he would have thrown it all out if that could have bought him a real, loving family—the kind you saw in movies, the kind you dreamed about in the middle of the night. Instead, he had this empty ache in his heart.

And that made watching Pellea and her father all the more effective. From his position in the entryway, he could see her bending lovingly over her father and dropping a kiss on his forehead. She talked softly to him, wiping his forehead with a cool, damp cloth, straightening his covers, plumping his pillow. The love she had for the man radiated from her every move. And he felt very similarly. She was obviously a brilliant bit of sun in his rather dark life.

"How are you feeling?" she asked.

"Much better now that you're here, my dear."

"I'm only here for a moment. I must get back. The masked ball is tonight."

"Ah, yes." He took hold of her hand. "So tonight you and Leonardo will announce your engagement?"

"Yes. Leonardo is prepared."

"What a relief to have this coming so quickly. To be able to see you protected before I go…"

"Don't talk about going."

"We all have to do it, my dear. My time has come."

Pellea made a dove-like noise and bent down to kiss his cheek. "No. You just need to get out more. See some people." Rising a bit, she had a thought. "I know. I'll have the nurse bring you to the ball so that you can see for yourself…."

"Hush, Pellea," he said, shaking his head. "I'm not going anywhere. I'm comfortable here and I'm too weak to leave this bed."

Reluctantly, she nodded. She'd known he would say that, but she'd hoped he might change his mind and try to take a step back into the world. A deep, abiding sadness settled into her soul as she faced the fact that he wasn't even tempted to try. He was preparing for the end, and nothing she said or did would change that. Tears threatened and she forced them back. She would have to save her grieving for another time.

Right now, she had another goal in mind. She was

hoping to prove something to Monte, and she was gambling that her father would respond in the tone and tenor that she'd heard from him so often before. If he went in a different direction, there was no telling what might happen. Glancing back at where Monte stood in the shadows, she made her decision. She was going to risk it—her leap of faith.

"Father, do you ever think of the past? About how we got here and why we are the way we are?"

He coughed and nodded. "I think of very little else these days."

"Do you think about the night the castle burned?"

"That was before you were born."

"Yes. But I feel as though that night molded my life in many ways."

He grasped her hand as though to make her stop it. "But why? It had nothing to do with you."

"But it was such a terrible way to start a new regime, the regime I've lived under all my life."

"Ugly things always happen in war." He turned his face away as though he didn't want to talk about it. "These things can't be helped."

She could feel Monte's anger beginning to simmer even though she didn't look at him. She hesitated. If her father wasn't going to express his remorse, she might only be doing damage by making him talk. Could Monte control his emotions? Was it worth it to push this further?

She had to try. She leaned forward.

"But, Father, you always say so many mistakes were made."

"Mistakes are human. That is just the way it is."

Monte made a sound that was very close to a growl. She shook her head, still unwilling to look his way, but ready to give up. What she'd hoped for just wasn't going to happen.

"All right, Father," she began, straightening and preparing to get Monte out of here before he did something ugly.

But suddenly her father was speaking again. "The burning of the castle was a terrible thing," he was saying, though he was speaking so softly she wondered if Monte could hear him. "And the assassination of the king and queen was even worse."

Relief bloomed in her chest. "What happened?" she prompted him. "How did it get so out of control?"

"You can go into a war with all sorts of lofty ambitions, but once the fuse is lit, the fire can be uncontrollable. It wasn't supposed to happen that way. Many of us were sick at heart for years afterwards. I still think of it with pain and deep, deep regret."

This was more like it. She only hoped Monte could hear it and that he was taking it as a sincere recollection, not a rationalization. She laced her fingers with her father's long, trembling ones.

"Tell me again, why did you sign on with the rebels?"

"I was very callow and I felt the DeAngelis family had grown arrogant with too much power. They were rejecting all forms of modernization. Something was needed to shake the country up. We were impatient. We thought something had to be done."

"And now?"

"Now I think that we should have moved more slowly, attempted dialogue instead of attack."

"So you regret how things developed?"

"I regret it deeply."

She glanced back at Monte. His face looked like a storm cloud. Wasn't he getting it? Didn't he see how her father had suffered as well? Maybe not. Maybe she was tilting at windmills. She turned back to her father and asked a question for herself.

"Then why do you want me to marry Leonardo and just perpetuate this regime?"

Her father coughed again and held a handkerchief to his lips. "He'll be better than his father. He has some good ideas. And your influence on him will work wonders." He managed a weak smile for his beloved daughter. "Once you are married to Leonardo, it will be much more difficult for anyone to hurt you."

She smiled down at him and blotted his forehead with the damp cloth. He wouldn't be so sure of that if he knew that at this very moment, danger lurked around her on all sides. Better he should never know that she was carrying Monte's child.

"I must go, Father. I've got to prepare for the ball."

"Yes. Go, my darling. Have a wonderful time."

"I'll be back in the morning to tell you all about it," she promised as she rose from his side.

She hurried toward the door, jerking her head at Monte to follow. She didn't like the look on his face. It seemed his hatred for her father was too strong for him to see what a dear and wonderful man he really was. Well, so be it. She'd done her best to show him the truth. You could lead a horse to water and all that.

But they were late. She had a path laid out and a routine, and now she knew she was venturing out into the unknown. At her usual time, she never met anyone in the halls. Now—who knew?

"We have to hurry," she said once they were outside the room. She quickly looked up and down the empty hallway. "I've got to meet Leonardo in just a short time." She started off. "Quickly. We don't want to meet anyone if we can help it."

The words were barely out of her mouth when she heard loud footsteps coming from around the bend in the walkway. Only boots could make such a racket. It had to be the guards. It sounded like two of them.

"Quick," she said, reaching for the closest door. "In here."

Though she knew the castle well, she wasn't sure what door she'd reached for. There was a library along this corridor, and a few bedrooms of lower-ranking relatives of the Granvillis. Any one of them could have yielded disaster. But for once, she was in luck. The door she'd chosen opened to reveal a very small broom closet.

Monte looked in and didn't see room for them both. He turned back to tell her, but she wasn't listening.

"In," she whispered urgently, and gave him a shove,

then came pushing in behind him, closing the door as quietly as she could. But was it quietly enough? Pressed close together, they each held their breath, listening as the boots came closer. And closer. And then stopped, right outside the door.

Pellea looked up at Monte, her eyes huge and anxious. He looked down at her and smiled. It was dark in the closet, but enough light came in around the door to let him make out her features. She was so beautiful and so close against him. He wanted to kiss her. But more important things had cropped up. So he reached around her and took hold of the knob from the inside.

There was a muttering conversation they couldn't make out, and then one of the guards tried the knob. Monte clamped down on his lower lip, holding the knob with all his might.

"It's locked," one of the guards said. "We'll have to find the concierge and get a key."

The other guard swore, but they began to drift off, walking slowly this time and chattering among themselves.

Monte relaxed and let go of the knob, letting out a long sigh of relief. When he looked down, she was smiling up at him, and this time he kissed her.

He'd been thinking about this kiss for so long, and now, finally, here it was. Her lips were smooth as silk, warm and inviting, and for just a moment, she opened enough to let his tongue flicker into the heat she held deeper. Then she tried to pull away, but he took her head in his hands and kissed her longer, deeper, and he felt her begin to melt in his arms.

Her body was molded to his and he could feel her heart begin to pound again, just as it had when they'd almost been caught. The excitement lit a flame in him and he pulled her closer, kissed her harder, wanted her all to himself, body and soul.

It was as though he'd forgotten where they were, what was happening around them. But Pellea hadn't.

"Monte," she finally managed to gasp, pushing him as hard as she could. "We have to go while we have the chance!"

He knew she was right and he let her pull away, but reluctantly. Still, he'd found out what he needed to know. The magic still lived between them and they could turn it on effortlessly. And, he hoped, a bit later, they would.

But now she opened the door tentatively and looked out. There was no one in the hall. She slipped out and he followed and they hurried to her gate, alert for any hint of anyone else coming their way. But they were lucky. She used a remote to open the gate as they approached. In seconds, they were safely inside.

The moment the gate closed, Monte turned and tried to take her into his arms again, but she backed away, trying hard to glare at him.

"Just stop it," she told him.

But he was shaking his head. "You can't marry Leonardo. Not when you can kiss me like that."

She stared at him for a moment. How could she have let this happen? He knew, he could tell that she was so in love with him, she could hardly contain it. She could protest all she wanted, he wasn't going to believe her. If she wasn't very careful, he would realize the precious secret that she was keeping from him, and if that happened, they would both be in terrible trouble.

Feeling overwhelmed, she groaned, her head in her hands. "Why are you torturing me like this?

He put a finger under her chin and forced her head up to meet his gaze. "Maybe a little torture will make you see the light."

"There's no light," she said sadly, her eyes huge with tragedy. "There's only darkness."

He'd been about to try to kiss her again, but something in her tone stopped him and he hesitated. Just a few weeks before, their relationship had been light and exciting, a romp despite the dangers they faced. They had made love, but they had also laughed a lot, and teased and played and generally enjoyed each other. Something had changed since then. Was it doubt? Wariness? Or fear?

He wasn't sure, but it bothered him and it held him off long enough for her to pivot out of his control.

"Gotta go," she said as she started for the gate, prepared to dash off again.

He took a step after her. "You're not planning to tell Leonardo I'm here, are you?" he said. His tone was teasing, as though he was confident she had no such plans.

She turned and looked at him, tempted to do or say something that would shake that annoying surety he had.

But she resisted that temptation. Instead, she told the truth.

"I'm hoping you won't be here any longer by the time I get back."

He appeared surprised. "Where would I go?"

She shook her head. It was obviously no use to try, but she had to make her case quickly and clearly. "Please, Monte," she said earnestly. "Go back the way you came in. Just do this for me. It will make my life a whole lot easier."

"Pellea, this is not your problem. I'll handle it."

She half laughed at his confidence. "What do you mean, not my problem? That's exactly what you are. My problem."

"Relax," he advised. "I'm just going to work on my objective."

"Which is?"

"I told you. I'm here to kidnap you and take you back to the continent with me."

"Oh, get off it. You can't kidnap me. I'm guarded day and night."

"Really? Well, where were your wonderful guards when I found my way into your chambers?"

She didn't have an answer for that one so she changed the subject. "What's the point? Why would you kidnap me?"

He shrugged. "To show them I can."

She threw up her hands. "Oh, brother."

"I want to show the Granvillis that I've been here and taken something precious to them."

Her eyes widened. "You think I'm precious?"

His smile was almost too personal. "I know you are. You're their most beautiful, desirable woman."

That gave her pause. Was she supposed to feel flattered by that? Well, she sort of did, but she wouldn't admit it.

"Gee, thanks. You make me feel like a prize horse." She shook her head. "So to you, this is just part of some war game?"

The laughter left his gaze. "Oh, no. This is no game. This is deadly serious."

There was something chilling in the way he said that. She shivered and tried to pretend she hadn't.

"So you grab me. You throw me over your shoulder and carry me back to your cave. You go 'nah nah nah' to the powers that be in Ambria." She shrugged. "What does that gain you?"

He watched her steadily, making her wonder what he saw. "The purpose is not just to thumb my nose at the Granvillis. The purpose is to cast them into disarray, to make them feel vulnerable and stupid. To throw them off their game. Let them spend their time obsessing on how I could have possibly gotten into the castle, how I could have possibly taken you out without someone seeing. Let them worry. It will make them weaker."

"You're crazy," she said for lack of anything else to say. And he was crazy if he thought the Granvillis would tumble into ruin because of a kidnapping or two.

"I'd like to see them tightening their defenses all around," he went on, "and begin scurrying about, looking for the chinks in their armor. There are people here who watch what they do and report to us. This will give us a better idea of where the weak spots are."

She nodded. She understood the theory behind all this. But it didn't make her any happier with it.

"So when you get right down to it, it doesn't have to be me," she noted. "You could take back something else of importance. The tiara, for instance."

Something moved behind his eyes, but he only smiled. "I'd rather take you."

"Well, you're not going to. So why not just get out of my hair and go back where you came from?"

He shook his head slowly, his blue eyes dark with shadows. "Sorry, Pellea. I've got things I must do here."

She sighed. She knew exactly what he would be doing while she was gone. He would be in her secret room, checking out what was going on all over the castle. Making his plans. Ruining her life. A wave of despair flooded through her. What had she done? Why hadn't she been more careful?

"Arrgghh!" she said, making a small wail of agony.

But right now she couldn't think about that. She had to go meet Leonardo or he would show up here.

"You stay out of my closet room," she told him with a warning look, knowing he wouldn't listen to a word she said. "Okay?" She glared at him, not bothering to wait for an answer. "I'll be back quicker than you think."

He laughed, watching her go, enjoying the way her

hips swayed in time with her gorgeous hair. And then she was gone and he headed straight for the closet.

To the casual eye, there was nothing of note to suggest a door to another room. The wall seemed solid enough. He tried to remember what she'd done to close it, but he hadn't been paying attention at the time. There had to be something—a special knock or a latch or a pressure point. He banged and pushed and tried to slide things, but nothing gave way.

"If this needs a magic password, I'm out of luck," he muttered to himself as he made his various attempts.

He kicked a little side panel, more in frustration than hope, and the door began to creak open. "It's always the ones you don't suspect," he said, laughing.

The small room inside was unprepossessing, having space only for a computer and a small table. And there on the screen was access to views of practically every public area, all over the castle. A secret room with centralized power no one else knew about. Ingenious.

Still, someone had built it. Someone had wired it. Someone had to know electronics were constantly running in here. The use of electricity alone would tip off the suspicious. So someone in the workings of the place was on her side.

But what was "her side" exactly? That was something he still had to find out.

The sound of Pellea's entry gong made him jerk. He lifted his head and listened. A woman's voice seemed to be calling out, and then, a moment later, singing. She'd obviously come into the courtyard.

Moving silently, he made his way out of the secret room, closing the door firmly. He moved carefully into the dressing area, planning to use the high wardrobe as a shield as he had done earlier, in order to see who it was without being seen. As he came out of the closet and made his way to slip behind the tall piece of furniture, a pretty, pleasantly rounded young woman stepped into the room, catching sight of him just before he found his hiding place.

She gasped. Their gazes met. Her mouth opened. He reached out to stop her, but he was too late.

She screamed at the top of her lungs.

CHAPTER FOUR

MONTE MOVED LIKE LIGHTNING but it felt like slow motion to him. In no time his hand was over the intruder's mouth and he was pulling her roughly into the room and kicking the French door closed with such a snap, he was afraid for a moment that the glass would crack.

Pulling her tightly against his chest, he snarled in her ear, "Shut the hell up and do it now."

She pulled her breath into her lungs in hysterical gasps, and he yanked her more tightly.

"Now!" he demanded.

She closed her eyes and tried very hard. He could feel the effort she put into it, and he began to relax. They waited, counting off the seconds, to see if anyone had heard the scream and was coming to the rescue. Nothing seemed to stir. At last, he decided the time for alarm was over and he began to release her slowly, ready to reassert control if she tried to scream again.

"Okay," he whispered close to her ear. "I'm going to let go now. If you make a sound, I'll have to knock you flat."

She nodded, accepting his terms. But she didn't seem

to have any intention of a repeat. As he freed her, she turned, her gaze sweeping over him in wonder.

"Wait," she said, eyes like saucers. "I've seen you before. You were here a couple of months ago."

By now, he'd recognized her as well. She was Pellea's favorite maid. He hadn't interacted with her when he'd been here before, but he'd seen her when she'd dropped by to deal with some things Pellea needed done. Pellea had trusted her to keep his presence a secret then. He only hoped that trust was warranted—and could hold for now.

But signs were good. He liked the sparkle in her eyes. He gave her a lopsided smile. "I'm back."

"So I see." She cocked her head to the side, looking him over, then narrowing her gaze. "And is my mistress happy that you're here?"

He shrugged. "Hard to tell. But she didn't throw anything at me."

Her smile was open-hearted. "That's a good sign."

He drew in a deep breath, feeling better about the situation. "What's your name?" he asked.

"Pellea calls me Kimmee."

"Then I shall do the same." He didn't offer his own name and wondered if she knew who he was. He doubted it. Pellea wouldn't be that reckless, would she?

"I've been here for a couple of hours now," he told her. "Pellea has seen me. We've been chatting, going over old times."

Kimmee grinned. "Delightful."

He smiled back, but added a warning look. "I'm

sure you don't talk about your mistress's assignations to others."

"Of course not," she said brightly. "I only wish she had a few."

He blinked. "What do you mean?"

She shrugged, giving him a sly look. "You're the only one I know of."

He laughed. She had said the one thing that would warm his heart and she probably knew it, but it made him happy anyway.

"You're not trying to tell me your mistress has no suitors, are you?" he teased skeptically.

"Oh, no, of course not. But she generally scorns them all."

He looked at her levelly. "Even Leonardo?" he asked.

She hesitated, obviously reluctant to give her candid opinion on that score. He let her off the hook with a shrug.

"Never mind. I know she's promised to him at this point." He cocked an eyebrow. "I just don't accept it."

She nodded. "Good," she whispered softly, then shook her head as though wishing she hadn't spoken. Turning away, she reached for the ball gown hanging in front of the wardrobe. "I just came by to check that the gown was properly hung and wrinkle-free," she said, smoothing the skirt a bit. "Isn't it gorgeous?"

"Yes, it is."

"I can't wait to see her dancing in this," Kimmee added.

"Neither can I," he murmured, and at the same time, an idea came to him. He frowned, wondering if he should trust thoughts spurred on by his overwhelming desire for all things Pellea. It was a crazy idea, but the more he mulled it over, the more he realized it could serve more than one purpose and fit into much of what he hoped to accomplish. So why not give it a try?

He studied the pretty maid for a moment, trying to evaluate just how much he dared depend on her. Her eyes sparkled in a way that made him wonder how a fun-loving girl like this would keep such a secret. He knew he had better be prepared to deal with the fallout, should there be any. After all, he didn't have much choice. Either he would tie her up and gag her and throw her into a closet, or he would appeal to her better nature.

"Tell me, Kimmee, do you love your mistress?"

"Oh, yes." Kimmee smiled. "She's my best friend. We've been mates since we were five years old."

He nodded, frowning thoughtfully. "Then you'll keep a secret," he said. "A secret that could get me killed if you reveal it."

Her eyes widened and she went very still. "Of course."

His own gaze was hard and assessing as he pinned her with it. "You swear on your honor?"

She shook her head, looking completely earnest. "I swear on my honor. I swear on my life. I swear on my…"

He held a hand up. "I get the idea, Kimmee. You really mean it. So I'm going to trust you."

She waited, wide-eyed.

He looked into her face, his own deadly serious.

"I want to go to the ball."

"Oh, sir!" She threw her hands up to her mouth. "Oh, my goodness! Where? How?"

"That's where you come in. Find me a costume and a nice, secure mask." He cocked an eyebrow and smiled at her. "Can you do that?"

"Impossible," she cried. "Simply impossible." But a smile was beginning to tease the corners of her mouth. "Well, maybe." She thought a moment longer, then smiled impishly. "It would be fun, wouldn't it?"

He grinned at her.

"Will you want a sword?" she asked, her enthusiasm growing by leaps and bounds.

He grimaced. "I think not. It might be too tempting to use it on Leonardo."

"I know what you mean," she said, nodding wisely.

He got a real kick out of her. She was so ready to join in on his plans and at the same time, she seemed to be thoroughly loyal to the mistress she considered her best friend. It was a helpful combination to work with.

He lifted his head, looking at the ball gown and thinking of how it would look with his favorite woman filling it out in all the right places. "All I want to do is go to the ball and dance with Pellea."

"How romantic," Kimmee said, sighing. Then her gaze sharpened as she realized what he might be describing. "You mean…?"

"Yes." He nodded. "Secretly. I want to surprise Pellea."

Kimmee gave a bubbling laugh, obviously delighted with the concept. "I think Leonardo will be even more surprised."

He shook his head and gave her a warning look. "That is something I'll have to guard against."

She sighed. "I understand. But it would be fun to see his face."

He frowned, wondering if he was letting her get a little too much into this.

"See what you can do," he said. "But don't forget. If Leonardo finds out…" He drew his finger across his throat like a knife and made a cutting sound. "I'll be dead and Pellea will be in big trouble."

She shook her head, eyes wide and sincere. "You can count on me, sir. And as for the costume…" She put her hand over her heart. "I'll do my best."

Pellea returned a half hour later, bristling with determination.

"I've brought you something to eat," she said, handing him a neatly wrapped, grilled chicken leg and a small loaf of artisan bread. He was sitting at a small table near her fountain, looking for all the world like a Parisian playboy at a sidewalk café. "And I've brought you news."

"News, huh? Let me guess." He put his hand to his forehead as though taking transmissions from space.

"Leonardo has decided to join the national ballet and forget all about this crazy marriage stuff. Am I right?"

She glared at him. "I'm warning you, don't take the man lightly."

"Oh, I don't. Believe me." He began to unwrap the chicken leg. He hadn't eaten for hours and he was more than ready to partake of what she'd brought him. "So what is the news?"

"Leonardo talked to his father and we've decided to move the wedding up." Her chin rose defiantly. "We're getting married in two days."

He put down the chicken leg, hunger forgotten, and stared at her with eyes that had turned icy silver. "What's the rush?" he asked with deceptive calm.

The look in his gaze made her nervous. He seemed utterly peaceful, and yet there was a sense in the air that a keg of dynamite was about to blow.

She turned away, pacing, thinking about how nice and simple life had been before she'd found him lurking in her garden that day. Her path had been relatively clear at the time. True, she had been fighting her father over his wish that she marry Leonardo. But that was relatively easy to deal with compared to what she had now.

The irony was that her father would get his wish, and she'd done it to herself. She would marry Leonardo. She would be the first lady of the land and just about impervious to attack. Just as her father so obsessively craved, she would be as safe as she could possibly be.

But even that wasn't perfect safety. There were a thousand chinks in her armor and the path ahead was perilous. Everything she did, every decision she made, could have unforeseen repercussions. She had set a course and now the winds would take her to her destination. Was it the best destination for her or was it a mirage? Was she right or was she wrong? If only she knew.

Looking out into the courtyard, Pellea shivered with a premonition of what might be to come.

Monte watched her from under lowered brows, munching on a bite of chicken. Much as she was trying to hide it, he could see that she was in a special sort of agony and he couldn't for the life of him understand why. What was her hurry to marry Leonardo? What made her so anxious to cement those ties?

Motivations were often difficult to untangle and understand. What were hers? Did it really mean everything to her to have her father satisfied that she was safe, and to do it before it was too late? Evidence did suggest that he was fading fast. Was that what moved her? He couldn't think what else it could be. But was that really enough to make her rush to Leonardo's arms? Or was there something going on that he didn't know about?

"I suppose the powers that be are in favor of this wedding?" he mentioned casually.

She nodded. "Believe me, everything around here is planned to the nth degree. Public-relations values hold sway over everything."

"I've noticed. That's what makes me wonder. What's the deal with this wedding coming on so suddenly? I would think the regime would try to milk all the publicity they could possibly get out of a long engagement."

"Interesting theory," she said softly, pretending to be busy folding clothes away.

"Why?" he asked bluntly. "Why so soon?"

"You'd have to ask Leonardo about that," she said evasively.

"Maybe I will. If I get the chance." He looked at her sharply, trying to read her mind. "I can't help but think he has a plan in mind. There has to be a reason."

"Sometimes people just want to do things quickly," she said, getting annoyed with his persistence.

"Um-hmm." He didn't buy that for a minute. The more he let the idea of such a marriage—the ultimate marriage of convenience—linger in his mind, the more he hated it. Pellea couldn't be with Leonardo. Everything in him rebelled at the thought.

Pellea belonged to him.

That was nonsense, of course. How could she be his when he wouldn't do what needed to be done to take that responsibility in hand himself? After all, he'd refused to step up and do the things a man did when making a woman his own. As his old tutor might say, he craved the honey but refused to tend to the bees.

Still in some deep, gut-level part of him, she was his and had been since the moment he'd first laid eyes on her. He'd put his stamp on her, his brand, his seal. He'd held her and loved her, body and soul, and he wanted her available for more of the same. She was his, damn it!

But what was he prepared to do about it?

That was the question.

He watched her, taking in the grace and loveliness of her form and movement, the full, luscious temptation of her exciting body, the beauty of her perfect face, and the question burned inside him. What was he prepared to do? It was working into a drumbeat in his head and in his heart. What? Just exactly what?

"You don't love him."

The words came out loud and clear and yet he was surprised when he said them. He hadn't planned to say anything of the sort. Still, once it was out, he was glad he'd said it. The truth was out now, like a flag, a banner, a warning that couldn't be ignored any longer. And why not? Truth was supposed to set you free.

And she didn't love Leonardo. It was obvious in the way she talked to him and talked about him. She was using him and he was using her. They had practically said as much in front of him—though neither had known it at the time. Why not leave it out there in the open where it could be dealt with?

"You don't love him," he said again, even more firmly this time.

She whirled to face him, her arms folded, her eyes flashing. "How do you know?" she challenged, her chin high.

A slow smile began to curl his lips. As long as they were speaking truth, why not add a bit more?

"I know, Pellea. I know very well. Because…" He paused, not really for dramatic effect, although that was what he ended up with. He paused because for just a second, he wondered if he really dared say this.

"Because you love me," he said at last.

The shock of his words seemed to crackle in the air.

She gasped. "Oh! Of all the…" Her cheeks turned bright red and she choked and had to cough for a moment. "I never told you that!"

He sat back and surveyed her levelly. "You didn't have to tell me with words. Your body told me all I would ever need to know." His gaze skimmed over her creamy skin. "Every time I touch you your body resonates like a fine instrument. You were born to play to my tune."

She stood staring at him, shaking her head as though she couldn't believe would have the gall to say such things. "Of all the egos in the world…"

"Mine's the best?" he prompted, then shrugged with a lopsided grin. "Of course."

She held her breath and counted to ten, not really sure if she was trying to hold back anger or a smile. He did appear ridiculously adorable sitting there looking pleased with himself. She let her breath back out and tried for logic and reason. It would obviously be best to leave flights of fancy and leaps of faith behind.

"I don't love you," she lied with all her heart. Tears suddenly threatened, but she wouldn't allow them. Not now. "I can't love you. Don't you see that? Don't ever say that to me again."

Something in her voice reached in and made a grab for his heartstrings. Had he actually hurt her with his careless words? That was the last thing he would ever want to do.

"Pellea." He rose and reached for her.

She tried to turn away but he wouldn't let her. His arms came around her, holding her close against his chest, and he stroked her hair.

"Pellea, darling…"

She lifted her face, her lips trembling. He looked down and melted. No woman had ever been softer in his arms. Instantly, his mouth was on hers, touching, testing, probing, lighting her pulse on fire. She kissed him in return for as long as she dared, then pulled back, though she was still in the circle of his embrace. She tried to frown.

"You taste like chicken," she said, blinking up at him.

He smiled, and a warm sense of his affection for her was plain to see. "You taste like heaven," he countered.

She closed her eyes and shook her head. "Oh, please, Monte. Let me go."

He did so reluctantly, and she drew back slowly, looking toward him with large, sad eyes and thinking, *If only…*

He watched her, feeling strangely helpless, though he wasn't really sure why. With a sigh, she turned and went back to pacing.

"We have to get you out of here," she fretted while he sat down again and leaned back in his chair. "If I can get you out of the castle, do you have a way to get back to the continent?"

He waved away the very concept. "I'm not going anywhere," he said confidently. "And when I do go, I'll take care of myself. I've got resources. No need to worry about me."

She stopped, shaking her head as she looked at him. How could she not worry about him? That was pretty much all she was thinking about right now. She needed him to leave before he found out about the baby. And even more important, she wanted him to go because she wanted him to stay alive. But there was no point in bringing that up. He would only laugh at the danger. Still, she had to try to get him to see reason.

"There is more news," she told him, leaning against the opposite chair. "Rumors are flying."

He paused, the chicken leg halfway to his mouth. He put it down again and gazed at her. "What kind of rumors?"

She turned and sank into the chair she'd been leaning on. "There's talk of a force preparing for an Ambrian invasion."

He raised one sleek eyebrow and looked amused. "By whom?"

"Ex-Ambrians, naturally. Trying to take the country back."

His sharp, all-knowing gaze seemed to see right into her soul as he leaned closer across the table. "And you believe that?"

"Are you kidding?" She threw her hands up. "I can see it with my own eyes. What else are you doing here?"

He gave her another view of his slow, sexy smile. "I came to kidnap you, not to start a revolution. I thought I'd made that perfectly clear."

She leaned forward, searching his eyes. "So it's true. You are planning to take over this country."

He shrugged, all careless confidence. "Someday, sure." His smile was especially knowing and provocative. "Not this weekend though. I've got other plans."

He had other plans. Well, wasn't that just dandy? He had plans and she had issues of life and death to contend with. She wanted to strangle him. Or at least make him wince a little. She rose, towering over him and pointing toward her gateway.

"You've got to go. Now!"

He looked surprised at her vehemence, and then as though his feelings were hurt, he said, "I'm eating."

"You can take the food with you."

He frowned. "But I'm almost done." He took another bite. "This is actually pretty good chicken."

She stared at him, at her wit's end, then sank slowly back into the chair, her head in her hands. What could she do? She couldn't scream for help. That could get him killed. She couldn't pick him up and carry him to the doorway. That would get *her* killed. Or at least badly injured. She was stuck here in her chambers, stuck with the man she loved, the father of her child, the man whose kisses sent her into orbit every time, and everything depended on getting rid of him somehow. What on earth was she going to do?

"I hate you," she said, though it was more of a moan than a sentence.

"Good," he responded. "I like a woman with passion."

She rolled her eyes. Why couldn't he ever be serious? It was maddening. "My hatred would be more effective if I had a dagger instead," she commented dryly.

He waved a finger at her. "No threats. There's nothing quite so deadly to a good relationship. Don't go down that road."

She pouted, feeling grumpy and as though she wasn't being taken seriously. "Who said we had a good relationship?"

He looked surprised. "Don't we?" Reaching out, he took her hand. "It's certainly the best I've ever had," he said softly, his eyes glowing with the sort of affection that made her breath catch in her throat.

She curled her fingers around his. She couldn't help it. She did love him so.

She wasn't sure why. He had done little so far other than make her life more difficult. He hadn't promised her anything but kisses and lovemaking. Was that enough to give your heart for?

Hardly. Pellea was a student of history and she knew very well that people living on love tended to starve pretty quickly. What began with excitement and promises usually ended in bleak prospects and recriminations.

The gong sounded, making her jump. She pulled away

her hand and looked at him. He shrugged as though he regretted the interruption.

"I'll take my food into the library," he offered. "Just don't forget and bring your guest in there."

"I won't," she said back softly, watching him go and then hurrying to the entryway.

It was Magda, her hairdresser, making plans for their session. The older woman was dressed like a gypsy with scarves and belts everywhere. She was a bit of a character, but she had a definite talent with hair.

"I'll be back in half an hour," she warned. "You be ready. I'm going to need extra time to weave your hair around the tiara. It's not what I usually do, you know."

"Yes, I know, Magda," Pellea said, smiling. "And I appreciate that you are willing to give it a try. I'm sure we'll work something out together."

Magda grumbled a bit, but she seemed to be looking forward to the challenge. "Half an hour," she warned again as she started off toward the supply room to prepare for the session.

Pellea had just begun to close the gate when Kimmee came breezing around the corner.

"Hi," she called, rushing forward. "Don't close me out."

Pellea gave her a welcoming smile but didn't encourage her to come into the courtyard. "I'm in a bit of a hurry tonight," she warned her. "I've got the hairdresser coming and…"

"I just need to give your gown a last-minute check

for wrinkles," Kimmee said cheerfully, ignoring Pellea's obvious hint and coming right on in.

"Where is he?" she whispered, eyes sparkling, as she squeezed past.

"Who?" Pellea responded, startled.

Kimmee grinned. "I saw him when I was here earlier. You were out, but he was here." She winked. "I said hello." She looked around, merrily furtive. "We spoke."

"Oh."

Pellea swallowed hard with regret. This was not good. This was exactly what she'd hoped to avoid. Kimmee had kept the secret before, but would she again?

"He is so gorgeous," Kimmee whispered happily. "I'm so glad for you. You needed someone gorgeous in your life."

Pellea shook her head, worried and not sure how to deal with this. "But, Kimmee, it's not like that. You know I'm going to marry Leonardo and…"

"All the more reason you need a gorgeous man. No one said it had to be a forever man." Her smile was impish. "Just take some happiness where you can. You deserve it."

She looked at her maid in despair. It was all very well for her to be giving shallow comfort for activities that were clearly not in good taste. But here she was, hoisted on her own petard, as it were—taking advice that could ruin her life. But what was she going to do—beg a servant not to gossip? Might as well ask a bird not to fly

Of course, Kimmee was more than a mere servant.

In many ways, she had always been her best friend. That might make a difference. It had in the past. But not being sure was nerve-wracking. After all, this was pretty much a life-or-death situation.

She closed her eyes and said a little prayer. "Kimmee," she began nervously.

"Don't worry, Pel," Kimmee said softly. She reached out and touched her mistress's arm, her eyes warm with an abiding affection. She'd used the name she'd called Pellea when they were young playmates. "I'm just happy that…" She shrugged, but they both knew what she was talking about. "I'd never, ever tell anyone else. It's just you and me."

Tears filled Pellea's eyes. "Thank you," she whispered.

Kimmee kissed Pellea's cheek, as though on impulse and nodded. Then suddenly, as she noticed Monte coming into the doorway to the library, she was the dutiful servant once again. "Oh, miss, let me take a look at that gown."

Monte leaned against the doorjamb, his shirt open, his hair mussed, looking for all the world like an incredibly handsome buccaneer.

"Hey, Kimmee," he said.

"Hello, sir." She waved, then had second thoughts and curtsied. As she rose from her deep bow, Pellea was behind her and Kimmee risked an A-OK wink to show him plans were afoot and all was going swimmingly. "I hope things are going well with you," she added politely.

"Absolutely," he told her. "I've just had a nice little meal and I'm feeling pretty chipper."

She laughed and turned back to her work, completed it quickly, and turned to go.

"Well, miss, I just wanted to check on the gown and remind you I'll be here to help you get into it in about an hour. Will that suit?"

"That will suit. Magda should be through by then." She smiled at the young woman. "Thank you, Kimmee," she said, giving her a hug as she passed. "I hope you know how much I appreciate you."

"Of course, miss. My only wish is for your happiness. You should know that by now."

"I do. You're a treasure."

The maid waved at them both. "I'll be back in a bit. See you."

"Goodbye, Kimmee," Monte said, retreating into the library again.

But Pellea watched her go, deep in thought. In a few hours, she would be at the ball, dancing with Leonardo and preparing to have their engagement announced. People would applaud. Some might even cheer. A couple of serving girls would toss confetti in the air. A new phase of her life would open. She ought to be excited. Instead, she had a sick feeling in the pit of her stomach.

"Get over it," she told herself roughly. She had to do what she had to do. There was no choice in the matter. But instead of a bride going to join her fiancé, she felt like a traitor going to her doom.

Was she doing the right thing? How could she know for sure?

She pressed both hands to her belly and thought of the child inside. The "right thing" was whatever was best for her baby. That, at least, was clear. Now if she could just be sure what that was, maybe she could stop feeling like a tightrope walker halfway across the rope.

And in the meantime, there was someone who seemed to take great delight in jiggling that rope she was so anxiously trying to get across.

CHAPTER FIVE

TURNING, PELLEA MARCHED into the library and confronted Monte.

He looked up and nodded as she approached. "She's a good one," he commented on Kimmee. "I'm glad you've got such a strong supporter nearby."

"Why didn't you tell me you'd seen her, actually chatted with her?" Pellea said, in no mood to be mollified. "Don't you see how dangerous that is? What if she talks?"

He eyed her quizzically. "You know her better than I do. What do you think? Will she?"

Pellea shook her head. "I don't know," she said softly. "I don't think so, but…"

She threw up her hands. It occurred to her how awful it was to live like this, always suspicious, always on edge. She wanted to trust her best friend. Actually, she did trust her. But knowing the penalty one paid for being wrong in this society kept her on her toes.

"Who knows?" she said, staring at him, wondering how this all would end.

It was tempting, in her darkest moments, to blame it

all on him. He came, he saw, he sent her into a frenzy of excitement and—she had to face it—love, blinding her to what was really going on, making her crazy, allowing things to happen that should never have happened.

But he was just the temptor. She was the temptee. From the very first, she should have stopped him in his tracks, and she'd done nothing of the sort. In fact, she'd immediately gone into a deep swoon and hadn't come out of it until he was gone. She had no one to blame but herself.

Still, she wished it was clearer just what he'd been doing here two months ago, and why he'd picked her to cast a spell over.

"Why did you come here to my chambers that first time?" she asked him, getting serious. "That day you found me by the fountain. What were you doing here? What was your purpose? And why did you let me distract you from it?"

He looked at her coolly. He'd finished the chicken and eaten a good portion of the little loaf of bread. He was feeling full and happy. But her questions were a bit irksome.

"I came to get the lay of the land," he said, leaning back in his chair. "And to see my ancestral castle. To see my natural home." He looked a bit pained.

"The place I was created to rule," he added, giving it emphasis that only confirmed her fears.

"See, I knew it," she said, feeling dismal. "You were prepared to do something, weren't you?"

"Not then. Not yet." He met her gaze candidly. "But soon."

She shook her head, hands on her hips. "You want to send Leonardo and his entire family packing, don't you?" That was putting a pleasant face on something that might be very ugly, but she couldn't really face just how bad it could be.

He shrugged. "There's no denying it. It's been my obsession since I was a child." He gave her a riveting look. "Of course I'm going to take my country back. What else do I exist for?"

She felt faint. His obsession was her nightmare. She had to find a way to stop it.

"That is exactly where you go wrong," she told him, beginning to pace again. "Don't you see? You don't have to be royal. You don't have to restore your monarchy. Millions of people live perfectly happy lives without that."

He blinked at her as though he didn't quite get what she was talking about. "Yes, but do they make a difference? Do their lives have meaning in the larger scheme of things?"

She threw out her arms. "Of course they do. They fall in love and marry and have children and have careers and make friends and do things together and they're happy. They don't need to be king of anything." She appealed to him in all earnestness, wishing there was some way to convince him, knowing there was very little hope. "Why can't you be like that?"

He rose from the desk and she backed away quickly,

as though afraid he would try to take her in his arms again.

But he showed no intention of doing that. Instead, he began a slow survey of the books in her bookcases that lined the walls.

"You don't really understand me, Pellea," he said at last as he moved slowly through her collection. "I could live very happily without ever being king."

She sighed. "I wish I could believe that," she said softly.

He glanced back over his shoulder at her as she stood by the doorway, then turned to face her.

"I don't need to be king, Pellea. But there is something I do need." He went perfectly still and held her gaze with his own, his eyes burning.

"Revenge. I can never be fulfilled until I have my revenge."

She drew her breath in. Her heart beat hard, as though she was about to make a run for her life.

"That's just wicked," she said softly.

He held her gaze for a moment longer, then shrugged and turned away, shoving his hands down deep into his pockets and staring out into her miniature tropical forest.

"Then I'm wicked. I can't help it. Vengeance must be mine. I must make amends for what happened to my family."

She trembled. It was hopeless. His words felt like a dark and painful destiny to her. Like a forecast of doom.

There was no doubt in her mind that this would all end badly.

It was very true, what Monte had said. His character needed some kind of answer for what had happened to his family, some kind of retribution. Pellea knew that and on a certain level, she could hardly blame him. But didn't he see, and wasn't there any way she could make him see, that his satisfaction would only bring new misery for others? In order for him to feel relief, someone would have to pay very dearly.

"It's just selfish," she noted angrily.

He shrugged and looked at her coolly. "So I'm selfish. What else is new?"

She put her hand to her forehead and heaved a deep sigh. "There are those who live for themselves and their own gratification, and there are those who devote their lives to helping the downtrodden and the weak and oppressed. To make life better for the most miserable among us."

"You're absolutely right. You pay your money and you take your chances. I'd love to help the downtrodden and the poor and the oppressed in Ambria. Those are my people and I want to take care of them." He searched her eyes again. "But in order for me to do that, a few heads will have to roll."

The chimes on her elegant wall clock sounded and Pellea gasped.

"Oh, no! Look at the time. They're going to be here any minute. I wanted to get you out of here by now."

She looked around as though she didn't know where to hide him.

He stretched and yawned, comfortable as a cat, and then he rose and half sat on the corner of the desk. "It's all right. I'll just take a little nap while you're having your hair done."

"No, you will not!"

"As I remember it, your sleeping arrangements are quite comfortable. I think I'll spend a little quality time with your bedroom." He grinned, enjoying the outrage his words conjured up in her.

"I want you gone," she was saying fretfully, grabbing his arm for emphasis. "How do you get in here, anyway? Tell me how you do it. However you get in, that's the way you're going out. Tell me!"

He covered her hand with his own and caressed it. "I'll do better than that," he said, looking down at her with blunt affection. "I'll show you. But it will have to wait until we leave together."

She looked at his hand on hers. It felt hot and lovely. "I'm not going with you," she said in a voice that was almost a whimper.

"Yes, you are." He said it in a comforting tone.

Her eyes widened as she glanced up at him. He was doing it again—mesmerizing her. It was some sort of tantalizing magic and she had to resist it. "No, I'm not!" she insisted, but she couldn't gather the strength to pull her hand away.

He lifted her chin and kissed her softly on the lips.

"You are," he told her kindly. "You belong with me and you know it."

She felt helpless. Every time he touched her, she wanted to purr. She sighed in a sort of temporary surrender. "What are you going to do while I'm at the ball?" she asked.

"Don't worry. I'll find something to while away the time with." He raised an eyebrow. "Perfect opportunity, don't you think? To come and go at will."

She frowned. "There are guards everywhere. Surely you've seen that by now."

"Yes. But I do have your security setup to monitor things. That will help a lot."

"Oh." She groaned. She should never have let him see that.

She shook her head. "I should call the guards right now and take care of this once and for all."

"But you won't."

Suddenly, a surge of adrenaline gave her the spunk she needed to pull away from his touch, and once she was on her own, she felt emboldened again.

"Dare me!" she said, glaring at him with her hands on her hips.

He stared back at her for a long moment, then a slow grin spread over his handsome face. "I may be careless at times, my darling, but I'm not foolhardy. Even I know better than to challenge you like that."

The entry gong sounded. She sighed, all the fight ebbing out of her. "Just stay out of sight," she warned him. "I'll check in on you one last time before I go to the ball." She gave him a look of chagrin. "Unless, of course, you've left by then." She shrugged. "But I guess I won't hold my breath over that one."

He nodded. "Wise woman," he murmured as he watched her go. Then he slipped into her bedroom and closed the door before she'd let the hairdresser into the compound.

It was a beautiful room. The bedding was thick and luxurious, the headboard beautifully carved. Large oils of ancient landscapes, painted by masters of centuries past, covered the walls. He wondered what they had done with all the old portraits of his ancestors. Burned them, probably. Just another reason he needed his revenge.

But that was a matter to come. Right now he needed sleep.

He sat on the edge of her bed and looked at her bedside table, wondering what she was reading these days. What he saw gave him a bit of a jolt.

Beginning Pregnancy 101.

Interesting. It would seem Pellea was already thinking about having children. With Leonardo? That gave him a shudder. Surely she wasn't hoping to have a baby in order to reassure her father. That would be a step too far. And if she just had a yen for children, why choose Leonardo to have them with?

Making a face, he pushed the subject away. It was too depressing to give it any more attention.

He lay down on her sumptuous bed and groaned softly as he thought of the times he'd spent here. Two months ago everything had seemed so clean and simple.

A hungry man. A soft and willing woman. Great love-making. Good food. Luxurious surroundings. What could be better? He'd come back thinking it would all be easy to recreate. But he'd been dead wrong.

The wall clock struck the quarter hour again and tweaked a memory. There had been a huge, ancient grandfather clock in his mother's room when he was a child. There was a carved wooden tiger draped around the face of the timepiece and it had fascinated him. But even as he thought of that, he remembered that his mother had kept copies of her jewelry in a secret compartment in that clock.

What a strange and interesting castle this was. There were secret compartments and passageways and hiding places of all kinds just about everywhere. A few hundred years of the need to hide things had spurred his ancestors into developing ingenious and creative places to hide their most precious objects from the prying eyes and itching fingers of the servants and even of the courtiers. Life in the castle was a constant battle, it seemed, and it probably wasn't much different now.

Looking around Pellea's room, he wondered how many secret places had been found, and how many were still waiting, unused and unopened, after all these years. He knew of one, for sure, and that was the passageway that had brought him here twice now. He was pretty sure no one else had used it in twenty-five years. What else would he find if he tapped on a few walls and pressed on a few pieces of wood trim? It might be interesting to find out.

Later. Right now he needed a bit of sleep. Closing his eyes, he dreamed of Pellea and their nights together. He slept.

Pellea stood looking down at Monte, her heart so full of love, she had to choke back the tears that threatened. Tears would ruin her makeup and that was the last thing she would have been able to handle right now. She was on the edge of an emotional storm as it was.

Everyone had gone. She'd even sent the two men who were supposed to guard the tiara out into the hall to wait for her. And now she was ready to go and make the announcement that would set in stone her future life and that of her baby. But she needed just one more moment to look at the man she loved, the man she wished she were planning to marry.

If only they had met in another time, another place. If only circumstances were different. They could have been so happy together, the two of them. If there was no royalty for him to fight for, if her father was still as hale and hearty as he'd been most of her life, if her place weren't so precarious that she needed it bolstered by marrying Leonardo...

There were just too many things that would have to be different in order for things to work out the way they should, and for them to have a happy life. Unfortunately that didn't seem to be in the cards for her.

As for him—oh, he would get over it. He would never know that the baby she would have in a few months was really his. He was the only man she'd ever loved, but she had been very careful not to tell him that. She was pretty sure he'd had romances of one kind or another for years. It wouldn't be that hard for him. There would always be beautiful and talented women ready to throw themselves at him in a heartbeat.

Of course, if he did do as he threatened and try to take his country back by force, the entire question would be moot and they might all have to pay the ultimate price. Who knew?

In the meantime, she wanted just a moment more to watch him and dream….

When he woke an hour or so later, she was standing at the side of the bed. His first impression was benignness, but by the time he'd cleared his eyes, her expression had changed and she was glaring down at him.

"I don't know why you're still here," she said a bit mournfully. "Please don't get yourself killed while I'm at the ball."

He stretched and looked up at her sleepily. She was dressed to the hilt and the most beautiful thing he'd ever seen. His mother's tiara had been worked into a gorgeous coiffure that made her look as regal as any queen. Her creamy breasts swelled just above the neckline of her gown in old-fashioned allure. The bodice was tight, making her waist look tiny, as though he could reach out and pick her up with his two hands and pull her down…

His mouth went dry with desire and he reached for her. Deftly, she sidestepped his move and held him at bay.

"Don't touch," she warned. "I'm a staged work of art right now and I'm off to the photographer for pictures."

A piece of art was exactly what she was, looking just as she appeared before him. She could have walked right out of a huge portrait by John Singer Sargent, burnished lighting and rich velvet trimmings and all.

He sighed, truly pained. She looked good enough to ravish. But then she always did, didn't she?

"Forget the ball," he coaxed, though he knew it was all for naught. "Stay here with me. We'll lock the gate and recreate old times together."

"Right," she said, dismissing that out of hand, not even bothering to roll her eyes. She had other things on her mind right now. "The pictures will take at least an hour, I'm sure. Leonardo will meet me there and we'll go directly to the ball."

He frowned, feeling grumpy and overlooked for the moment. "Unless he has an unfortunate accident before he gets there," he suggested.

She looked at him sharply. "None of that, Monte. Promise me."

He stretched again and pouted. "When do you plan to make the big announcement?" he asked instead of making promises he might not be able to keep.

She frowned. "What does that matter?" she asked.

He grinned. "You are so suspicious of my every mood and plan."

Her eyes flashed. "With good reason, it seems."

He shrugged. "So I won't see you again until later?"

"No. Unless you decide to go away. As you should." She hesitated. She needed to make a few thing clear to him. He had to follow rules or she was going to have to get the guard to come help her keep him in line.

Right. That was a great idea. She made a face at herself. She was truly caught in a trap. She needed to keep him in line, but in order to do that, she would be signing his death warrant. There was no way that was going to happen.

At the same time, he showed no appreciation for the bind she was in. If he didn't feel it necessary to respect the rules she made, she couldn't have him here. He would have to understand that.

Taking a deep breath, she gave him the facts as she needed them to be.

"Once the announcement is made, our engagement will be official and there will be no more of anything like this," she warned him, a sweep of her hand indicating their entire relationship. "You understand that, don't you?"

His eyes were hooded as he looked up at her. "I understand what you're saying,"

"Monte, please don't do anything. You can't. I can't let you. Please have some respect."

His slow, insolent smile was his answer. "I would never do anything to hurt you."

She stared at him, then finally did roll her eyes. "Of

course not. Everything you do would be for my own good, wouldn't it?"

There was no escaping the tone of sarcasm in her voice. She sighed with exasperation and then the expression in her eyes changed. She hesitated. "Will you be gone?" she asked.

He met her gaze and held it. "Is that really what you hope?"

She started to say, "Of course," but then she stopped, bit her lip and sighed. "How can I analyze what I'm hoping right now?" she said instead, her voice trembling. "How can I even think clearly when you're looking at me like that?"

One last glare and she whirled, leaving the room as elegantly as any queen might do.

He rose and followed, going to the doorway so that he could watch her leave her chambers, a uniformed guard on either side. She could have been royalty from another century. She could have been Anne Boleyn on her way to the tower. He thought she was pretty special. He wanted her to be his, but just how that would work was not really clear.

Right now he had a purpose in mind—exploring the other side of the castle where his family's living quarters had been. That was the section that had burned and he knew it had been recently renovated. He only hoped enough would be left of what had been so that he could find something he remembered.

It would seem the perfect time to do it. With the ball beginning, no one would be manning their usual places.

Everyone would be gravitating toward the ballroom for a look at the festivities. A quick trip to Pellea's surveillance room was in order, and then he would take his chances in the halls.

The long, tedious picture-taking session was wrapping up and Pellea waited with Kimmee for Leonardo to come out. The photographers were taking a few last individual portraits of him.

"Shall I go check on the preparations for your entrance to the ballroom?" Kimmee asked, and Pellea nodded her assent.

It had been her experience that double-checking never hurt and taking things for granted usually led to disaster. Besides, she needed a moment to be alone and settle her feelings.

Turning slowly, she appraised herself in the long, full-length mirror. Was that the face of a happy woman? Was that the demeanor of a bride?

Not quite. But it was the face of a rather regal-looking woman, if she did say so herself. But why was she even thinking such a thing? She would never be queen, no matter what. Monte might be king someday, but he would never pick her to be his wife. He couldn't pick someone from a traitor's family to help him rule Ambria, now could he?

The closest she would get to that was to marry Leonardo. Did that really matter to her? She searched her soul, looking for even the tiniest hint of ambition and couldn't find it. That sort of thing was important to her father, but not to her. If her father weren't involved, she would leave with Monte and never look back. But that was impossible under the circumstances.

Still, it was nice to dream about. What if she and Monte were free? They might get on a yacht and sail to the South Seas and live on an island. Not an island like Ambria with its factions always in contention and undermining each other. A pretty island with coconut trees and waterfalls, a place that was quiet and warm and peaceful with turquoise waters and silver-blue fish and white-sand beaches.

But there was no time to live in dreams. She had to live in the here and now. And that meant she had to deal with Leonardo.

She smiled at him as he came out of the sitting room.

"All done?" she asked.

"So it seems," he replied, then leaned close. "Ah, so beautiful," he murmured as he tried to nuzzle her neck.

"Don't touch," she warned him, pulling back.

"Yes, yes, I know. You're all painted up and ready to go." He took her hand and kissed her fingers. "But I want to warn you, my beauty, I plan to touch you a lot on our wedding night."

That sent a chill down her spine. She looked at him in surprise. He'd never shown any sexual interest in her before. This put an ominous pall on her future, didn't it? She'd heard lurid tales about his many mistresses and she'd assumed that he knew their marriage would be for advantage and convenience only, and not for love or for anything physical. Now he seemed to be having second thoughts. What was going on here?

She glanced at Kimmee who'd just returned and had heard him as well, and they exchanged a startled glance.

Leonardo took a call on his mobile, then snapped it shut and frowned. "I'm sorry, my love," he told her. "I'm afraid I'm going to have to let the guards escort you to the ballroom. I'll be along later. I have a matter that must be taken care of immediately."

Something in his words sent warning signals through her.

"What is it, Leonardo?" she asked, carefully putting on a careless attitude. "Do we need to man the barricades?"

"Nothing that should trouble you, my sweet," he said, giving her a shallow smile that didn't reach his eyes. "It seems we may have an interloper in the castle."

"Oh?" Her blood ran cold and she clenched her fists behind the folds of her skirt. "What sort of interloper?"

He waved a hand in the air. "It may be nothing, but a few of the guards seem to think they saw a stranger on one of the monitors this afternoon." He shook his head. "We don't allow intruders in the castle, especially on a night like this."

He sighed. "I just have to go and check out what they caught on the recorder. I'll be back in no time."

"Hurry back, my dear," she said absentmindedly,

thinking hard about how she was going to warn Monte.

"I will, my love." He bowed in her direction and smiled at her. "Don't do any dancing without me," he warned. Turning, he disappeared out the door.

Pellea reached out to steady herself to keep from keeling over. She met Kimmee's gaze and they both stared at each other with worried eyes.

"I told him to go," she fretted to her lifelong friend and servant. "Now he's probably out running around the castle and about to get caught. Oh, Kimmee!"

Kimmee leaned close. "Don't worry, Pel," she whispered, scanning the area to make sure no one could overhear them. "I'll find him and I'll warn him. You can count on me."

Pellea grabbed her arm. "Tell him there is no more room for error. He has to get out of the castle right now!"

"I will. Don't you worry. He'll get the message."

And she dashed off into the hallway.

Pellea took a deep breath and tried to quiet her nerves. She had to forget all about Monte and the trouble he might be in. She had to act as though everything were normal. In other words, she would have to pretend. And it occurred to her that this might be a lesson for the way things would be for the rest of her life.

CHAPTER SIX

MONTE WAS BACK FROM EXPLORING and he was waiting impatiently for Kimmee to make good on her promises and show up with a costume he could wear to the ball.

He'd been to the other side of the castle and he'd seen things that would take him time to assimilate and deal with emotionally. It could have been overwhelming if he'd let it be. He'd barely skimmed through the area and not much remained of the home he'd lived in with his loving family. Most of what was rebuilt had a new, more modern cast.

But he had found something important. He'd found a storeroom where some of the rescued items and furniture from his family's reign had been shoved aside and forgotten for years. A treasure trove that he would have to explore when he got the chance. But in the short run, he'd found his mother's prized grandfather clock. More important, he'd found her secret compartment, untouched after all these years. That alone had given him a sense of satisfaction.

And one of the items he had found in that secret

hiding place was likely to come in very handy this very night.

But right now, he just wanted to see Kimmee appear in the gateway. He knew she'd been helping with the photo shoot, but surely that was over by now. If she didn't come soon, he would have to find a way to go without a special costume—and that would be dangerous enough to make him think at least twice.

"Don't give up on me!"

Kimmee's voice rang out before the gong sounded and she came rushing in bearing bulky gifts and a wide smile.

"I've got everything you need right here," she claimed, spreading out her bounty before him. "Though I'm afraid it's all for naught."

"Once more, you save the day," he told her as he looked through the items, thoroughly impressed. "I'm going to have to recommend you for a medal."

"A reward for costume procurement?" she asked with a laugh. "But there's more. I'm afraid you won't be able to use this after all."

"No?" He stopped and looked at her. "Why not?"

"The castle is on stranger alert." She sighed. "You must have gone exploring because some of the guards claim they saw you—or somebody—on one of the hall monitors."

"Oh. Bad luck."

She shrugged. "Leonardo is looking into it and he seems pretty serious about it. So Pellea sent me to tell you to get out while the getting's good, because there's no time left." She shook her head, looking at him earnestly. "I went ahead and brought you the costume, because I promised I would, and I knew you'd want to see this. But I don't think it would be wise to use it. You're going to have to go, and go quickly."

"Am I?" He held up the coat to the uniform and gazed at it.

"Oh, I think you'd better," she said.

"And I will." He smiled at her. "All in good time. But first, I want to dance with Pellea."

Her face was filled with doubt but her eyes were shining. "But if you get caught…?"

"Then I'll just have to get away again," he told her. "But I don't plan to get caught. I've got a mask, don't I? No one will be sure who I really am, and I'll keep a sharp eye out." He grinned. "Don't worry about me. I'm going to go try this on."

"Well, what do you know?" She sighed, wary but rather happy he wasn't going to give up so easily. "Go ahead and try it on. I'll wait and help with any last-minute adjustments."

He took the costume up as though it were precious—and in a way it was. He recognized what she'd found for him—the official dress uniform of Ambrian royalty from the nineteenth century—a uniform one of his great-great-grandfathers had probably worn. He slipped into it quickly. It all fitted like a glove. Looking in the mirror, he had to smile. He looked damn good in gold braid and a stiff collar. As though he was born to wear it.

When he walked out, Kimmee applauded, delighted with how it had worked out.

"Here's your mask," she said, handing it to him. "As you say, it will be very important in keeping your identity hidden. And it's a special one. Very tight. Very secure." She gave it a sharp test, pulling on the band at the back. "No one will be able to pull it off."

"Exactly what I need. Kimmee, you're a genius."

"I am, aren't I?" She grinned, pleased as punch. "Believe me, sir, I take pride in my work—underhanded as it may be."

He shook his head. "I don't consider this underhanded at all."

And actually, she agreed. "I'll just think of it this way—anything I can do to help you is for the good of the country."

He looked at her closely, wondering if she realized who he was. But her smile was open and bland. If she knew, she wasn't going to let it out. Still, it was interesting that she'd put it that way.

"I've got to hurry back," she said as she started toward the gate. "I'm helping in the ladies' powder room. You pick up all the best rumors in there."

"Ah, the ladies like to talk, do they?" he responded, adjusting his stand-up collar.

"They like to impress each other and they forget that we servants can hear, too." She gave him a happy wave. "I'll let you know if anything good turns up."

He nodded. "The juicier the better."

She laughed as she left, and he sobered. He'd been

lighthearted with Kimmee, but in truth, this was quite an emotional experience for him.

He took one last look in the mirror. For the first time in many years, he felt as if he'd found something he really belonged to, something that appealed to his heart as well as his head. It was almost a feeling of coming home.

And home was what he'd missed all these years. Without real parents, without a real family, he'd ached for something of his own.

He'd had an odd and rather disjointed life. For his first eight years, he'd been the much beloved, much cosseted Crown Prince of Ambria, living in the rarified air of royal pomp and celebrity. His mother and father had doted on him. He'd shown every evidence of being as talented and intelligent as his position in life warranted, and also as pleasant and handsome as a prince should be. Everyone in his milieu was in awe of him. The newspapers and magazines were full of pictures of him—his first steps, his first puppy, his new Easter clothes, his first bicycle. It was a charmed life.

And then came the coup. He still remembered the night the castle burned, could still smell the fire, feel the fear. He'd known right away that his parents were probably dead. For an eight-year-old boy, that was a heavy burden to bear.

That night, as he and his brother Darius were rushed away from the castle and hustled to the continent in a rickety boat, he'd looked back and seen the fire, and even at his young age, he'd known his way of life was crumbling into dust just as surely as the castle of his royal ancestors was.

He and Darius were quickly separated and wouldn't see each other again until they were well into adulthood. For the first few weeks after his escape, he was passed from place to place by agents of the Ambrian royalty, always seeing new contacts, never sure who these people were or why he was with them. People were afraid to be associated with him, yet determined to keep him safe.

As the regime's crown prince, he was in special danger. The Granvillis had taken over Ambria and it was known that they had sent agents out to find all the royal children and kill them. They didn't want any remnants of the royal family around to challenge their rule.

Monte finally found himself living in Paris with an older couple, the Stephols, who had ties to the monarchy but also a certain distance that protected them from scrutiny. At first, he had to hide day and night, but after a year or so, the Stephols got employment with the foreign service and from then on, they were constantly moving from one assignment to another, and Monte lived all over the world, openly claiming to be their child.

He grew up with the best of everything—elite private schools, vacations in Switzerland, university training in business. But he was always aware that he was in danger and had to keep his real identity a secret. The couple treated him with polite reserve and not a lot of affection—as though he were a museum piece they were protecting from vandals but would return to its proper shelf when the time came. They had no other children and were sometimes too cool for comfort. The couple was very closely knit and Monte often felt like an interloper—which he probably was. They were kind to him, but somewhat reserved, and it was a lonely life. They obviously knew he was special, though he wasn't sure if they knew exactly who he was.

He knew, though. He remembered a lot and never forgot his family, his country or that he was royal. That in itself made him careful. He remembered the danger, still had nightmares about it. As he got older, it was hard not being able to talk to anyone about his background, not having someone he could question, but he read everything he could about his homeland and began to understand why he had to maintain his anonymity. He knew that some saw him as cold and removed from normal emotions. That wasn't true. His emotions were simmering inside, ready to explode when the time was right.

Coming back to Ambria had done a lot to help put things in order in his mind. Finding Pellea had confused the issue a bit, but he thought he could handle that. Now, putting on the uniform that should have been his by rights cemented a feeling of belonging in him. He was the Crown Prince of Ambria, and he wanted his country back.

Monte DeAngelis, Crown Prince of Ambria, walked into the ballroom annex in a uniform that reflected his position, and he did it proudly. He knew the authorities were looking for him and it would only take one careless action, one moment of inattention, to make them realize he was the intruder they were searching for.

But he was willing to risk it. He had to. He needed to do this and he was counting on his natural abilities and intelligence to keep him from harm. After all, he'd had to count on exactly those for most of his life, and his talents had so far stood him in good stead. Now for the ultimate test. He definitely expected to pass it.

The announcer looked up at him in surprise and frowned, knowing that he'd never seen this man before in his life. He got up from his chair and came over busily, carrying papers and trying to look as though he were comfortably in charge.

"Welcome," he said shortly, with a bow. "May I have the name to be announced?"

Monte stood tall and smiled at him.

"Yes, you may. Please announce me as the Count of Revanche," he said with an appropriately incomprehensible Mediterranean accent, though he was blatantly using the French word for revenge.

The man blinked, appearing puzzled. "And Revanche is…?"

"My good man, you've never visited our wonderful region?" Monte looked shocked. "We're called the wine country of the southern coast. You must make a visit on your next holiday."

"Oh," the man responded dutifully, still baffled. "Of course." He bowed deeply and held out his arm with a flourish. "If you please, Your Highness."

He reached for the loudspeaker and made the announcement.

"Ladies and gentleman, may I present His Highness, the Count of Revanche?"

And Monte held his head high as he navigated the steep stairway into the ballroom.

Heads turned. And why not? Obviously, no one had ever heard of him before, and yet he was a commanding presence. He could see the wave of whispering his entrance had set off, but he ignored it, looking for Pellea.

He picked her out of the crowd quickly enough. For a moment the sight of all those masks blinded him, but he found her and once he'd done that, she was all he could see. She stood in the midst of a small group of women and it seemed to him as though a spotlight shone down on her. In contrast to the others around her, the mask she wore was simple, a smooth black accent that set off the exotic shape of her dark eyes and allowed the sparkling jewels of the tiara to take center stage. At the same time, the porcelain translucence of her skin, the delicate set of her jaw, the lushness if her lips, all added to the stunning picture she made in her gorgeous gown. She was so utterly beautiful, his heart stopped in his chest.

He began to head in her direction, but he didn't want to seem over-anxious, so he made a few bows and gave out a few smiles along the way.

Only a few stately couples were dancing as he entered the cavernous room, but he knew how this sort of ball operated, having been to enough of them on the continent. The older people did most of the dancing at first, and the music was calm and traditional. Then the younger ones would filter in. By a certain hour, rocking rhythms and Latin beats would be the order of the day, and the older people would have retreated to drink in the bar or queue for the midnight buffet table.

That was the structure, but it wasn't really relevant to his plans. He just wanted Pellea in his arms. Now all he had to do was to get there and claim her.

Many of the women had noticed him right away. In fact, a few were blatantly looking him over. One pretty little redhead had actually lowered her mask in order to wink at him in outright invitation.

Meanwhile, Pellea hadn't even noticed his arrival. She was deep in conversation with another woman, both of them very earnest. It was quite evident that the subject of their talk was more likely to be the state of world affairs than the latest tart recipe. But what did that matter? She was looking so beautiful, if one had to pick out a queen from the assemblage, she would take the night.

Why did that thought keep echoing in his mind? He turned away, reminding himself that the question was out of order. He wasn't going to think about anything beyond the dancing tonight. And in order to get things started, he decided to take the little redhead up on her offer.

She accepted his invitation like a shot and very soon they were on the dance floor. It was a Viennese waltz, but they managed to liven it up considerably. She chatted away but he hardly heard a word she said. His attention was all on Pellea.

As he watched, Leonardo asked her to dance, and she refused him, shaking her head. He looked a bit disgruntled as he walked away, but his friends crowded around him and in a moment, they all went straight for the hard liquor bar, where he quickly downed a stiff one.

Monte smiled. Fate seemed to be playing right into his hands. The music ended and Monte returned the redhead to her companions. He gave her a smile, but not many words to cherish after he was gone. Turning, he headed straight toward Pellea.

As he approached, she looked up and he saw her eyes widen with recognition behind her mask. She knew who he was right away, and that disappointed him. He'd hoped to get a bit of play out of the costume and mask before he had to defend himself for showing up here.

But then he realized the truth, and it warmed his heart. They would know each other in the dark, wouldn't they?

Not to say that she was pleased to see him.

"You!" she hissed at him, eyes blazing. "Are you crazy? What are you doing here?"

"Asking the most stunning woman in the room to dance with me." He gave her a deep bow. "May I have the honor?"

"No!" She glared at him and lifted her fan to her face. She was obviously finding it hard to show her anger to him and hide it from the rest of the people in the room at the same time. "Didn't Kimmee tell you that you'd been seen?" she whispered.

"Kimmee delivered your message and I acknowledge it. But I won't be cowed by it." He gave her a flourish and a flamboyant smile that his mask couldn't hide. "I have a life to live you know."

"And this stupid ball is that important to your life?" she demanded, trying to keep her voice down and astounded that he could be so careless.

Didn't he care? Or did he see himself as some kind of superhero, so over-confident in his own abilities that he scoffed at danger? In any case, it was brainless and dangerous and it made her crazy.

"Oh, yes, this ball is very important," he answered her question. His smile was slow and sensual. "It may be my last chance to dance with you. Believe me, Pellea, there is nothing more important than that."

She was speechless, then angry. How did he do it, again and again? Somehow he always touched her emotions, even when she knew very well that was exactly what he was aiming at. She felt like a fool, but she had to admit, a part of her that she wasn't very proud of loved it.

Monte knew he'd weakened her defenses with that one and he smiled. It might sound glib and superficial, but he meant every word of it.

She was beautiful, from head to toe, and as he gazed at the way the tiara worked perfectly with her elaborate ensemble, he thought about his memories of his own mother wearing it, and a mist seemed to cloud his eyes for a moment. In many ways, Pellea fitted into the continuity of culture here in Ambria the way no other woman he'd ever met could do. It was something to keep in mind, wasn't it?

Out of the corner of his eye, he saw Leonardo coming back into the room and looking their way, frowning fiercely. Monte smiled and glanced at Pellea. She'd seen him, too.

"We'd better get out on the dance floor or we'll be answering questions from Leonardo in no time," he noted. "He has that mad inquisitioner look to him tonight."

Quickly, she nodded and raised her arms. He took her into his embrace and they began to sway to the music.

"This is all so wrong," she murmured, leaning against his shoulder. "You know this is only going to anger him."

He glanced over at Leonardo, who was scowling, his friends gathered around him. Angering Leonardo was the least of his worries right now. He was gambling that the man wouldn't see him as the intruder he'd been studying on the castle monitoring system.

If he'd arrived in more normal attire, that might have been a problem. But because he'd appeared in such an elaborate costume, claimed to be royal and seemed to fit so well with the others who were here, he hoped Leonardo wouldn't connect him with the intruder until it was too late.

At first glance, he would have to say that he'd been right. Everything was influenced by context.

"I see that your handsome and valorous swain is celebrating his fool head off tonight," he noted as Leonardo threw back another shot of Scotch.

"Yes," she whispered. "He's already had too much. It's becoming a habit of his lately. I'm going to have to work on that."

He gazed down at her and barely contained the sneer he felt like using at her words. "Are you?"

"Yes." She lifted her chin and met his gaze defiantly. "After we're married."

She said the word loud and clear, emphasizing it to make sure he got her drift. And now he did sneer. He got it all right. He just didn't want to accept it.

He whirled her in a fancy turn, then dipped her in a way that took her breath away. But she was half laughing at the same time.

"Oh, that was lovely," she told him, clinging to him in a way that sent his pulse soaring.

"Your lover boy didn't like it," he told her blithely.

"Maybe not," she admitted, looking back at where Leonardo was standing a bit apart from his friends and watching her. "But you have to admit, until you arrived, all in all, he seems to be happy tonight."

"Why wouldn't he be?" He pulled her up against his chest and held her there for a beat too long, enjoying the soft, rounded feel of her body against his. "And you, my darling," he added softly. "Are you happy?"

Her dark eyed gaze flickered up at him, then away again. "You know the answer to that. But I'm prepared to do my duty."

That was an answer that infuriated him and he was silent for a moment, trying to control himself. But he couldn't stay angry with her in his arms. He looked down at her and his heart swelled. When was he going to admit it? This trip had been completely unnecessary. He'd already gathered all the reconnaissance data he needed on his last visit to Ambria. He'd only come for one thing. Trying to turn it into a Helen-of-Troy kidnapping of the enemy's most beautiful woman was just fanciful rationalizing. He'd come to find Pellea because he needed to see her. That was all there was to it. But now that he knew about this insane wedding to a Granvilli monster, he wanted to get her out of here with more urgency. She had to go. She couldn't marry Leonardo. What a crime against nature that would be!

And yet, there was the problem of her father. No matter what he might think of the man, if he ripped her away from him by force, without first convincing her to go, she would never forgive him. Knowing how important family was, and how traumatic it could be when it was torn apart, he might never forgive himself.

He had to find a way to make her come with him. Somehow.

He dipped her again, pulling her in close and bending over her in a rather provocative way. "I promise you, Pellea," he said, his voice rough and husky. "I swear it on my parents' graves. You will be happy."

Her heart was beating hard. She stared at him, not sure what he was up to. He was making promises he couldn't possibly keep. She didn't believe a word of it.

"You can't decide on my happiness," she told him bluntly. "It's not up to you."

"Of course not," he said, his bitterness showing. "I suppose it's up to your father, isn't it?"

She drew her breath in and let resentment flow through her for a moment. Then she pushed it back. It did no good to let emotions take over at a time like this.

"I know you hate my father," she said softly, "and you may have good reason to, from your point of view."

"You mean from a reasonable perspective?"

She ignored his taunt and went on.

"But I don't hate him. I love him very much. My mother died when I was very young and he and I have been our only family ever since. He's been everything to me. I love him dearly."

He pulled back, still holding her loosely in his arms. "You'd choose him over me?" he asked, his voice rough as sandpaper.

Her eyes widened. His words startled her. In fact, he took her breath away with the very concept. What was he asking of her? Whatever he was thinking, he had no right to put it to her that way.

And so she nodded. "Of course I would choose him. He and I have a real relationship. With you, I have…"

Her voice trailed off. Even now she was reluctant to analyze what exactly it was that they had together. "With you I had something that was never meant to last," she said finally.

He stared at her, wondering why her words stung so deeply. Wondering why there was an urge down in him that was clawing its way to the surface, an urge to do what he'd only bantered about, an urge to throw her over his shoulder as his own personal trophy, and fight his way out of the castle.

Kidnap her. That was the answer. He would carry her off and hide her away somewhere only he could find her. The need swelled inside him, almost choking him with its intensity. He was flying high on fantasy.

But he came back down to earth with a thump. What the hell was wrong with him? That whole scenario was just sick. He had no more right to force her into any-thing than he had to force anyone. If he really wanted her that badly, he would have to find a way to convince her to want him just as much. And so far, that wasn't working.

She preferred to stay with her father.

But that wasn't fair, to put it that way. Her father was her only living relative and he was very ill. Of course she was protective of him and wanted to stay with him. Her tenderness and compassion were part of what he loved about her.

"So I guess I come in third," he mentioned with de-ceptive calm. "Behind your father and Leonardo." He glanced back at her fiancé waiting for this long dance to end. "Maybe I ought to have a talk with your lover boy."

She drew her breath in sharply. "Stay away from him, Monte. The more he drinks the more dangerous he'll be."

She was passionate and worried, but also confused and torn and not at all sure how to handle this. Here she was in the same room with the man she loved and even in his arms, and just a stone's throw away from the man she was pledged to marry.

Let's face it, he was the man she *had* to marry, no way around it. She was pregnant. She needed a husband. Without one, she would be persona non grata in this community. And if those in charge ever figured out who the baby's father was, her child would be an outcast as well.

She really didn't have much choice in the matter. In a country like this, living in this rarefied sliver of the society as she did, and caring for her father as she did, there was no option to play the free spirit and defy the culture's norms. She needed protection. It was all very well to love Monte, but he would never marry her. She had to provide for her child—and herself. No one else was prepared to do it for her.

No one but Leonardo, and for that—though Monte might never understand it—she would be forever grateful to the man.

Leonardo knew she was pregnant, though he didn't know who the father was. He didn't really care. It wasn't love he was looking for in their relationship. It was the factions she represented, the power she could help him assemble, and the prestige of her name. Though her father had been mistrusted for a time because he had worked with the old DeAngelis regime, years had passed now, and his reputation was clear. Now, the magic of the old days and the old regime was what mattered. People were said to hold him in such high esteem, his reputation rivaled that of the Granvillis. And that was one reason Leonardo wanted her on his side.

It was well understood between the two of them. She was getting something she needed from him and he was getting something he needed from her. If Monte had just stayed away, everything would be going along as planned.

But Monte had appeared out of nowhere once again and upset the apple cart. She loved him. She couldn't deny it. And he was the father of her child, although he didn't know it. And here he was, inserting himself into the equation in a way that was sure to bring misery to them all. Did she have the strength to stop him? So far, it didn't seem possible.

The music finally came to an end. She knew Leonardo was waiting for her to return to her spot and she was resigned to it. Reluctantly, she began to slip out of Monte's arms.

But he didn't want to let her go.

"Do you find it oppressively hot in here?" he murmured close to her ear, his warm breath tickling her skin.

"Oh, I don't know, I guess…"

He didn't wait for a full answer. In the confusion of couples coming and going every which way to get on and off the dance floor, he maneuvered her right out the open French doors onto the dimly lit and almost empty terrace. As the small orchestra struck up a new tune, they continued their dance.

"Monte," she remonstrated with him. "You can't do

this. You're not the only one who wants to dance with me, you know."

"I know that very well," he said. "Why do you think I felt I had to resort to these guerilla tactics to have my way with you?"

She laughed low in her throat and he pulled her into the shadows and kissed her. His kiss was music by Mozart, sculpture by Michelangelo, the dancing of Fred Astaire. He was the best.

Of course, she wasn't exactly an expert on such things. Her experience wasn't extensive. But she'd had make-out sessions with incredibly attractive men in her time, and she knew this was top-tier kissing.

He started slowly, just barely nipping at her lips, and, as she felt herself enjoying the sensation and reaching for more of it, he found his way into the honey-sweet heat of her mouth, using his tongue to explore the terrain and sample the most tender and sensitive places.

She knew she was being hypnotized again and for the moment, she didn't care. His slow, provocative touch was narcotic, and she fell for the magic gladly. If he had picked her up and carried her off at that moment, she wouldn't have protested at all.

But he'd kept the clearer head and he pulled back.

"Oh, Monte, no," she sighed, the sweetness of his lips still branding hers. She felt so wonderful in his arms, like a rose petal floating downstream. The music, the cool night air, his strong arms around her—what could be better?

"Please," she whispered, reaching for him again.

"Not now, my darling," he whispered back, nuzzling behind her ear. "There are people nearby. And there are things that must be done."

"Like what?" she murmured rather sulkily, but she was beginning to come back to her senses as well and she sighed, realizing that he was perfectly right to deflect her. "Oh, bother," she muttered, annoyed with herself as her head cleared. "There you go, flying me to the moon again."

He laughed softly, dropping one last kiss on her lips. "There will be plenty of time for that later," he promised.

"No there won't," she said sensibly. "I'll be married. And if you think you're going to be hanging around once that has happened, you'd better think again."

She couldn't help but wince as she let herself imagine just how bereft her world was going to be.

But she managed to keep a fiercely independent demeanor. "There are certain lines I swear I will never cross."

He gazed at her, his blue eyes clouded and unreadable. "What time is the announcement planned for?" he asked her.

She looked up at him in surprise. "Just before the midnight buffet," she answered, then frowned, alarmed. "Wait. Monte! What are you planning to do?"

"Who, me? Why would you think I was planning anything at all?"

"Because I know you." She planted her hands on his

shoulders and shook him. "Don't do it! Whatever you're planning, don't!"

He pretended to be wounded by her suspicion, though his eyes were sparkling with laughter. "I can't believe you have so little faith in me," he said.

She started to respond, but then her gaze caught sight of something that sent her pulse racing. "Leonardo," she whispered to Monte. "He's found us."

"Oh, good," he said. "I've been wanting to talk to him."

CHAPTER SEVEN

PELLEA DREW IN A SHARP BREATH, filled with dread as she watched Leonardo approach.

"I'll hold him off if you want to make a run for it," she told Monte urgently, one hand gripping his shoulder. "But go quickly!"

"Why would I run?" he said, turning to meet the man, still holding her other hand. "I've been looking forward to this."

"Oh, Monte," she whimpered softly, wishing she could cast a spell and take them anywhere else.

Leonardo's face was filled with a cold fury that his silver mask couldn't hide.

"Unhand my fiancée, sir," he ordered, his lip curling and one hand on the hilt of the sword at his side. "And identify yourself, if you please."

Monte's smile was all pure, easy confidence. "You don't allow hand holding with old friends?" he asked, holding Pellea's hand up where Leonardo could see his fingers wrapped around hers. "Pellea and I have a special connection, but it's nothing that should concern you."

"A special connection?" Leonardo repeated, seeming momentarily uncertain. "In what way?"

"Family connections," Monte explained vaguely. "We go way back." But he dropped her hand and clicked his heels before giving Leonardo a stiff little bow. "Allow me to introduce myself. I'm the Count of Revanche. Perhaps you've heard of me?"

Leonardo looked a bit puzzled, but much of his fury had evaporated and a new look of interest appeared on his long face. "Revanche, is it?"

"Yes." Monte stuck out his hand and gave the man a broad smile. It was fascinating how the hint of royalty always worked magic, especially with dictator types. They always seemed a little starstruck by a title, at least at first. He only hoped the sense of awe would last long enough to save him from ending up in a jail cell.

"It is a pleasure to meet you at last, Leonardo," he said heartily. "I've heard so much about you. I'm hoping the reality can compete with the legend."

Leonardo hesitated only a moment, then stuck out his own hand and Monte shook it warmly.

"Have I heard of you before?" he asked.

Monte gave a grand shrug. "That's as may be. But I've heard of you." He laughed as though that was quite a joke. "Your father and I go way back."

"My father?" Leonardo brightened. "How so?"

Monte nodded wisely. "He's meant a great deal to me in my life. In fact, I wouldn't be the man I am today without his strong hand in my early training."

"Ah, I see." Leonardo began to look downright welcoming. "So he has mentored you in some way."

Monte smiled. "One might say that. We were once thick as thieves."

Leonardo actually smiled. "Then you will be happy to know he is going to make an appearance here tonight."

Monte's confidence slipped just a bit, but he didn't let it show. "Is he? What a treat it will be to see him again. I'll be happy to have a drink with him."

"Well, why not have a drink with me while we await his arrival?" Leonardo suggested. He was obviously warming to this visiting count and had forgotten all about the manhandling of his future bride. "Come along, Pellea," he said, sweeping them back into the ballroom with him. "We must make sure our guest is well supplied with refreshment."

Her gaze met Monte's and she bit her lip. She could see what he was doing, but she didn't like it at all. The moment an opportunity arose, she would help him make a run for it. That was the only thing she could see that would save him. This manly bonding thing couldn't last once the truth began to seep out.

But Monte gave her a wink and his eyes crackled with amusement. He was obviously having the time of his life fooling someone who didn't even realize he was dealing with his worst enemy.

They made their way to the bar, and by the time they got there, a crowd of Leonardo's friends and hangers-on had joined them.

"Come," Leonardo said expansively. "We must drink together."

"Of course," Monte agreed cordially. "What are we drinking?"

The bartender slapped a bottle of something dark and powerful-looking on the bar and everyone cheered.

"We must share a toast," Monte said, holding his glass high. "Let us drink to destiny."

"To destiny!"

Each man downed his drink and looked up happily for more. The bartender obliged.

"And to fathers everywhere," Monte said, holding his glass up again. "And to General Georges Granvilli in particular."

"Well. Why not?" Leonardo had just about decided Monte was the best friend he'd ever had by now. He pounded him on the back at every opportunity and merrily downed every drink Monte put before him.

Pellea watched this spectacle in amazement. But when Monte offered her a glass, she shook her head.

"Pellea, come share a toast with us," he coaxed, trying to tempt her. "I'll get you something fruity if you like."

She shook her head firmly. "No. I don't drink."

He blinked at her, remembering otherwise and sidling a bit closer. "You drank happily enough two months ago," he said to her quietly. "We practically bathed in champagne, as I remember. What's changed?"

She flashed him a warning look. "That was then. This is now."

He frowned, ready to take that up and pursue an answer, but Leonardo wrapped an arm around his neck and proclaimed, "I love you, man."

"Of course," Monte said with a sly smile. "You and I are like blood brothers."

Pellea blanched. Was she the only one who got a chill at hearing his words?

"Blood brothers." Leonardo had imbibed too much to be able to make head nor tails of that, but it sounded good to him.

Monte watched him with pity. "You don't understand that," he allowed. "I'm going to have to explain it to you. But for now, trust me." He raised his glass into the light, glad no one seemed to notice that he had never actually drunk what was in it. "Blood brothers under the skin."

"Are we, by God?" Leonardo was almost in tears at the thought.

"Yes," Monte said with an appropriate sense of irony. "We are."

Pellea shook her head. She could see where this was inevitably going and knew there would probably be no announcement of their engagement tonight. Unless Monte volunteered to prop the man up for it, and that wasn't likely.

All in all, this appeared to be a part of his plan. Didn't he understand that it would do no good? The announcement would be made, one way or another, before the wedding, and that was only two days away. He couldn't stop it. She couldn't let him.

He caught her eye, gesturing for her to come closer.

"Do you think Georges will really make an appearance?" he whispered to her.

She shook her head. "I have no idea. I haven't seen him in months. They always say he is in France, taking the waters for his health. For all I know, he's been right here this whole time, watching television in his room."

Monte glanced at Leonardo, who was laughing uproariously with a couple of his mates. One more toast and it was pretty obvious he wouldn't be capable of making an engagement announcement.

"Wait here, my love," he said softly. "I have to finish what I've started."

"Monte, no!" She grabbed his arm to keep him with her, but he pulled away and joined the men at the bar.

"A final toast," he offered to Leonardo. "To our new and everlasting friendship."

"Our friendship!" cried Leonardo, turning up his glass and taking in the contents in one gulp. Then, slowly, he put the glass down. Staring straight ahead, his eyes glassy, he began to crumble. His knees went first, and then his legs. Monte and a couple of the others grabbed him before he hit the ground. A sigh went through the crowd. And, at the same time, bugles sounded in the hallway.

"The General is coming!" someone cried out. "It's General Georges."

"Prepare for the arrival of the General."

Shock went through the crowd in waves, as though no one knew exactly what to do, but all realized something had to be done. Their leader was coming. He had to be welcomed in style.

One of Leonardo's friends sidled up to Monte. "We've got to get him out of here before his father comes," he whispered urgently. "There'll be hell to pay. Believe me, the old man will kill him."

Monte looked at the limp young gentleman who thought he was going to marry Pellea and had a moment of indecision. What did he care if Georges saw his son like this? It wasn't his problem.

And yet, in a way, it *was* his fault. Leonardo was not his enemy. His rival, yes. But it was Leonardo's father who was his mortal enemy. And perhaps it would be just as well if Georges wasn't distracted by focusing his rage on his hapless son.

Because he did plan to face him. How could he avoid the confrontation he'd spent his life preparing for?

"Let's go," he said to the man who'd approached him. "Let's get him to his chambers before his father gets here."

He looked back at Pellea, signaling her to his intentions. But she wasn't paying attention any longer. A servant had come to find her.

"My lady, your father is ill and asking for you," he said nervously.

Pellea reacted immediately. "My father! Oh, I must go."

Monte stopped her for only a moment. "I'll meet you at your father's room as soon as I can make it," he told her.

She nodded, her eyes wide and anxious. "I must go," she muttered distractedly, and she hurried away.

Monte looked back at the task at hand and gritted his teeth. It wasn't going to be a pretty chore, but it had to be done.

"Let's get him out of here," he said, hoisting Leonardo up with the assistance of two other men. And, just as they heard Georges arrive at the main ballroom entrance, they slipped out the side door.

"I'll be back, Georges," Monte whispered under his breath. "Get ready. We've got business between us to settle. Old business."

Monte slipped into Pellea's father's room and folded his form between the drapes to keep from being seen. Pellea was talking to the doctor and her father seemed to be sleeping.

The doctor began to pack his black bag and Pellea went to her father's bedside. Monte watched and saw the anguished love in her face as she leaned over the man. There was no denying this simple truth—she adored her father and she wouldn't leave him.

Monte closed his eyes for a moment, letting that sink in. There was no way he would be able to take her with him. All his kidnapping plans—in the dust. In order to get her to leave he would have to render her unconscious and drag her off, and that wasn't going to happen.

When the idea had first formed, he'd assumed she would come at least semi-willingly. Now he knew that was a fantasy. Her love for her father was palpable. She would never leave while he was still alive. And yet, how could he leave her behind? How could he leave her to the tender mercies of the Granvillis? The more he saw of her, the more he got to know her, the more he felt a special connection, something he'd never felt with a woman before. He wanted her with him.

But more than that, he wanted her safe. Leaving her here with Leonardo would be torture. But what could he do?

Invade, a voice deep in his soul said urgently. *The sooner the better.*

Yes. There really was no other option left.

So he would return to the continent empty-handed. Not quite what he'd promised his supporters waiting for him in Italy.

But all was not lost on that score. He had another plan—something new. Instead of kidnapping their most desirable woman, he would take their most valuable possession.

He was going to steal the tiara.

"Please tell me how he really is," she said anxiously to the doctor. "Don't sugarcoat anything. I need to know the truth." She took a deep breath and asked, "Is he in danger?"

"In other words, is he going to die tonight?" Dr. Dracken translated. "Not likely. Don't worry. But he is very weak. His heart is not keeping up as it should." He hesitated, then added, "If you really want me to be blunt, I'd have to say I wouldn't give him much more than six months. But this sort of thing is hugely unpredictable. Next year at this time, you might be chiding me for being so pessimistic."

"Oh, I hope so," she said fervently as she accompanied him to the door. "Please, do anything for him that you can think of."

"Of course. That's my job, Pellea, and I do the best I can."

The doctor left and Monte reached out and touched her as she came back into the room.

"Oh!" She jumped back, then put her hand over her heart when she realized it was him. "Monte! You scared me."

"Sorry, but once I was in, I was going to startle you no matter how I approached it."

She looked at him with tragic eyes. "My father…" Her face crumpled and she went straight into his arms and clung to him.

"Yes," he said, holding her tenderly, stroking her hair. "I heard what the doctor said. I'm so sorry, Pellea. I truly am."

She nodded. She believed him.

"He's sleeping now. The doctor gave him something. But a little while ago he was just ranting, not himself at all." She looked up into his face. "They are bringing in a nurse to stay with him tonight and tomorrow I'm going to sit with him all day."

He nodded, and then he frowned, realizing his fingers were tangling in her loosened hair. She was wearing it down. All the fancy work Magda had put into her coiffure was gone with the wind.

"Pellea, what happened to the tiara?" he asked.

She drew back and reached up as though she'd forgotten it was gone. "The guards took it back to its museum case," she said. She shook her head sadly. "I wonder if I'll ever get to wear it again."

He scowled, regretting that he'd let her get away before doing what he'd planned to do. Unfortunately, this threw a spanner into the works. Oh, he was still going to steal the thing. But now he was afraid he would have to do some actual breaking and entering in order to achieve his objective.

But when he looked at her again, he found her studying him critically, looking him up and down, admiring the uniform, and the man wearing it. He'd lost the mask somewhere, but for the rest, he looked as fresh as he had at the beginning of the evening.

"You know what?" she said at last, her head to the side, her eyes sparkling. "You would make one incredibly attractive Ambrian king."

He laughed and pulled her back into his arms, kissing her soundly. Her arms came up and circled his neck, and she kissed him back. Their bodies seemed to meet and fit together perfectly. He had a quick, fleeting thought that this might be what heaven was made of, but it was over all too soon.

She checked that her father was sleeping peacefully, then turned to Monte again. "Come sit down and wait with me," she said, pulling him by the hand. "And tell me what happened in the ballroom after I left. Did the General actually appear?"

He shook his head. "I didn't stay any longer than you did. With all the chaos that ensued upon Leonardo's… shall we call it a fall from grace…?"

He flashed her a quick grin, but she frowned in response and he sobered quickly, looking abashed.

"There you were, rushing off to see to your father. People were shouting. No one knew exactly what was going on for quite some time. And I and all my new mates picked up your fiancé and carried him to his rooms."

"I'm glad you did that," she said. "I would hate to think of what would have happened if his father had seen him like that."

"Yes," he said a bit doubtfully. "Well, we tucked him into his bed and I nosed around a little."

"Oh?"

"And I find I need to warn you of something."

She smiled. "You warning me? That's a twist on an old theme, isn't it?"

"I'm quite serious, Pellea." He hesitated until he had her complete attention. "Did it ever occur to you that you might not be the only one with a video monitoring system in this castle?"

She shrugged. "Of course. There's the main security center. Everyone knows that."

"Indeed." He gave her a significant look. "And then there's the smaller panel of screens I found in a small room off Leonardo's bedroom suite. The one that includes a crystal-clear view of your entryway."

Her eyes widened in shock. "What?"

He nodded. "I thought that might surprise you. He can see everyone who is coming in to see you, as well as when you leave."

She blanched, thinking back over what she'd done and who she'd been with in the recent past. "But not…" She looked at him sideways and swallowed hard.

"Your bedroom?" He couldn't help but smile at her reaction. "No. I didn't see any evidence of that."

"Thank God." But her relief was short-lived as she began to realize fully the implications of this news.

She frowned. "But how is it monitored? I mean…did he see you when you arrived? Or any of the other times you've come and gone?"

"I'm sure he doesn't spend most of his time sitting in front of the monitor, any more than you do."

"It would only take once."

"True."

"And how about when you arrived this time?"

Monte hesitated, then shrugged and shook his head. "I didn't come in through your entryway."

She stared at him, reminded that his mode of entering the castle was still a mystery. But for him to say flat-out that he didn't use the door—that was something of a revelation. "Then how…?"

He waved it away. "Never mind."

"But, Monte, I do mind. I want to know. How do

you get into my courtyard if you don't come in the way everyone else does?"

"I'm sorry, Pellea. I'm not going to tell you."

She frowned, not liking that at all. "You do realize that this leaves me in jeopardy of having you arrive at any inopportune moment and me not able to do anything about it."

He'd said it before and now he said it again. "I would never do anything to hurt you."

"No." She shook her head, her eyes deeply troubled. "No, Monte. That's not good enough."

He shrugged. He understood how she felt and sympathized. But what could he do? It was something he couldn't tell anyone about.

"It will have to do. I'm sorry, Pellea. I can't give away my advantage on this score. It has nothing to do with you. It has everything to do with my ability to take this country back when the time comes."

She searched his eyes, and finally gave up on the point. But she didn't like it at all. Still, the fact that Leonardo was secretly watching who came to her door was a more immediate outrage.

"Oh, I just can't believe he's watching my entryway!"

Monte grinned. "Why are you so upset? After all, you're watching pretty much everyone in the castle yourself."

"Yes, but I'm just watching general walkways, not private entrances."

"Ah, yes," he teased. "That makes all the difference."

"It does. I wouldn't dream of setting up a monitor on Leonardo's gate."

He raised one eyebrow wisely. "Yes, but you're not interested in him. And he is very interested in you."

She thought about that for a few seconds and made a face. "I'm going to find his camera and tape it up," she vowed.

He looked pained. "Don't do that. Then he'll know you're on to him and he'll just find another way to watch you, and you might like that even less. The fact that you know about the camera gives you the advantage now. You can avoid it when you need to."

She sighed. "You're probably right," she said regretfully. It would have felt good taping over his window into her world.

There was a strange gurgling sound and they both turned to see Pellea's father rising up against his pillows.

"Father!" she cried, running to his side. "Don't try to sit up. Let me help you."

But he wasn't looking at his daughter. It was Monte he had in his sights.

"Your Majesty," he groaned painfully. "Your Royal Highness, King of Ambria."

Monte rose and faced him, hoping he would realize the man standing in his bedroom was not the king he'd served all those years ago, but that king's son. This was the first time anyone had mistaken him for his father. He felt a strange mix of honor and repulsion over it.

"My liege," Pellea's father cried, slurring his words. His thin, aged face was still handsome and his silver hair still as carefully groomed and distinguished as ever. "Wait, don't go. I need to tell you. I need to explain. It wasn't supposed to happen that way. I…I didn't mean for it to be like that."

"Father," Pellea said, trying to calm him. "Please, lie back down. Don't try to talk. Just rest."

"Don't you see?" he went on passionately, ignoring her and talking directly to the man he thought was King Grandor. "They had promised, they'd sworn you would be treated with respect. And your queen, the beautiful Elineas. No one should have touched her. It was a travesty and I swear it cursed our enterprise from the beginning."

Monte stood frozen to the spot. He heard the old man's words and they pierced his heart. It was obvious he had a message he'd been waiting a long time to deliver to Monte's father. Well, he was about twenty-five years too late.

He slid down into his covers again, now babbling almost incoherently. Pellea looked up with tears in her eyes.

"He doesn't know what he's saying," she said. "Please go, Monte. You're only upsetting him. I'll stay until the nurse comes."

Monte turned and did as she asked. His emotions were churning. He knew Pellea's father was trying to make amends of sorts, but it was a little too late. Still, it was good that he recognized that wrong had been done.

Wrong that still had to be avenged.

CHAPTER EIGHT

KNOWING PELLEA WOULD BE BUSY with her father for some time, Monte made a decision. He planned to make a visit to General Georges. Why not do it now?

A deadly calm came over him as he prepared to go. This meeting with the most evil man in his country's history was something he'd gone over a thousand times in his mind and each time there had been a different scenario, a different outcome. Which one would he choose? It didn't matter, really. They all ended up with the General mortally wounded or already dead.

The fact that his own survival might be in doubt in such an encounter he barely acknowledged and didn't worry about at all. His destiny was already set and included a confrontation with the General. That was just the way it had to be.

He strode down the hallways with confidence. He knew where the cameras were and he avoided them with ease. One of Leonardo's compadres had pointed out the General's suite to him as they'd carried Leonardo past it, and he went there now.

Breaking into the room was a simple matter. There

were no guards and the lock was a basic one. He'd learned this sort of thing as a teenager and it had stood him in good stead many times over the years.

Quietly, he slipped into the darkened room. He could hear the General snoring, and he went directly into his bedroom and yanked back the covers on his bed, ready to counter any move the older man made, whether he pulled out a gun or a cell phone.

But the man didn't move. He slept on. He seemed to have none of the effete elegance his son wore so proudly. Instead, he was large and heavy-set, but strangely amorphous, like a sculpture that had begun to melt back into a lump of clay.

"Wake up," Monte ordered. "I want to talk to you."

No response. Monte moved closer and touched the dictator. Nothing changed.

He glanced at the things on the bedside table. Bottles of fluid and a box of hypodermic needles sat waiting. His heart sank and he turned on the light and looked at the General again.

His eyes were open. He was awake.

The man was drugged. He lay, staring into space, a mere burnt-out shell of the human being he had once been. There wasn't much left. Monte realized that he could easily pick up a pillow and put it over the General's face…and that would be that. It would be a cinch. No problem at all. There wasn't an ounce of fight left in his enemy.

He stood staring down at the General for a long, long time and finally had to admit that he couldn't do it. He'd always thought he would kill Georges Granvilli if he found him. But now that he'd come face to face with him, he knew there was nothing left to kill. The man who had murdered his parents and destroyed his family was gone. This thing that was left was hardly even human.

Killing Georges Granvilli wouldn't make anything any better. He would just be a killer himself if he did it. He wasn't worth killing. The entire situation wasn't worth pursuing.

Slowly, Monte walked away in disgust.

He got back to the courtyard just moments before Pellea arrived. He thought about telling her where he'd been and what he'd seen, but he decided against it. There was no point in putting more ugliness in her thoughts right now. He could at least spare her that.

He was sitting by the fountain in the twilight atmosphere created by all the tiny fairy lights in her shrubbery when she came hurrying in through the gate.

"Monte?" she asked softly, then came straight for him like a swooping bird. As she reached him, she seized his face in her hands and kissed him on the lips, hard.

"You've got to go," she said urgently, tears in her eyes. "Go now, quickly, before they come for you."

"What have you heard?" he asked her, reaching to pull her down into his lap so that he could kiss her sweet lips once more.

"It's not what I've heard," she told him, snuggling in closely. "It's what I know. It's only logic. When all this chaos dies down and they begin to put two and two together, they'll come straight here looking for you. And you know what they'll find."

He searched her dark eyes, loving the way her long lashes made soft shadows on her cheeks. "Then we'd better get the heck out of here," he said calmly.

"No." She shook her head and looked away. "You're going. I'm staying."

He grimaced, afraid she still didn't understand the consequences of staying. "How can I leave you behind to pick up the pieces?"

"You have to go," she told him earnestly. She turned back to look at him, then reached up to run her fingers across the roughness of his barely visible beard, as though she just couldn't help herself. "When Leonardo wakes up, he's going to start asking around and trying to find out just who that man at the ball was. He'll want to know all about you and where you've been staying. And this time, they won't leave my chambers alone. They'll search with a fine-tooth comb and any evidence that you've been here will be…"

Her voice trailed off as she began to face the unavoidable fact that she was in as much danger as he was. She looked at him, eyes wide.

He was just thinking the same thing. It was torture to imagine leaving her behind. He'd turned and twisted every angle in his mind, trying to think of some way out, but the more he agonized, the more he knew there was no good answer. Unless she just gave up this obsession with staying with her father, what could he do to make sure she was protected while he was gone?

Nothing. Nothing at all.

He did have one idea, but he rejected it right away. And yet, it kept nagging at him. What if he showed her the tunnel to the outside? Then, if she was threatened, she could use it to escape.

They were bound to come after her, and even if they couldn't find any solid evidence of her ties to him, they would have their suspicions. Luckily her position and the fact that her father was so highly placed in the hierarchy would mean the most they would do at first was place her under house surveillance—meaning she would be confined to her chambers. But if her father died, or Leonardo became insanely jealous, or something else happened, all that might fall apart. In that case, it would be important for her to have a way to escape that others didn't know about. That was what made it so tempting to give her the information she needed.

Still, it was crazy even to contemplate doing that. Deep down, he didn't believe she would betray him on purpose. But what if she was discovered? What if someone saw her? His ace in the hole, his secret opening back into the castle which he and his invading force would need when he returned to claim his country back would be useless. He just couldn't risk that. Could he?

"And Monte," she was saying, getting back to the subject of her thoughts. "Leonardo's father is not a nice man."

"No?" Monte thought of the burned-out hulk he'd just been visiting. "What a surprise."

"I'm serious. Leonardo has at least some redeeming qualities. His father? None."

He looked at her seriously. "And do those redeeming qualities make him into a man you can stomach marrying?"

She avoided his eyes. "Monte…"

His arms tightened around her. "You can't kiss me the way you just did and then talk about marrying Leonardo. It doesn't work, Pellea. I've told you that before and nothing's changed." He kissed her again on her mouth, once, twice, three times, with quick hunger that grew more urgent with each kiss. He pulled her up hard against his strong body, her softness molding against him in a way that could quickly drive him crazy. Burying his face in her hair, he wanted to breathe her in, wanted to merge every part of her with every part of him.

She turned in his arms, reaching up to circle his neck, arching her body into his as though she felt the same compulsion. He dropped kisses down the length of her neck and heard her make a soft moaning sound deep in her throat. That alone almost sent him over the top, and the way her small hands felt gliding under his shirt and sliding over the muscles of his back pretty much completed the effort.

He wanted her as he'd never wanted a woman before, relentlessly, fiercely, with an insatiable need that raged through him like a hurricane. He'd felt this way about her before, but he hadn't let her know. Now, for just a few moments, he let her feel it, let her have a hint of what rode just on the other side of his patience.

She could have been shocked. She could have considered his ardor a step too far and drawn back in complete rejection. But as she felt his passion overtaking him and his desire for her so manifest, she accepted it with a willingness of her own. She wanted him, too. His marriage of the emotional need for her with the physical hunger was totally in tune with her own reactions.

But this wasn't the time. Resolutely, she pushed him back before things went too far.

He accepted her lead on it, but he had to add one thing as she slipped out of his arms.

"You belong to me," he said fiercely, his hand holding the back of her head like a globe. "Leonardo can't have you."

She tried to shake her head. "I'm going to marry him," she insisted, and though her voice was mournful, she sounded determined. "I've told you that from the moment you came today. I don't know why you won't listen."

This would be so much easier if she could tell him the truth, but that was impossible. How could he understand that she needed Leonardo even more than he needed her? She was caught in a web. If she didn't marry Leonardo, she would be considered an outcast in Ambrian traditional society.

Out-of-wedlock births were not uncommon, but they were considered beyond the pale. Once you had a baby out of wedlock, you could never be prominent in society. You would always have the taint of bad behavior about you. No one would trust your judgment and everyone would slightly despise you.

It wasn't fair, but it was the way things were.

He held her in a curiously stiff manner that left her feeling distinctly uncomfortable.

"You don't love Leonardo," he said. He'd said it before, but she didn't seem to want to accept it and act upon the fact. Maybe he should say it again and keep saying it until she realized that some things were hard, basic truths that couldn't be denied or swept under the rug.

She pulled away from him and folded her arms across her chest as though she were feeling a frost.

"I hate to repeat a cliché," she said tartly, "but here goes. What's love got to do with it?"

He nodded, his face twisted cynically. "So you admit this is a royal contract sort of wedding. A business deal."

"A power deal is more like it. Our union will cement the power arrangements necessary to run this country successfully."

"And you still think he'll want you, even if he begins to suspect…"

"I told you, love isn't involved. It's a power trade, and he wants it as much as I need it."

"Need it?" He stared at her. "Why do you 'need' it?"

She closed her eyes and shook her head. "Maybe I put it a little too strongly," she said. "I just meant… Well, you know. For my father and all."

He wasn't sure he bought that. There was something else here, something she wasn't telling him. He frowned, looking at her narrowly. He found it hard to believe that she would prefer that sort of thing to a love match. But then, he hadn't offered her a love match, had he? He hadn't even offered her a permanent friendship. So who was he to complain? And yet, he had to. He had to stop this somehow.

"Okay, I see the power from Leonardo's side," he said, mulling it over. "But where do you get yours?"

She rose and swayed in front of him, anger sparking from her eyes. She didn't like being grilled this way, mostly because she didn't have any good answers.

"For someone who wants to be ruler of Ambria, you don't know much about local politics, do you?"

He turned his hands palms-up. "If you weren't such a closed society, maybe I could be a bit more in the know," he pointed out.

She considered that and nodded reluctantly. "That's a fair point. Okay, here's the deal. Over the years, there have been many factions who have—shall we say—strained under the Granvilli rule for various reasons. A large group of dissenters, called the Practicals, have been arguing that our system is archaic and needs updating. For some reason they seem to have gravitated toward my father as their symbolic leader."

Monte grunted. "That must make life a bit dodgy for your father," he noted.

"A bit. But he has been invaluable to the rulers and

they don't dare do anything to him. And anyway, the Practicals would come unglued if they did."

"Interesting."

"The Practicals look to me as well. In fact, it may just be a couple of speeches I gave last year that set them in our direction, made them think we were kindred souls. So in allying himself with me, Leonardo hopes to blunt some of that unrest."

He gazed at her in admiration and surprise. "Who knew you were a mover and a shaker?" he said.

She actually looked a bit embarrassed. "I'm not. Not really. But I do sympathize with many of their criticisms of the way things are run. Once I marry Leonardo, I hope to make some changes."

Was that it? Did she crave the power as much as her father did? Was it really all a bid for control with her? He found that hard to believe, but when she said these things, what was he to think?

He studied her for another moment, then shrugged. "That's what they all say," he muttered, mostly to himself.

She was tempted to say something biting back, but she held her tongue. There was no point in going on with this. They didn't have much more time together and there were so many other things they could be talking about.

"Have you noticed that so far, no one seems to know who you really are?" she pointed out. As long as they didn't know who he was, his freedom might be imperiled, but his life wouldn't be. And if they should somehow realize who it was they had in their clutches… She hated to think what they might do.

"No, they don't, do they?" He frowned, not totally pleased with that. "How did *you* know, anyway? From the other time, I mean."

"You told me." She smiled at him, remembering.

"Oh. Did I?" That didn't seem logical or even realistic. He never told anyone.

"Yes, right from the first." She gave him a flirtatious look. "Right after I saved you from the guards, you kissed me and then you said, 'You can tell everyone you've been kissed by the future king of Ambria. Consider yourself blessed.'"

"I said that?" He winced a bit and laughed softly. "I guess you might be right about me having something of an ego problem."

"No kidding." She made a face. "Maybe it goes with being royal or something."

"Oh, I don't know about that." After all, he hadn't blown his cover all these years—except, it seemed, with her. "I think I do pretty well. Don't you think I blend in nicely with the average Joes?"

She shook her head, though there was a hint of laughter in her eyes. "Are you crazy? No, you do not blend in, as you so colorfully put it. Look at the way you carry yourself. The arrogance. There's no humility about you."

"No humility?" He was offended. "What are you talking about? I'm probably the most humble guy you would ever meet."

She made a sound of deprecation. "A little self-awareness would go a long way here," she noted as she looked him over critically. "But I could see that from the start. It was written all over you. And yet, I didn't kick you out as I should have."

"No, you didn't." Their gazes met and held. "But we did have an awfully good weekend, didn't we?"

"Yes." She said it softly, loving him, thinking of the child they had made together. If only she could tell him about that. Would he be happy? Probably not. That was just the way things were going to be. She loved him and he felt something pretty deep for her. But that was all they were destined to have of each other. How she would love to spend the next fifty years in his arms.

If only he weren't royal and she weren't tied to this place. If only he didn't care so much about Ambria. They could have done so well together, the two of them. She could imagine them walking on a sandy beach, chasing waves, or having a picnic by a babbling brook, skipping stones in the water, or driving around France, looking at vineyards and trying to identify the grapes.

Instead, he was planning to invade her country. And that would, of necessity, kill people she cared about. How could she stand it? Why hadn't she turned him in?

"Why does it matter so much to you, Monte?" she asked at last. "Why can't you just leave things alone?"

He looked up, his eyes dark and haunted. "Because a very large wrong was done to my family. And to this country. I need to make things right again. That's all I live for."

His words stabbed into her soul like sharp knives. If this was all he lived for, what could she ever be to him?

"Isn't there someone else who could do it?" she asked softly. "Does it have to be you?"

Reaching out, he put his hand under the water raining down from the fountain. Drops bounced out and scattered across his face, but he seemed to welcome them. "I'm the crown prince. I can't let others fight my battles for me."

"But you have brothers, don't you?"

He nodded. "There were five of us that night. Or rather, seven. Five boys and twin girls." He was quiet for a moment, remembering. "I hunted for them all for years. I started once I enrolled in university in England. I studied hard, but I spent a lot of time poring over record books in obscure villages, hoping to find some clue. There was nothing."

He sighed, in his own milieu now. "Once I entered the business world and then did some work for the Foreign Office, I developed contacts all over the world. And those have just begun to pan out. As I think I told you, I've made contact with two of my brothers, the two closest to me in age. But the others are still a mystery."

"Are you still looking?"

"Of course. I'll be looking until I find them all. For the rest of my life if need be." He shrugged. "I don't know if they are alive or not. But I'll keep looking." He turned and looked at her, his eyes burning. "Once we're all together, there will be no stopping us."

She shook her head, unable to imagine how growing up without any contact with his family would have affected this young Ambrian prince.

"What was it like?" she asked him. "What happened to you as a child? It must have been terrible to grow up alone."

He nodded. "It wasn't great. I had a wonderful family until I was eight years old. After that, it was hit or miss. I stayed with people who didn't necessarily know who I was, but who knew I had to be hidden. I ended up with a couple who were kind to me but hardly loving." He shrugged. "Not that it mattered. I wasn't looking for a replacement for my mother, nor for my father. No one could replace either one of them and I didn't expect it."

"Why were they hiding you?"

"They were trying to keep the Granvillis from having me killed."

"Oh." She colored as though that were somehow her fault. "I see."

"We were all hidden. From each other, even. You understand that any surviving royals were a threat to the Granvilli rule, and I, being the crown prince, am the biggest threat of all."

"Of course. I get it."

"We traveled a lot. I went to great schools. I had the sort of upbringing you would expect of a royal child, minus the love. But I survived and in fact, I think I did pretty well."

"It wasn't until I found my brother Darius that I could reignite that family feeling and I began to come alive again. Family is everything and I had lost mine."

"And your other brother?"

"A young woman who worked for an Ambrian news agency in the U.S. found Cassius. He was only four during the coup and he didn't remember that he was royal. He'd grown up as a California surfer and spent time in the military. Finding out his place in life has been quite a culture shock to him. He's trying to learn how to be royal, but it isn't easy for a surfer boy. I only hope he can hold it all together until we retake our country."

The old wall clock struck the time and it was very late, well after midnight. She looked at him and sighed. "You must go," she told him.

He looked back at her and wondered how he could leave her here. "Come with me, Pellea," he said, his voice crackling with intensity. "Come with me tonight. By late morning, we'll be in France."

She closed her eyes. She was so tired. "You know I can't," she whispered.

He rose and came over to kiss her softly on her full, red lips. "Then come and get some sleep," he told her. "I'll go just before dawn."

"Will you wake me up when you go?" she asked groggily.

"Yes. I'll wake you."

And would he show her his escape secrets? That was

probably a step too far. He couldn't risk it. He had to think of more lives than just their two. So he promised he would wake her, but he didn't promise he would let her see him go.

She lay down in her big, fluffy bed and he lay down on her long couch, which was almost as comfortable. He didn't understand why she wouldn't let him sleep beside her. She seemed to have some strange sense of a moral duty to Leonardo. Well, if it was important to her, he wasn't going to mess with it. She had to do what she had to do, just like he did. Lying still and listening to her breathe on the bed so near and yet so far, he almost slept.

CHAPTER NINE

THE MOMENT PELLEA WOKE, she knew Monte was gone. It was still dark and nowhere near dawn, but he was gone. Just as she'd thought.

She curled into a ball of misery and wept. Someday she would have his child to console her, but right now there was nothing good and beautiful and strong and true in her life but Monte. And he was gone.

But wait. She lifted her head and thought for a moment. He'd promised to say goodbye. He wouldn't break his promise. If he didn't tell her in person, he would at least have left a note, and there was nothing. That meant…he was still somewhere in the castle.

Her heart stopped in her throat. What now? Where could he be? Dread filled her since, surely, he would get caught. He would be killed. He would have to leave without saying goodbye! She couldn't stand it. None of the above was tolerable. She had to act fast.

Rising quickly, she went to the surveillance room with the security monitors and began to study them. All looked quiet. It was about three in the morning, and she detected no movement.

Maybe she was wrong. Maybe he had gone without saying goodbye. Darn it all!

That's when she saw something moving in the museum. A form. A tall, graceful masculine form. Monte! What was he doing in the museum room?

The tiara!

She groaned. "No, Monte!" she cried, but of course he couldn't hear her.

And then, on another panel, she saw the guards. There were three of them and they were moving slowly down the hallway toward the museum, looking like men gearing up for action. There was no doubt in her mind. They'd been alerted to his presence and would nab him.

Her heart was pounding out of her chest. She had to act fast. She couldn't let them catch him like this. They would throw him in jail and Leonardo would hear of it and Monte's identity would be revealed and he would be a dead man. She groaned.

She couldn't let that happen. There was only one thing she could do. She had to go there and stop it.

In another moment she was racing through the hallways, her white nightgown billowing behind her, her hair a cloud of golden blond, and her bare feet making a soft padding sound on the carpeted floors.

She ran, heedless of camera positions, heedless of anyone who might step out and see her. Who would be watching at this time of night anyway? Only the very men she'd seen going after Monte. She had one goal and that was to save his singularly annoying life. If only she could get there in time.

The museum door was ajar. She burst in and came face to face with Monte, but he was standing before her in handcuffs, with a guard on either side. Behind them, she could see the tiara, glistening on its mount inside the glass case. At least he didn't have it in his hands.

She stared into Monte's eyes for only a second or two, long enough to note the look of chagrin he wore at being caught, and then she swung her attention onto the guards.

"What is going on here?" she demanded, her stern gaze brooking no attitude from any of them. She knew how to pour on the superior pose when she had to and she was playing it to the hilt right now. Even standing there barefoot and in her nightgown she radiated control.

The guards were wide-eyed. They knew who she was but they'd never seen her like this. After a moment of surprised reaction, the captain stepped forward.

"Miss, we have captured the intruder." He nodded toward Monte and looked quite pleased with himself.

She blinked, then gestured toward Monte with a sweep of her hand. "You call this an intruder?" she said sternly, her lip curling a bit in disdain.

"Uh." The captain looked at her and then looked away again. "We caught him red-handed, Miss. He was trying to steal the tiara. Look, you can see that the lock was forced open."

"Uh." The second in command tugged on the captain's shirt and whispered in his ear.

The captain frowned and turned back to Pellea, looking most disapproving.

"I'm told you might have been dancing with this gentleman at the ball, Miss," he said. "Perhaps you can identify him for us."

"Certainly," she said in a sprightly manner. "He's a good friend of Leonardo's."

"Oh." All three appeared shocked and Monte actually gave her a triumphant wink which she ignored as best she could. "Well, there may be something there. Mr. Leonardo, is it?"

Just his name threw them for a loop. Everyone was terrified of Leonardo. They shuffled their feet but the captain wasn't cowed.

"Still, we found him breaking into the museum case," he noted. "You can't do that."

"Is anything missing?" she asked, looking bored with it all.

"No. We caught him in time."

"Well then." She gave a grand shrug. "All's well that ends well, isn't it?"

The captain frowned. "Not exactly. I'm afraid I have to make a report of this to the General. He'll want to know the particulars and might even want to interview the intruder himself."

Not a good outcome. Monte gave her a look that reminded her that this would be a bad ending to this case. But she already knew as much.

"Oh, I doubt that," she said airily. "If you have some time to question him yourself, I think you will find the problem that is at the root of all this."

The captain frowned. He obviously wasn't sure he

liked the interference being run by this know-it-all from
the regime hierarchy. "And that is?"

She sighed as though it was just so tedious to have to
go over the particulars.

"My good man, it was a ball. You know how men get.
This one and Leonardo were challenging each other to a
drinking contest." She shrugged elaborately. "Leonardo
is now out cold in his room. I'm sure you'll find this
fellow…" She gestured his way. "…who you may know
as the Count of Revanche, isn't in much better shape. He
may not show it but he has no clue what he's doing."

The guards looked at Monte. He gave them a par-
ticularly mindless grin. They frowned as Monte added a
mock fierce look for good measure. The guards glanced
away and shuffled their feet again.

"Well, miss," said the captain, "What you say may
be true and all. But he was still found in the museum
room, and the lock was tampered with and that just isn't
right."

Pellea bit her lip, biding for time. They were going
to be sticklers, weren't they? She felt the need of some
reinforcement. For that, she turned to Monte.

"Please, Your Highness, tell us what you were doing
in the museum room."

He gave her a fish-eyed look before he turned to the
guards and gave it a try.

"I was…" He managed to look a little woozy. "I was
attempting to steal the tiara." He said it as though it were
a grand announcement.

"What on earth!" she cried, feeling all was lost and wondering what he was up to.

"Don't you understand?" he said wistfully. "It's so beautiful. I wanted to give it back to you so that you could wear it again."

She stared at him, dumbfounded at how he could think this was a good excuse.

"To me?" she repeated softly.

"Yes. You looked enchanting in it, like a fairy-tale princess, and I thought you should have it, always." His huge, puppy-dog eyes were doing him a service, but some might call it over the top for this job.

"But, it's not mine," she reminded him sadly.

"No?" He looked a bit puzzled by that. "Well, it should be."

She turned to the guards. "You see?" she said, throwing out her hands. "He's not in his right mind. I think you should let me take him off your hands. You don't really want to bother the General with this trifle, especially at this time of night. Do you?"

The captain tried to look stern. "Well, now that you mention it, miss…"

She breathed a sigh of relief. "Good, I'll just take him along then."

They were shuffling their feet again. That seemed to be a sign that they weren't really sure what they should be doing.

"Would you like one of us to come along and help you handle him?" the captain asked, groping for his place in all this.

"No, I think he'll be all right." She took hold of his hands, bound by the handcuffs, and the captain handed her the key. "He usually does just what I tell him," she lied happily. She'd saved him. She could hardly contain her excitement.

"I see, miss. Good night, then."

"Good night, Captain. Men." She waved at them merrily and began to lead Monte away. "Come along now, Count," she murmured to him teasingly. "I've got you under house arrest. You'd better do what I tell you to from now on."

"That'll be the day," he said under his breath, but his eyes were smiling.

Once back in her courtyard, they sat side by side on the garden bench and leaned back, sighing with relief.

"You're crazy," she told him matter-of-factly. "To risk everything for a tiara."

"It's a very special tiara," he reminded her. "And by all rights, it belongs to my family."

"Maybe so, but there are others who would fight you for it," she said, half closing her eyes and thinking about getting more sleep. "You almost pulled it off," she added.

"Yes."

She turned to look at him. "And you actually seemed to know what you were doing. Why was that? Have you been moonlighting as a jewel thief or something?"

He settled back and smiled at her. "In fact, I do know what I'm doing around jewelry heists," he stated calmly.

"I apprenticed myself to a master jewel thief one summer. He taught me everything he knew."

She frowned at him for a long moment. It was late. Perhaps she hadn't heard him correctly. But did he say…?

"What in the name of common sense are you talking about?" she said, shaking her head in bewilderment. "Why would you do such a thing?"

He shrugged. "I wanted to learn all I could about breaking into reinforced and security-protected buildings. I thought it would be a handy talent to have when it came time to reassert my monarchy on this island nation."

She stared at him in wonder, not sure if she was impressed or appalled. But it did show another piece of evidence of the strength of his determination to get his country back. This was pretty obviously an ambition she wasn't going to be able to fight.

Sighing, she shook her head and turned away. "Well, maybe you should go back for a refresher course," she noted.

He raised an eyebrow. "What are you talking about?"

She looked back at him. "Well, you didn't get the tiara, did you?"

"What makes you say that?" He smiled and reached back and pulled something out of the back of his shirt and held it up to the light, where it glittered spectacularly.

"You mean this tiara?" he asked her.

She stared at it as it flashed color and fire all around the room. "But I saw it in the case in the museum."

"You saw a copy in the case." He held it even higher and looked at it, admiring its beauty. "This is the real thing."

She was once again bewildered by him. "I don't understand."

"What you saw was a replica. My grandmother had it made years ago. I remembered that my mother had it in a secret hiding place. I went over to that side of the castle and, lo and behold, I found it."

"That's amazing. After all this time? I can hardly believe it."

"Yes. It seems that most of my family's private belongings were shoved into a big empty room and have been forgotten. Luckily for me."

She shook her head. "But now that you have the tiara, what are you going to do with it?"

"Take it back with me." He tucked it away and leaned over to take her hand in his. "If I can't take their most beautiful woman from them, at least I can take their prized royal artifact." He smiled. "And when you think about it, the tiara actually belongs to me. Surely you see that."

She laced her fingers with his and yearned toward him. "You're just trying to humiliate them, aren't you? You would have preferred to do it by stealing me away, but since that's not possible, you take the tiara instead."

"Yes," he said simply. "The answer is yes."

"But…"

"Don't you understand, Pellea? I want them thrown off-center. I want them to wonder what my next move might be. I want them to doubt themselves." The spirit of the royal warrior was back in his eyes. "Because when I come back, I'm going to take this country away from them."

He sounded sure of himself, but in truth, here in the middle of the night, he was filled with misgivings and doubts. Would he really be able to restore the monarchy? Would he get his family back into the position they'd lost twenty-five years before? Night whispers attacked his confidence and he had to fight them back.

Because he had to succeed. And he would, damn it, or die trying. No doubts could be allowed. His family belonged here and they would be back. This was what his whole life had been aimed at.

It was time to go. Actually, it was way past time to go, but he had run up against the wall by now. He had to follow the rules of logic and get out of here before someone showed up at Pellea's gate. It was just a matter of time.

But there was something else. He had made a decision. He was going to show Pellea the tunnel. There was no other option. If he couldn't take her with him, he had to give her some way to escape if things got too bad.

He was well aware of what he was doing—acting like a fool under the spell of a woman. If he were watching a friend in the same circumstances, he would be yelling, "Stop!" right now. Every bit of common sense argued against it. You just didn't risk your most important advantages like that.

After all, there were so many imponderables. Could he trust her? He was sure he could, and yet, how many men had said that and come out the loser in the end? Could he really take a woman who claimed she was going to marry into the family of the enemy and expect her to keep his confidences? Was he crazy to do this? He knew he was risking everything by placing a bet on her integrity and her fidelity—a bet that could be lost so easily. How many men had been destroyed putting too much trust in love?

For some reason the lyrics to "Blues in the Night" came drifting into his head. But who took their advice from old songs, anyway?

He had to trust her, because he had to protect her. There was nothing else he could do.

"Pellea," he said, taking her into his arms. "I'm going."

"Oh, thank God!" She held his face in her hands and looked at him with all the love she possessed. "I won't rest easy until you get to Italy."

He kissed her softly. "But I need you to do me a favor."

"Anything."

He was looking very serious. "I want you to keep a secret."

She smiled. "Another one?"

He touched her face and winced, as though she was

almost too beautiful to bear. "I'm going to show you how I get into the castle."

Her face lost its humor and went totally still. She understood right away how drastic this was for him. He'd refused even to hint at this to her all along. Now he was going to show her the one ace in the hole he had—the chink in the castle's armor. Her heart began to beat a bit faster. She knew very well that this was a heavy responsibility.

"All right," she said quietly. "And Monte, please don't worry. I will never, ever show this to anyone."

He looked at her and loved her, loved her noble face, loved her noble intentions. He knew she meant that with all her heart and soul, but he also knew that circumstances could change. Stranger things had happened. Still, he had to do it. He couldn't live with himself if he didn't leave behind some sort of escape route for her.

He frowned, thinking of what he was doing. It wouldn't be enough to show her where it was. The tunnel was old and dark and scary. He remembered when he'd first tried to negotiate it a few weeks before. He'd always known about it—it was the way he and his brothers had escaped on that terrible night all those years ago. And it had been immediately obvious no one had used it since. That was the benefit of having strangers take over your castle. If they made themselves hateful enough, no one would tell them the castle secrets.

When he'd come through, in order to pass he'd had to cut aside huge roots which had grown in through cracks. For someone like Pellea, it might be almost impossible.

It would be better if she came partway with him so that she would see what it was like and wouldn't be intimidated by the unknown.

"Bring a flashlight," he told her. "You're going to need it."

She followed him. He took her behind the fountain, behind the clump of ancient shrubs that seemed to grow right out of the rocks. He moved some smaller stones, then pushed aside a boulder that was actually made of pumice and was much lighter than it looked. And there, just underfoot, was a set of crumbling steps and a dank, dark tunnel that spiraled down.

"Here it is," he told her. "Think you can manage it?"

She looked down. It would be full of spiders and insects and slimy moss and things that would make her scream if she saw them. But she swallowed hard and nodded.

"Of course," she said, trying hard to sound nonchalant. "Let's go."

He showed her how to fill in the opening behind her, and then they started off. And it was just as unpleasant a journey as she'd suspected it would be. In twenty-five years, lots of steps had crumbled and roots had torn apart some walls. The natural breakdown of age was continuing apace and wouldn't be reversed until someone began maintaining the passageway. Even with a flashlight, the trip was dark and foreboding and she was glad she had Monte with her.

"Just ahead there is a small window," he told her. "We'll stop there and you can go back."

"All right," she said, shuddering to think what it was going to be like when she was alone.

"How are you feeling?" he said.

"Nauseated," she said before she thought. "But I'm always sick in the morning lately."

As soon as the words were past her lips she regretted them. How was it that she could feel so free and open to saying anything that came into her head when she was with him? And then she ended up saying too much. She glanced at him, wondering if he'd noticed.

He gave no sign of it. He helped her down the last set of stairs and there was the thin slit of a window, just beginning to show the dawn coming out over the ocean. They stopped and sat to rest. He pulled her close, tightening his arm around her and kissing her cheek.

She turned her face to accept his lips and he gave her more. Startled, she found in the heat of his mouth a quick arousal, calling up a passionate response from her that would have shocked her if she hadn't already admitted to herself that this man was all she ever wanted, body and soul. She drew back, breathless, heart racing and he groaned as she turned away.

"Pellea, you can't marry Leonardo. I don't care how much your father wants you to. It won't end up the way he hopes anyway. Nothing like that ever does. You can't sell your soul for security. It doesn't work."

"Monte, you don't really know everything. And you can't orchestrate things from afar. I've got to deal with the hand I've been dealt. You won't be here and you won't figure in. That's just the way it has to be."

"You don't understand. This is different. I'm making you a promise." He hesitated, steeling himself for what he had to do. "I'm going to move up operations. We'll invade by midsummer. I'll come and get you." He brushed the loose curls back from her face and looked at her with loving intensity. Here in the gloom, she was like a shining beacon in the dark.

"Leonardo's brand of protection won't do you any good by then. I'll be the one your father will have to look to."

His words struck fear into her heart. She turned, imploring him.

"No, Monte. You can't do that. You'll put yourself and all your men in danger if you try to come before your forces are ready. You can't risk everything just for me." She reached up and grabbed the front of his shirt in both hands. "I can't let you do that."

He gazed back steadily. "We'll have right and emotion on our side. We'll win anyway."

"Monte, don't be crazy. You know life doesn't work like that. Just being right, or good, or the nicest, doesn't win you a war. You need training and equipment and the manpower and…"

He was laughing at her and she stopped, nonplussed. "What is it?"

"You sound as though you've taken an army into the field yourself," he told her. "If I didn't know better, I would think you were a natural-born queen."

She flushed, not sure whether he was making fun of her. "I only know I want you safe," she said, her voice trembling a bit.

He took her into his arms. "I'll be safe. You're the one who needs protecting. You're the one ready to put your trust in the Granvillis."

She shook her head. "It's not like that," she said, but he wasn't listening.

He gazed at her, his blue eyes troubled. "I'll do anything I have to do to keep you from harm."

"You can't do it. You can't invade until you're ready."

"We'll get ready." He lifted her chin with his finger. "Just don't ruin everything by marrying Leonardo."

She turned away. Another wave of nausea was turning her breathless.

"What is it?" he said.

She shook her head. "I'm…I'm just a little sick."

He sat back a moment, watching her. "Have you been having that a lot lately?"

She couldn't deny it. She looked up and tried to make a joke out of it. "Yes. I imagine the situation in the world brings on nausea in most sane people at least once a day."

He frowned. "Possibly." A few bits of scattered elements came together and formed a thought. He remembered the way she seemed to want to protect her belly. The book at her bedside. The sudden aversion to alcohol. "Or maybe you're pregnant."

She went very still.

"Are you, Pellea? Are you pregnant?"

She paled, then tried to answer, but no words came out of her mouth.

"You are."

Suddenly the entire picture cleared for him. Of course. That explained everything—the reluctance to recreate the love they'd shared, the hurry to get him out of her hair, the rush to marry Leonardo. But something else was also clear. If she was pregnant, he had no doubt at all that the baby was his.

What the hell!

"You're pregnant with my baby and you weren't going to tell me about it?"

Outrage filled his voice and generated from his body. He shook his head, unable to understand how she could have done this. "And you plan to marry Leonardo?" he added in disbelief.

That rocked him back on his heels. He couldn't accept these things. They made no sense.

"Pellea…" He shook his head, unable to find the words to express how devastated he was…and angry.

She turned on him defensively. "I have to marry *someone*," she said crisply. "And you aren't going to marry me, are you?"

She held her breath, waiting for his response to that one, hoping beyond all logic.

He stared at her, rage mixing with confusion. He couldn't marry her. Could he? But if she was carrying his child… This was something new, something he hadn't even considered. Did it change everything? Or was everything already set in stone and unchangeable?

He turned away, staring out at the ocean through the tiny window in the wall. She waited and watched the emotions crossing in his face and knew he wrestled with his feelings for her, his brand-new feelings for his child, and his role as the crown prince and a warrior king. He was torn, unprepared for such big questions all at once. She had to give him a bit of space. But she'd hoped for more. It wasn't like him to be so indecisive.

And, as he didn't seem to be able to find words that would heal things between them, her heart began to sink. What was the use of him telling her that they had to be together if he wasn't prepared to take the steps that might lead to something real? If he would never even consider making her his wife?

He had a lot of pride as the royal heir to Ambria. Well, she had a bit of pride herself. And she wasn't going anywhere without a promise of official status. If she wasn't good enough to marry, she would find another way to raise her child.

He turned back, eyes hard and cold as ice. "You have to come with me," he said flatly.

She was already shaking her head. "You know I can't go with you while my father lives."

Frustration filled his face and he turned away again, swearing softly. "I know," he said at last, his hands balled into fists. "And I can't ask you to abandon him."

"Never."

"But, Pellea, you have to listen…"

Whatever he was about to say was lost to history. An alarm went off like a bomb, echoing against the walls of the castle, shaking it to its foundations. They turned, reaching for each other, and then clinging together as the walls seemed to shake.

He looked questioningly at her. "What is it?" he asked her roughly.

"The castle alarm," she said. "Something must have happened. I haven't heard an alarm like this since…since Leonardo's mother died."

He stepped back, listening. "I thought for a moment it was an earthquake," he muttered, frowning. "Do you think…?"

"I don't know," she said, answering his unspoken question.

The alarm continued to sound. Pellea put her hands over her ears.

And just as suddenly as it had begun, it stopped. They stared at each other for a long moment.

"I'm going back," she said.

He nodded. He'd known she would. He had never wanted anything more strongly than he wanted her to come with him and yet he knew she couldn't do it. He was sunk in misery such as he'd never known before—misery in his own inability to control things. Misery in leaving behind all that he loved. And even the concept of a new baby that he would take some time to deal with.

"One more thing," he noted quickly. "Come here to the window." He waited while she positioned herself to look out. "Listen to me carefully. When you escape, wait until you get out into the sunlight, then look out across that wide, mowed field and you will see a small cottage that looks like something left over from a fairy tale. Go directly to it, ask for Jacob. I'll warn him that you may be coming. He will take you to the boat that will transfer you to the continent."

"If I escape," she amended softly, feeling hopeless.

He grasped her by the shoulders. "You will. One way or another, you will. And when you do, you'll come to me. Do you swear it?"

She nodded, eyes filling with tears.

"Say the words," he ordered.

"I swear I'll come to you," she said, looking up through her tears.

He stared into her eyes for a long moment, then kissed her.

"Goodbye," she said, pulling away and starting up the steps. "Good luck." She looked back and gave him a watery smile. "Until Ambria is free," she said, throwing him a kiss.

"Until Ambria is free," he saluted back. "I love you, Pellea," he called after her as she disappeared up the stairs. "And I love our baby," he whispered, but only to himself.

He would be back. He would come to claim what was his, in every way, or die trying. Cursing, he began to race down the stairs.

CHAPTER TEN

PELLEA GOT BACK without anyone knowing that she'd been gone and she covered up the escape tunnel exactly as Monte had in the past. She didn't find out what the alarm had been about until Kimmee came by with her breakfast.

"I guess the old General is really sick," she said, slightly in awe. "Can you believe it? I thought that man would be immortal. Anyway, someone went in to give him his morning coffee and thought he was dead. So they set off the alarm. Leonardo is furious."

"But he's not really dead."

"Not yet. But they say he's not far from it."

Despite everything, Pellea was upset. "How sad to come all this way home after all this time without really having a chance to see anyone he cares for," she said.

"Maybe," Kimmee said. "Or maybe," she whispered, leaning close, "the meanness finally caught up with him."

"Don't speak that way of the sick," Pellea said automatically, but inside, she agreed.

Still, she had a hard time dwelling on the sad condition

of the man who had been Ambria's leader for all her life. Mostly, she was thinking about Monte and his pledge to invade very soon, and she was sick at heart. She knew what danger he would be putting himself and his men in if he invaded now. If he did this just because of her and he was hurt—if anyone was hurt—she would never forgive herself.

Leonardo came by before noon. She went to meet him at the gate with her heart in her throat, wondering what he knew and what he was going to suspect. He looked like a man seriously hung-over and rather distracted by his current situation, but other than that, he seemed calm enough.

"Hello, my dear," he said. "I'm sure you've heard about my father."

"Yes. Leonardo, I'm so sorry."

"Of course, but it's not unexpected. He's been quite ill, you know. A lot worse than we'd told the people. It's a natural decline, I suppose. But for that moron to start the alarm as though he were dead!" He shook his head. "I've dealt with him." He slapped his gloves against his pant leg and looked at her sideways. "That was quite a night we had, wasn't it? I'm afraid we never did get around to announcing our engagement, did we?"

She realized he was asking her, as though he wasn't quite sure what had happened the night before. What on earth would she tell him? Nothing. That was by far the wisest course.

"No, we didn't," she said simply.

He studied her face. "Does that mean that the wedding is off?" he asked musingly.

She hesitated, not really sure what he wanted from her. "What do you think?" she asked him.

He made a face. "I think there was someone at the ball who you would rather marry," he said bluntly.

"Oh, Leonardo," she began.

But he cut her off. "Never mind, darling. We'll have to deal with this later. Right now I've got my hands full. I've got my father's ill health to come to terms with. And then there are the plans for succession."

"Why? What's going on?"

"You haven't heard?"

"No. Tell me."

"You know that my father arrived last night. They brought him in from France. I hadn't seen him for weeks. I didn't realize…" He stopped and rubbed his eyes. "My father is a vegetable, Pellea. I'm going to have to file for full custodial rights. And every little faction in the castle is sharpening its little teeth getting ready to try to grab its own piece of power." He shook his head. "It's a nightmare."

"Oh, Leonardo, I'm so sorry."

"Yes. It's all on me now, my sweet. I don't know if I have time for a marriage. Sorry."

Leonardo shrugged and turned to leave, his mind on other things. Pellea watched him go and sighed with relief. That was one hurdle she wasn't going to have to challenge at any rate.

Not that it left her in the clear. She was still pregnant.

She was still without a husband. What would become of her and her baby? She closed her eyes, took a deep breath and forced herself to focus. She had to think. It was time to find some new answers.

Pellea went to sit with her father later that day. He was much better. She wasn't sure what the doctor had given him, but she could see that his mind was clear once again and she was grateful.

She chatted with him for a few minutes and then he surprised her with a pointed question.

"Who was that man who was here yesterday?" he asked.

"The doctor?" she tried evasively.

"No. The other man. The one I momentarily mistook for King Grandor."

She took in a deep breath. "It was his son, the crown prince. It was Monte DeAngelis."

"Monte?" He almost smiled. "Oh, yes, of course it was Monte. I remember him well. A fine, strapping lad he was, too." He shook his head. "I'm so glad to see that he survived."

She paused, then decided to let honesty rule the day. "He makes a pretty good grown man as well," she said quietly.

"Yes." His gaze flickered up to smile at her. "I saw him kissing you."

"Oh." It seemed her father hadn't been as out of it as she had supposed. Well, good. He might as well know the truth. Did she have the nerve to go on with the honesty? Why not? What did she have to lose at this point?

"I'm in love with him, Father. And I'm carrying his child."

There. What more was there to say? She waited, holding her breath.

He closed his eyes and for a moment she was afraid what she'd said was too much for him.

"I'm so sorry, Father," she said, leaning over him. "Please forgive me."

"There's nothing to forgive," he said, opening his eyes and smiling at her. "Not for you at any rate. I would assume this is going to put an end to my plans for you to marry Leonardo."

She shook her head, sorry to disappoint him. "I'm afraid so."

He frowned. "The powers that be won't like it."

"No."

For the next few minutes he was lost in thought. She tidied things in the room and got him a fresh bottle of water. And finally, he took her hand and told her what he wanted to do next.

"I'd like to see the doctor," he said, his voice weak but steady. "I think we'd better make some plans. I'm about to leave this life, but I want to do something for you before I go."

"No, Father, you don't have to do anything more for me. You've done everything for me my whole life. It's enough. Just be well and stay alive for as long as you can. I need you."

He patted her hand. "That is why I need the doctor. Please see if you can get him right away."

She drew in her breath, worried. "I'll go right now."

The doctor came readily enough. He'd always been partial to Pellea and her father. After he talked to the older man, he nodded and said, "I'll see if I can pull some strings."

"Good," her father said once he was gone. "Leonardo will have his work cut out for him fighting off all the factions that will try to topple his new rule. He doesn't have time to think about me. I'm of no use to him now anyway and in no condition to help him." He took his daughter's hand in his and smiled at her. "The doctor will get me permission to go to the continent to see a specialist. And I'll need you to go along as one of my nurses."

"What?" She could hardly believe her ears. They were going to the continent. Just like that. Could it really be this easy?

"Are you willing?" he asked her.

"Oh, Father!" Pellea's eyes filled with tears and her voice was choked. "Father, you are saving my life."

Arriving in Italy two days later, Pellea was more nervous than ever. She wanted to see Monte again, but she was afraid of what she would find when she did. After all, how many times and in how many ways had he told her that he would never marry her? She knew there wasn't much hope along those lines.

And there was more. She knew very well that the

excitement of a clandestine affair was one thing. The reality of a pregnant woman knocking on the door was another. He might very well have decided she wasn't worth the effort by the time he got home. Was that possible? She didn't like to think so, but reality could be harsh and cold.

Still, one thing was certain. She had to go to him. She had to let him know that she was not in danger any longer, that she was not marrying Leonardo, and that her well-being was not a reason to launch an invasion. She was no longer in Ambria and no longer in need of any sort of rescue. The last thing in the world she wanted was to be the catalyst for a lot of needless killing.

She'd left her father in a clinic in Rome and she'd traveled a few hours into the mountains to the little town of Piasa where she knew Ambrian ex-patriots tended to gather. She found his hotel, and with heart beating wildly, she went to the desk and asked for him.

"He's not seeing visitors, miss," the concierge told her. "Perhaps if you left your name…"

How could she leave her name? She wasn't staying anywhere he would be able to find her. She turned away from the hotel desk in despair, losing hope, wondering where she could go.

And then, there he was, coming out of an elevator with two other men, laughing at something someone had said. Joy surged in her heart, but so did fear, and when he looked up and saw her, her heart fell. He didn't look happy to see her. He seemed almost annoyed.

He excused himself from the other men and came

toward her. He didn't smile. Instead, he pressed a room key into her hand.

"Go to room twenty-five and wait for me," he told her softly. Then he turned on his heel and went back to the men, immediately cracking a joke that made them laugh uproariously, one even glancing back at where she stood. Had he told them why she was here? Was he making fun of her? Her cheeks flamed crimson and, for just a moment, she was tempted to throw the key in his face and storm out.

Luckily, she calmed down quickly. There was no way she could know what he'd said to the other men, or even what he was thinking. He might have needed some sort of ruse to maintain his situation. She had no way of knowing and it would be stupid of her to make assumptions. Taking a deep breath, she headed for the elevator.

She found her way to the room, and despite her sensible actions, she was still numb with shock at the way he'd acted. Just as she'd feared, he was another person entirely when he wasn't in the castle of Ambria. What was next? Was he going to hand her money to get lost? And if he did that, how would she respond? She was sick at heart. This wasn't what she'd hoped for.

She paced the room for a few minutes, but she was so tired. After a few longing looks at his bed, she gave in to temptation and lay down for a rest. Very quickly, she fell asleep.

But not for long. The next thing she knew, someone was lying next to her on the bed and kissing her ear.

"Oh!" she said, trying to get up.

But it was no use. Monte was raining down kisses all over her and she began to laugh.

"What are you doing?"

"Some people welcome with flowers," he told her with a sweet, slow grin. "I do it with kisses. Now lie still and take it like a woman."

She giggled as he dropped even more kisses on her. "Monte! Cut it out. I'm going to get hysterical."

"Do you promise?"

"No! I mean… Oh, you know what I mean."

He did, and he finally stopped, but his hand was covering her belly. "Boy or girl?" he asked her softly.

She smiled up at him, happiness tingling from every inch of her. "I don't know yet."

"It's hard to believe."

She nodded. "Just another miracle," she said. "Are you happy about it?"

He stared into her eyes for a long moment before answering, and she was starting to worry about just what his answer was going to be, when he spoke.

"*Happy* isn't a strong enough word," he told her simply. "I feel something so strong and new, I don't know what the word is. But there's a balloon of wonderfulness in my chest and it keeps getting bigger and bigger. It's as though a new world has opened at my feet." He shrugged. "And now that you're here, everything is good."

She sighed. "I was worried. The way you looked when you saw me…"

"In public you'll find I am one person, Pellea. In

private, quite another. It's a necessary evil that some-one in my position has to be so careful all the time." He traced her lips with his finger. "But with you, I promise always to be genuine. You'll always know the real me, good or bad."

She was listening, and it was all very nice, but she still hadn't heard certain words she was waiting for. She told him about what had happened at the castle, and how she had accompanied her father for his visit to the specialist.

"I hope they can do something for him," she said.

"Does he plan to go back?"

"Oh, I'm sure he does. His life is in Ambria."

He nodded thoughtfully. "You're not going back," he said, as though he had the last word in the decision.

"Really?" She raised an eyebrow. "And just what is going to keep me here?"

"I am."

She waited. There should be more to that statement. But he frowned as though he was thinking about some-thing else. She was losing her patience.

"I've got to get back to my father," she said, rising from the bed and straightening her clothing.

Monte rose as well. "I'm going with you," he said firmly.

She looked up at him in surprise. "But...you hate him."

"No." He shook his head. "I hate the man he used to be. I don't hate the man he is today."

"You think he's changed?"

"I think we all have." He pulled her close. "And anyway, there are no good jewelers here in Piasa. I need to go to Rome. I need a larger city to find a real artist."

"Why would you want a jeweler?"

"I need a good copy made."

"Of the tiara?" She scrunched up her face, trying to figure out what he would want that for.

"In a way. I'd like to find someone who could reproduce the main part of the tiara as…" He smiled at her. "…as an engagement ring."

Her eyes widened. "Oh."

He kissed her on the mouth. "Would you wear a ring like that?"

And suddenly she felt as though she were floating on a cloud of happiness. "I don't know. It would depend on who gave it to me."

"Good answer." And he kissed her again, then took her two hands in his and smiled down at her. "I love you, Pellea," he said, his feelings shining in his eyes. "My love for you is bigger than revenge, bigger than retribution, bigger than the wounds of the past. I'm going to take care of all those things in good time. I'm going to get my country back. And when I take over, I want you with me, as my queen. Will you be my wife?"

She drew in a full breath of air and laughed aloud. There they were. Those were the words she'd been waiting for.

"Yes, Monte," she said, reaching for the man she loved, joy surging in her. "With all my heart and soul."

Welcome to your new-look
By Request series!

Wedding Wishes

LIZ FIELDING · CHRISTIE RIDGWAY · MYRNA MACKENZIE

By Request

Royal Seductions: Diamonds

LUCY MONROE · LUCY GORDON · NATALIE RIVERS

By Request

Misbehaving with the Millionaire

KIMBERLY LANG · MARGARET MAYO · LEE WILKINSON

By Request

RELIVE THE ROMANCE WITH THE BEST OF THE BEST

This series features stories from your favourite authors that are back by popular demand—and, now with brand new covers, they look even better than before!

See the new covers now at:
www.millsandboon.co.uk/byrequest

A sneaky peek at next month...

By Request

RELIVE THE ROMANCE WITH THE BEST OF THE BEST

My wish list for next month's titles...

In stores from 16th May 2014:

❑ Misbehaving with the Millionaire –
Kimberly Lang, Margaret Mayo & Lee Wilkinson

❑ Hot Summer Nights! –
Kelly Hunter, Cara Summers & Emily McKay

In stores from 6th June 2014:

❑ Royal Seductions: Diamonds –
Michelle Celmer

❑ Wedding Wishes – Liz Fielding,
Christie Ridgway & Myrna Mackenzie

3 stories in each book - only £5.99!

Available at WHSmith, Tesco, Asda, Eason, Amazon and Apple

Just can't wait?

Visit us Online

You can buy our books online a month before they hit the shops! **www.millsandboon.co.uk**

0514/05

Special Offers

Every month we put together collections and longer reads written by your favourite authors.

Here are some of next month's highlights— and don't miss our fabulous discount online!

On sale 6th June   On sale 6th June   On sale 6th June

Save 20%
on all Special Releases

Join our *EXCLUSIVE* eBook club

FROM JUST £1.99 A MONTH!

Never miss a book again with our hassle-free eBook subscription.

★ Pick how many titles you want from each series with our flexible subscription

★ Your titles are delivered to your device on the first of every month

★ Zero risk, zero obligation!

There really is nothing standing in the way of you and your favourite books!

Start your eBook subscription today at www.millsandboon.co.uk/subscribe

The World of Mills & Boon

There's a Mills & Boon® series that's perfect for you. There are ten different series to choose from and new titles every month, so whether you're looking for glamorous seduction, Regency rakes, homespun heroes or sizzling erotica, we'll give you plenty of inspiration for your next read.

By Request
Back by popular demand!
12 stories every month

Cherish™
Experience the ultimate rush of falling in love.
12 new stories every month

INTRIGUE...
A seductive combination of danger and desire...
7 new stories every month

Desire™
Passionate and dramatic love stories
6 new stories every month

nocturne™
An exhilarating underworld of dark desires
3 new stories every month

For exclusive member offers go to
millsandboon.co.uk/subscribe

WORLD_ M&Ba

Which series will you try next?